" . . . a love letter to America . . ."

An award-winning novelist and journalist, W.J. Weatherby was born in the north of England where the story of THE MOONDANCERS opens, but he has spent most of his adult life in the United States. He first came as a special correspondent for the prestigious *Manchester Guardian*, like Horatio Thomas in THE MOONDANCERS. His account of a friendship across racial lines in the Deep South, *Love In The Shadows*, was selected as one of the best books of the year by James Baldwin and has recently been optioned for a movie. Another book about a friendship with film star Marilyn Monroe, *Conversations With Marilyn*, was serialized in the *Ladies Home Journal* and numerous other magazines and newspapers throughout the world. He was awarded an Edgar from the Mystery Writers of America for his first novel, *Death Of An Informer*. He is also the author of *Goliath*, a novel anticipating the assassination attempt on the Pope. He describes his latest novel, THE MOONDANCERS, as "a love letter to America at a time when people have doubts about the American Dream and may need reminding of what makes it come true—the free spirit of a Moondancer."

"And hand in hand, on the edge of the sand,
They danced by the light of the moon"
—Edward Lear, *The Owl and the Pussy-Cat*

The Moondancers

W. J. Weatherby

A Dell/Quicksilver Book

Published by
Quicksilver Books, Inc.
in association with
Dell Publishing Co., Inc.
1 Dag Hammarskjold Plaza
New York, N.Y. 10017

Dell (R) TM 681510, Dell Publishing Co., Inc.

ISBN: 0-440-06189-X

Printed in the United States of America

First printing—March 1983

To my Kath—my mother

To my Moondancer friends,
George and Kenneth Hendrix
One will have to make the mountain top for both
now

And in memory of
Abner Parker, Senior

Prologue

Kathleen Tracy.

Kath . . .

I first heard of her when I was a boy. "Kathleen Tracy," grown-ups used to say, "That girl was downright wicked." It was enough to win a boy's interest. I soon learned she was a beautiful redhead who had killed in a fit of passion—some said she killed her lover, some said her father. It made her seem a very romantic figure to me and I tried to find out all I could about her.

Only two photographs existed—one when she was ten taken by a local artist whose name has been forgotten and the other when she was nineteen, the work of the famous American Civil War photographer, Mathew Brady. As a boy I used to study both photographs for hours, but neither of them conveyed the woman I came to "know." I was grown-up myself by the time I learned enough to understand her and the dream that obsessed her.

I was greatly aided in this understanding by the unpublished journals of a foreign correspondent named Horatio Thomas, who worked for the same newspaper I did, *The Manchester Guardian,* but a hundred years before.

"I have been there," wrote Horatio Thomas.

"I have been to the little terraced house in the cobbled back street where she was born, to the cotton factory where she worked and dreamed, to the city prison where she awaited her execution. People are no longer hanged for murder there, but I have stood where the scaffold was set up for her and the noose was placed around her neck.

"I have seen the thatched cottage where the hangman lived.

"I have walked in the woods where she and her father went poaching and where she met her lover.

"I have climbed the heather-covered hills where the police found her. . . ."

It was Horatio Thomas who provided me with the key to Kath's life—that her dream had finally come true, though not in the way she had expected.

"According to ancient legends," Horatio Thomas noted, "we must be worthy of our dreams before they can come true. The moon is said to hold the key. Its reflected light is in close touch with our subconscious." (He wrote this before Freud.) "Those who know the secret of how to make their dreams come true are often called Moondancers. . . ."

The Moondancers began as an attempt to capture the American Dream of just over one hundred years ago. What I discovered was that then as now, the American Dream is real . . . but only for those individuals free enough to be themselves.

W.J.W.

New York City

The Moondancers

1

Go back over a hundred years, back up the river of time before planes or cars or telephones were invented.

Go back to early in September, 1864, to the great industrial city of Manchester in the north-west of England.

The Industrial Revolution had done its worst there, slashing through the green countryside to throw up huge factory chimneys belching black smoke across the northern sky. Gone were the settled ways of English rural life as farm workers crowded into Manchester and the surrounding cotton towns in search of jobs.

There was a new spirit of restlessness in this part of England, with widespread fears of riots among the unemployed and talk of a war with America to distract everybody. Change, even violent change, was in the air, and the hangman was kept busy.

That year there had been six hangings already in the north of England, and another was scheduled in Manchester—a young woman.

Frank Butler, the northern hangman, had become a well-known figure, but it was a lonely life. People acted as if you were outside society, with more in common with the criminals you hanged than with respectable folk. This angered Frank because he felt he deserved the same respect as any other craftsman.

Tall and well-built with the dark good looks of the Black

Irish, he was only twenty-four, young for an established executioner. But his father had been the northern hangman for 18 years before him, and in the last year Frank sometimes acted as his assistant for gambling money. When his father collapsed and died in the middle of a hanging at Liverpool Prison, Frank completed the execution so efficiently that he was immediately asked to become the new hangman. Frank wasn't keen to accept the unpopular job (even more unpopular after so many recent hangings), but it was that or factory work. Frank was too much of a countryman to enjoy working inside with machines, and the hangman's pay, though not great, was enough to finance his passion—gambling at cards or dice in remote Lancashire pubs, where he hoped no one would recognise him.

He lived in a thatched cottage in the hills above the town of Stockport. He seldom went down into Stockport, which was usually half hidden by a damp mist from the cotton mills, and the only time he travelled to the city of Manchester beyond was when he was needed at the prison for a hanging.

The next hanging there was a young woman from Stockport. He didn't know who she was, but it wouldn't be the first time he'd hanged a woman. It didn't worry him at all. People all died the same way on the scaffold. What sex they were made no difference, just their age and height and weight, the vital statistics that determined the length of the drop.

The day of the woman's hanging was warm and sunny, one of those perfect English late summer days. Not a day for leaving the world, the young hangman thought as he stared out of the back window of his hillside cottage. The sky was a deep blue, the color of forget-me-nots, and the sun gleamed on the buttercups covering the grassy slopes. The bright light made his head ache. He had been out late gambling—and losing—and drinking heavily in a pub in Rochdale, and he'd gone home with a woman in her late thirties, a big blonde who had drained the life out of him. She'd worked him all night, and he'd had no rest until he returned to the cottage close to dawn. She was the second woman he'd had that week. It was always that way before a hanging. He had an almost feverish need for excitement. Gambling, drinking, women, especially women, as if he had to have a sense of making life just before taking it. It was a soft way of thinking. His father was never like that.

He boiled some water from a nearby stream for coffee—very strong and black. He had to be clear-headed by eight o'clock. That was the time they'd bring her out. The warm early morning air coming off the hills ruffled the window curtains, and he wondered if the prisoner could glimpse the beautiful day just beginning through her cell window—it was enough to break down anyone whose life on earth was running out. Hangings, he thought, should be held on one of those hopelessly rainy days that seemed like the end of the world in Manchester.

It was unlike him to have such thoughts. He usually had a gambler's attitude toward life and death. You played for high stakes, and if your luck turned bad, you accepted it with a shrug, even if it meant your life. Or that was the idea. He tried not to think about the prisoner until the time of execution, and then it was too late to affect him. To stop thinking of her now, he hurriedly went out into the small backyard enclosed by a high wooden fence and robbed the chickens there of half a dozen eggs. The cock began to crow.

He fried the eggs with several thick slices of ham and home-made bread, and then washed it all down with more black coffee. He always ate a hearty breakfast before a hanging. It wasn't a job to do on an empty stomach. The prisoner's guilt or innocence was none of his business. His own responsibility was to make sure they didn't suffer too much. It had to be fast and sure.

At seven o'clock, Frank put on his black hangman's suit and whistled to his black stallion grazing on the grassy hillside behind the cottage. The stallion came at a gallop and was quickly saddled. He almost forgot to get his pistol from the cottage. It hadn't become a habit yet. He had started carrying it two weeks ago after a group of workers in the center of Manchester had tried to pull him off his horse. They had been friends of an unemployed dock worker he had hanged the week before in Liverpool; he had never even learned what the man's crime was and yet they blamed him. Why didn't they attack the judge or the police chief instead of him? The hangman was only doing a job.

The police had warned him that this young woman being hanged today was popular with the unemployed cotton workers so, in riding to the prison, he was careful not to pass through any crowded areas. He bypassed the town center of Stockport in the valley and also the outlying cotton districts of Manchester with their grim rows of box-like brick houses all alike and huddled together. The dark narrow streets had pavements worn smooth by boots and clogs rushing to the factories in the early morning and coming back at night. Factory whistles were blowing along his whole route.

The black-suited hangman with his brooding Black Irish looks, erect on the black stallion, appeared an eerie figure against the bright early morning sky, but not many people were in the streets to see him. The factories had already started work. He thought he was going to make it unrecognized. But not far from the prison, a woman held up a young boy as he rode past, and he heard her shout, "Now you can say you've seen . . . *the hangman!*" She cried after him: *"Hired killer!"* It made him angry so he slapped the stallion into a gallop. He was only doing a job, didn't she understand that? His youth made him very sensitive about public opinion; his father had been indifferent even when they nicknamed him "The Strangler." The cry echoed again behind him: *"Hired killer!"*

The dark walls of Manchester Prison soon reared up against the blue sky. He was early, and workmen were still setting up the gallows, for hangings were still public ceremonies. A large crowd had already gathered even though it was so early. Some of them had been there all night to make sure of a good view. Many of them were cotton workers with worn cloth caps and scarves tied tightly round their necks. Men were walking through the crowd with trays of food for sale. It might have been a holiday outing.

Frank galloped past them as fast as possible. The stallion felt his concern through his tightening leg muscles, and responded with a great surge that sent its hooves clicking madly over the cobblestones. Then someone recognised him, and there were angry shouts and boos and clenched fists gestured at him. Part of the crowd began to move forward to cut him off, but the stallion responded even more strongly with no trace of fear, and the huge prison gates opened quickly and they galloped inside, with the crowd outside baying like frustrated hounds. He patted the stallion, whose heavy breathing was making faint clouds in the early morning air. "Good boy."

"You just made it," said one of the prison guards, slamming the gates shut. They sometimes played cards together before a hanging, but there wasn't time today.

The angry shouts from outside went on and on.

Hired killer!

"The bastards," said the young hangman, leaping off the stallion. He stood listening to the crowd outside, exchanging anxious looks with the prison guard. They were worse than he had ever known them. Hard times had incensed them, bringing out their violence. Didn't they realize someone had to do the hangman's job, and he did it as well as it had ever been done? His father, "The Strangler," often miscalculated the length of the drop and the prisoner was slowly throttled to death. But he had made an execution as scientific as possible, as befitted the times they lived in. He had not only worked out a foolproof mathematical formula for estimating the drop, but he had speeded up the time of a hanging—the prisoner was often brought from his or her cell and hanged while the prison clock was still striking eight. The mental suffering was as brief as possible. He took a real pride in his work. But people didn't appreciate it. They wanted to take their guilt out on him.

Frank remembered when his father had kept a beer house in Stockport and people came to buy a pint mug of beer just to stare at him as if he were some weird, exotic beast in the zoo—or maybe even Death's personal assistant from the next world. It never seemed to occur to people that he was doing their work for them. Let them outlaw capital punishment if they didn't want a hangman. He didn't believe it had much effect anyway. Crime was increasing in the country. It hadn't deterred this young woman he was hanging today. He had overheard people talking about her. She had murdered her employer, someone said, but then he had walked away so he wouldn't learn any more. He didn't like to know *anything* about the person he was hanging. Nothing personal anyway. He didn't even like to see them before they were marched out on the morning, and then it was too late to get to know them, to have any feeling for them. He always had someone else weigh and measure them the night before. And he always wore a hood so they wouldn't see his face—the face of the person sending them into the next world. It was a carefully worked-out procedure. Very professional—and very impersonal.

Frank washed his hands in a prison bathroom and manicured his nails. He liked to be as neat as a surgeon when he handled the noose and slipped it round the neck. He made sure it was the finest Indian hemp imported specially from Bombay. He wanted no frayed strands or other mishaps. He had seen enough with his father.

Then he studied the prisoner's statistics. She was 124 pounds, a sturdy bitch. But then she was tall for a woman—5 feet 10 inches. She was also young, only eighteen, and that made a difference. The muscles were more active, more responsive to stress, more resistant. He better be on the safe side, and allow an extra foot in the drop. He made a quick calculation in his head, as unemotional as a bank clerk, and then he was ready.

The doctor was drunk as usual. He was a mild old man who could only endure watching a hanging if his feelings were dulled with Scotch whisky. It was very unprofessional, but it didn't matter much as he didn't have anything to do with the actual hanging. In fact, he often left Frank to examine the body and check that the prisoner was dead while he went off to the bathroom, presumably to vomit. He only came because his practice was in a poor district and he needed the fee.

"Morning, doctor."

There was a mumble in reply and a vacant look. Frank could smell the Scotch on his breath.

The usual small group, including the governor, an ex-army colonel, went out to the gallows with a larger number of guards than usual. A way had to be cleared through the noisy, aggressive crowd and wooden barriers erected in front of the gallows. Frank was surprised to see the High Sheriff of Lancashire join them. Robert Bennington very seldom attended a hanging. This must have special political significance—perhaps because she had killed her employer and the workers were demonstrating in her favor. But Frank tried not to think about it. He just had his job to do. What she had done was no concern of his. Everyone was the same to the hangman. What was it his father used to say? Death has no favorites.

The gallows had brick walls with planking on top and, above that, two beams and a crossbar with the rope dangling. He just had time to test the rope and the drop when the clock began to strike and the gates were opening again and they were bringing her out. Immediately the mood of the crowd changed. The angry cries and boos were drowned in thunderous cheers. Those at the front pressed against the barriers and the police had to beat them back. The sunlight glinted on their helmets as they charged.

Frank waited patiently for her, ice cold. At first all he could see was the top of her head—a crown of red hair among the dark uniformed prison guards. A prison chaplain in a surplice was intoning as they walked: "In the midst of life, we are in death. . . ."

They came up to the steps to the scaffold as the clock continued to strike. Her arms were tied and guards were on each side of her, almost caressing her, trying clumsily to help her up the steps. But they weren't needed. She was a cool one. Her step was firm, even buoyant, showing no excitement or fear. There was just one worrying moment. Halfway up the steps, she stopped and faced the sun with a sensuous expression, feeling the warmth on her skin for a last time. There was a sudden hush, everyone fearing a last-minute breakdown. The guards closed in on her. But to their relief, they didn't need to act. After a few moments, she began to move again, climbing the steps.

And as they came on to the platform close to the hanging noose, her face calm and not even tired or strained looking, he saw her for the first time . . . and beneath his black executioner's hood, he paled, badly shocked.

He knew that face.

It wasn't a face you could ever forget.

He hadn't seen her for four years. She had grown taller and filled out. But it was her all right.

He stared fixedly at her, unable to move, relieved his shocked reaction was hidden under the hood.

That face—he had dreamed of it many times.

He studied her as if they were alone together. Everyone else was blotted out the moment he saw her.

Beneath a crown of dark, thick red hair he had once rubbed his hands through was a strong-boned face with large brown sensuous eyes, thick, arched eyebrows, a wide, expressive mouth, and a chin that expressed determination without spoiling her beauty. My God, she had grown into a beautiful woman. His eyes roved down her body, the wide shoulders and big uptilted breasts, clearly outlined even in the thick, coarse prison smock, and the narrow waist he had once caressed as he lay on top of her, and what was beneath that he had been the first one to try to enter and would have been successful but for the arrival of some gamekeepers. He had looked for her many times since, feeling a sense of frustration, of something unfinished, but he had never seen her . . . until now.

They were all looking at him, waiting in a rough circle round the gallows. The clock had stopped striking. He was late. It was as if he had lost his will power and had been mesmerized by her. All he knew was that he couldn't hang her. He had never been so moved by a woman. She was only fourteen then, but she was already big and sensuous-looking with a strange, earthy quality she didn't know she possessed. He had been just twenty, with no shortage of women, and yet he had been drawn to her at the first look, and then just at the moment of taking her—and she had been a virgin then—he had lost her . . . until now.

He had never seen her again except in his dreams.

Until now.

They were all looking strangely at him as if beginning to suspect something was wrong. The governor. The chaplain. The high sheriff. Even the drunken doctor.

Even her.

Reluctantly, he gripped the noose—the four-strand hemp he had tested with a 200-pound weight—and slipped it over her head. He felt the thick red hair and the soft skin, but he daren't let his fingers linger. At the touch of the rope, her mouth tightened, but she gave no other sign of her feelings. She certainly had guts. He had known people empty their bowels or even faint at that moment.

Next came the small cotton bag like a flour sack to drop over her head.

"Leave it off," she said firmly. "I want to see to the end."

The governor, who was nervously poking the plank floor with a walking stick, glanced across at the high sheriff and shrugged. The prisoner was supposed to die with face covered, but a rule could be broken. All that mattered now was to get it over with.

The young hangman continued to stare at her.

He had found her again—but was it too late?

His gambler's instinct was aroused.

He *couldn't* spring the trap on her and yet, if he refused, someone else would do it. The result would be the same. She would disappear on what his father used to call "the unknown journey" and then he would never have her.

But what could he *do*—now—at this last moment?

The chaplain would soon be reaching the signal for the drop: "Lord Jesus, receive her spirit. . . ."

The governor said impatiently, "Let's proceed."

He looked at the governor, at the tight little circle round the gallows, and then he stared back at her. Her eyes were watching the crowd beyond the barriers. A heavy silence had fallen over the massed faces. Everyone was waiting for him.

There was no way out.

The execution would have to take place.

He was going to lose her for a second and last time, and he didn't even know her name.

"What is she called?" he murmured to a guard standing near.

"Kathleen," the man said, peering at him.

Kathleen.

Kath. . . .

"Carry on," snapped the governor.

The moment had come. . . .

2

When Kathleen Tracy was ten years old, a grand thing happened. She sat for her photograph. Photography was in its infancy then, and for her face to appear on special paper in a silver frame—the same face she saw in the mirror every day of her life—was a fantastic happening that made her tenth birthday the most wonderful she had ever had.

A local artist friend of her father's had made himself a photographic box on long legs, and he sat her on a wall near the beer house, told her not to move a muscle, and then disappeared under the black cloth covering his camera.

It didn't take long, not nearly as long as the artist had once taken to sketch her Dad with a pencil (and then it hadn't looked very like him). She sat very still for just a few minutes. Suddenly there was a noise like a rifle shot. And then it was all over. She didn't believe it was serious, but some kind of joke of her Dad's and his friends. But that night the artist came to their house with the photograph in a silver frame. It not only looked like her, but made her seem very grown-up. When her mother and the boys saw it, they were all jealous and wanted one, too. But it wasn't their birthday.

The photograph made Kath take herself more seriously. You were a Somebody if you had your picture taken. At first she lifted it out of its special place in her drawer and stared at it at least a hundred times a day. Her interest gradually dwindled, until after a few weeks she only looked at it when she got up and again when she went to bed, and then the time came when it began not to look like her and it stayed in her drawer.

The old black-and-white photograph didn't capture the color of her hair or the clearness of her skin, but it did convey her beauty and her independence even at that age. At ten, she looked like fourteen, with the bold expression of someone used to caring for herself. Her hair was red like her father's and she had the legendary temper of an Irish redhead. Her mother, who was English, used to greet her occasional explosions of temperament with the warning, "Whom the gods wish to destroy they first make angry." But her father, all Irish from County Rosscommon, who had a temper, too, claimed it was proof of her distinction among the heathen English.

That photograph was Kath's most treasured possession, not only for itself but because it recorded a special time in her life—what she came to remember as the end of her happiness. Although her family was poor, it had never occurred to Kath until then that she wasn't happy. You made the best of what you had. She lived with her parents and three younger brothers in one of the crammed terraced houses in the backstreets of Stockport. The old cotton town was originally built in a valley, but it had grown rapidly up the hillsides so that its streets were on many different levels, connected by steep stone steps. The Romans had once had an army camp nearby and the people had a hard, durable look as if they were directly descended from those days, as lasting a part of the valley as the cobblestones in the old streets and the hard rock of the hills.

The river Mersey moved slowly through the center of the town, already half-choked with waste from the cotton mills and other factories that dotted the valley and the green hillsides. Beyond the town to the north lay the scattered houses and little farms that led to the crowded outskirts of the sprawling city of Manchester, and on the other side to the south there was a complete contrast—the largely unspoilt moorlands that were unmarked except for occasional villages with ancient parish churches (and tolling bells on Sunday mornings) and country inns and the big estate of Heaton Hall behind its high stone wall and acres of woodland filled with game.

The town of Stockport and the hills beyond were all the world Kath knew. At ten, she hadn't even been to the city of Manchester. She never asked herself whether she was happy. She presumed she was. Being unhappy was being ill and Kath was never ill. Sometimes she worried that her mother didn't love her as much as her three younger brothers, Harold, John, and Peter, but she was her father's favorite and that was what mattered.

Joseph Tracy was a man-and-a-half in young Kath's eyes. He was the kind of Irishman who could hold you spellbound with his stories. A big man with a loud voice and an expressive face, he was popular at the factory and people always welcomed his company at the beer-house. Kath sometimes had to wait outside for hours, but he always brought her out a lemonade and his friends made a big fuss of her. She had a certain status as Joseph Tracy's daughter. They would put her on one of the outside tables and look at her as if she were for sale and they were thinking of buying her and taking her home. "You got a beauty there, Joe," they'd say and her Dad would look proud. That was how her photograph came to be taken. The artist saw her sitting outside the beer-house and went home for his camera. He didn't know it was her birthday. That was just her good luck. The family had had no money for presents because it was rent week, but the photograph was better than any present. And then afterwards her Dad took her poaching in the grounds of Heaton Hall, just her and him, and they came home with two hares and a pheasant. They all sat down to a hare dinner, and her Dad kept them all laughing with his stories, even though they had heard most of the stories before. As her Dad said, it wasn't the story that mattered so much as how you told it, and he always told them differently every time. She never got tired of listening to him.

After that, her happiness began to fall apart. She remembered the exact day. It was a week after her birthday. She had just got home from school when she saw her Dad and several of his friends coming up the narrow cobbled street. Two of them were holding him by the arms and his face was very pale and grim. She rushed out to meet them. "Your Dad's had an accident, Kath," one of them said. Her Dad said nothing, didn't even look at her, his eyes half-closed and full of pain. She could smell the painkiller—the Scotch whisky that was too costly to drink, but was used in the case of illness. Then she saw the bloody bandage on his left hand and his eyes widened, looking at her, and she saw more of the pain and fear in his usually bright eyes. He had caught his hand in a factory machine and lost two of his fingers. Yes, and more than that. A part of his spirit, too, though Kath didn't realize it at first.

He stayed in bed all that day and the next, his face to the wall, no longer talking and laughing, not even wanting the beer his friends brought him. Kath thought he would soon be his old self. She watched when her mother changed the bandage and she saw the short, red stumps of the two fingers, and later she asked her Dad if they would grow back. "Never, Kath," he told her and his voice broke.

The missing fingers were bad enough, but to see her Dad so down was a great shock. It was Kath's first real experience of violence and loss. That not even her father was safe shattered her sense of security. If he had soon returned to his old loud self, it might not have had such a traumatic effect on her, but he never seemed to recover his self-confidence and eventually he lost his job at the factory because he was afraid of the machines. He couldn't work with them any more so there was no job for him. There were then four children to support, none old enough to work—Kath at ten was the oldest. He went out each day looking for a job, but times were bad, and he never seemed to find more than a few days' casual work.

He grew increasingly bitter. Kath noticed with a sinking heart that he never seemed to laugh anymore or tell any stories. Often his thoughts were elsewhere when she spoke to him, and he didn't reply. As if this weren't bad enough, other misfortunes struck the family. Her mother's gold wedding ring disappeared and nobody could find it. Then the rent money in the old tobacco box on the mantlepiece was missing—all of it. Her Dad said the back door had been forced late at night, but Kath felt her mother looking at her with suspicious eyes. Two policemen in uniform came to the house, but they didn't find the money, although they questioned everybody, and, it seemed to Kath, asked her more questions than anyone. It was truly a terrible time and she began to realise this was how it felt to be unhappy.

The little terraced house had only two bedrooms—one for her parents and the other for her and her brothers with home-made wooden bunks up to the ceiling—and you could hear through the thin plaster walls. Often Kath had lain awake listening to her parents talking, arguing, or having sex, her Dad grunting as if he were going up a steep hill and her mother suddenly crying out in a mixture of pleasure and pain. She hadn't known what they were doing until one of the girls at school who had had two Dads told her all about it.

This night when her happiness ended, she heard him get up and tell her mother he was going downstairs to the outside lavatory in the backyard. She sensed something more important was going on by his casual tone and his cautious step on the creaky old stairs. His whole manner seemed so secretive. She knew him so well that she could guess he was up to something. She wondered why her mother didn't notice and follow him down. Even if she were half asleep, all the years with him should have warned her.

Kath caught him at the front door with everything that was his in two old cardboard suitcases. One spare shirt, one spare pair of socks. There wasn't much. He seemed shocked when he saw her coming down the stairs. He was obviously afraid she'd give him away. He ought to have known her better than that. He put his finger to his lips. She whispered, "You're going away?"

He nodded. "I have to, Kath."

"Where are you going?" she asked in a tone of dread, her world tumbling all around her.

"To America, Kath." His eyes brightened in the old way. "To the New World." He had the front door open and a full moon cast a strange unearthly glow over his face. "Over there, darlin', are big chances for everybody. Not like here. Dreams come true there, Kath. Poor men can get rich. It's paradise compared with England. There's nothing for me here. I'll just waste away. But there I've got a chance as good as anyone else. You do understand, love, don't you? I've *got* to go."

"Yes," she whispered, "I know." Tears sprang to her eyes

"Oh, Dadda, I'll miss you so much. All our good times together. The beer-house and, oh, the poaching—" Her voice rose into a cry and he put his right hand over her mouth.

"You'll wake the whole house, darlin'."

"Take me with you, Dadda."

"I can't, my darlin'. I would if I could. But I must go alone. It's something a man must do by himself." He gripped her tightly so she felt the hard stumps of his missing two fingers, and he kissed her on the mouth. "I'll send for you, Kath. Just as soon as I'm settled."

"Promise?"

"I promise."

"Where will you go?"

"New York. That's where the ship docks. I may go to Virginia where the English gents settled. Or out west where my father's cousin went. I fancy the state of Kansas where the cowboys are. Or I may make so much money in New York I won't want to move anywhere else." He chuckled and then put a finger to his lips, afraid the low sound had been audible upstairs. "I must be off, Kath, or I'll miss the train."

She couldn't let him go just like that with nothing to remember her by.

"Wait a minute."

Before he could argue, she was up the stairs. Harold stirred in his sleep, but didn't waken as she opened her drawer. She crept past the next bedroom where her mother was sleeping. When she got downstairs again, she thought he'd gone. Then she noticed the front door was open. He was waiting outside.

"Here. Take it with you to remember me by." It was her photograph. "It still looks a bit like me."

The sky was still dark. He picked up his suitcases. It was as if she were watching him in slow motion. None of it was real. Say it's all a dream. But, as if to show her it was really happening, he leaned down and kissed her again, his lips hard on hers, and then he was walking away down the narrow street, trying not to make a noise on the cobblestones, his head down as if he daren't look back.

She let him go, watching him grow smaller and smaller in the early morning fog. She hoped he'd turn and wave at the end of the street and when he didn't, she rushed out to call after him and then remembered he didn't want the others to wake. So with tears rolling down her face, she let him vanish round the corner. When would she ever see him again? But it was for the best, she told herself. Her Dad was right. There was nothing for him in Stockport. But there were all kinds of opportunities in America. Of course there were wild people there, but her Dad was too clever to get involved with them. He'd be true to himself, but he'd do well in America.

She went slowly back into the silent house and closed the front door. The house suddenly felt much colder and lonesome. She was left now just with her mother and her three brothers. She hadn't the same feeling for them as for her father. She felt very alone as she crept up the stairs, careful not to wake anyone. They would know soon enough.

3

The next morning Kath tried to keep out of her mother's way. She heard her asking the boys, "Have you seen your Dad?" and she stayed out in the backyard and then left early for school. Her mother wouldn't be fooled by any lies.

By the time she returned in the afternoon, her mother was convinced he'd had an accident. How she could think that was beyond Kath. Her mother was avoiding facing the truth. She'd been to the beer-house and even to the factory to talk to his friends. She sat at the kitchen table as if waiting for him to come home as she had done so many times in the past when he was out drinking. But the past was over.

Kath went to bed early to get away from the pale, worried face, the pointless waiting. She pretended to be asleep when her brothers came up, but she lay awake long after they were snoring, wondering if her Dad was on the ship yet, still trying to accept he was gone. His parting promise helped to keep her going and was always in her thoughts: "I'll send for you, Kath." Make it soon, Dadda. *Soon.* I don't want to stay here now without you, she thought. They don't need me—or even want me.

It was next morning that one of her Dad's beer-house friends came by and had a whispered conversation with her mother in the kitchen. They both looked very grim. The man left, and when they all sat down to breakfast, her mother told them,

"Your father has gone away." Kath didn't speak, she couldn't, she'd show that she knew already, but Harold said eagerly as if it must be good news, "Where to? Where's he gone? Are we going there, too?"

Her mother obviously didn't know how much she should tell them. She wasn't yet sure he'd gone for good. All she'd been told was that he'd been seen getting on the early morning train for Liverpool—and Liverpool was the port from where ships sailed for America. And she had discovered his old suitcases and his few clothes were gone, too. She finally decided not to answer Harold's question and there was a long, uneasy silence at the breakfast table. All the boys knew now that something was wrong, very wrong. Their mother's ashen, worried face had closed up into a sad, silent mask. They couldn't reach her. She had closed them out—usually it was only Kath.

Later that day the next-door neighbor's wife, Ernestine Walker, came by with more news. The missing gold wedding ring had turned up in a local pawnbroker's. Kath's mother went there immediately and learned who had pawned it. Then she remembered the missing rent money. He had been raising his fare to America any way he could.

That night Kath heard her crying in the next room in the lonely bed. She knew now her man wasn't coming back. It was the first time Kath had ever known her to cry. Usually she didn't show her feelings. It made Kath's world seem even more insecure. There was no one now to lean on. She was more alone than ever.

Next morning at the breakfast table, her mother's feelings were hidden again except for a quick, angry look in her eyes at any mention of him. Soon nobody referred to him in front of her.

"He's left us," Harold said indignantly in the backyard.

"He had to," Kath told him. "There was nothing for him here."

"Why didn't he take us with him?"

"Where's the money coming from?"

Harold didn't understand. That was why Dadda wouldn't send for him or any of the rest of them, only her.

In the first few weeks, Kath continued to miss him terribly.

But she wasn't miserable like her mother. She kept telling herself he had done right. There was nothing for him in Stockport. Nothing. He would have wasted himself here. There—in America—he had a chance. After school, she used to go up in the hills behind Stockport and look as far westwards as possible, as if she might see her father on the horizon coming for her. She waited for the mailman every day.

Eventually after three months, a letter did come—very brief and formal and addressed to her mother. He wrote merely that he had gone to America in search of work and he would write again and send money. Love to all. They waited for more news to come, Kath for a special message for her alone ("I'll send for you, Kath"), her mother for money. They all listened for the mailman, but as the days and weeks went by, Kath was the only one who didn't give up hope.

The letter they had received had no address for them to write to—he said he wasn't settled yet—but it was postmarked *Richmond, Virginia.* Kath studied a sketchy map of the state of Virginia in her school geography book and learned the names of the places there by heart—Richmond, the Shenandoah Valley, Charleston, Chesapeake Bay. . . . Was her Dad in Richmond still or was he living now in one of those other romantic-sounding places? Had he settled by now and was saving up to send for her?

It was then the dream began. Night after night she had the same dream—of America like the Garden of Eden in the Bible, a paradise of green slopes and cool streams and flowering fruit trees. And she and her Dad were there, just the two of them like Adam and Eve, to be happy ever after. But then something happened. She was never sure what except it was something concerning her father. She always awoke trembling, in a cold sweat, wondering what the dream meant.

She didn't discuss it with any of the family, not even with Harold who was closest to her age. She could tell by her mother's attitude that she thought his long silence meant he must be dead, perhaps killed by some wild American gunmen, but Kath knew better. Joseph Tracy wasn't dead. He would send for her one day as soon as he could. He *would*.

The weeks dragged on, then one fine afternoon a gypsy cart

came down the street, an old gypsy woman behind a lean donkey crying out, "Rag and bones." The gypsies were dealers in junk with romantic reputations; they were said to live on the road in caravans, never settled houses, and to be able to predict the future. Kath's mother, who didn't like them, said all gypsies were thieves and not to open the front door when they called out. But Kath couldn't resist running out to watch the old woman ride by on her cart. The old woman saw her and stopped.

"What's your name, pretty girl?" the old gypsy asked, her hooded eyes peering down at Kath.

"Kathleen Tracy," replied Kath proudly.

"Let me see your hand, child."

Kath held out her right hand and the old gypsy woman studied it with a grave face.

"What do you see?" Kath asked at last.

The old woman took Kath's face in one of her hard withered hands. "The Shadow of Death, child. You will have to go through the valley of The Shadow of Death and be reborn." The old woman's hooded eyes had a faraway expression. "You will have to journey along the perilous path of enlightenment. It will not be easy." She squeezed Kath's face. "But never lose your dream. You will reach the heights of fulfillment. Then you will learn the secret of what makes dreams come true." She released Kath's face then and cracked her whip over the lean, sad-looking donkey and was gone. Kath didn't move even when the cart had disappeared up the hill. She stood thinking about the old gypsy's prediction. What had it meant?

She'd learn the answer one day, but in the meantime she had to survive. Her mother had a job in a factory and also worked in a grocery store in Stockport for several hours at night. With no money coming from America, she had to struggle on alone. She had applied for poor relief and to one of the local private charities, but with no success. Thousands of unemployed workers had filled the lists already. She was told to wait. Kath did odd jobs in the town after school and cooked for the family. What her mother's earnings bought was so little, the leftovers at the butcher's and the greengrocer's, that she soon turned back to another source of supply—poaching.

Her Dad had passed on his skills to her. They had spent so much time together. On days when he didn't work at the factory, if he didn't spend too long with his friends drinking beer, then the two of them went poaching in the grounds of Heaton Hall. Her Dad knew where the wall was low enough to climb over. "They've got so much they can spare us a little," he told her as he set up his traps. If he hadn't been drinking, he'd use his short sawn-off rifle. Hares or pheasants, it was mostly. Sober, he could hit a hare at a hundred yards in open country, and he taught her to shoot equally well. He said she was ready when, shooting at a playing card he placed in the fork of an oak tree, she shot twice leaving only one bullet hole in the card. At first she thought one of the shots had missed, but then she noticed the hole was slightly enlarged—one bullet had followed the other almost exactly. "You're ready, Kathleen," her Dad had said. In those days he always used her full name when he was especially proud of her.

After that test, he let her accompany him all the way into the grounds of Heaton Hall, and the time came when he let her shoot her first hare. They had seen it on the edge of a dense wood and he had called to it in hare language, a sharp, low cry that made the hare stand up on its hind legs and wait for him. "Quickly, Kath," he'd said, handing her the gun. He'd drunk too much for a long shot, his hands were trembling. She felt excited before her first kill, but at that distance the hare meant no more to her than the target on the oak tree. She'd sighted and shot almost without thinking, and the hare, a good seventy yards away, staggered back and slowly slumped over. It was still breathing when they reached it. Blood was seeping out of a bullet hole through its neck. Only its frightened eyes were alive. Kath suddenly realised what she had done. But as she stood staring, feeling sick, her Dad grabbed the dying hare and twisted its neck and its eyes glazed over. It was like putting out a light. She turned away and threw up. Her Dad acted as if he hadn't noticed. He stuffed the dead hare in a secret pocket of his long coat that reached to his ankles. It had special pockets for poaching that her mother had stitched in.

They had been ready to leave when a gamekeeper, who had heard the shot, came rushing out of the wood. "Run, Kath," her Dad cried, and off they dashed with the gamekeeper after them. He was soon gaining on her, so her Dad told her to run one way and he ran another, and of course the gamekeeper followed her Dad because he had the hare and the gun weighing him down. Gallant her Dad was. She ran all the way home and waited outside for her Dad. But he didn't come. The police did. They had been passing the main gates of Heaton Hall as he ran out just ahead of the gamekeeper. Bad luck, that was all. Everyone had it sooner or later. Without the police interfering, her Dad would easily have outrun the gamekeeper. He was in jail for a few days and then was fined fourteen shillings, which his friends collected at the factory and the beer-house. The boss at the factory also owned Heaton Hall and warned him he'd lose his job if he was caught poaching again. That was the last time she went poaching with him. Soon after he lost his two fingers and life was never the same again.

He had taken his short sawn-off rifle with him to America, but Kath was able to borrow another gun from an old poacher whose rheumatism had made him retire. She agreed to give him a hare every time she went out.

The first time alone she was scared. She tried to persuade Harold, who was only two years younger, to go with her, but he wouldn't—he was even more scared. She was more of a boy than Harold or her other two younger brothers would ever be. She should have been born a boy instead of a girl. Her mother said she was a tomboy, but didn't mean it as praise. "You're a young lady, Kathleen. Act like one." Her mother never liked anything she did, not even now, after all these years and all her efforts to make up for her Dad's absence.

So she went poaching for their dinner by herself. She was tired of cooking the butcher's leftovers, old bones with hardly any meat, and hearing her brothers complain they were still hungry as if it were her fault. She remembered the fat hares and pheasants to be had at Heaton Hall.

That first time alone she was nearly arrested by a policeman. Her secret pockets were all full. He guessed what she had been doing. She decided to be honest. "I've killed three hares to feed hungry kids," she said looking up at him. He stared down at her, astonished. He gave it some thought. "Go on, girl," he said at last and let her run away.

She waited a week to get her courage back and then went out again. She tried some of her Dad's special tricks, feeding the pheasants with raisins soaked in gin to get them drunk and unable to escape. She picked the fattest and wrung their necks and put them in her secret pockets. Killing no longer bothered her. You had to eat. She went poaching at least once a week. Summer passed quickly that way . . . then winter . . . the year was over and then another and still her Dad didn't send for her.

It was very cold that winter and her feet crunched on the frosty ground of Heaton Hall. It was what her Dad called "giveaway weather"—they could hear you coming. At least not many gamekeepers seemed to be out in the grounds. Probably too cold even for them. Kath knew the language of the birds from scaring them in the fields the previous summer for a shilling a week, enough to buy her mother a four-pound loaf. Far off a blackbird squawked, and she stopped to listen. That could be a sign that other people were in the area. But there were no more squawks so she crept on very slowly, trying to minimise the noise.

The wind through the pine trees sounded the way she imagined the sea did—the sea her Dad had crossed to get to America. There was a new moon in the cold night sky. The moonlight always made her feel strange, touching something inside her, but a new moon was extra special like the beginning of a fresh period in her life. She hadn't known it was the night of a new moon. She had got up before dawn because her Dad had told her the old men who lived by poaching always did it by moonlight.

A blackbird squawked suddenly quite close, then again and again with a frantic tone, and there was a flurry of wings in some nearby bushes as the bird rose to escape from some intruder. It was a clear warning of danger, but it had come too late for her. A tall dark figure stepped out of the trees ahead, holding a double-barrelled shotgun that made her sawn-off little gun look like a toy. "Move another yard and I'll let daylight into you," a gruff man's voice told her.

Kath froze. There was no escape this time. She waited for his next move.

"Come here," said the voice, "let me see you."

She stepped forward into the moonlight.

Suddenly there was a deep laugh.

"You're only a kid—a girl."

She was near enough to see him now. He wasn't that old himself—about nineteen or twenty. Tall and dark with big black eyes and flashing white teeth. Too big for her to deal with. His hand pulled off her knitted cap and her red hair fell out over her shoulders. He unbuttoned her coat, and his other hand touched her swelling breasts that annoyed the tomboy in her so much.

"You're not a kid," he said. "You're already a woman."

He stood examining her. His eyes took in the angry face, the full breasts, the narrow waist, the strong thighs. She was four- teen now, already big and with a sexual look she didn't know she had.

He gave her a boyish grin. "You're the first pretty poacher I ever saw." He rubbed a hand through her hair. She pulled back and the shotgun rose in her face. "No running, Red. I can shoot as good as you can any time." He grinned again, enjoying himself. "You're in my power, Red. I can hand you over to the gamekeepers or. . . ."

He stared at her slyly. He seemed very young then, a boy in a man's body; he had some filling out to do yet. She began to hope. Presumably he wasn't one of the gamekeepers the way he was talking.

"I'll make you an offer, Red. You got something I want, I got something you want—namely, your freedom. We can do an exchange, make a deal."

"I don't follow you, mister," Kath said.

"You want your freedom, don't you, girl? You want to get out of here and go home, don't you? Then you got to give me something in return. Follow me." The shotgun gestured to- wards the woods. "We'll go somewhere quieter where we won't be disturbed. The gamekeepers are probably all drunk, but don't count on it."

She hesitated. She didn't want to follow him anywhere. She

wondered whether to run for it, but she didn't want both barrels in her back.

"Come on, walk."

She felt she had no choice. She *had* to do what he said. She began to walk ahead of him under the overhanging trees.

"Anybody tell you you got nice legs, Red?" he asked, close behind her.

Oh, she thought, that's what he's got on his mind. A boy-man with the urge. She stopped.

They were well into the woods. It was very still and dark. There were no sounds, not even bird cries.

"There," he said, pointing to a patch of grass under a big weeping willow. He took off his coat and dropped it on the ground. He didn't seem to feel the cold.

"Lie down," he said, grinning at her.

"No," she said, hunching her shoulders, trying to look more like a kid. "I'm not ready for that—"

"You're plenty ready."

She stood, hands on hips, staring defiantly at him.

The shotgun pointed at her.

"Don't be a little fool. You don't want me to give you to the gamekeepers. You'll enjoy it. I'll be very gentle with you. You'll see."

She could tell by his expression how worked up he was. If he'd been a grown man, she'd have had more hope, but a boy like him just wanted to satisfy himself.

"Not now," she said. "I'm not ready for a man—"

A big hand pushed her down and suddenly he was on top of her. He was hard-muscled and strong. She struggled, but she couldn't hold him off. One of his big rough hands was under her skirt, feeling between her legs, while his wet, hot lips were on her swelling nipples. She tried to scream, but he covered her face with his other hand. Her skirt was up now and she felt him moving up between her thighs. She rocked violently back and forth trying to stop him, but he held her tightly and thrust upwards. He was very excited. Suddenly she felt a hardness stab inside her and a sharp pain upwards through her body, and she clenched her teeth, waiting for more, but there was a noise at the back of them . . . voices . . . the squawk of birds . . . warnings of danger close by.

She held her breath, pushing at him, but he seemed reluctant to stop, still thrusting upwards between her legs, trying to find his way back in, ignoring the danger, but the voices grew louder behind them and at last he cursed angrily and tore himself away from her unwillingly, completely frustrated, and stood up over her, listening.

There seemed to be more voices and the crackling sounds of people coming through the undergrowth near them. Closer and closer, until it seemed to Kath that they must be in sight across the clearing.

He pulled up his trousers, grim-faced.

"We'll have to finish it another day, Red," he panted.

She got up warily, watching him.

He grabbed her by the hair and kissed her. "Run, you little fool. It's the gamekeepers," and then he was off through the bushes with not even a backward look—like her Dad that last morning.

She ran the other way and came unexpectedly close to the voices, but she ducked down as the gamekeepers rushed past and no one saw her. They had shotguns, but luckily no dogs. When she reached home, she emptied her pockets on the kitchen table. It was enough for at least three meals for them all. Then she went up to bed at last. Harold woke up briefly and said hello and then went back to sleep. He was the only one of her brothers she liked. His manchild's face had a look of her Dad. Her lack of feeling for the others embarrassed her because she thought she ought to like them all. They were her family, her blood. Perhaps it was possible to love people without liking them.

She lay awake for a long time, thinking. The man's dark handsome face kept coming back to her. At first he made her angry, but then her mind turned to the sensation he had started in her. It was something new and disturbing, a feeling of the woman in her she could no longer deny. The tomboy she had been was now only a part of the childhood she had left behind. The incident in the wood marked the turning point. She wondered if she would ever see him again.

4

When Kath was fifteen, she went to work full-time at the factory. She had often paused on the way home from school outside the towering gray stone building with the smoky high chimney and listened to the hum of the machines and wondered what went on inside. Now her clogged feet joined all the others that wore the cobblestones smooth on the road up the hill to the high factory gates. Her time had come.

Work began at six o'clock in the morning. It was cold then, and her mother gave her an old shawl like the other women wore to the factory. Kath draped it over her head and shoulders the way she had seen Mexican women wear a mantilla in a picture at school. It made her feel romantic and mysterious.

Becoming part of the grown-up world excited her. Nobody could call her a child any more. She was officially a woman now! The first time she was paid she ran all the way home with her wages and at dinner that night, she watched the rest of the family eat, thinking "My wages bought that food in their stomachs." She felt very proud of herself.

The rows of heavy gray machines fascinated her. They did such complicated manufacturing, almost as clever as human beings, and she was their master. She had a sense of power for the first time in her life. The machines had a regular rhythm, almost a sort of mechanical music, and they went on and on, bang-clang-whang, all day long.

At first she was shy with the other women—some of them were old enough to be her mother, but they soon made her part of the gang, part of the hard joking and laughter and gossip over the machines, making the hours pass faster. Most of the gossip was about men. How selfish they were, how foolish, how dirty, what lousy lovers, she was surprised what women said when they were alone together, men wouldn't like it, yet none of them seemed to want to be without a man. Half the younger women were pregnant. Men were their only escape from the factory—from the caged-up feeling it gave you.

Kath's excitement, her enjoyment of the change in her life, soon passed. You got too tired. The long hours six days a week and the sense of confinement wore her down. She had to stay with the noisy machines hour after hour without a break. She no longer felt like their master, but their slave. They demanded constant attention. The cotton dust crept down her throat and made her cough and her eyes run. The dampness irritated her skin. She came to hate being shut up in the grim, damp building all day, and even when the time came when she could leave, she felt drained of energy, and yet she still had to go home to cook. The boys were home first from school, but they wouldn't do any cooking, not even Harold. They said it was a woman's work. It made her long more than ever for her Dad to rescue her. Perhaps he wouldn't even recognise her now. The photograph in the silver frame that she had given him was now a picture of someone else—someone who had been as free as a bird in the sky and now was caged.

She longed to escape from the cage. The factory, cooking for the rest of the family, sleep—that was her existence, it was no life. Her dream had dimmed a little over the years, but she was still sure she would go to America to her Dad one day. Perhaps he had been wounded in the civil war there or had been caught poaching and had been imprisoned by the Americans. He was probably waiting to make his fortune and then he'd feel he was ready for her. There were any number of possible explanations. In the meantime, she had to stick it out.

Some of the men at the factory made passes at her. They always went after a new girl and the very young ones, who might be virgins, had a special attraction. They seemed to sense

Kath was ready; they came round her like tomcats, the married ones worse than anyone. It was as if the incident in the wood at Heaton Hall had made her bloom. Her body didn't feel her own any more. A wild animal was loose inside her, barely under control. She knew she had to be careful. This was the time when you could get trapped for life. She was determined not to give herself to anyone like so many of the girls did. Get pregnant by one of the men and she'd be condemned to this way of life forever. She'd never escape from the cage.

Nancy, one of the older women who had befriended her, warned her: "Don't be flattered just because a man wants you, Kath. Get something back for it. I mean much more than just a few minutes of pleasure when he does it to you. With your looks, you should be able to better yourself. Just learn to play your cards right. You've got some aces."

It was Nancy who first suggested the factory owner was interested in her. She hadn't paid much attention until then. He was old enough to be her Dad. She noticed him coming by often after that and how he stared at her body as she leaned over the machines. She waited for him to speak, but he took his time. It wasn't shyness. He was too old for that, too old and too shrewd, a big heavy man with an air of authority, used to getting his own way. The boss.

She was sixteen when he made his first move. It surprised her in spite of all the attention he'd given her, because by then she'd convinced herself he'd hold off because he was married. He came by when it was her turn to stop the machines—the other girls had all left. The factory was a big empty shell. Every sound echoed on the stone floor. She heard his footsteps before she saw him. He sat on the edge of a machine and began talking to her as if they already knew each other intimately. He wasted no time. He explained his wife was an invalid, bedridden with no hope of recovery. She hadn't long to live. Then he put a big hairy hand on Kath's arm and added quietly that it was years since she'd been a real wife to him. He was desperate for a young woman. He was frank with her. He wanted *her.*

Kath was shocked by his bluntness and nervous at being alone with him. She gazed at the tufts of black, greying hair on his hand, unsure how to reply. After all, he was the boss. She was saved by the sound of footsteps on the stone floor on the far side of the factory. Probably the night-watchman.

"I'll give you time to think about it," he said quickly and disappeared down the lane of silent machines.

She was now forced to make a decision about her life. She wished she had someone she completely trusted to advise her. She couldn't mention it to her mother. They didn't communicate. Her mother had never even discussed sex with her. It was something sinful outside marriage—an unmentionable. There was only Nancy to talk it over with and she knew what Nancy would say. "It's your big chance, Kath. But don't make it too easy for him. A man doesn't respect a girl he gets too easy. Make your conditions before you do more than cuddle. Ask for marriage when his wife dies or nothing doing. You can strike it rich, girl, and be mistress of Heaton Hall."

Kath wasn't sure she wanted to pay the price. Part of her thought like Nancy, part like her mother. This was the time she needed her father. It was a conflict she couldn't resolve on her own. She needed time. "You'll miss your big opportunity," Nancy told her. "Wish it was me. I'd have said 'Yes' as soon as he asked me." But she wasn't Nancy.

She tried to avoid him, but it was impossible. He was there every day, pressuring her to meet him after work. She wondered if she would lose her job if she turned him down. She tried to keep him dangling until she made up her mind. She told him she wasn't interested in just being with a man, she was looking for a husband. At first he laughed. Didn't take her seriously. Marriage wasn't what he wanted from her. He tried to get close to her at the machines, but she kept her distance and always walked home with some of the other girls. He kept on asking her. But she made it clear she wouldn't do what he wanted until he promised to marry her when his wife died. She never expected him to agree. And she didn't care. She really didn't want to get involved with him. He didn't attract her in any way.

At last, to her astonishment, he came by early one morning when the machines were still warming up, and whispered, "You're keeping me awake at night." She said nothing, but just pretended to concentrate on the machines. "All right," he said,

"let's do it the way you want it. When my wife dies . . . yes."
He glanced round to make sure no one was looking and then
pressed her hand. "Meet me in the stables at the Hall tonight."
He pressed her hand again.

"You promise?" she said.

"Yes, I promise." He eyed her body as if he now had the
right to do it openly. "Call me Edward . . . Kath."

He waited for her reply. She felt trapped in a situation she
didn't want. He was old enough to be her Dad.

"At eight," he said, "when it's dark."

She told Nancy.

"Oh, love, how wonderful!" Nancy kissed her. It only depressed her more. She thought of not showing up. But he had
met her terms. "You can handle him," Nancy said. "He won't
give you a hard time. It's not like a young feller."

It was the night of a full moon, and Kath stared up at the
moonlight and felt slightly dizzy as she climbed the wall of
Heaton Hall—the broken part her Dad had showed her. She
nearly turned back. But she steeled herself. Nancy was right—
she could handle him. She had no choice if she wanted to get
away from the factory.

The stables were in darkness, the moonlight reflecting on
one of the windows. She heard the horses stirring in their stalls.
Perhaps he wasn't coming. But then suddenly he spoke out of
the darkness. "I'm over here."

He had made a bed of straw and he pulled her down on it.
She had hoped a bit of caressing and kissing would satisfy the
old man, but he became very excited and rough and wanted to
go all the way with her. She tried to slip away from him, but
he was very strong. He rolled on top of her, breathing heavily.

"Let me."

"No—"

"Let me. I've got to get to know you—my future wife. Let
me do it. Now. . . ."

She couldn't get away. She wished it was the young man in
the wood. He had opened the way for this old man. She kept
thinking of what she was gaining from it—being his wife would
save her from her present life. She tried to imagine it was her
Dad and then perhaps she could like him more. He had the

same heavily built, hairy body as her Dad and also the same big square hands (though he had all his fingers). He panted and grunted when he was on top of her like her Dad had sounded through the bedroom wall—and at last he pained her with the size of him, and finally she was caught up in the feeling of it and it no longer mattered who was doing it to her. She was only sorry he had been the one to do it first. She had a sense of letdown at the end. He lay back as if completely drained, panting heavily.

"Can I go now?" she murmured.

He put a hand on her breasts.

"Call me Edward."

"Edward, can I go now?"

"Is that all you've got to say to me? Did you enjoy yourself? Tell me you did."

"Yes, yes." Anything to get away and be by herself. She heard the horses moving in their stalls. She felt as bound to this man as they were.

Next day at the factory he wanted to meet again that night. She told him she had to be home early. The next night then. "You've hooked him," Nancy said. "All you've got to do is not let him go until you've got him on dry land—at the altar!"

They met the next night and he wanted to do it again. She decided to keep him to two nights a week at the most and she made sure they took precautions. She didn't want to get trapped with a baby at sixteen, not until they were married. She was bringing no bastards into this world. She talked to Nancy who had been with a great many men, even soldiers, and then she made him wear a sheath, even though he complained it dulled his enjoyment and might make him impotent. No such luck. To get through it without angering him, she sometimes imagined he was someone else—sometimes the dark young man in the wood. When they were alone, he was often kind and affectionate, but his manner at the factory was distant and gave nothing away. It was a strange relationship that never seemed to develop much beyond a sexual level.

He gave her money. She bought a new red shawl and let her mother have what was left. He began to give her money regularly. Her mother never asked where it came from, but she said once, "We can manage without the extra," a strange, accusing expression in her eyes. Another time she told Kath, "You need to go to church more often, Kathleen." Her father had been born a Catholic, but never went to church. Her mother didn't like Catholics and brought up the children as Anglicans. Kath went to the Parish Church most Sundays, but it didn't mean much to her. She felt as if God never answered her prayers, that He had abandoned her. One Sunday, without telling her mother, she went in a Catholic church, but she didn't feel any different. God would probably only answer her prayers when she gave up her present life, but she was trapped in it. She admitted nothing to her mother. She and her mother weren't any closer than they had ever been. There had always been something that soured their relationship—something Kath didn't understand. What she was doing was better than poaching, that she did know. They ate better, and nobody, nothing, suffered but herself. But she wasn't doing it for the money, but for the future—the Hall, the estate, a change of life, no more struggling, no more poverty, no more cotton dust. She was doing it to escape from the cage. Edward was insurance in case something *had* happened to her Dad. Surely God in the end helped those who helped themselves.

Some rich people from Chester came to stay at the Hall for a week and Edward took the men out fox-hunting. The dogs chased a red fox into the factory as they were all at work. Several of the girls screamed and stood on their chairs. The fox streaked under one of the machines. The dogs were too big to follow it and stood in front of the machine howling and pawing the stone floor with frustration. Edward had the machine dismantled. The little fox, its red fur stiff with fear, was revealed crouched in a corner. It gave a low, despairing cry as the dogs pounced and tore it to pieces. Edward gave her a triumphant grin, one of those vain peacock male looks, and he seemed surprised by her horrified stare. The next time they met in the stables, he mentioned it.

"It was cruel," she told him.

"No more cruel than poaching."

"A poacher kills quickly. Just imagine what torture that poor fox went through as it listened to the machine being taken out and the dogs' howls getting nearer. It must have been as bad as waiting to be hanged."

"You women don't understand such things," he said grumpily. He was particularly rough with her that night. He was still excited by the fox-hunt. She might have been the fox. He penetrated her as if he were thrusting a knife into her. She felt the pain up through her body. He didn't even notice, but moaned with satisfaction. His own pleasure—that was all he cared about.

They had been meeting twice a week in the stables for over a year when his wife died at last, a sudden heart attack after breakfast. When the news sped round the factory, Kath struggled hard to hide her happiness. She felt like cheering. Now she'd get her reward for all those nights on the stable floor. She'd give up the factory and go to live at the Hall and one day he would die, too, and then it would all be hers. She would be rich and free. She could go and find her Dad and share it all with him. It came at the right time in every way. She and her mother weren't getting on. When she went out to meet Edward, her mother always seemed to be at the door. "Where are you going so late?" she'd ask with accusing eyes. Her mother wanted to get married again—to the grocer she worked for in the evenings—but she couldn't until she had confirmation her husband was dead. And he wasn't. He *wasn't*.

On an impulse, she told the foreman she was giving up her job. She'd never go to the factory again. She couldn't wait to do it until after she saw Edward. She had to do it immediately. It was a wonderful feeling, something she had wanted to do for so long. The foreman was very off-hand, he didn't care, there were plenty of other people waiting for work.

She met Edward that night. He told her to wait until after the funeral, but she insisted. She arrived at the stables feeling very lighthearted, and at first she didn't notice that he wasn't sharing her happiness. He was solemn and distant. "How long's the official mourning?" she asked. "When can the wedding take place?"

He didn't reply.

"What's wrong?" she demanded at last.

Then he told her—as bluntly as he had once expressed his

desire for her. There was going to be no wedding, at least for her. He was going to marry someone else, a woman in Chester who was rich, too. It made good business sense to merge their two fortunes, he told her with a satisfied smile. Of course he and Kath could go on meeting in secret. She hadn't lost him, he added complacently. He didn't even mention his promise or try to apologize.

She was slow to understand. She didn't want to believe it. Then his meaning hit her. *He wasn't going to marry her.* It was almost as big a shock as if her Dad had written to say he wasn't ever going to send for her. Her dream of life in Heaton Hall had kept her going through all the long days in the factory and the cotton dust and through the intimate meetings with him and the sex, the *sex.*

"But you promised me," she cried.

"I said I would if I could," he hedged. "But the situation has changed."

"I've already given up my job."

"That was very foolish of you. Never mind, I'll make sure you get it back."

Get it back! Back to the factory. Back to the cage—the prison. For ever and ever. With no hope of escape. He didn't seem to understand what he had done to her, that he had crushed her dreams. He came closer to her. Her blood began to pound. She wanted to push him away. His promise had been a lie, he'd *never* intended to marry her. She'd endured his old hairy body, all those times being pawed over and treated like an animal, for *nothing* at the end of it. She felt . . . defiled. She could have torn out her vagina in disgust with herself and with him. He must think she had no real feelings, that she was just one of the factory girls to be used any way he wanted.

He put a big hand on her breasts and pressed hard, crushing the nipples. She could smell the whisky on his breath. He was always at his worst when he was drinking.

"Please, Edward. . . . Please, stop it."

He ignored her. He tried to kiss her, but she turned her face away. He felt angrily for her buttocks.

"You're mine," he whispered, his heavy body pressing against hers. "This won't make any difference to us." Both hands now cupped her buttocks and pulled her to him. "I'll show you, Kath—"

"Get away from me!" He was treating her cheaply, like a prostitute. She struggled to break his grip, but the more she fought him, the more excited he grew.

"That's right, my little tigress," he murmured thickly, his whisky breath in her face. "I'll show you who's the master." He forced her dress down over her shoulders and put a hand between her legs. "You little bitch, you'll do what I say."

"Get off me, Edward. I hate you," she cried, but he wasn't listening. He had her dress up above her waist. He was going to force himself into her. She struggled wildly, but he was too strong. He bent her back, pushing between her legs, pressing her to the floor.

She panicked. Her hand felt instinctively for something secure to keep her balance. If she fell to the straw, she'd be completely in his power. He'd have her again. Her fingers touched a knife for cutting leather that a groom had left on a bench. Hardly aware of what she was doing in her rising panic, Kath seized the knife and struck out blindly. She felt it cut into him and he shrieked like a wounded animal. At once his grip on her relaxed. She felt him collapsing backwards. Blood was gushing through his silk shirt. His heavy body fell in a heap on the straw, his eyes already glassy, unseeing. He didn't move.

She was ready to run, then she realised he was no longer a threat. Her panic slowly ebbed away. Her mind cleared and she knelt down to examine him. But as soon as she saw his face close up and touched his cheek, she knew he was dead, suddenly aged and shrunken as if someone had pulled out a plug and all the life had drained away. Oh, Kathleen Tracy, she thought desperately, what a terrible thing you have done! Shock rocked her back on her heels. She had *killed* him, she had ended his life. The bloody knife lay on the floor at her feet. She kicked it away from her. If only that could undo what had happened! She put her hands to her face to blot out the sight of him and stood like that for a long time.

She waited until she was completely calm, until her nerves no longer seemed to be out of control. It had been as easy to kill Edward as a hare or a pheasant, and the thought horrified

her. Dear God, she thought, forgive me, but she was aware
only of a great silence, a terrifying loneliness.

When she looked again, the blood had stopped flowing. His
shirt and the thick straw were sodden with it. The horses
smelled the blood and moved restlessly in their stalls. Edward
had always been worked up sexually by the horses' smell; that
was one reason why he wanted to meet in the stables. He was
a very sick, repressed old man . . . and now he was dead.

She steeled herself. She knew what she had to do and she
hoped she had the strength. She turned her back on the body.
It no longer seemed like Edward lying there but just a lifeless
hulk. She walked slowly to the wooden double doors, knowing
she was leaving the stables for the last time. One of the stallions
reared up and stamped the floor as she passed his stall. Then
she was out in the cold fresh air.

As Kath walked up the terraces to the Hall, her long red hair
streaming behind her, she stared at the dark horizon as if hoping that her Dad would appear to rescue her. But there was no
escape now—anywhere. It was then she began to appreciate the
enormity of what she had done. She had destroyed not only her
dream of leaving the factory, but of going to America, of seeing
her Dad again—she had destroyed it all, everything had come
tumbling down.

The Hall seemed to mock her as she approached, her shoes
crunching on the gravel, tearing at her nerves. Now the big
black-and-white house would never be hers.

She hesitated before ringing the heavy iron doorbell. There
was no turning back once she did that. But she knew she *had*
to do it. The ringing echoed far away in the bowels of the great
house.

The old butler came. He knew who she was. He stared at her
with distaste.

"What do you want?" he snapped.

"You better call the police," Kath said very distinctly, her
heart thumping madly. "I've just killed your master."

The old butler's mouth sagged open.

"Look in the stables," she told him impatiently.

Then suddenly she knew she couldn't go through with it.
She couldn't lose her dream.

She ran. She heard the old butler shout. But she was soon too far away to hear any more. She ran down the terraces, across the driveway, through the woods, and over the wall. She ran as if they were after her already—the police. She ran until her heart beat against her chest and she panted for air.

At first she ran towards home, but she knew there was no refuge with her mother, and the neighbors would see her come down the street.

So she ran the other way—towards Hayfield and the heather-covered moors leading to the great Kinder Scout mountain range where she and her father had once climbed and picnicked.

She ran for hours. Some gypsies let her sit on the back of their cart for a few miles. She remembered the old gypsy woman's prediction. Was this what she had meant by the Shadow of Death?

She reached the moors when it was growing dark. She sheltered at night behind one of the dry stone walls, but she nearly froze to death. They found her late the next day. Local sheep farmers had reported seeing her. They remembered her red hair. Police with dogs came across the moors. She climbed high up the rocks, refusing to give herself up. But the police cut off her retreat and surrounded her close to the top of Kinder Scout. When they marched her down, all that she could think of was that her dream was lost forever.

5

They held her in the ancient Stockport jail until her trial. The cold stone building was below the cobbled marketplace, and many times Kath had passed the barred windows on the way to shopping in the market. Once she had asked her mother, "What kind of people do they put in jail?," and her mother had replied, "Wicked people."

Her mother came to see her the second day. By then, Kath was longing to talk to the family, to explain herself. The long hours alone with her thoughts had been a torture. She rushed to her mother to hug her, expecting her love and sympathy.

Her mother said coldly, "Why did you do this wicked act, Kathleen? Our family has always had a good name until now."

Kath tried to explain. "I didn't mean to kill him. It just happened—"

"Excuses, Kathleen! Remember, whom the gods wish to destroy, they first make angry. Your father had a violent temper, too. You've inherited his no-good, evil side." She was as hard-eyed as the prison guards, as distant as the chaplain who had come that morning. "You were involved with a married man. Nothing good can come of lust. I tried to bring you up as well as the boys, but you had too many of your father's bad ways. All you can do now in the time left to you is to repent and ask for forgiveness and prepare to meet your Maker."

Oh, it was cold. There had never really been any love between them and there was none now. Kath was relieved when her mother was ready to leave. It was better to be alone. But at the cell door, her mother suddenly stopped and came back. One last thing remained to be said between them.

"I've been in two minds whether to tell you this, Kathleen," she said coldly. "But this may be the last time we'll talk freely together. I think you should know the truth about yourself before you go to meet your Maker. You're not my daughter." Kath's heart gave a jump. "Your mother died when you were born, several years before your father and I were married."

She said it with obvious satisfaction. There might be a murderess in the family, but she didn't share the same blood. She'd make sure the neighbors knew. Kath examined her as if she had never seen her before—this strange woman named Victoria Tracy. Kath wasn't shocked by the news, but strangely relieved. It made sense. It explained the lack of feeling between them and why her mother—no, not her mother, her Dad's second wife—had always been warmer to the boys. They were *her* children. Only her Dad had really loved her. She was totally alone now at the very time in her life when she needed somebody—somebody to care.

"Who was my mother?" she asked softly.

"I never knew her and your father never talked about her."

All Kath's resentment flared up. She cried so the guards outside must have heard, "Don't come back. You've done your duty. You can have a good conscience at church on Sunday."

Victoria Tracy's pale, thin face tightened. "You're still arrogant—like the Devil, Kathleen. Your temper blinds you. You need to ask the Lord's forgiveness before it's too late. You've betrayed our family just like your father did. You're sinners of the same flesh."

"He went to America to get away from you!" Kath yelled angrily.

The cell door clanged, and Victoria Tracy was gone down the bare passageway with the hard cold stone floor and the nauseous prison smell.

* * *

The trial in Manchester was like a dream to Kath. It was hardly real that all these important people in this old ornate building were there because of her—an unknown factory girl. One violent, impulsive act had made her famous. The eyes of everyone in the courtroom kept returning to her. They went endlessly over the killing of Edward, draining it of all meaning. She refused to plead guilty. She hadn't meant to kill him, she'd been trying to get away from him. And all eyes were on her as she spoke quietly but firmly. Oh, that she could have had all this attention without killing anyone.

She felt completely isolated in the crowded courtroom. There might have been a barrier between her and the rest of humanity. She saw her ex-mother sitting at the back, but there was no recognition between them. The only one of the family she wanted to talk with was Harold, but he was probably too young to come to the jail or perhaps his mother wouldn't let him. He was in the courtroom on the last day and gave her a shy wave. She nodded, her face set in her public mask, afraid of showing any feelings before the crowd of strangers. She was determined not to reveal any weakness or what she had done would lose all meaning. She had to be strong, and her firm chin jutted out. Her Dad would understand she had had no choice. And perhaps her mother, her real mother, whoever she was, would have understood, too. She wouldn't get a chance to ask her Dad about her mother now. She'd have liked to know something about her.

Kath had accepted from the beginning that she was going to die—from that very first moment when she stood over the body and knew Edward was dead. An eye for an eye—that was the way it went always unless they proved you were crazy and she wasn't crazy. She might have been out of her mind in that brief flash of rage when she did it, but not now. She was as sane as the elderly judge in the courtroom. No excuses. She didn't want any. She was prepared to die. Like the hare or the pheasant.

* * *

During the trial, a crowd of unemployed cotton workers demonstrated outside the courtroom. Their shouts were clearly audible to Kath as she sat in the dock. It took her a long time to realise they were on her side. Police on horseback, wielding heavy truncheons, dispersed them, but they came back.

It was a strange contrast: the cold legal ritual inside the courtroom and the emotional violence outside. The elderly judge in his tall white wig flinched at each roar from the street.

When Kath was sentenced, there was another demonstration, bigger and angrier. While Kath was listening to the elderly judge's formal words, standing very straight, pale but expressionless, hardly realising what the reedy old man's voice was saying, two of the courtroom's stained glass windows were smashed. Nine workers and two policemen were taken to a local hospital with minor injuries.

"The court won't be intimidated," the elderly judge snapped. "Your vicious crime deserves the maximum sentence," he told Kath with an angry face. "But we also trust it will prove to the mob outside that they are not above the law. You are sentenced to be hanged by the neck until you are dead. . . ."

My God, she thought, they're going to *hang* me. She had expected to pay with her life, but the thought of the gallows and the hanging noose horrified her. But there was no escape.

The demonstration started again in the evening. Marches, banners, speeches. To Kath in her cell, it sounded like a war. All this because of me, she thought with amazement. They have more feeling for me than my own family. I won't be alone when I'm hanged. They'll come and watch as if I'm like a travelling circus. I'll be a star!

All that she really regretted was that now she'd never go to America. She'd have to see her Dad on the other side—in heaven or hell. Then she wept for the first time, but only because there was nobody to see her.

A note was smuggled in to her. It was tucked in with her food. It was from Nancy at the factory.

"They won't let me come to see you. But don't give up hope, Kath. You have many friends outside trying to help you."

Next day, a striking figure with her long red hair flowing over her dull prison garb, she was moved to Manchester Prison in a closed carriage to await her public execution. The cotton workers massed outside the prison and kept a round-the-clock vigil in front of the gates. Kath was one of them, a symbol of rebellion against oppression, a refusal to be treated like a slave.

It also helped that she was young and beautiful. The cotton workers had lacked a martyr to rally round and urge them on. Their leaders were quick to see Kath's usefulness as a cause.

A petition was drawn up, asking the government to reprieve her. Soon fifty thousand signatures had been collected. A delegation went to London to present the petition to Sir George Grey, the Home Secretary, but he refused to meet them, and so they had to leave the pages of signatures with his secretary.

But the government was worried. Robert Bennington, the High Sheriff of Lancashire, was summoned to London for an on-the-spot evaluation. Kath heard about it from one of the prison guards who was friendly. She hardly dared to hope. Before then, she had never heard of the High Sheriff. Now her life depended on him. He came to see her before he left for London—a small, plump, greying man whose manner reminded her of Edward. Used to the easy life. But he was courteous and interested in what happened to her. He was worried about the demonstrations of the workers and her effect on them. She could tell that by the questions he asked. Would she be willing to plead guilty in exchange for a reprieve? She looked at him. The grey eyes were kindly. No, sir, she told him at last, otherwise what she had done would have no meaning. He seemed disappointed and her hope dimmed, but all the next day her thoughts followed him to London. Perhaps he would find a way to save her.

* * *

Unlike the sheriffs of the American Wild West, which was just then opening up, the High Sheriff of Lancashire was not a peacekeeping officer. He didn't even carry a gun. He was in reality a wealthy landowner, a key figure in the paternal system of the England of his time, and a local political controller of considerable power who reported to the government in London on conditions in the county of Lancashire.

The 180-mile journey to the capital was a long one in those days. The High Sheriff had to get up before dawn at his country mansion outside Manchester. A new moon, like the remains of a big celestial cheese, was still glowing in the early morning sky as Robert Bennington's horse-drawn carriage set off down the winding gravel driveway to take him to the nearest railway station.

Growing up in the age of horses, the aging High Sheriff was suspicious of train travel. He sat by the train window watching uneasily the changing English landscape flash by at an incredible 50 miles an hour.

On the outskirts of several towns, he saw clusters of unemployed workers standing at street corners like potential mobs. They made him even more uneasy. There was unemployment in the Lancashire cotton mills because of the American civil war then in its third bloody year, and thousands of people were on poor relief. The threat of violence was always present as the cities turned into industrial slums and only one man in thirty had a vote—and no woman. Perhaps if they executed this young woman, the High Sheriff thought, it would be enough to start a riot. He was going to London to recommend a reprieve. Lancashire couldn't afford any more trouble. And after all it was a crime of passion, not a cold-blooded premeditated murder. The more romantic French on the other side of the Channel would probably have acquitted her altogether.

He was met at the London railway station by a representative of the Home Secretary and immediately taken to present his on-the-spot evaluation personally.

Sir George Grey, a seasoned London politician and a born aristocrat, greeted him rather condescendingly, but the High Sheriff was used to that. Londoners regarded the North as primitive, the people who lived there as crude, uncultured—mere savages! He didn't let it deter him from putting the case for reprieving the young woman, Kathleen Tracy, as strongly as possible. It was foolish to provide the cotton workers with a martyr at such a confused, violent time. They needed to be placated, not provoked. As he spoke, he could visualize that pale face and that long red hair. She was too young, too beautiful, too full of life to die. He *must* save her.

When he finished his report, he was greeted by a few tense moments of total silence, except for the wheezy ticking of an old grandfather clock beside a bust of Queen Victoria at the time of her accession. The Queen looks much older and dumpier now, the High Sheriff thought, watching the Home Secretary's face for any sign of how his argument had been received. But it was impossible to read those grave, impassive features, and yet the High Sheriff knew that at that moment the fate of Kathleen Tracy was being decided. Surely they wouldn't be so foolish as to invite trouble. But this man no more understood Lancashire than if it was one of the outposts of the empire— India or Australia. He was used to London's solid status quo, life with secure unchanging foundations, and today in Lancashire was like standing on shifting sands, no more solid than that. Everything could change overnight. No wonder politicians like the Home Secretary were full of fear—and fear seldom made the right decisions.

Suddenly the Home Secretary began to speak, his voice strong and confident. Having now made his decision, he had no doubt it was the right one. He couldn't afford any doubts. The High Sheriff searched his face again, but it gave nothing away as he spoke.

"You must remember, Bennington, I have to look at the effect on the whole country. Unrest is rampant everywhere, not only in Lancashire. All it needs is one careless move, a spark, to set off a riot, a series of riots, even an uprising. That spark could come from anywhere—even from overseas across the Atlantic."

He gestured at a wall map facing him. It showed North America with the latest battle positions in the civil war marked with blue and gray flags.

"All eyes are on America," he said. "If Lincoln and the North win and the American experiment in democracy appears to have been successful, it could inspire fresh demands here for parliamentary reform, for a greater share of the national pie. Every damned radical and back-street troublemaker will come crawling out of the woodwork waving American flags." Sir George's thin lips curled with distaste. "We can't control what happens in North America, Bennington, unless the government decides to intervene there on the side of the South, but we can avoid any careless moves here. We certainly can't afford any signs of weakness, any suggestions of backing down before mob pressure. We must give an appearance of strength, not weakness."

"Reprieving her wouldn't be weakness," protested the High Sheriff, realising then what the Home Secretary's decision would be. "There was a case earlier this year of a man who murdered a woman because she broke off their engagement. His death sentence was commuted to imprisonment."

"Yes, because three Home Office doctors certified he was insane. This young woman's not insane."

"No," the High Sheriff agreed sadly, "she isn't. Far from it."

"That was the Townley case you referred to. There was widespread indignation he wasn't hanged. Even the Prime Minister condemned what he called 'benevolence mongers' for having sympathy for a murderer. Lord Palmerston's a great believer in hanging—not for vengeance, but as a deterrent."

The Home Secretary leaned forward, clasping his well-manicured hands, and said firmly, "This young woman must hang."

* * *

Kath heard the news late that night from the friendly guard. "They've turned you down, love," he said gently. The next day the demonstrations started again, but now she didn't care. They couldn't save her. Nobody could. Not even her Dad. She tried to make herself angry about the High Sheriff's failure. Then she wouldn't be scared.

And she remembered the old gypsy woman's prediction. This was certainly the Shadow of Death. But would she be reborn again?

6

Now that all hope had gone, Nancy was allowed to come in her Sunday best—the ratty fur coat and faded brown leather shoes they used to joke about. Nancy sat holding her hand, not knowing what to say.

"I'm sorry, Kath," she brought out at last. "I blame myself, love, for pushing you into it. He was no good for you, the old bastard." She bit her lip to hold back the tears. "You're famous, you know, Kath. Everybody's outside demonstrating for you. They're on your side."

"It won't do any good, Nancy. It's over for me. They've decided."

Nancy's tears ran then. Kath didn't want that, it only weakened her. She tried to get Nancy to gossip about the factory and the girls and who was pregnant and by whom, the way they used to talk over the machines.

Soon Nancy was giggling and making her laugh about her men—the machines'd make better lovers than some of them, she said. Kath almost forgot where she was until the guard rapped on the bars.

"Time to go."

It all came back then with a rush.

"Oh, Kath."

Nancy kissed her in tears and ran.

* * *

The last morning.

It was sunny and beautiful—"a great day to be alive," her Dad would have said.

My God, she told herself, I should be up in the hills above Stockport instead of waiting for the hangman. It still wasn't quite real, as if she were living a dream and any moment would wake up, perhaps to look into her father's face.

She hadn't slept well, going over Edward's death and imagining the hanging—the drop. Her mind wouldn't stop. When eventually she fell asleep, she had the recurring dream from childhood—of America as a paradise overshadowed by something that was happening to her father. She awoke as she always had without knowing what. Even on this last day, she wasn't to learn the meaning of the dream. When she got up, she checked in a mirror the friendly guard brought that her weariness didn't show in her face. She didn't want them to see any signs of weakness.

The news that she was already up must have gone round the prison because the governor came in to see her very early. He intended to be kind, but he was rather stiff and formal in telling her there was no last-minute reprieve. Then it was the turn of the chaplain with his fussy, pompous talk about a God she didn't recognise, God who sounded like a prison governor and employed fools like the chaplain. She had felt out of touch with the real God since going with Edward. When she tried to pray, she felt more alone than ever. This chaplain couldn't help her.

Then he was gone and there was nobody else—nobody she cared about to say good-bye to.

She was offered a hearty breakfast: bacon and eggs, toast and tea. The prison doctor had probably put bromides in the food to deaden her reactions. But she'd be dead soon enough, she wanted to feel *everything* right up to the end. She pushed the tray away untouched.

They came then wanting to cut her hair to make the hangman's work easier, but she refused to let the big prison scissors touch her long red tresses. No drugs, no prison haircut. She'd die her own way.

The friendly guard came shortly before eight o'clock. His name was George, he told her. He struggled for something

helpful to say and finally mumbled, "It won't take long, love.
It's soon over. And then . . . no more worries." He pressed her
hand and then hurried away. Nancy and he represented all the
people she'd grown up with, the people who made do with very
little and remained cheerful most of the time, able to make a
joke even in bad times. They were her people.

Then the procession came for her. They tied her arms. "You
don't need to," she protested, but they did it anyway. They
were taking no chances. Then, with a guard on each side, she
was led out down the bare stone corridor with the nauseous
prison smell, past the other cells. Faces were pressed against the
bars and several men called out to her—friendly greetings,
cries of good luck, "We're with you, Kath." They were her
people, too, whatever society said about them outside.

The prison was suddenly full of noise, loud, angry, protesting
sounds. Hangings always upset the other prisoners, but this
reaction was extraordinary. The prisoners beat out a protest
with tin cups on the bars or stone floors, their voices raised in
angry roars. The noise drowned the voice of the chaplain reciting "In the midst of life, we are in death. . . .," and obviously
scared the others in the procession. The governor and the High
Sheriff were pale. Kath's masklike face suddenly relaxed in a
slight smile. Her people were giving her a good send-off. This
was the right way to go. And she knew then she wouldn't break
down. The anger of the other prisoners seemed to send a surge
of anger through her.

Then they were outside the gates and she was surprised by
the size of the crowd waiting on the common. A great roar went
up when people saw her. Extra guards surrounded the procession and police on horseback reinforced those at the barriers. The crowd pushed forward, but the police line held. The
procession hurried on.

She felt the sun on her face as she climbed up to the scaffold—*the gallows.* A magnificent blue sky was at the back of
the noose. She'd have given anything at that moment to see the
end of this day, even if it meant remaining in prison for the rest
of her life. But that kind of thinking was dangerous. Suppressing everything with iron control, she tried to be unaware of
what was happening around her, to clear her head of anything

that might break her down. Remember what George the friendly guard had said: "It won't take long, love. . . ." Hurry now.

The small group moved ahead of her, including the governor, standing erectly as if back in the army, and the little doctor who staggered and looked drunk. There, too, was the High Sheriff who had failed to get her a reprieve. They all watched her closely, but she stared straight ahead—at the hanging rope. She tried not to let it frighten her. The hooded hangman was standing behind it. She stopped and faced him. He was a big, muscular man with a very loose, youthful stance. He was staring at her. She could see his dark, bright eyes under the hood. He disturbed her so she turned away, her eyes on the gallows.

They had brick walls with planking on top and, above that, two beams and a crossbar with the rope dangling.

She was aware then of the noise of the crowd—the angry cries and boos turning to thunderous cheers for her—and above it all the clock striking the hour of eight. The crowd pressed against the barriers and the police beat people back. The sunlight glinted on the police helmets as they charged.

The young hangman was still staring fixedly at her. His eye glanced down at her body, the wide shoulders and big uptilted breasts clearly outlined even in the thick, coarse prison smock. She was aware of a long pause . . . of impatient looks at the hangman. She could see the dark eyes flash strangely beneath the hood. It was almost as if the hangman recognised her.

They were all waiting in a rough circle round the gallows. The clock had stopped striking. The hangman was late. He was standing as if paralysed. Why was he taking so long? George the friendly guard had been wrong. The seconds of anticipation weighed down on her. Time after time she imagined the fatal drop, breaking her neck, but the hangman continued to stand in front of her doing nothing. His eyes had such a strange look of surprise and uncertainty. What was he waiting for? Did they want to break her down first?

They were all staring at the hangman—the governor, the chaplain, the High Sheriff, even the drunken doctor. Was something wrong?

Kath steeled herself to wait, and at that moment the hangman moved forward and slipped the noose over her head. The hemp felt shockingly rough against her neck. It tightened slowly. The hangman seemed to pause again. She was aware of some feeling that shouldn't have been there, a strange, powerful reaction from him. She waited for him to move again, expecting every moment to be her last. The waiting was anguish now. Would she be aware of the drop, the sudden jerk? Or would it break her neck instantly? She bit her lip until she tasted blood, trying to remain in control.

The governor said impatiently, "Let's proceed."

A heavy silence had fallen over the crowd as if everyone sensed something was wrong.

The chaplain said with a meaningful look at the hangman, "Lord Jesus, receive her spirit," and then waited.

Nothing happened.

The chaplain paused uncertainly, confused, and then slowly repeated, "Lord Jesus," and then louder, "receive her spirit. . . ."

Then suddenly the spell was broken. The hangman moved close to her. He began to adjust the rope around her neck with fumbling fingers. She could hear his heavy breathing. Everyone watched him with impatient expressions. Kath felt the hemp tighten, cutting her skin. The end was near now. At that moment she wished she had been stronger, but she hadn't enough faith in herself for this world. . . .

Finally the hangman stood back, satisfied, and he gestured to the chaplain: "Lord Jesus," the chaplain began again, "receive her spirit. . . ."

The hangman pulled the lever.

The wooden platform gave way under her feet.

She dropped like a stone into the darkness. . . .

7

A twitch, a shudder, then a hint of awareness.

In the darkness that lay like a heavy shroud, there was a glimmer of light somewhere.

And suddenly . . . *pain.*

Intense, burning pain that fired the nerves to a screaming pitch and stirred the senses.

The mind flickered.

Pain cut through millions of exploded cells and smashed circuits. Connections were made again in the brain.

Slowly consciousness crept back, a faint feeling of herself in the vacuum of darkness.

She still possessed a body—a body that could still suffer in what must surely be the next world.

This all enveloping darkness must be . . . hell.

She tried to swallow and at once located the cause of all the pain. Her throat was on fire—the fire of hell. It was agony even to force her saliva down. This was certainly not the transcendent world of the spirit she had been told about; existence was still on a physical level.

The light now was stronger beyond her swollen, bruised eyelids. She saw intense red flashes—blinding sunset streaks. Slowly she pushed open her sore eyelids and, swallowing again with nerve-wracking pain, she peered out fearfully at this afterlife.

What she saw looked very familiar, very earthly.

Kath quickly closed her eyes and then opened them again. The vision was the same.

A plain room with a bed—and she was in the bed.

A flat, white-washed wall.

A window, and through the window, a glimpse of a field and a grassy hillside. A black horse. The sky. Sunlight.

The next world looked just like the one she'd left.

"You're awake!"

A tall man in the doorway—dark, youngish, oddly familiar. Smiling. She tried to turn her head and the pain increased. Her hands went up to soothe her throat and felt a rough bandage. That brought her back to earth.

"Ugh. . . ." She coughed and it was torture. "I'm . . . still . . . alive," she murmured painfully.

The young man sat on the edge of the bed and grinned down at her.

"You certainly are, Red. The only one of my victims to be hanged and to survive."

"What . . . happened?" She was shocked. She really was alive!

"Yours truly here saved your neck."

Her neck didn't feel "saved." She swallowed painfully, unsure if she wanted life at this price. She couldn't speak without agony.

"Well, I know it doesn't feel great right now, Red. Your neck must be sore as hell and I'm sorry about that, I really am, but it had to look real, you understand." He stared into her eyes, waiting for a response. She glared at him.

He went on apologetically: "I had to adjust the rope so your neck wasn't broken. It needed a very careful calculation in split seconds—and all in my head! A change in the drop formula! Tricky mental arithmetic! You just swung there, and then I had to get it over with in time to cut you down before you throttled to death. There was no other way to do it. But you have my apologies for the pain, Red."

He showed big, even white teeth in a flash of pride in what he'd done. "I only just succeeded. It was a near thing as your throat will tell you. Another fraction of an inch and you'd have been a goner, Red. Luckily nobody was keen to examine you. They felt even more guilty than usual, you being young and a woman—and beautiful. It was made easier because the good doctor was drunk. They all left it to me and I fooled them."

He laughed and looked for her approval. There was no response. She'd fainted.

"I'll tell you the rest later, Red."

* * *

When Kath awoke again, it was dusk and she was lying on a blanket in a backyard near a row of cages—rabbits and pigeons peered out at her. Somewhere close by she could hear the cluck-cluck of chickens. There was no sign of the young man. But the fresh air felt good.

She tried to swallow and her throat burned as much as before. The pain was intense, but the air from the hills continued to soothe her. It was good to be alive after all. This was the rebirth the old gypsy woman had promised. She had passed through the Valley of the Shadow of Death and made a fresh start. She hadn't lost her dream. Now she had to reach the heights of fulfillment. Nothing else mattered.

At the back of her was a thatched cottage. She wondered where she was and who the man was. Why did he seem familiar? What had he called her—*Red?* Some memory hovered on the edge of consciousness, but remained unclear.

"Feel like something to drink? Might ease your throat a little."

There he was again, standing over her. She stared up at the big black boots and strong muscular thighs in black pants and the grin. He wasn't so old.

"Try a few drops of water."

He knelt beside her, lifted her head up, and put a glass to her lips. The cold stream water felt good on her parched throat, but it was torture swallowing even a few drops. She blacked out again.

* * *

She slept for a long time. When she awoke, it was daylight. An oil-lamp was burning, and she saw that she was back in the bed and she had nothing on but a man's shirt. He must have undressed her. Her body immediately felt self-conscious, but he hadn't touched her in any way that mattered. She imagined his face—pale and dark, with fierce, passionate eyes. There was a smell of him about the shirt she wore. Then suddenly she remembered who he was—the young man in the woods at Heaton Hall that time who had tried to rape her!

Immediately she pushed the blanket aside and put her feet on the floor. She had to get out of there. She felt weak on her feet. Her clothes were piled on a chair. She began to dress with nervous fingers. She had to get away. This man wasn't to be trusted. What he'd done once, he could do again. She hadn't come back to life for that.

"Where d'you think you're going, Red?"

He was there in the doorway, formidable, big-muscled, grinning.

"I've . . . gotta . . . go." Her throat burned, but the pain was bearable now.

"You'd be spotted as soon as you reached the road. The girl with the red hair. Bandage round your neck. Your face is well-known, Red. Your family lives only a few miles from here. You'd be recognised all right. Kathleen Tracy back from the dead! You might get hanged a second time as a witch—with me alongside you. I'm not going to let that happen, Red."

He barred her way.

"Look," she said, "How did you get into all this anyway?"

"Don't you know?" He backed off and gave her a mock bow. "I'm the hangman—Frank the hangman."

She sat up and glared at him. Her hand touched the bandage round her neck.

"It was you who gave me this?"

"I saved your life. But for me, you'd be lying in your grave at the prison."

"But for you, I wouldn't have been nearly raped when I was only fourteen years old. You ought to be ashamed of yourself."

"You remember." He was strangely pleased. "It meant a lot to you, too, Red."

"That's not something to forget, a near rape. And don't call me Red. That's not my name."

"I'll call you what I like, Kathleen. You ought to thank the good Lord we-er-met in that wood, otherwise I wouldn't have known you on the scaffold and I'd have gone ahead and hanged you. Look, Red, relax. You've got to stay here until we decide what to do. Everybody thinks you're good and dead, even your family. As far as the world's concerned, Kathleen Tracy no longer exists, at least not on this earth. I'm the only one who knows."

She touched her throat. The flesh burned.

"How did you fool them?"

"I'm trying to tell you, Red. I saved your life. I fixed the rope so it wouldn't break your neck. Then I cut you down before you could be throttled and told the doctor you were dead. He was half drunk and was satisfied to leave it all to me. I put you in the coffin, had the coffin carried to the hangman's workshop, took you out and put some weights in and then let them bury the coffin. Somebody who's hanged only rates a burial in the prison grounds, but it was a very nice, dignified funeral. You'd have been pleased with it, Red." He grinned at her. "The body and belongings belong to the hangman. I sent most of your belongings to your family, but I kept some clothes for you that you'll need and also your poaching knife. Then I stayed in the prison until nightfall. While the guards were changing on the gates, I took you out on my horse under a blanket."

"Where am I now?"

"In my cottage outside Stockport."

"My home—"

"You have no home. You're dead."

Silence as she thought carefully about that.

"No one knows I'm alive? *No one?*"

"No one but me."

"And you won't tell?"

"It's more than my own neck's worth."

She slowly relaxed. She'd have to come to terms with him.

He went in the backyard and returned with a basket full of eggs. He broke half a dozen into a big bowl and added some milk and stirred it all up and then gave the bowl to her. She had a hard time swallowing the mixture, but she got it down. She felt better after that.

"Some blood's come through your bandage. We better change it."

He was very gentle. Surprisingly so. The dried blood stuck to the bandage and he eased it off her neck very carefully.

"Let me look at it," she said.

"It's not pretty, Red."

She stood in front of the mirror and examined her neck. The rope had cut deeply into the flesh and left a raw wound and a big black bruise tinged with blood. It was so *ugly*. She was marked for life.

"You did that to me, you bastard."

"Had no choice, Red. Had to make it look real. Saved your life, didn't I? You owe me that."

"I owe you nothing. And stop calling me Red!"

"Calm down, girl." He put a big hand on her shoulder and began to caress her face with his other hand, careful not to touch her throat. She tried to stop his caresses. He said indignantly, "You ought be nice to me after what I did for you."

"You did nothing—except *this.*" Her hand touched her neck. It spoiled her looks.

"I could have killed you."

"Murderer!"

"That's my job. I'm the northern hangman—it's legal. You're the murderer."

"The man I killed deserved it."

"That's what they all say. Accept responsibility for what you did."

"I wouldn't expect a man to understand. Do you accept responsibility for what you do?"

"Don't be so serious, Red. Lie down with me." He began to unbutton his shirt. "It's about time you and me had some fun. Come on, let's finish what we started."

"You're crazy. I'd rather lie down with—with that horse out there."

"You owe me a good time for saving your life."

"I owe you this neck wound."

"You don't seem to understand me. The body belongs to the hangman. In other words, Kathleen, you're mine."

"I'm not a body. I'm still alive."

"Dead or alive, you belong to me!"

He put his strong-muscled arms around her waist and tried to kiss her. She couldn't break his grip. She slapped him hard.

"You witch! Look, you better treat me nice—that is, if you want to go on living. If I throw you out of here, they'll find you and hang you again. This time for keeps."

"I'm not letting you try raping me again."

"I'll do what the hell I want. This is my home. You'll do what I say here, girl."

"I'm not your prisoner, Mister Hangman."

"Damn you, you owe me your life. Don't you understand that, you ungrateful little bitch?" He was clearly amazed by her ingratitude.

"You talk like you own me. Nobody does."

He grabbed her and kissed her on the lips. She bit him hard so that blood trickled down his chin and he howled.

"You vixen," he roared and he tried to back her into a corner. She broke away from him and went into the bedroom and slammed the door. She pushed the heavy wooden bed against it. He tried to force open the door, but the bed was wedged against the wall and shook and creaked but didn't move. She heard him curse angrily. There was a smash as if he'd thrown something against a wall. Then she heard the back door open, and through the window, she saw him calling his horse. The black stallion came at a gallop, very dark against the clear sky. He jumped on it as if he were in a rage and went at a great speed down the hill and out of sight.

The cottage was suddenly quiet. She wondered if she had done right. Why couldn't she go along with him if it meant survival? She had nowhere else to go, and he was young and not bad-looking—better than Edward. But then, she told herself, that was in another life. She was beginning all over again and this time she was not giving herself away to *anyone*.

* * *

He returned shortly before dawn. She heard the black stallion gallop up the hillside and his voice shouting at it. He sounded drunk. Now for trouble, she thought, ready for a violent siege. She turned up the oil lamp and checked on the bed and the door. She wished she had a gun. Any kind of a gun. Or her poaching knife, but he had that.

He made a great deal of noise entering the cottage. She heard glasses clink and a bottle open—the pop of the cork sounded like a pistol and made her even more nervous.

Then a long silence. Any moment she expected an attack on the door. Drink might give him extra strength to burst in. But nothing happened. She sat waiting, eyes on the door. Then she heard a low, familiar noise. He was snoring.

She lay back. It was safe now for her to sleep, too. But first she had to plan what she was going to do. She couldn't stay here with this crazy fellow. She couldn't stay in Stockport—she'd be recognised. She had to start an entirely new life somewhere else, somewhere no one knew her. And she didn't have any money to do it with. Not a penny. She lay awake, unable to sleep, thinking about it. Then suddenly she knew where she was going.

8

Kath heard him moving around in the late morning. She lay there listening. There was a loud bang on the door. She shot up in the bed, ready to resist an attack. "Breakfast," he shouted.

She hesitated. It could be a trap, but she didn't want to seem scared of him. That might make him act really crazy. She decided to take a risk. She didn't have much choice. She had to eat. He could starve her out eventually. She might as well face him now when she was still strong.

She moved the bed away from the door and went out to him, ready to fight. She'd have no more chance there than cornered in the bedroom. What she needed was space. She could probably outrun him. She had to make the backyard and then the hillside and outrun him as she had the gamekeepers.

He was sitting at the kitchen table eating a heap of fried eggs and bacon. He looked pale and hungover.

"Morning, Red. I did you some eggs. Didn't think you'd be up to eating bacon yet. Needs chewing. Hard to swallow."

She sat at the table on the far side from him and slowly ate the eggs, chewing slowly, watching him. Swallowing was still very painful; every time she tried, it brought back the scene on the scaffold—the drop, the great jerk, the burning sensation, and the pain, my God, the pain.

"Feel better, Red?"

"A little," she murmured, waiting for some trick.

"You acted like a little bitch last night," he said cheerfully.

"You acted like a real bastard. Like I'm on this earth just to give you pleasure. Well, I'm not."

"Let's cut it out for now." He held his head, elbows on the table. "I'm not in good shape this morning."

"You sounded drunk when you came home."

"I was, Red. You drove me to it."

"Well," she said softly, "you won't have me to bother you much longer."

"Say that again. I don't follow you, Red."

"I'm going away."

"Where?"

"Liverpool."

That surprised him. "Liverpool? That hell hole? Whatever for?"

"I've decided to go to America and start a new life. It's possible there, you know. A new life in the New World." She sat up straight and her voice rose with confidence. "My Dad's there. I'm going to find him."

He stared at her incredulously.

"Where is he? Which part of America?"

"Virginia."

"That's a big state. Where in Virginia?"

"I don't know, but I'll find him. A letter he sent years ago was postmarked Richmond, but he may not be still there."

He laughed. "You're a bigger gambler even than me. It's a long, long way to America, Red. Have you worked out how you're going to get there?"

"By ship. I can't walk."

"Have you any money?"

She hesitated. She didn't want to tell him too much about herself. "Not just at present."

He sat back, grinning at her.

"What's wrong with you?" she demanded.

"You'll get a long way without money, Red. Half the people in England would go to America to try to change their luck if they had the price of a boat ticket."

"I'll find a way."

He examined her determined face.

"How?"

"I'll get to Liverpool first. Then I'll look into what a passage to America by steamship costs. Then I'll examine my prospects. Perhaps I'll stowaway."

"They'll catch you and throw you off."

"You sound like you don't want me to go."

"I don't. I didn't save your life from hanging to let you give it to the Americans—or end up a prostitute in Liverpool."

"Why did you save me then?"

He leered at her. "I told you already."

"You better find someone else. When I say I'm going to America, I mean it. My father is very important to me."

"But your body belongs to me. That's the hangman's right."

"He has rights to the dead but not the living."

She no longer felt afraid of him. She sensed his boyish confusion. Hangman, gambler, woman-chaser—he was thoroughly mixed up, not grown up. She could manage him.

He stood up abruptly and went to the window and stared out. The black stallion was standing patiently in the field. It looked very strong and handsome as it moved gracefully along a low stone wall, waiting for his call. The sight seemed to move him. He rubbed his eyes.

"I could sell this cottage easily enough," he said softly. "And the rabbits and pigeons and the chickens. I've had a couple of good offers for them. But it would mean leaving him out there behind. I couldn't take him. We've been together since I was a boy. Perhaps I could send for him and have him shipped over."

"What are you saying?" Kath asked, watching his pale brooding face.

"I'm going to America with you."

"Oh, no, you're not."

"There's nothing left here for me. I need to start a new life, too, Red. Being the hangman's no life for a young man. Nobody wants to know you. They point you out in the street as if you're some freak in a travelling circus. I only took the job because my father wanted me to succeed him when he was dying. It seemed a secure trade, steady employment. Not as dull as a factory job. Even a little excitement now and then. Or that's the way I saw it when I started. But I feel different now. I don't want to be hated. For God's sake, I have to carry a gun."

He turned away from the window and faced her. His eyes were sombre. "I've burnt my boats now anyway by saving you. By faking it. It's too risky to continue. A little fool like you might give me away. I don't want to go to prison. But if I give it up, what am I going to do? There are no jobs, not even in the factories, and I'd hate a factory job. Besides, Red, you really are mine, whether you see it or not. I won you fair. I'm not letting you get away from me any more'n I'd lose my winnings in a card game."

"I'm going to America—on my own!" she cried angrily. "You're not coming with me."

But he ignored both her anger and her arguments. He kept her locked up all the next day. She heard him negotiating the sale of the cottage to a man with a deep bass voice. One condition was that the buyer had to look after the black stallion until he sent for it.

The time came when he was ready to leave. He walked across the field and talked to the black stallion for a long time and then he walked back and the stallion watched him without moving. He was sad and angry. It was the first time Kath realised an animal could mean as much as another human being.

"You'd think that horse was a person," she said.

"Better than most people I know," he grunted.

He and the horse exchanged a final look across the field and then he followed her down the hill. Her red hair was cut shorter and was hidden by a man's cloth cap. She was dressed in men's clothing—trousers, a sweater, boots, a cotton scarf round her neck, though her red shawl and other women's clothes were in her shoulder bag that he had given her. She tried to walk like a man with long strides. Her new life had begun—or it would begin as soon as she could get rid of *him*.

9

The train was fun. A monster puffing a trail of smoke that faded slowly away in the air behind them. Kath had never travelled so fast before and she loved it. Speed was exciting. It brought the same kind of sensations as danger. Fifty miles an hour through the Lancashire countryside and the growing industrial spread of factories and back-to-back houses. Tall factory chimneys belching smoke even more vigorously than the train. Stockport was soon left behind in the valley—and, with it, her whole life. She felt no sadness, not even when she stared back and saw the hills behind the town and the shadows of the dry stone walls she had known as a child with her Dad. She was too excited.

Many of the people on the train were going to the Assize Courts in Liverpool—lawyers, clerks, plaintiffs, defendants, witnesses—their talk reminded Kath of her trial. She tried to sit very quietly so no one would notice her. She had kept the scarf round her neck, but she was still very self-conscious about the rope wound, it was such a giveaway and so ugly. She hoped she would pass as a youth, at least until they reached the ship.

Several people stared curiously at her, but that may not have meant anything. Travellers on trains were probably more curious and alive than other people—they were going farther and faster and had to be sharp-witted. Perhaps, too, she was worth a look. When the hangman gave her some of his clothes and she put them on, tightening his belt several extra holes and rolling up the trouser legs a little, he whistled and said, "You make a damn good-looking boy, too. Now all the women will be eyeing you, Red." Several did on the train, but she wasn't sure whether they were admiring, just curious or saw through her disguise. You could count on fooling men more than women.

He sat watching her with a sardonic smile. Of course he had done a lot of travelling already so this journey was no big thing to him. Hanging people took you to many places. He had even been to London once—unless he was lying. Young men like him boasted a great deal. They were very unsure of themselves.

She was surprised how little luggage he had brought. One big leather bag. No more than her Dad had taken with him. "Travelling light leaves you free," he said. Maybe he didn't have much—just the cottage and the black stallion and he couldn't take them with him. She tried to find out where he was carrying the money he was paid for the cottage and his savings from his hangman's pay, but he never let her see even when he took out the money for the train tickets. He didn't trust her. They didn't trust each other.

She wondered why he was accompanying her really. She didn't believe it was because of her, though you could never be sure with young men—sex was their weakness even more than booze or gambling. Perhaps he also wanted to leave his past behind, the life of a hangman and all the folk he'd killed. She studied his face anew for signs of cruelty and sadism, and then she reminded herself she'd killed someone, too, but that had been different, on an impulse, in a sudden rage, whereas his hangings were cold and premeditated and for money. Working in a factory like a slave was bad enough, but to hang people for money—that was inhuman! His dark good looks obviously concealed hidden depths. He looked Black Irish. She didn't believe the legend that Black Irish were descended from survivors of the Spanish Armada shipwrecked on the Irish coast, but her Dad had told her they were deep, brooding, often violent people. This man certainly had a strong presence for someone so young. She felt his closeness like a magnet.

She must have been staring at him in a peculiar way, because he asked her, "What's wrong with you?"

"Nothing." She turned her face to the train window to hide her feelings. At that speed, the green and gray countryside seemed to be moving away from them, rushing back to Stockport behind them like on a magic carpet. It made horse travel seem very unexciting.

Liverpool was another big shock. Her first big city! She'd never even been to Manchester except in a closed police carriage to the court and then later to the prison. You couldn't count that. Besides, it was in her other life. The size of the buildings and the crowds thronging the railway station and the streets outside made her shy at first. She felt very country and inexperienced in the city. But the hangman surprised her by seeming as much at home as he was in the Stockport area. He led her quickly out of the railway station to a line of hansom cabs and told the first cabbie to take them "to the docks." On the way he asked where the ships for America docked and directed the cabbie there.

Soon they were going at a fast pace through the Liverpool streets, so much broader and flatter and busier than the Stockport streets she was used to. Kath's head turned this way and that not to miss anything, and then suddenly in the far distance she glimpsed what she'd been waiting for—the sea! It looked immense, stretching far ahead until it reached the sky. It was disappointingly muddy close up rather than the bright clean blue she had expected, but it was still the ocean her Dad had sailed on eight years ago and which she was now going to follow him on. He seemed much closer already!

A forest of masts blocked the view, then there was a river on which white sailed ships with all kinds of foreign flags glided inwards. They went across a swing bridge along the pier and entered a huge dock where hundreds of steamers were being loaded and unloaded. Sailors of all colors were running along the dock, giving Kath, who knew only English people and mainly inland factory workers, a sense of new, strange worlds.

A line of tall steamships, waiting for the morning tide, towered above the hansom cab, and she could see sailors, bare to the waist, working on the decks.

Frank paid off the cabbie and then slowly eyed the nearest ships. They weren't good enough. He led her past four ships before he saw one that satisfied him.

"Wait here," he told her brusquely and strode up the narrow gangplank and disappeared. He was gone a long time. A big, weatherbeaten sailor coming from the city and smelling strongly of whisky asked Kath if she needed a job. He spat into the water as he looked her up and down.

"There's work for a cabin boy," he said, "And you look like a strong lad. I'm the cook." He leered at her. "I'll treat you good. We might even get to be . . . *friends.*"

She shook her head, trying not to speak in case she sounded too girlish.

The big sailor had evil eyes. He gave her a mean look and went on to the ship that the hangman had boarded. He made the gangplank shake precariously. Kath noticed the ship's name for the first time: The *Raleigh.* Probably named after Sir Walter Raleigh the adventurer she had read about in school. She waited some more. The next ship was being loaded with heavy machinery—she watched the dockworkers sweating and straining to finish before the tide. That ship was called the *St. Clare.* She liked that name better.

Frank's face appeared above her. He gestured for her to join him on the ship. She ran up. The ship was moving slightly in the muddy water like something alive. She had to be careful not to stumble over coils of rope and seamen's luggage. Live animals were tied up on the deck, and the bloody carcasses of sheep and pigs waited to be cut up.

"We've got a cabin," Frank told her. "I had to bribe the captain. We sail soon."

Something about his pleased manner worried her. "Have I got my own cabin?" she asked anxiously.

"We're sharing one," he told her with a grin. "I told the captain we were brothers." He winked at her.

"I don't want to share."

"No share, no ship. I'm doing all the paying, you ungrateful little bitch. Do you want to be left behind?"

No, she didn't, but she'd have to work something out to save herself from him. It would be a long voyage. Maybe she could sleep on deck away from him under the stars. If it was safe. She remembered the cook's evil eyes.

A fat, grey-bearded man joined them. He wore a stained blue uniform open at the neck. An old naval officer's cap at a jaunty angle half-covered a wild mop of curly grey hair.

"This your brother?" he wheezed, little bloodshot eyes examining Kath from head to foot.

"That's right, Captain," the hangman said pleasantly.

"Nice-looking boy. Welcome to the good ship *Raleigh* of the North Atlantic Line." The old captain winked at Frank. "Better keep him in the cabin at night."

"I will," said the young hangman, grinning at Kath.

She sensed the old captain had seen through her disguise but he didn't care. It seemed like a rough ship and at sea the only law would be the captain's. She'd have to be very careful.

"We sail in an hour," said the captain. "I'm waiting for one more passenger—a very important personage." There was a click of horses' hooves on the dock below. "Here he is now."

Two hansom cabs had arrived, the horses breathing heavily as if they had been racing. Out of the first cab stepped an exotic figure—a slightly built Indian with a dusky face and a white turban. Kath had never seen an Indian before and he intrigued her. She leaned over the rail to get a closer look at him. But another man then emerged from the cab who interested her even more. He looked English, a lean, elegant man in a white suit and a wide-brimmed hat. She had never seen a man in a white suit before. He was obviously the boss. He stood lazily waiting while the little Indian went over to the other cab and lifted out a seemingly endless collection of trunks, suitcases and boxes, some bigger than himself. He lined them up neatly on the quay. The Englishman slowly counted the assembled luggage. Twenty-two pieces.

"Travelling light, Mr. Thomas?" the captain shouted.

The white-suited figure waved jovially.

"Got to be ready for all emergencies, Captain."

Kath watched open-mouthed. This man had a grand style she had never seen before. She said quickly, "Who is he?"

The captain chuckled at her ignorance. "You don't know

who he is, boy?" She shook her head. "That's Horatio Thomas."

The way the captain said it the name was obviously famous, but it meant nothing to Kath. She watched the man in the white suit pay off the two cabbies with a lordly gesture. The cabbies touched their caps respectfully. The others on deck were watching the scene below, too. She was even more curious about who this Horatio Thomas was. Maybe a duke or a prince.

Well, she thought, I bet I find out all about him before we reach America.

Whatever he was, he was only a man.

And she might have need of him.

As an ally.

Against the hangman . . . or the cook.

America was a long way off. Anything could happen on the journey across the Atlantic. She had a moment of fear, but then her hand went to her neck. I've already survived a hanging, she told herself. I can survive this. My second life is only just beginning.

10

The man in the white suit wasn't a duke or a prince. He was a journalist—a famous war correspondent. Kath had never heard of him because she never read newspapers.

Journalism was at its most personal and adventurous. Scoops often depended on finding the fastest way to get a story back to the editor. The telegraph was in its infancy and couldn't be depended on.

Horatio Thomas had been called after his parents' childhood hero, England's great one-eyed, one-armed admiral of the fleet, Horatio Lord Nelson, killed sixty years before in the Battle of Trafalgar. Thomas had made his own name famous in covering the Crimean War for the prestigious *Manchester Guardian*. Twice he'd beaten the *London Times's* veteran war correspondent, William H. Russell, to front-line scoops. He'd helped to make pioneer nurse Florence Nightingale a household name back home. He'd described the disastrous Charge of the Light Brigade from such close range that he'd been hit in the left leg by shrapnel from Russian cannons— slight fleshy wounds that hadn't stopped him from staying until the end of the battle. His *Guardian* reports had blasted the incompetency of the English generals, were read aloud in the House of Commons, and nearly brought down the government.

After the Crimean War, he headed eastwards and covered

the Indian Mutiny. In the midst of the bloodiest fighting, he rescued a young Sikh from a charge of fixed bayonets and thereby acquired a body servant for life, though he did his best to discourage him. "I travel alone," he told the grateful young Sikh. It had no effect. The young Sikh had decided this was his chance to hitch his future to a star and escape from the poverty of India, and he couldn't be shaken off. He soon became indispensable in discovering the fastest way to get a story through to the *Guardian* ahead of Thomas's rivals as well as acting as interpreter, cook, and general Man Friday.

From India, Horatio Thomas returned home to England and found himself famous. Even Queen Victoria wanted to meet him. He went first to Manchester to see his editor. They had corresponded, but never met. The *Manchester Guardian,* like other newspapers at the time, was an all-male office and the editor was worried that his famous war correspondent might turn out to be one of the new liberated women who wrote under male pseudonyms—two titled ladies had done that in the Middle East and recently returned home to embarrass their editors in London. So there was much relief in the *Guardian* office when "Horatio Thomas" turned out to be a genuine white-suited male, even though he was very flamboyant by Manchester standards.

Horatio Thomas was introduced to the *Guardian* staff and then had lunch alone with the editor at the Reform Club, the staid headquarters of local liberalism. Every head looked up as the doors of the dining-room swung open and Horatio Thomas strode in. The members were not used to such theatrical entrances. They watched intently as the head waiter led Thomas and the editor to a table in a private corner.

"You've created a sensation," the editor said with a smile. He studied Horatio Thomas carefully. The lean, elegant appearance and lazy manner were deceptive. So, too, was his cynical attitude. He talked as if he were tired of England, and was scathing about its class system. Yet this was the same man who had risked his life several times in getting a story, who had slept on the ground with front-line troops, and had helped army doctors to remove the wounded soldiers from the battlefield to emergency hospitals. This much the editor knew from Horatio

Thomas's work and mentions of him in official dispatches. That was all the editor knew. The first contact between them had been when Horatio Thomas mailed a story from the Crimea. Thomas had gone out to the war on borrowed money in the hope of becoming a war correspondent for some newspaper back home. He had tried the *Guardian* first. When the editor read his first story—colorful, newsy, evocative, precise— Thomas didn't need to try anywhere else. He was both a good reporter and a good writer, a rare combination. He was hired immediately.

Horatio Thomas also studied the editor. The man's quiet, scholarly manner obviously concealed great journalistic shrewdness. Thomas was anxious to learn what his next assignment was going to be. He had only been in England two days and already he was restless. Over lunch they seemed to discuss everything—Russia's empire dreams, the Untouchables in India, social unrest in England—everything except what Thomas wanted to know. At last, over coffee and brandy, he put it bluntly: "Where do I go next?"

The editor glanced round to make sure no one could hear. The other members had all gone back to discussing their own business. The club's staid surroundings had returned to normal.

"There's only one place now for a war correspondent," the editor told him. "America! I want you to cover the end of the Civil War. We've depended too much on Reuters. We need our own man there. The *Times* had Russell, but he offended the Lincoln government by an unflattering description of the Union Army at Bull Run. They wouldn't let him near the front again so he came home."

"He should have gone south and covered the war from the other side. Russell's got too comfortable, too successful. He no longer wants to rough it."

"One problem," said the editor, "is that the TransAtlantic cable still isn't working. It was completed six years ago, but it broke down after only a few weeks. You'll have to depend on the steamships. That means stories are at least two weeks old by the time they reach Liverpool and we can collect them."

"At least the *Guardian* will save money and stories won't have to pass through the American army censors. I understand they're hard on reporters." Horatio Thomas drained his brandy thoughtfully. "It's a problem for my Indian assistant to work out. Ram's a genius at finding ways and means for fast deliveries. It'll give him something to do on the way over."

The *Guardian* editor was very favorably impressed by Thomas's quick, practical response. "The American Civil War is very important to us here. It will greatly influence our future, Thomas. If the North wins, a victory for Abraham Lincoln and the American experiment in democracy, then our society will be forced to become more democratic. All the reforms that were conveniently shelved at the time of the Crimean War will have to be re-introduced. At the start of the Civil War, I was convinced that the South would win its independence, but now I'm not so sure—"

"The North will win," Thomas said firmly. "This is a different kind of war. It'll be won by the side with the most armament factories. And that's the North. This war makes even the Crimean conflict seem old-fashioned."

The *Guardian* editor nodded. "I think we here, like the government in London, have tended to misread the situation in America because President Lincoln is a new kind of politician, unique to America, a real man of the people. We haven't got a clear picture of him."

"With all due respect," Horatio Thomas said, "I think you gave too little attention to both his inaugural address and his Gettysburg speech. They were important statements. So, too, was his message to the working people of the city here when they declared their support for his stand against slavery at that mass meeting at the Manchester Free Trade Hall. Lincoln didn't reply to them lightly. He addressed Manchester, the north of England, because he knew the south, especially the government in London, was unsympathetic. I think you should have responded as a paper, a mouthpiece of the people, to what he was saying."

"That's precisely why I'm sending you to America," the *Guardian* editor told him. "I trust your judgment, Thomas. Give us an eye-witness account of Lincoln and the civil war. I suspect he's much more interested in keeping the Union together than in the emancipation of the slaves, but find out and tell us. And when the war's over, tell us about the peace—how Lincoln keeps his promises. Politicians seldom do. Tell us what happens to the former slaves, to race relations in this new democracy. That is the acid test. What happens there will decide our future, too, for the next century or more. It's a great turning point in western civilization, Thomas. You're going on a great story, much greater than the Crimean War. Once the civil war is over, the railroads will open up the whole of the American continent. That will revolutionize the cattle market. There'll be another war out there—a war over the cattle and the land."

"The wild west!" Horatio Thomas cried enthusiastically. "That's what I really want to see. Private wars on the range, duels at high noon—the cowboys certainly need a war correspondent. It seems as if I'm not going to be home again for a long time," he added with satisfaction.

"I anticipate the Civil War will be over next year," the editor said. "The losses on both sides are too great for the bloodshed to last much longer. Then you'll need several months to cover the start of the peace and go west."

"It'll be a costly trip."

"Some European and Empire newspapers will share the expenses in exchange for the use of your reports. Just keep the expenses reasonable. Come home when you get homesick." The editor pushed back his chair. Their business was done. He had no small talk. "Ready?" When they were walking back to the *Guardian* office across St. Ann's Square, he asked Thomas, "Have you ever read that young French aristocrat's book, *Democracy in America?* What was his name?

"Alexis Charles Henri Clerel de Tocqueville," said Horatio Thomas.

"Ah, yes, de Tocqueville. It's thirty years since he wrote it, but it's still got a few lessons for us today. Here, let's see if they have a copy in one of the local bookshops." They had. The *Guardian* editor bought a leather-bound copy and presented it to Thomas. "Here—you're following in de Tocqueville's footsteps thirty years later. You might like to read his book on the ship to pass the time and compare your impressions with his."

"The American Dream thirty years later," said Horatio

Thomas. "The latest version of paradise. Human beings will look everywhere for perfection but in themselves."

The editor paused outside the *Guardian* building. "Just one thing before we part, Thomas. Don't tell anyone that you're going. We want to keep an element of surprise. I don't want the *Times* to know until we publish your first report from over there. They'll be green with envy and very annoyed they let Russell come home."

"I'm seeing Russell for a drink at his London club tomorrow after I've been to the Palace to meet the Queen, but I won't say a word about going to America. I'm also going to talk to Charles Dickens about his impressions of America—"

"Yes, Dickens is very responsive to American democracy and the need for a dose of it here, but he isn't blind to any of its shortcomings. Get him on American prisons if you want to hear a blast from him. But don't tell him you're going. That London literary world is all interconnected and full of gossips."

"Nobody will know I've gone except you, I promise you. I'll cross the Atlantic in one of the smaller steamships. That way it won't leak out."

"You should leave within the week."

"I'll take the first steamship leaving Liverpool after tomorrow."

And that was the *Raleigh*.

* * *

They had one-and-a-half cabins—a large one for Horatio Thomas and his luggage, and a much smaller one for Ram, which he had to share with one of the other passengers, a morose German. Thomas was scathing about the facilities of the *Raleigh*. "I've not felt so shut in since I visited that prison in Calcutta. If this was the best we could get, Ram, we should have waited. The damn civil war's been going on for three years without us, a few more days wouldn't make any difference, except to our comfort! I'm astonished, Ram, that you allowed us to be dumped on a steamship like this. Have you seen those animals tied up on deck? It's more like a zoo or a sheep farm than a TransAtlantic steamship!"

The young Sikh said nothing, but let Horatio Thomas rage on. He had learned that was best when Thomas was in a mood like this. The Englishman never complained in really tough situations, but occasionally, at times like this, he became loud and angry as if letting off steam so he could then be calm and in complete control. Englishmen didn't usually show their feelings—they were bottled up people, so they had to sound off occasionally. Ram waited patiently for Thomas to run down.

"Mr. Thomas?"

It was the captain. He'd obviously heard Thomas's angry outburst. Ram opened the cabin door.

"Is anything wrong?"

The captain's eyes were bloodshot and his voice was slurred. Spots of beer froth were on his beard. Ram was afraid for a moment that the half-drunk captain would be a target for the remains of Thomas's irritation, and there would be a row that would make the voyage unpleasant. But the English journalist was too experienced a traveller to do that. He smiled slightly and said in his most relaxed English drawl, "We're coping manfully, Captain. Our needs are small."

"Anything you want, Mr. Thomas, just let me know."

"My assistant will draw up a list of our requirements, Captain."

The captain blinked, unsure how to respond to that. He rubbed his bloodshot eyes and withdrew.

Thomas began to unpack one of his bags. Ram helped him in silence. The harangue was over. Thomas took out a map of America and began to mark on it the latest front-line positions. "I'll be sending my first story from Washington," he said as he worked. "You'll have to get it to New York and then onto a steamship. We'll have to work out where it should be picked up. Even saving a few hours is important."

Ram leaned forward to study the map. "It may be possible to save time by using one of the Irish ports—Queenstown, Crookhaven, or Greencastle. A day could be saved by telegraphing summaries from there."

"A day could make all the difference in beating the *Times*," Horatio Thomas said.

As they leaned over the map, they both felt the engines pound under their feet, and the steamship shuddered slightly and began to move away from the dock. There were excited cries from up on deck. The transatlantic voyage had begun.

* * *

Horatio Thomas went on deck to watch. He was in time to see the captain and several of the engineers, armed with big clubs, driving a group of stokers back down below. The stokers were drunk and wanted to get off the ship.

The captain waved jovially when he saw Thomas.

"Everything's under control," he cried. He looked almost as drunk as the stokers.

There were sandbanks at the mouth of the river and the water had to be high enough to float the steamship over them. It was just high enough, the sandbanks a dark shadow under the water. A pilot-boat went as far as Holyhead and then the steamship was on its own. The voyage across the Atlantic began under a leaden sky, and the coast of England was soon lost in rainy darkness.

Thomas went to bed early. He put in his ear-plugs—he had super-sensitive hearing and couldn't sleep soundly without them—but this night, the first at sea, he tossed and turned and finally took out the ear-plugs and sat up and opened the book the *Guardian* editor had given him—de Tocqueville's *Democracy in America*. The steamship, the dark sea, the journey were all soon forgotten as he went back thirty years with the young Frenchman's book. De Tocqueville had gone to America convinced the democracy there would soon spread to Europe, the same feeling the English had now. De Tocqueville wrote: "I sought there the image of democracy itself, with its inclinations, its character, its prejudices, and its passions, in order to learn what we have to fear or to hope from its progress."

What had de Tocqueville found? Horatio Thomas turned the pages excitedly as if the answer were important to his own quest. "Nothing struck me more forcibly than the general equality of condition among the people," concluded the young French aristocrat. But he had rejected the common American claim that equality meant freedom or that democracy signified liberty. As conditions in America became more equal, de Tocqueville claimed that Americans seemed more and more to take pride not in their individuality, in their personal liberties, in their freedom, but rather in their sameness. "Every citizen, being assimilated to all the rest, is *lost in the crowd,* and nothing stands conspicuous but the great and imposing image of the people at large." De Tocqueville wrote that increasingly Americans had subordinated their concern for the liberties and freedom of the individual to their new respect for—or fear of—the majority. There was a real danger of what De Tocqueville called "the tyranny of the majority."

Horatio Thomas put the book down and stared up at the cabin ceiling that seemed so close to his head. Was the Frenchman influenced by his own aristocratic background, or had he touched on a fatal flaw in the new democracy? Surely the answer would be plain now, thirty years later. It was an exciting prospect, and the cabin suddenly seemed much too confining. He had to get some fresh air if he was to have any chance of sleep.

Thomas heard someone above him on the deck, someone whose heavy tread creaked the old woodwork. He would have company up there. He put a topcoat over his pyjamas and dropped a double-barrelled pistol he had brought back from India into a pocket of the topcoat. Some of these small, cheap ships recruited their crews from the streets. The drunken stokers had acted like riff-raff. You had to take precautions living among them in the middle of nowhere.

He crept past the next cabin where Ram was sleeping and went quickly up the ladder to the deck.

A full moon lit up the ship. It was a calm night with a clear sky. The sea looked glassy in the moonlight. Thomas breathed deeply enjoying the fresh sea smell after the stuffiness of the cabin. Some of the animals became restless at the sight and smell of him and strained at their ropes. He couldn't see anybody else on deck. But there was a movement beyond the animals under a tarpaulin covering one of the lifeboats. At first Thomas thought it must be an animal struggling to get out. The tarpaulin bulged and moved as a body—or bodies—heaved beneath it. There was a low cry from somewhere in the lifeboat —it could have been a young animal, but then there was a gruff curse and that was certainly a man.

Horatio Thomas strode quickly over to the lifeboat and

pulled back the tarpaulin. The big, heavily built cook was struggling with a red-haired youth. He had the youth face down on the floor of the lifeboat. The youth's trousers were rolled down to the thighs exposing plump buttocks, and the cook's huge hairy hands were squeezing the cheeks apart.

Thomas grabbed the cook's massive shoulder and pulled him back. The cook turned furiously and punched at Thomas. He was much bigger and heavier than the English journalist, who stepped back until he felt the ship's rail behind him. Thomas took out the double-barrelled pistol and pointed it at the big man. But it didn't check him. The cook moved closer.

"Don't be a fool," Thomas told him. Thomas was reluctant to shoot and the cook seemed to know it. He lunged at Thomas like a bull. Thomas hit him in the face with the pistol.

The cook roared with pain, but kept coming.

"I'll kill you if I have to," Thomas said. "It's not worth your life."

The cook charged. Horatio Thomas, in pressing the trigger, aimed for his shoulder, but the cook ducked his head as he came in and received both barrels in his face. He gave a terrible cry and, with both hands to his bloody, shattered face, he staggered sideways against the rail, was unable to steady himself, and went over backwards. He fell like a sack and made a great splash as he hit the sea. He disappeared and didn't come back to the surface. Thomas stared down at the dark sea, shocked. He had seen many people killed, but he had never killed anyone himself before. But the brutal cook had given him no choice.

"Quick," he told the red-haired youth, "Go to my cabin—the second one below."

The youth disappeared.

"Man overboard!" Thomas shouted.

A look-out on the far side of the ship took up the cry: "Man overboard!"

It occurred to Thomas that the look-out should have seen the fight and raised the alarm already. Perhaps he had been aware of the attempted rape. Maybe it was his turn next. Thomas decided not to get involved. The crew would stand together against him.

When the captain came hurrying up on deck, pulling on an old sweater, Thomas knew nothing. His pistol, still warm, was safely back in his pocket. He told the captain he'd been reading in his cabin and had heard someone fall overboard. That was all. He'd have to risk the look-out—if the man had been aware of the attack on the youth, he'd probably keep quiet about it. What was there to gain?

The captain stopped the steamship and sent out a search party in the lifeboat. The sea was calm and silvery under the moonlight. There was no sign of anything or anybody. They were alone far out in the Atlantic beneath the stars. It was an unsettling feeling. The lifeboat circled the ship in bigger and bigger circles. It was out for nearly half-an-hour before the captain gave up and called it in. By then he had discovered that two people were missing—the ship's cook and one of the passengers, a youth. Thomas watched a tall, young black-haired man talking urgently with the captain. He seemed very upset. Someone said he was the youth's elder brother.

Thomas went down to his cabin. Ram was standing outside like a guard. He gave Thomas a strange look.

"I promised not to let anyone in but you," he said.

"Promised him?"

"Her."

Thomas hurried in. The youth was sitting on one of the trunks. Youth, hell! He saw his error immediately. He leaned down and ripped open the youth's shirt. Big women's breasts, strapped down, were revealed.

Horatio Thomas, irritated that he'd been fooled, said sharply, "No wonder the cook was worked up."

"He didn't know," she replied quietly, watching him. "That cook was more interested in young boys than women. I was trying to tell him I was no boy, but he wouldn't listen. He was too excited. I think he would have raped me anyway. He was in a mad raping mood."

"What were you doing on deck at night?"

"Sleeping. I thought I'd be safe in the lifeboat. I didn't even sleep with my knife in my hand." She took out an ugly-looking blade with a crude homemade wooden handle. "This was my poaching knife. It'll cut up a deer, so it certainly would cut up a man. But I didn't have time to get it out."

She was holding the torn high collar of her shirt tightly round her neck. Horatio Thomas grew suspicious. He pulled away her hand, revealing the deep rope marks.

"That comes from a hanging," Thomas said. "Who are you?"

"Kathleen Tracy of Stockport," she replied quickly, then regretted saying so much, a hand to her mouth.

Something twitched in Horatio Thomas's memory at the name, but he couldn't place it. Something to do with the cotton workers in Manchester. But he couldn't remember the details, except that a woman had been hanged.

"How did you get that mark?"

"He gave it to me."

"Who's he?"

She didn't reply.

Horatio Thomas told her impatiently, "Your brother's on deck searching for you. He's very worried. You better tell him you're safe."

"He's not my brother." Her hand touched her neck. "He was the one who gave me this. He's worse than that man you shot. He's the hangman."

"He was to hang you? What happened? Tell me the truth now. It's your only chance. I'll know if you're lying."

How could she tell him about her rebirth that the old gypsy fortune-teller had predicted, the second chance to make her dream come true? He wouldn't understand.

"What's your relationship with this hangman?" Thomas asked.

"We have no relationship. Why do you think I was sleeping in the lifeboat? I crept away while he was playing cards with the captain. It wasn't safe being in the same cabin with him."

Horatio Thomas stared at the wild-eyed, pretty face. She was only seventeen or eighteen—a young girl's peak, like a young tree, full of sap, juicy. She'd bring the beast out in most men.

"What is your plan?" he asked gently.

She gave him an innocent, defenseless look. "Can I stay here? We'll be in America in a few days."

"Stay here—in this cabin? In *my* cabin?" Horatio Thomas was appalled. "There's hardly enough room for me."

"Please, Mr. Thomas."

"You know my name?"

"I know you're rich and famous?"

"Not so rich. Journalists don't get rich."

"You're a *journalist?* A newspaper writer?" She seemed very disappointed.

"What did you think I was?"

"I didn't know to be honest with you, Mr. Thomas. Don't get me wrong. I'm sure you're a fine man. Newspaper writers have to be very clever. A girl can trust you." Her big, sensuous eyes stared up at him. "Please, can I stay? I'll be no trouble to you, Mr. Thomas—"

"Trouble? You've already caused me to kill a man."

"That wasn't my fault."

No, he thought, it wasn't. He was being unfair.

She must have sensed he was weakening, because she said quickly in a scared tone, "If I go out there, I'll not be safe. Not with him. And nobody'll stop him, not on this boat. They're all on his side. He's friendly with the captain. You can't shoot them all." Her eyes opened wider. "I've got to get to America to find my father. I'll be all right once I find him. Until then I'm in danger from that man out there." She tried to read what his reaction was. "You're a gentleman, Mr. Thomas. I know I'll be safe with you."

He took two steps and stopped in front of a trunk. "You see how little space there is. There's none for another person. You can't possibly stay here. You can't."

But in the end she did. Ram made her a bed on the floor. He looked very disapproving.

"We can't send her out to a fate worse than death," Thomas snapped. Probably Ram thought he was going to sleep with her. Well, perhaps out of gratitude, she might. . . .

He lay down on the bed. She was on the floor wrapped in a blanket.

"Goodnight," he said.

"Thanks for everything, Mr. Thomas. Goodnight."

Then silence. Her gratitude didn't go that far.

Thomas got up.

"You better have the bed. I sleep badly wherever I am. The floor won't make any difference to me."

"You sure, Mr. Thomas?" she murmured sleepily.

"Yes, I'm sure."

She didn't say, "We can share the bed together," but waited for him to get out and then she silently took his place, half-asleep already.

Horatio Thomas lay on the floor listening to her even breathing in the bed. He felt frustrated, as if she had got the better of him. The moonlight came through the cabin window and he could see her breasts rise with her breathing, the nipples uptilted. She's had enough attempted rapes for one night, he thought turning over, trying to find a comfortable position on the hard cabin floor. The *Manchester Guardian* would be proud of my self-control, he told himself with a smile. Eventually he put in his ear-plugs, but he was still aware of her breathing, the even rise and fall of her breasts in the moonlight. Why did this woman have such an effect on him?

* * *

Kath felt strangely secure with the English journalist. He was a stranger and yet he was obviously a gentleman. While she was with him, she was safe from Frank and the crew, all the dangers of the outside world. It was a feeling her father had given her when she was a child. Dear God, she thought, let me stay with him until I'm safely on my way in America. . . .

* * *

The next few days—and nights—dragged.

Not only the sleeping accommodations, but the eating and toilet arrangements caused many irritating problems. Also Ram was less help than usual. He acted as if he didn't like Kath. Perhaps he's jealous, Horatio Thomas thought impatiently, and maybe he fears she's taking over his meal ticket. The young Sikh snubbed all her attempts to be friendly. She tried to get him to explain why he wore a turban. He pretended not to hear and walked out of the cabin, his black eyes flashing with anger.

"Sikhs don't believe in cutting their hair," Thomas grunted from where he was studying a map of Washington. "It's to prove their devotion to God. The word 'Sikh' means disciple."

"And all his hair's under the turban?"

"Coiled and plaited and fastened with a comb called a *kanga*."

"Where does he come from?"

"The Punjab in northern India near China and Afghanistan. Punjab means five rivers. It's a very fertile land as well as being a gateway to the rest of India and is always being invaded. This makes the Sikhs very united and great warriors. They have to be great warriors to survive. The circular steel bracelet Ram wears on his right wrist symbolises the unity of the Sikhs. The circle has always meant a lot in Indian thought and teaching."

"How do you know so much about India?"

"I lived there for months."

"You ever been to America before?"

"No, this is my first visit."

"Where in America are you going?"

"The front-line of the Civil War in Virginia—"

"My Dad was in Virginia. Perhaps he still is. Can I go with you?"

He shook his head firmly. "No, I'm going first to Washington—to interview President Lincoln if I can."

Enough is enough, he thought. It's all take and no give with you, my girl. He stared at the sexual expression in her eyes. He wondered how much it was deliberate, how much unconscious —she was such a strange mixture of feminine shrewdness and childish innocence. He'd be relieved when the ship docked and he saw the last of her. She was too much of a responsibility.

Added to the problems of logistics was the fear of being caught hiding her. The captain had come to the cabin and questioned Thomas closely. It was hard to tell if he knew anything or if he was just trying to impress Thomas. She had hidden in one of the largest trunks. The captain kept staring round the cabin. His eyes seemed to focus on the trunk as if he felt her presence. Thomas waited, inwardly tense but outwardly very relaxed. Ram entered as a diversion, wearing a clean red turban.

"Did you hear any sounds on deck that night?" the captain asked the young Sikh. "Any sounds of a fight?"

Ram shook his head.

"And you, Mr. Thomas, you heard no fight?"

"No . . . just the sound of someone going overboard. Why do you ask about a fight?" Had the look-out talked?

"Just wondered, that's all." The captain's bloodshot eyes were impossible to read as he looked from Thomas to Ram. "There are two people missing. It's possible one of them's still on the ship." He examined the cabin again and once more his eyes seemed unusually interested in the large trunk. "We're searching the ship. Have you checked your cabin?"

"There's hardly enough room for me here, Captain," Horatio Thomas said with a relaxed smile, his hand clenched in his pocket.

"You'd be surprised where people can hide." Again the captain's eyes roamed the cabin, and then he nodded to them both and left. His steps sounded unsteady as he went up on deck.

Horatio Thomas didn't dare to leave the cabin after that. He kept the door locked. Twice during the night he heard someone turn the door handle. Perhaps it was the dark man, her so-called brother. He had come by several times during the day, but he had knocked then. Thomas never let him into the cabin, but talked to him at the door. He didn't trust the man. Black Irish could be tricky, unpredictable, sometimes violent. The girl was afraid of him—or so she said.

"I don't believe . . . he . . . went over the side," the dark man had said.

"Someone went over."

"Not . . . him."

"Why do you say that?"

The man shrugged, staring at Thomas. He was powerfully built, and simmered with suppressed hostility.

He knocked again later. Thomas nearly didn't open the door, but it was better to face trouble.

The man regarded him with angry eyes. Thomas braced himself. The man said fiercely, "You ought to know she's a woman in disguise. And dangerous. She killed a man."

"Why do you tell me this now?" Thomas asked. "What is it to me? Tell the captain."

The man said angrily, "I'm not going to let her escape from

me. I've carried her this far. Wherever she is, I'll find her." He
looked very young and wild—the Black Irish could be passionate. It was the other side of their violent brooding nature.

Thomas said soothingly, "Get some sleep, man."

The other stared at him as if ready to attack him. Thomas's
hand was on the double-barrelled pistol in his pocket. But then
suddenly the man rushed away.

"He knows I'm here," Kath said, opening the lid of the
trunk. Two air holes had been cut in the far side close to the
wall, but she was relieved to breathe naturally again. He
watched her breasts rise and fall.

"He said you killed someone."

"He's lying."

"Who was it? Tell me the truth."

Kath was silent.

"I thought there was something about your name, something
I read in the papers when I came back to England." He stared
at her. "I want the truth."

She gave him her innocent expression. "I killed someone like
you did. He was . . . trying to take advantage of me." She added
quickly, "How do you plan to get me out of here, Mr.
Thomas?"

"In that," Thomas said, pointing to the trunk.

"And take me to Washington to meet President Lincoln?"

"No, I've helped you enough, young lady." She had killed
someone, she had caused him to kill someone—she was *trouble.* It was time to drop her.

But during the night, Thomas had an idea. He wanted his
first story from America to make a big impression back home.
An interview with Lincoln would be all right, but how much
stronger it would be if it had a dramatic connection with England—with Manchester, as Lincoln had sent the working people of Manchester a message of thanks for their support! What
if he introduced Lincoln to one of those working people—a
young woman who used to work in a factory not far from
Manchester? Thomas had learned that much about Kath and he
had the true journalist's failing that he was willing to give up
everything for the sake of a story. All his misgivings about
Kath, his satisfaction at the thought of getting rid of her, were

forgotten. What did it matter if she had killed someone? he rationalized. He would take her to Washington to present her to Lincoln and *then* he would drop her.

During the last night before the *Raleigh* docked in New York, the weather changed drastically. The sea became restive, choppy. Rain lashed the deck, soaking the animals. A storm moving up the coast from Florida was about to overtake them.

Thundering knocks came on the door. Black Irish shouted, "Let me in! I know what you're doing in there!"

"Don't open the door," Kath whispered. "He sounds crazy. Storms affect some people that way. Like the moon."

He banged and banged on the cabin door, still shouting. Thomas sat with his hand on the pistol.

"I know she's in there. Let me in!"

Suddenly the whole ship lurched as if given a great blow from a giant fist. They heard Black Irish hurled against the steps leading to the deck. He bothered them no more. Nobody on the steamship had time for anything for the next few hours but personal survival. It was the kind of tropical storm that Thomas had never experienced before, that seemed to clutch the steamship in a vast hand and move it this way and that in huge tidal waves. The whole ship shuddered and groaned, and something crashed down on the deck above their heads. The animals moaned. Luggage rolled up and down Thomas's cabin. He and Kath clung to the bed as the *Raleigh* seemed to turn over, battered by both the wild sea and the roaring wind in ever stronger onslaughts.

"Nature's much wilder here," Kath cried as the sea crashed against the cabin window and she was thrown against Thomas.

"Bigger," Horatio Thomas shouted back, steadying her, aware of her body against his.

The steamship plunged and then rose again. They couldn't feel the engines any more. The *Raleigh* could have been out of control. The noise of the ocean and the wind drowned out everything.

The oil-lamp went out, leaving them in total darkness. There wasn't even a glimmer of light from the window. The sea covered it with a curtain of spray as waves lashed against the sides. This made their situation even more frightening. She clung to him. He put his arms round her. It was the nearest he had got to her. She was very soft and warm. Her breasts were pressed against him.

"We'll be all right," he whispered. "This is just our introduction to America." He kissed her on the neck. She turned her head away. Damn her, he thought. Even now she doesn't want to give anything in return.

He persisted. He caressed her hair and held her close to him as the steamship was rocked by the wild sea. He felt her breasts against his chest and the softness of her back against his hand. But she kept her head down and gave him no encouragement to go any further.

The storm went on and on with no sign of relenting. She went to sleep finally in his arms. He watched the sea roar up and cover the cabin window again.

Then slowly, as dawn approached, the winds began to slacken, the waves to fall back.

When at last the storm was over, the steamship was within sight of the American coast.

America. . . .

Even the usually calm English journalist was excited.

The land of the American Dream. . . .

He woke Kath up.

"Look!"

She pressed her face to the cabin window.

"I made it!" she cried happily. "I made it to America."

"Quiet," Horatio Thomas hissed. They couldn't take any chances even now.

There was a knock at the door.

They both tensed.

But it was only Ram.

"*Waheguru,*" he said, his black eyes flashing, a new white turban covering his head.

"What does that mean?" she asked him.

"Wonderful Lord!" he replied. "I pray all night and so the storm cannot harm us." He was so pleased that he was willing even to talk to her—and also he expected to see the last of her as soon as the *Raleigh* docked.

Horatio Thomas wondered how he was going to break it to the young Sikh that she was going with them.

11

Familiar noises and smells, the shouts of stevedores—at first sight, the dock didn't seem very foreign. People spoke the same language, more or less. There were shouts and curses in other languages, but you heard that in Liverpool, too. Sailors and dockworkers were like gypsies—they came from everywhere and nowhere.

Frank Butler didn't have much sense of being in America. When he was outside Thomas's cabin, the storm had flung him against a wall and knocked him out. His head still ached. But even so, his young, passionate nature was interested in only one thing—getting Kath back. His gambler's sense of proportion made this all important, the New World a mere background to the great game of chance he was involved in. He had won her, but he had been cheated out of his winnings so far. She was *his*, not the English journalist's. He had given up everything for her. It had become an obsession with him. Nothing could begin in America until he got her back—until he won the game. But Kath meant even more than that to him. She had become the focus of his feelings, the side of him that had been suppressed in his cold hangman's work. Saving one of his victims had made up for all the others. Kath was his salvation. He needed her desperately.

He was one of the first off the *Raleigh* onto Manhattan Island. He didn't look around, but just stood where he couldn't be seen behind a loading shed and waited for the   . He didn't have to wait long. Perhaps they hoped to beat him to it and make a quick getaway.

The Indian servant came first carrying one end of a large black trunk with a sailor at the other end. It was about six feet long—long enough for her. They puffed as if it were heavy. She weighed over 120 pounds; he remembered from the time he estimated the drop in Manchester.

He watched them stagger down the gangplank with the black trunk, the journalist in his fancy white suit walking calmly behind them. Their other luggage was left on the ship to be collected later. The large trunk was obviously special. That was a giveaway. The journalist wasn't as smart as he thought he was.

They laid the trunk gently down on the quay. The journalist walked away to say good-bye to the captain. Frank wondered how he could outwit the other two. Then the Indian servant told the sailor to stay with the trunk while he went on board to get something he'd forgotten. That was Frank's chance.

Money soon persuaded the sailor to change sides. By then the Indian had disappeared, and the journalist, deep in conversation with the captain on deck, had his back to them. Together, they carried the trunk into an empty warehouse that resounded with their footsteps. It weighed about right for her, Frank was sure as he caressed the sides of the trunk. He still felt no excitement at being in America; his thoughts were wholly on her and outwitting the smart-aleck journalist—it was like a fever of jealousy, of frustration, that raged through him. He had given up *everything* for her, and yet she had treated him so badly. It wasn't revenge he wanted as he leaned over the trunk so much as that long delayed satisfaction. He was too young to be so thwarted by the journalist.

The large trunk was locked. He took out his pocket knife and worked for a long time on the heavy lock. Slowly he was able to force open the trunk lid. It groaned like a human being and then the wood gave a loud, cracking sound. He heaved up the lid and looked inside with a triumphant expression, expecting to see her curled up there with a cowed, frightened, hellishly attractive face that would be all his.

Instead there was only a pile of books.

Books about America.

Atlases, histories . . . heavy, leather-bound books. . . .

He had been tricked!

He gave a bellow of rage and ran out of the warehouse back to the *Raleigh*. There was no sign of the journalist now on deck or the Indian servant, but the captain came swaying down the gangplank.

"Are they still on board?" Frank cried.

"You mean Mr. Thomas?" the captain asked, his speech slurred, already celebrating the steamship's safe arrival.

"Yes, the journalist in the fancy suit. Where is he?"

"You've just missed him. He went off in a horse-and-buggy, him and his Indian assistant."

"Where did they go?"

"A famous man like Mr. Thomas isn't held up," the captain said evasively. "They let him in without fuss. He had a letter of introduction to one of the Custom House officers and they let him through in double-quick time. He was in a big hurry."

"Where was he going?"

The captain hesitated.

Frank gave him a handful of money.

"To Washington, I heard him say—to see the President in the White House."

"How do I get to Washington?"

"You don't give up easy, do you?"

"Can you take me there?"

"No, it's overland. A long way. Even for an important man like Mr. Thomas, there's no easy way."

* * *

The captain was right about that, as Horatio Thomas, Ram and Kath had already discovered. It was a long way to Washington. Kath had expected America to be completely different from all that she had known before, a wonderful place where everything was easy, but the first impressions were a big letdown. This was all too close to the hard, struggling world she already knew. She tried to keep up her hopes as she left the docks, which were no prettier than Liverpool's. Could this be a country where dreams came true? she wondered, recalling the old gypsy woman's talk of a journey along "the perilous path

of enlightenment." Was that to be in America? Was life to test
her still more? She steeled herself for what lay ahead as she sat
beside Horatio Thomas and Ram. The carriage they had hired
took them no farther than the river. They crossed the Hudson
in a ferry, then boarded a crammed, crowded train, little more
than a long box on wheels with a double row of seats, to
Philadelphia. There were smoking cars for men and non-smokers for women. As Kath was still dressed as a man, they sat in
the smoker. An immense iron stove occupied the center, boiling the atmosphere so that they all gently sweated. The doors
opened and slammed continually for a procession of people
who included conductors and youths selling newspapers and
food. The other passengers were a mixed lot of European faces
and everyone talked to everyone else and, by English standards, asked the most personal questions. There was no priva-
cy, no polite silence between strangers. Ram feared another
outburst from Thomas as a man opposite interrogated him
about his life, but the English journalist chatted easily in the
most friendly way, skillfully turning the conversation so that he
was soon the one asking the questions. The man told his life
story at great length and Thomas listened with apparent interest. "Ah," he said expansively at one point, "this is American
democracy on wheels. Everyone is equal. No first class or second class. Just segregation of smokers and non-smokers."

It seemed to please him. He told Ram his first impression of
America was of somewhere vast and friendly and unfinished—a
different stage in the world's evolution from what you found
in Europe. It reminded him of a book that had caused a great
scandal in England a few years before, Charles Darwin's *The
Origin of Species.* Darwin's ideas about natural selection and
the survival of the fittest, he said, were easier to understand in
a changing, pioneer society like this one. One of Darwin's
points had been that nature didn't create beauty for its own
sake, it had to have some use. A pioneer society like this one
was like that, everything had to have a use, whereas in England,
a more settled domesticated society, much was created just for
decoration. Here survival was harder because it was everybody
for himself or herself, there was no protection—as in nature at
its freest.

His approving, philosophical mood was shaken when they reached Philadelphia and had to change trains. When Ram was struggling over the transfer of all the luggage, a ticket-collector took one look at his dusky face and red turban and told him brusquely, "Negroes in the back." Ram paused with a heavy trunk on his shoulders. "In the back, you."

Thomas stepped forward. "In the back?"

"Not you, him."

"I thought we were in the United States of America."

"You're in Philadelphia," said the ticket-collector, carefully examining the white-suited figure in front of him and trying to assess how much trouble he might cause.

"You're fighting a war for the freedom of Negroes, my dear fellow. How can you discriminate against them in Philadelphia and make sense?" Thomas waved Ram on. "My friend here could pull rank if he wished. His ancestors could read and write when yours and mine were still running around naked with painted bodies." Thomas smiled pleasantly, allowing Kath to examine his teeth. They were a little uneven, she decided. "That's the greatness of this country. Whatever stage of evolution we have reached, we're all of equal importance here. I'm sure we misunderstood you." He surveyed the waiting train without bothering about the ticket-collector's reply. "I am on my way to meet President Lincoln. I can't possibly travel to Washington the way we did from New York, cooped up like so many chickens. I must get my rest. I'll need a whole sleeping-car for my party." He thrust some money into the ticket-collector's hand. "Please arrange it for me."

They were soon relaxing in a sleeping-car to themselves with sleeping berths and a lounge with armchairs. "Money can buy you anything in a frontier society," Thomas said with satisfaction. "Even virtue has to be practical. Charles Darwin should be with us. This country is a goldmine for a naturalist."

Thomas's talk of "stages of evolution" had caught Kath's attention. The old gypsy woman had talked as if there were stages in the evolution of a dream—along the perilous path of enlightenment to the heights of fulfillment. "Who's Charles Darwin?" she asked.

"Darwin's revolutionary, my dear. I don't mean political

revolution, but intellectual. He claims the human race wasn't just put here in its present state, but has evolved from lower animal orders. He was trying to show that transmutation of our species *had* occurred and that what he called natural selection, the preservation by the environment of specially well-adapted variations, was a possible explanation. You, my dear, will probably become a well-adapted variation yourself. America is full of them."

Thomas liked to hear his own voice, Kath thought. She wasn't sure she had understood him and she glanced at Ram to see his reaction, but he was concentrating on opening a bottle of wine for Thomas. The young Indian seldom questioned anything the English journalist said—to his face. Kath understood the influence of environment on a person. She was definitely different here than she was in Stockport in the factory. She felt far less confined and mechanical, more free and challenged to show what she was, what she could do. If she stayed in America, she'd become a different person than if she returned to Stockport. This new country would force her to discover herself—every inch of herself, including the bad parts. She remembered the Garden of Eden in the Bible—would she be tempted by the forbidden fruit as she had never been in England? Or had Edward been the forbidden fruit and she had fallen for the temptation? Was she to be tempted again in this, her second life, and would she fall again or would she be strong enough this time?

Thomas had gone on talking. " . . . Industrial development's a few years behind England, you know, but it's fast catching up. A hell of a lot of America's still farmland or desert. You can still grab a piece of it. There's no railroad yet across the whole country linking the east and west coasts. You can only get as far as Kansas. . . ."

Kansas—Kath remembered her father mentioning Kansas that early morning, the last time she had laid eyes on him.

The English journalist picked up de Tocqueville's *Democracy in America*. "Listen to this book written thirty years ago by a young Frenchman. It's still true." He read: " 'Why Democratic nations show a more ardent and enduring love of equality than of liberty. . . .'"' He glanced up at Kath to make sure she was listening.

"If you're equal, aren't you free, too?" Kath asked, trying to show interest to please him.

"Oh, no, my girl. You can have equality in slavery—or in prison. De Tocqueville makes the point that we have to decide whether the principle of equality is to lead us to servitude or to freedom. That's what this war is supposed to be about. What it's *really* about I hope we'll learn when we see President Lincoln." He examined Kath. "You must take off those ridiculous men's clothes. You must show the President the respect of being yourself." He smiled at her flushed face. "There's no longer any danger. You're in America now."

Kath felt her short hair.

"I can't make my hair grow."

"Wear a hat."

"I haven't got one."

"Buy one."

"I've got no money."

"You've come all the way to America with no money?" She didn't reply. "How are you going to search Virginia for your father with no money?" She gave no response so he answered his own question. She had crossed the Atlantic with no money, hadn't she? She had already proved she could survive without it. "All right, I'll buy you a hat. You can go to a hat shop with Ram as soon as we reach Washington. I'm introducing you to the President as Miss Manchester. You must look worthy of the honor."

"I'm not from Manchester. I'm from Stockport."

"What does it matter here, three thousand miles away? Nobody here has ever heard of Stockport. A lot of people probably haven't heard of Manchester. But at least we know the President has. So stop arguing. You're from Manchester. Good God, Stockport's only a few miles away, isn't it?"

Journalists weren't very honest, Kath thought. She had made one mistake in dealing with Thomas and that was in telling him her real name. If he used it in a newspaper story and someone in Stockport read it, she might be found out. But maybe they'd think it was another person with the same name. There were lots of Tracys in the world. She mustn't ever give her full address. Perhaps it was safer to be Miss Manchester, she told herself, staring through the window at America in the growing darkness. There wasn't much to see except the occasional house with its oil-lamps lit. Thomas was reading and sipping his wine. Ram was sitting down doing nothing for once. Perhaps he was meditating or praying. She fell asleep.

They reached Washington at six AM. Kath saw a vast mass of white marble towering above them, with colonnaded porticoes topped by an unfinished cupola with scaffold and cranes still in position. This was the unfinished Capitol building. Thomas was delighted. "Look at half-finished America," he cried, peering out.

There was a cleared space of mud with workmen's huts, and then streets of red brick houses and church spires. A line of hackney-coachmen, all black, awaited the people off the train. Horatio Thomas carefully selected a big burly coachman who looked powerful enough to help Ram with the luggage. Two coaches were needed. "Willard's Hotel," Thomas said when the luggage had been loaded at last.

They sped down Pennsylvania Avenue, a broad, unfinished boulevard lined with ailanthus trees and a variety of houses ranging from plank to marble, shacks to mansions. At the far end rose the great marble Treasury buildings. Most of the people on the muddy sidewalks were black domestic workers going to their jobs.

Willard's Hotel, which William Russell of the London *Times* had recommended to Thomas, was six stories high, a great square pile of heated, muggy rooms where members of Congress lived. A vast dining hall was crowded and the noise was tremendous. Spittoons were everywhere.

Ram noticed Thomas grimace at the noise. They wouldn't be staying here long. Thomas requested three rooms in the quietest part of the hotel and he insisted on inspecting them before paying a deposit. Then he told Ram to take Kath to buy a hat.

"Then, Miss Manchester, we'll go to the White House."

The White House, Kath thought. The American President's palace! My, perhaps her dream was starting to come true at last.

* * *

Kath stared with awe at the tall, loose-jointed man with bushy black whiskers and tired, sad eyes. This was the American equivalent of the Queen and here she was, Kathleen Tracy, meeting him and talking with him like they were equals.

Thomas had told the President she was born in Manchester which was of course a lie—she'd been born a good mile outside the Manchester boundary. But the President seemed very pleased and said he hoped the Manchester cotton workers weren't suffering too much because of the civil war blockade.

"Oh, no," she said to keep him pleased, though she didn't know much about it really. Her family hadn't suffered thanks to her poaching, but you couldn't tell the American President that.

"Where are you going to visit in America, Miss Tracy?" he asked politely, his great sad eyes staring at her as if he really cared. She wore a new hat with a feather that matched her red shawl, which she wore jauntily over her head and shoulders the way she had at the factory.

"I've come to find my father," she said, wondering if he could be of help. "The last I heard he was in Richmond, Virginia."

"In the front-line," the President said sombrely. "You may not be able to reach him until the war's over."

"But I must! I've waited so long—eight years."

"If I can help you, I will."

"Could you give me a letter—a sort of pass to get through the army lines?"

Horatio Thomas said quickly, "You mustn't bother the President, Kathleen."

"But he offered to help me!"

Lincoln laughed.

"That's quite right, I did. And I will." He called his secretary, a very formal-looking man standing nearby. She watched the President dictate a pass for her. "To whom it may concern. The President requests. . . ." He towered over everybody. She was surprised how poorly dressed he was, in a worn black frockcoat and trousers, a suit that was so old it fitted the angular curves of his big body. His huge feet were stuck in shabby slippers. Yet his clothes matched his lengthy awkwardness. He looked more like a country schoolteacher than any kind of ruler. He was typical, in fact, of the America she'd experienced so far—not at all snobbish or upper class, but down-to-earth like the people in Stockport, direct and open and just a little crude in accent and manners. One of her people.

"There you are, Miss Tracy," he said cordially. "It will be ready for you when you leave. I have asked the army to give you what help they can. But don't expect miracles. They are fighting a war. They will help you as they used to sell hogs in Indiana—as they run. Forward, I trust."

She said impulsively, "You make jokes like my Dad."

He laughed. "Give your Dad my best wishes when you catch up with him. For I know you will. You have come so far already. You're a young lady who gets what she wants."

"Oh, I hope so," she said.

He turned to Thomas. "I have arranged for you to see General Grant. He's here in Washington to report from the front. Just don't write anything he disapproves of or you may have to go back home to England like the *London Times* correspondent."

"The war may not last long enough for General Grant to read my reports, Mr. President," Thomas replied in the same bantering tone. Kath could see he really liked the American President and she was surprised, because the English journalist rarely seemed to like anyone.

"I hope you're right, Mr. Thomas. There's been more than enough bloodshed already."

"There's some fear in London that the war may be ended by bringing both sides together to fight a foreign war—perhaps against England."

"Never," Lincoln said firmly. "That's a rationalization by your London politicians to justify interfering. After this is over, we shall need a long period of peace, of reconstruction, to bind up the nation's wounds. It will take years."

"You'll have to run for a third term, Mr. President."

"No, I shan't be here, Mr. Thomas. It will be someone else's turn. Every dog must have its day—but no longer. History teaches us that."

The President walked with them to the reception room

where about a dozen people were waiting to see him, most of them dressed in simple working clothes. They crowded towards him. A woman at the front cried, "My son of seventeen has been sentenced to be executed for desertion. Please help him. You *must!*"

Lincoln looked distressed. "Take this lady's name," he told his secretary. "Please don't report that," he said to Thomas. "Desertion is a growing problem on both sides the longer the war lasts. Our army generals want to shoot all deserters for the sake of army discipline. But how can you shoot a boy of seventeen? He's had no say in causing the war. I can perhaps do something in private to help, but publicity won't help anyone but the enemy. You do understand, Mr. Thomas?"

"I have seen and heard nothing, Mr. President."

Lincoln shook hands quickly with the English journalist, wanting to retreat before anybody else could get to him. Kath was astonished at how available the American President was to the people. Her people.

"Good luck, young lady," he called to her and then the tall, loose-jointed figure was gone.

"It's very different from England," she said to Thomas.

"You mean the Queen in Buckingham Palace?" he replied. "We're an old society, this is a new one. This is democracy in action. We need a dose, too. But I hope he isn't taking America too far too fast and has calculated the risks he's taking. It could be dangerous if people aren't ready for it."

"What do you mean—dangerous?" she said. His talk was sometimes too complicated.

"He might get killed—and he knows it. War spreads like a plague. People get the habit of killing."

* * *

She was disappointed by the plainness of the White House. She had expected a grand castle, but it wasn't even as impressive as Heaton Hall, and its grounds were much smaller. But it matched Washington and its skyline dominated by the unfinished dome of the Capitol building. This wasn't the ancient city of London or Paris or Rome, but the new city of a young nation. A city at war.

Long lines of army wagons and artillery rumbled through the

endless, half-completed cobbled streets leading to the marshy wilderness on the outskirts. Squads of cavalry and lines of infantrymen could be heard passing through at all times of the day and night. The dust soon turned to mud. It was a small city that had grown artificially because of the civil war.

Schools, churches and public halls had been converted into military hospitals. Grim processions of wounded came from the railway station at Alexandria or the steamboat landing at Aquia Creek. After the latest battle in the fields of nearby Virginia, Washington had been flooded with strangers from other states searching for relatives or friends who had fought in the battle.

Several times Kath and Thomas coming from the White House were asked for the whereabouts of the military hospitals and had to admit they were strangers, too. They were also stopped by armed sentries patrolling the cobbled streets and the public buildings. Thomas was about to produce his *Guardian* credentials, but Kath flashed her pass from the President and they were allowed to proceed at once. It gave Thomas an idea. Perhaps her pass could be useful to him if he met any resistance from the army high command in the front line, for the Union officers were reputed to hate reporters. Several had been imprisoned and one nearly shot as a spy. Even Russell of the *Times* had been barred from the front. He decided not to drop her yet.

That night there was gunfire outside the city. It went on until dawn. Kath sat at the window watching the flashes in the night sky. The hotel manager told Thomas that the enemy—Confederate General Early and his army in the Shenandoah Valley—had reached the suburbs in July, and Grant had had to hold back part of his army (the Sixth Corps and one division of the 19th Corps) from the front to make sure Washington was protected.

Thomas was to see General Grant the next morning, but he wasn't surprised when the meeting was postponed until the following day. With the enemy on the doorstep, Grant had no time to answer an English reporter's questions. Thomas wrote his Lincoln story instead and gave it to Ram to send off. The young Sikh had arranged for a series of messengers to get it to

New York and on the first available fast steamship crossing the Atlantic.

He tried to reach the outskirts of the capital to see some of the action for himself, but soldiers refused to let him past the first fort. There were altogether forty forts surrounding Washington and lines of rifle pits dug by the infantry. It made the war seem very close. When he met a group of soldiers coming from the fort to spend the night in the city, he pretended to be looking for the military hospitals. He asked about the gunfire. One of the soldiers said, "It was only Mosby up to his tricks," and they all laughed and walked on.

Mosby?

Thomas was to remember the moment when he heard the name of Mosby for the first time. It meant nothing to him then. But when he arrived back at the hotel, he found the news had gone ahead of him. Kath was sitting in the big lobby talking to people. Americans liked to talk even more than the English. She was becoming more used to America and its mixed styles and more informal, easy-going attitude towards life and its opportunities.

"It was somebody called Mosby," she told Thomas. "With just a few men, he fooled them into thinking a whole army was attacking Washington. Everybody's mad at Mosby."

She laughed. This Mosby sounded like her Dad—a real hell-raiser. Horatio Thomas also reminded her a little of her father, though he wasn't half the man her Dad was. It annoyed her she had to wait on the English journalist; she wanted to be in charge of her own life. But at least these reminders of her Dad that life kept providing encouraged her that she was on the right track.

Thomas consulted the hotel manager about Mosby. He knew all about him. "The war has made him a famous name, Mr. Thomas. He harries our armies behind the lines north of Rappahannock and through the Shenandoah Valley. He doesn't fight according to the rules like General Lee and the rest of the southern army. He raids trains, army camps, even—as you saw yesterday—the capital here. With just a few men, he ties down thousands of ours. You can't help admiring him."

There was no more gunfire that day—Mosby and his men

had apparently disappeared again like ghosts—and General Grant kept his appointment the next morning.

The general was short and bearded and informal, nothing but a lieutenant-general's shoulder straps to show he wasn't a private. He was half-drunk, puffing at a cigar. He was quite affable until Thomas asked about the enemy raid.

Grant scowled. "There was never any danger. We're winning, don't you know, or hasn't the news reached the shores of England yet?"

"But Mosby, General—"

"So you know all about it," Grant snapped.

"The whole of Washington seems to know."

It was the wrong thing to say.

Grant became red in the face and shouted, "You can tell Washington that Mosby's finished, him and his whole band of outlaws. They're all as crazy as moondancers." Grant puffed on his cigar, becoming calmer. "We're going to stop him as part of the final push in Virginia. His reckless exploits boost the enemy's morale too much. We haven't been ruthless enough. From now on we're going to hunt Mosby down with everything we've got. One of my best officers will lead the hunt. Note the name—Custer. George Armstrong Custer. He's going to hunt Mosby and his damn guerrillas down like dogs. I'll introduce you to him. Wait here."

Horatio Thomas guessed it was an excuse for Grant to leave the room to get another drink. He returned after a long time with a youngish officer who was the exact opposite of Grant in style, his uniform pressed and finely tailored and full of the marks of rank and with a chestful of medals. He was tall with a big, golden moustache, a flamboyant, vain, ambitious man Thomas disliked on sight. But a reporter couldn't afford to show his personal feelings when he wanted some information.

"What's your first move against Mosby?" Thomas asked him politely.

Custer gave him a hard look.

"We captured three of Mosby's men outside Washington in yesterday's action. They were wearing our uniforms. We're going to hang them publicly as outlaws, as spies. That should tell Mosby we mean business. Print it on the front page." He patted his golden locks. "We want Mosby to know what we're doing."

He must think I'm an *American* journalist, Thomas thought. It won't be on my front page for at least a couple of weeks. But he didn't want to spoil Custer's performance in front of Grant, so he nodded obediently. Custer's voice boomed louder. The man was too vain to be realistic. He should know hanging was no answer.

* * *

When Horatio Thomas returned to the hotel, he looked for Kath in the crowded lobby. She wasn't there, but Ram was.

"Got another story for you," Thomas told him. "Mosby versus Goldilocks Custer. As soon as I've written it, I want you to get it off to New York immediately and catch the first ship. It's important it's published soon. It'll give people in England a clearer idea of how the war's going. Can you arrange for the same Irish delivery as you did for the Lincoln story?"

Ram nodded in a bored way. "Will all be taken care of." Thomas was interfering in his side of the business.

"Where's Miss Tracy?"

Ram glanced up at the ceiling. He never spoke of her if possible.

Thomas went upstairs to her room.

"Who is it?" She sounded scared.

"Me . . . Horatio Thomas."

She unlocked the door and let him in and then quickly locked the door again.

"What's happened?" he said.

Her big eyes grew even bigger.

"I've seen *him*."

Thomas's mind was half on his Mosby-Custer story and he didn't understand her at first.

"Who?"

"The hangman. I saw him outside the hotel. I've got to get out of here fast."

12

They found seats on a military train travelling to the front-line in Virginia. As the train left the capital, they could see the gallows being erected on a hill overlooking the Potomac River. Custer had chosen the most public place, visible for many miles, obviously hoping that Mosby and his men would see the hangings from the other side of the river.

Kath averted her face from the macabre sight. It brought back too many nightmare memories—and reminded her of *him*. She had been worried about him until the train started, and then she slowly relaxed. The gallows on the hill brought him back, all her fears. To distract herself, she chatted to the young Union soldiers in the coach, who were only too willing to forget their own fears of the front-line in conversation with a pretty redhead. They competed for her attention, lavishing her with compliments and boasting of their own manhood.

They seemed to be of all nationalities—the sons of Germans, Italians, Spaniards, Russians, French, Swedes, Poles, Greeks, they were all serving in this army. Could all these different people ever live in peace here, she wondered, when they couldn't in Europe? Like the city of Washington, their capital, there seemed to be an unfinished quality about Americans as if they had yet to be blended into one people. There was also a wildness here that there wasn't in England, where people were so much more settled. She remembered the feeling she had had during the storm on the ship—that nature on this side of the Atlantic was much more untamed than on the other side—and that went for human nature, too. There was a more dangerous quality to life here. So much remained to be discovered and explored. It was exciting and scary.

Beside her, Thomas was talking across the aisle to a thin, foxy looking man who worked for a Washington newspaper. He wasn't very friendly, but treated Thomas as a competitor. He soon walked away down the train to talk to some of the other soldiers. Thomas followed him and came back with the latest rumors. There was one circulating about a big battle outside Richmond in which thousands on both sides had been killed. And another about an attempt in Washington to kidnap the President. And on the train, General Sheridan's army paymaster was said to be aboard with $160,000 in pay for the Army of the Potomac. The only rumor Thomas believed was true was this last one. "They won't allow you in the rear of the train. There are armed guards. They've got something valuable back there."

Thomas put a newspaper over his face and his ear-plugs in and apparently went to sleep, but Kath went back to talking with the young soldiers sitting near her. They reminded her of her brother, Harold. She was talking to a soldier with fair hair and freckles who seemed very nervous when someone came down the aisle and sat opposite her.

"Hello, Red," said a familiar voice.

It was the hangman. He smiled sardonically at her and then told the young soldier, "You're talking to my woman, boy."

Kath said furiously, "You've no right to say that. I'm not your woman." She added more gently to the embarrassed young soldier, "Ignore him. He's crazy. Where are you from?"

"Boston," stammered the young soldier. "My parents came from England—from Cornwall."

Frank cut in, "I'm not crazy. Far from it. I've just come for my rights." He turned to face the young soldier and addressed him with a phony show of friendliness. "You know how little you can buy a woman for back in Washington? Women are so common they're not worth anything. They're walking the streets. Well, I saved this girl's life and I also paid her way across the Atlantic. Down South in the Confederacy, I'm told, that'd be enough to buy her for life. Slaves don't come that expensive."

"I'm not your slave," Kath snapped, blushing angrily.

"I don't think you should speak about the lady that way," said the nervous young soldier.

"You don't, don't you? And what are you going to do about it?"

Frank raised his hands as if to fight. The young soldier was confused, feeling trapped. The other soldiers began to watch, anticipating a good fight to distract them from their fears and boredom.

"You're *crazy,* just like I told you," Kath cried. She leaned over to the young soldier. "Don't fight over me. There'll be enough fighting when this train reaches the front-line."

"I'm staking my claim," Frank said, clenching his fists. "I'm going to teach this soldier here a lesson—and you, too."

Horatio Thomas lifted the newspaper off his face.

"Be careful you don't have to fight the whole Union Army!"

Frank immediately dropped all interest in the young soldier and angrily faced the English journalist.

"I'll fight you instead," Frank said fiercely. "You think you can move in and take over. Working class people like us don't matter—her or me. You feel we're just put on this earth for your pleasure or convenience."

"It's not my fault if she doesn't want you," Horatio Thomas drawled coolly.

"Look here, you," Frank cried, leaning forward with a mean expression, "You mesmerised her with your money and your fancy ways." He held out a clenched fist. "This is what'll bring you and her to your senses." He stood up. "Be a man instead of a tailor's dummy. Fight it out."

He grabbed the lapels of Thomas's jacket and pulled him to his feet, but before the two men could begin exchanging punches, the train gave a great lurch, throwing them back into their seats, and some of the young soldiers sprawling across the aisle. There was a tremendous roar and crash from somewhere near the front, and then the train braked and came to a sudden stop. The soldiers rushed to the windows. Part of the track had been torn up and the engine was lying on its side. The rest of the train was upright but stationary in some lonely, flat Virginia countryside.

"It's a raid," shouted a soldier and, a moment later, there were rifle and pistol shots outside along the whole length of the train and the thunderous sound of galloping horses. A blast from a shotgun shattered a window, spraying glass everywhere, and all the passengers dropped to the floor. There was no time to think about what to do. The door at the end of the coach was flung open, a pistol cracked overhead, and a man's voice cried, "Stay just where you are."

A young soldier made the mistake of getting up and immediately had a revolver stuck in his ribs.

"I told you, soldier, to stay where you are. Drop down again and this time don't try an' win any medals." The voice was casual but firm and commanded respect. The young soldier lost no time in obeying. "Now anybody with guns lay them in the aisle. Don't play any tricks or you won't see sundown, and that's a promise."

There were thumping sounds beneath the seats as guns were slid into the aisle.

"I wouldn't, soldier," warned the voice above them as someone hesitated. "You don't want to be a dead hero."

A soldier reluctantly laid his rifle with the other guns piled in the aisle.

"Just lie there and stay quiet."

Kath took a quick look at who was giving these orders. He was tall and lean and surprisingly young. She couldn't see much of his face beneath his dark wide-brimmed hat except that he had strong, sun-tanned features. His faded gray shirt and gray pants, tucked into worn leather cowboy boots, were the Confederate color but were worn with the independent style of an outlaw rather than an enemy soldier. She wondered whose side he was on—his own probably. He noticed her staring.

"That redhead! Who are you?" He came closer down the aisle. "Not bad-lookin' for a Yankee girl."

"I'm English!"

"So what are you doin' here in Virginia?"

"I'm looking for my father."

Astonishingly clear blue eyes examined her, and with one quick movement, he grabbed her shoulder bag. One hand quickly ripped it open and rummaged through while the other hand held the gun covering the rest of them.

"What's this?"

It was the Presidential pass. He saw Lincoln's signature. His sharp, knowing blue eyes were immediately suspicious. His tanned face hardened as he examined her more closely. "You some kind of government agent?"

"No, I—"

"You leave her alone!" Frank cried, getting up.

The revolver pointed at him.

"You stay out of this, mister."

"I'm with her."

The blue eyes examined Frank then and didn't seem to like much what they saw. "You both better come along with us," he grunted.

"But I'm going to find my father," Kath protested.

He ignored her.

An older bewhiskered man holding a double-barrelled shotgun came down the aisle.

Blue Eyes told him, "Bring the redhead and the fella with her. They may be into something the colonel should know about."

"Sacrifices in the holy war against Satan!" roared the bewhiskered man in a high preacher's tone.

The blue eyes went cold. "None of your crazy talk, Reverend. This is serious business."

"So is mine, my boy." The bewhiskered man made a big sign of the cross in the air. "This train's an agent of the Devil. We're doin' holy work in stoppin' it."

A shout came from outside. "All done, Bo."

"Time to get goin'," said Blue Eyes.

"Who are you?" Thomas asked him, standing up.

The gun covered the English journalist.

"We're Mosby Rangers, sir."

Mosby.

Horatio Thomas stepped forward. It was too good a chance to miss.

"I'm with her, too."

"Then bring him as well, Reverend."

"I have several pieces of essential luggage," Thomas said quickly. "I'll need help in carrying them."

"Anything valuable?" asked the bewhiskered gunman.

"To me, yes," replied Thomas. "But to you, no."

"Then leave them. We're not removal men, Fancy Pants."

Ram got up and followed Thomas. He was going, too, whether the raiders liked it or not. Nobody objected. Ram shouldered one of the trunks full of Thomas's clothes. Thomas grasped a suitcase of books and personal papers. The rest of the luggage had to be left.

Blue Eyes shouted back, "Bring several of the soldiers, too, Reverend. The Colonel asked for a few hostages."

As they all stepped off the train, other Mosby men were lifting iron boxes out of the next coach.

"Over $150,000 in crisp new banknotes!" one of them yelled.

"The Union army won't get paid this month," cried another, laughing as he loaded the iron boxes onto a wagon. Horses were patiently waiting by the side of the track where it had been uprooted by the raiders to stop the train. "Can you folk ride?" asked the bewhiskered man, gesturing with his shot-gun. Kath and Ram couldn't. The nearest Kath had ever come to riding a horse was when the local milkman in Stockport had let her sit on his big old carthorse when she was a child. Ram said you had to be rich in India to ride horses. He was found a place on the wagon carrying the iron boxes. He put the trunk he was carrying and the suitcase Thomas held on the wagon beside him. Kath was told to get up behind Thomas on a docile mare.

"She can't ride with him!" Frank shouted.

The shotgun was stuck in his face.

"Any more objections?" demanded the Reverend.

Frank glowered, but remained silent.

Blue Eyes then came galloping up before Kath could move and gathered her up to ride with him. Frank seemed to dislike that even more. The Mosby men laughed among themselves.

As the raiders and their prisoners rode away, soldiers began to hurry out of the train. They could be seen kneeling on the ground aiming their rifles, and there was a continual crackle of shots. But the raiders were too far away by then, riding fast towards the distant woods and the slopes of the high Virginia hills.

* * *

They rode for hours. The Mosby men rode fast but in a carefree style with little discipline. They were very cheerful after the successful raid. From their laconic conversation, it was clear they had known the paymaster with the money was on the train.

Kath noticed the other prisoners included not only several of the young soldiers she had talked with, very scared-looking now in their blue uniforms, but also the foxy-faced Washington journalist, who had discussed the war with Thomas. Mosby probably wanted publicity about the raid to scare Washington even more.

She didn't feel at all frightened. These men didn't scare her. She wasn't involved in their war; she didn't wear a blue uniform. She'd soon make their leader understand about Lincoln's pass and maybe this Mosby could help her, too, by giving her a pass for his territory. What mattered was that she was in Virginia at last.

Blue Eyes didn't talk to her; he seemed preoccupied with playing leader, but she was aware of his warmth and the hard muscles she clung to. This was a kind of man she hadn't met before, and she felt even more interested in him because he paid her so little attention. Beneath her, the fine white horse seemed to throb with life as it thrust its way up between the pine trees masking the hills. Pulling her red shawl closer, she felt more than ever like one of those mysterious Mexican women she had seen in a picture at school. They were shown on a horse with their man, a Mexican caballero with a reckless style much like the man she rode with, though more swarthy. She was so relaxed, so little worried, that she fell asleep.

Thomas also studied the Mosby men, less confident in his judgment than Kath. These were violent men—what did they intend to do with their prisoners? The young man Kath was riding with was nearest—he said he was from Texas when Thomas asked which part of America he came from, but he ignored the English journalist's other questions. Not rudely, but simply from lack of interest. On the far side of him was the older bewhiskered man known as the Reverend, who seemed half-drunk, nodding over his horse's neck, and behind were two sallow, big-boned men with short, black mustaches, who could have been Europeans or New Englanders. The Mosby Rangers were a mixed bunch—typical Americans, Thomas thought.

The long journey passed swiftly and peacefully. Thomas felt saddle sore by the time they reached the old stone farmhouse where Colonel Mosby was waiting for them. A big battle had recently been fought through the woods above the farmhouse. Not many trees were left standing, and the trunks of the survivors were all scarred with bullet and shrapnel holes. A row of apple trees nearer the farmhouse had been destroyed by cannon blasts. A few stumps showed above the short grass.

Kath stared at the ruined woods with horror. She had been prepared for wounded men, but not this wholesale destruction of nature. She imagined the scene in the woods of Heaton Hall where she had poached. These woods couldn't have been so different. Imagine a battle fought there at night, she thought. Soldiers, unable to see the enemy, forcing their way through the undergrowth, then stopping to listen as she had done. Then suddenly a surprise attack, like the appearance of the game-keepers. Musketry fire cutting through thick oak trees and spraying them with deadly splinters, heavy branches crashing down on their heads, finally fires started by artillery roaring through the treetops and the undergrowth trapping them and roasting them to death—them and the animals and the birds of the woods.

They left the ruined woods behind them, but as they neared the farmhouse, Kath saw part of the roof and a side wall were gone, but the living quarters at the back were intact. It was dusk as they came up the road. The wagon with the money was in the lead. The horses made soft, barely audible clip-clop sounds, but there must have been a look-out because people came out to greet them long before they reached the farmhouse. In the lead was a big red-faced woman Kath assumed was the farmer's wife—if the farmer had survived the battle that had destroyed his apple trees.

"Welcome home, boys," she called to them.

A successful raid called for a celebration, but this was a grim-faced reception, low-key, with no smiles. Blue Eyes sensed immediately that something had happened—something bad.

"Where's the Colonel?"

A man in a gray, wide-brimmed scout's hat thrust to the front of the welcoming group.

"Charlie Wyatt and Tom Straight and Ben Thrasher were captured outside Washington. The Colonel's gone to see what he can do for them."

The news spoiled the homecoming for everybody. There was no cause for celebration now. They dismounted in silence, the darkness now spreading across the flat farmland.

"Maybe we can rescue them," roared the Reverend.

"What do you think the Colonel's tryin' to do?" grunted Blue Eyes, petting his white horse.

Horatio Thomas wondered whether to mention Custer's scheme. He decided not to. It might make them even more suspicious.

Frank walked over to the white horse. Blue Eyes glanced quickly at him. It was a warning not to bother the weary stallion. It was a magnificent animal with a fine head carried high on an arched neck, a broad deep chest, and a high-set tail.

"Arab, isn't it?" Frank asked admiringly.

"That's right," said Blue Eyes, more friendly.

"I've got a mixture of Arab and Thoroughbred in England," Frank said, remembering. "He's got a quick intelligence, great stamina, and a sweet temper."

"Yeah," said Blue Eyes, stroking the long, fine mane, "they're a great horse. Someone told me they go back hundreds of years in the Arabian desert, famous for their courage and their beauty. Look at the limbs on him! He's a little short of a thousand pounds and about fifteen hands high. He used to belong to a general—a Yankee general."

"You men sound like you're talking about a woman," Kath told them, stroking the white horse.

Blue Eyes took off his dark wide-brimmed hat, showing long fair hair which he brushed back from his tanned forehead. "You wouldn't understand," he said slowly, "unless you've been around horses and know their ways. They're better company than a lot of women in my opinion." He replaced his hat and grinned at her, his teeth very white in his tanned face. "Horses don't try to possess you." He walked away with the horse in the direction of the barn.

They were all fed in the farmhouse. Kath helped the big red-faced farmer's wife to wash the dishes afterward and asked her about Mosby. The woman was glad to talk to another woman.

"Colonel Mosby has friends all over Northern Virginia. We call Loudoun, Fauquier, and Fairfax counties 'Mosby's Confederacy.' The Colonel is the law here since the war and all authority broke down. Look outside there," said the woman, pointing through the open window at the ruined woods. "We're in a sort of terrible No-Man's-Land. But the Colonel protects us. He even deals with horse thieves and other law-breakers, and we house and feed him and his men. The enemy's tried to get us to betray him by taking local farmers hostage, but we'll always be loyal to the Colonel. He's our friend and protector."

They slept in the barn with the Reverend as their guard. He was disgusted with the job. "Look, I wanna get some sleep. You try to move outta the barn, you're dead, okay?"

Thomas tried to calm his hostility.

"Where are you from?" he asked pleasantly.

"None of your business. My buddy, the Texan, Bo Blue Eyes, he come, therefore I come. I fight in any war against the Devil. Now you all get some sleep and don't move, hear?" He lay down on the straw, a whisky bottle by his side.

Soon they were all asleep except Horatio Thomas. Even with his ear-plugs in, he couldn't fall asleep. Rats rustled in the roof and birds cried across the fields, as if they were searching for the missing trees. Once Thomas got up to urinate in a corner. The Reverend sat up, gun in hand. When he saw what Thomas was doing, he chuckled and grunted, "Can't hold your liquor, huh?" and promptly rolled over and began snoring.

Shortly before dawn, a horse galloped off down the road.

The Reverend was awake at once and rushed to the door. He began to curse. "Why the hell didn't he wait for me?"

"What happened?" Thomas asked.

"The Texan's gone to find the Colonel. If I hadn't had you lot to look after, he'd have invited me along. Damn you!" And he took a swig of his whisky, lay down again, and soon was back to snoring.

They were allowed out for breakfast when the Reverend had had enough sleep. By then the sun was well up in a clear blue sky. In the brilliant light, the shattered trees and other signs of devastation looked very grotesque. Men sat against the tree stumps and played cards while their horses grazed in the fields. There was an air of anxious waiting about them all, about the whole farm.

The Reverend sat alone, nursing a hangover. Kath went over to him. The men playing cards watched her pass, but no one bothered her. There was a tight discipline under the apparently carefree style.

"I hope we won't be held long," she told the Reverend. "I need to get to Richmond."

Bloodshot eyes, half closed against the sunlight, regarded her coldly. "You'll never get to Richmond," he grunted. "The town's cut off. That devil Grant and his army of sinners have been trying to take Richmond for months."

"I'll get there somehow," she told him.

"Why do you want to get to Richmond anyway?" he asked suspiciously.

"My father was there and I want to find him."

"I was in Richmond before I joined the Colonel," the Reverend said, more friendly. "What's your Pa's name?"

"Joseph Tracy."

A hand on his head, he thought for a few moments. "Joe Tracy—No, I don't know any Joe Tracy. What kind of work does he do?"

"He came from England. He worked in a factory there. I don't know what he was doing in Richmond."

"*Was?* He's not still there?"

"That's what I've got to find out. We last heard from him eight years ago."

The Reverend laughed, showing broken, stained teeth. "Eight years, darlin'? That was before the siege, before the war even started. You mean you've heard nuthin' since then?"

"That's right."

The Reverend, sad-faced, took a quick drink. "Start of another day." He wiped his lips. "I sure hope you find your Pa. But that's a long time to be hearin' nuthin'. A lot's happened to Richmond in those eight years."

"I've *got* to find him."

The Reverend tipped his hat sympathetically. "If I can ever be of help, little lady, you just let me know—wherever you are and wherever I am. I'll do anything to help you on your way." The Reverend beamed. "Why, I'd even marry you!"

"I'm too young to settle down, thank you, Reverend," she said jokingly.

"I wasn't volunteerin' as a husband. I mean performin' your weddin' ceremony." He began to laugh when suddenly his expression changed. He stared tensely over her shoulder, his bloodshot eyes focussed on the far distance. "Someone's comin'," he murmured. That could mean trouble in this war. He stood up. The card-players stopped their game. The farmer's wife came out of the farmhouse, her face anxious.

At first Kath could see nothing in the bright sunlight, then a cloud of dust showed on the road steadily growing bigger. A group of horsemen were approaching. They were still unrecognisable to her when the Reverend roared with relief, "It's the Colonel."

There were about a dozen men, including the tall young Texan. Their faces were sombre. There was no good news. Riding at their head was a short, wiry man with an air of casual authority. This was Mosby. As he came closer, Kath noticed he had a fancy gray felt hat with a curling ostrich plume, a slight beard and stern, observant eyes. Kath was reminded of one of the oldtime English cavaliers, but he packed a Colt pistol instead of a sword. He jumped off his horse and strode into the farmhouse without speaking to anyone. The farmer's wife went in after him. A few moments later, Kath heard her cry out.

"What happened?" the Reverend roared to the other men. The tall young Texan patted his fine white stallion.

Nobody seemed keen to give the news.

"What happened to them?" asked the Reverend more quietly.

The young Texan swung easily off his horse.

"They were hanged," he said at last and went in the farmhouse.

"Those Yankee killers strung them up," said one of the other horsemen. "Charlie Wyatt, Tom Straight and Ben Thrasher were all hanged from trees like outlaws."

The Reverend cursed. It was like a litany of foul language. The card-players were all on their feet, shocked by the news, too. Several of them also cursed, but they couldn't match the Reverend. Horatio Thomas observed the change in them. Their lazy good-humour had vanished. Their faces were grim with suppressed violence, revengeful, their hands caressing the butts of their pistols. Perhaps Custer had miscalculated, Thomas thought.

The tall young Texan reappeared at the farmhouse door.

"The Colonel wants to see the prisoners," he said, tight-lipped, his blue eyes icy.

Horatio Thomas felt a chill of premonition.

13

They were brought into the farmhouse one by one. Kath was the first. She found Colonel Mosby sitting stern-faced behind a big hand-carved dining-table, a slight, almost frail-looking man but with piercing eyes and a steely determination. His ammunition belt with two revolvers was still round his waist, and he was wearing his cavalry boots with brass spurs. He was ready for action.

The news he'd brought had left him in a very sour mood. He interrogated her for a long time. The Lincoln pass and her wanting to get into Richmond, the besieged capital, made him very suspicious. He was worried that she might be a spy for Lincoln, and he tried to trap her into a lie by going back over and over again what she had told him.

Mosby seemed to be obsessed with the idea of spying, perhaps because he and his men had infiltrated the enemy lines, sometimes dressed up in Northern blue uniforms. Spying was part of their daily life; what they could do, so could others. Of course in a civil war like this one, spying was so easy, Kath thought. Both sides were part of the same family, spoke the same language. It was an incestuous struggle in which brother betrayed brother—or sister betrayed sister. At first Mosby wouldn't even accept that she was English. He had never heard of Stockport. Of Manchester, but not of Stockport. What did

people do there? What had *she* done? Why had a factory worker in Stockport come to Virginia?

"To look for my father?"

"You say you've come all the way from Stockport, England,
to look for your father?" Mosby said sharply, and she stared
back at those piercing eyes and replied firmly, "Yes, I've come
to find him."

Even her beauty aroused his suspicion. Spies were often
good-looking to win people's confidence, and many beautiful
women had already been caught spying for the North.

"Are you married?"

"No."

"Have you ever been married?"

"Not yet."

At last her persistence convinced him—or he said it did.
What also helped was the friendliness of the farmer's wife. She
spoke up for Kath. The woman's eyes were red with weeping.
After the interrogation was over, Kath went to her and asked
what the trouble was. The woman began to weep again. Her
husband—"My Ben"—had been one of the men hanged by
Custer.

Mosby was also slow to accept Horatio Thomas's *Guardian*
credentials. They could be forged, he said. There were Englishmen serving on both sides in the war. When Thomas told him
he'd talked with the Washington journalist on the train, Mosby
had the man brought in.

"You know this Englishman?" Mosby asked the foxy looking
journalist.

The competitive eyes gave Thomas a hard look.

"Never seen him before."

"But we talked on the train," Thomas protested.

"There are a lot of government agents running around claim-
ing to be reporters," the man told Mosby.

Kath stopped talking to the farmer's widow. "Mr. Thomas
is telling the truth," she said. "He was on the same steamship
coming from England with me, him and his Indian servant."

But this only renewed Mosby's suspicions of Kath—if
Horatio Thomas wasn't genuine, then perhaps she was a spy,
too, trying to cover up for him.

He had Ram brought in. The young Sikh in a clean white turban stood proudly before the Colonel. Mosby showed he knew a lot about India in questioning him. He asked Ram about the Sikh gurus. Who was Guru Nanak? "He was our first spiritual teacher," Ram told him solemnly, amazed that an American should know enough to ask such a question. "Guru Nanak lived from 1469 until 1539. He preached, 'To love God you must first learn to love one another'."

"And he was right about that," Mosby said grimly.

It was as if Ram had passed a test for them all. Mosby visibly relaxed and loosened his gun belt.

He smiled at Kath. "A beautiful woman is always suspicious in a war. You remind me of Lord Byron's poem, 'She walks in beauty like the night. . . .'" He told Thomas, "I want you and this Washington journalist to stay here in camp to witness what happens so you can go back and tell General Grant and that killer Custer."

"What are we going to witness?" Thomas asked.

"You'll see soon enough. Now I must examine the other prisoners," he said and instructed the Reverend who had brought in Ram to go for the young soldiers off the train. They arrived looking very young and scared. At least Mosby couldn't accuse them of being spies, dressed as they were in the enemy's blue uniforms.

* * *

The iron money boxes of General Sheridan's paymaster were opened in front of the farmhouse and the crisp new banknotes were solemnly counted and laid out in neat piles. Total: $154,-000.

Each of Mosby's men received $2,000. Several of them decided to ride into a nearby small town to buy new clothes. The tall young Texan decided he needed a haircut. Kath asked if she could accompany him so she could buy some soap. He said he would bring her some. She argued that he wouldn't bring the right kind. Her real reason for wanting to go was to get better acquainted with the Texan, because he seemed to be the man the others respected most after the Colonel. He might be useful. She would never admit to herself she was also attracted by him.

The Texan didn't look too pleased, but finally agreed to let her ride with him.

On the way down the road, he told her, "We're getting out of the Colonel's way. As you've already seen, the man's in a mean mood. He's going to explode one way or another, but it won't bring those boys back to life. No, sir, nobody comes back from a hanging."

That's where you're wrong, Kath thought humorously, and I'm here to prove it, but she didn't say anything. It might be dangerous to let them know that part of her past. The Colonel was obviously in a state of mind to strike out, to get revenge. She, too, had a bad feeling about what was going to happen.

The town was another victim of the war. It was a cluster of low, one-story buildings along a simple main street, and every house and store showed some marks of enemy guns. A whole wall of a church had collapsed, revealing the altar, but already the townspeople had started to repair it. The little town still had a lot of life. The stores were busy even though some had no windows, and so, too, was the barbershop.

There was a swivel chair facing a big wall mirror and a table with the usual assortment of colored bottles of hair oil, hair dye and hair restorer. The barber, big-eyed and balding, was at work on a customer who was hidden under a face full of lather and a white sheet covering the rest of him to protect his clothes. Two other men, both locals, were waiting for their turn. They eyed the tall young Texan and Kath—especially Kath—curiously, but didn't speak.

The Texan dropped lightly down on a wooden bench, stretched out his boots and picked up a magazine from a pile on the floor. He turned a few pages and then threw the magazine back on the pile. He acted as if he were bored and impatient. He said loudly to Kath: "I'd never buy a bottle of hair restorer from a bald barber, how about you?" Kath was embarrassed because the barber could hear. The Texan said even more loudly, "Business might look up if he got himself a fancy wig." And, nudging Kath with his elbow, he added, "The dye ain't no use, too, if you ain't got no hair."

He grinned at the barber, an open friendly grin, and then Kath realised he knew the barber and was teasing him. He'd been there before. But the barber's response obviously surprised him. Instead of grinning back, the barber seemed to become more and more nervous as he finished shaving the customer's face and cleaned him up. He kept looking toward the Texan as if trying to convey something without words. Finally the customer became impatient and whisked off the white sheet, revealing an army officer in uniform—a blue uniform.

The Texan sat forward, a hand on his knee, not far from his guns. Kath tensed, wondering what she should do in case of trouble. The Union officer was preoccupied with paying the barber and hadn't even noticed the Texan. The next customer got up to take his place in the swivel chair. The Union officer stood aside and it was then that he saw the Texan. His eyes scanned the whole of him down to his cowboy boots. The Texan obviously wasn't a local.

"Lookin' for somethin'?" drawled the Texan. It was a deliberate challenge.

"Thought I might know you from someplace," replied the Union officer carefully.

"Reckon not," said the Texan.

"You from these parts?"

"This ain't my home town if that's what you mean." He spoke in a deceptively casual way, the tension growing as the two men tested each other.

"Where you from then?"

"From Texas."

"You fought in the war?"

"I done my share."

The Union officer's hand dropped to his side near his gun. "On which side?"

It was as if the barber and the other customers, including Kath, were suspended in time, conscious of nothing but waiting for the Texan's reply.

"I asked you which side you fought on," said the Union officer, his voice sharper, more challenging.

The Texan stood up reluctantly.

"On Mosby's."

The Union officer went for his gun, but it wasn't half out of his holster by the time the Texan had his in his hand. He had drawn with astonishing speed. The Union officer paled and stood rigidly to attention as if expecting to be shot down. But the Texan merely covered him and drawled, "I want you to take this message back to your side. We don't kill people in cold blood the way you hanged three of our boys yesterday." He gestured with his gun towards the door. "Get goin'."

They watched the Union officer hurry down the short main street toward his horse.

"He'll be back soon with an army," said the barber.

"I guess I'll have to get my haircut another day," said the Texan, dropping his gun back in its holster. It was a most unusual pistol of a design Kath had never seen before and with a fine ivory handle.

"You mean that about the hangings?" asked the barber.

"Yeah," the Texan said slowly, "Charlie, Tom and Ben. They caught 'em outside Washington and hanged 'em high and left their bodies danglin' for folk to stare at. The Colonel shot 'em down with his rifle, broke their ropes."

"What's the Colonel goin' to do about it?"

The Texan shrugged. "Knowin' him, he'll have to do somethin'."

"This damn war gets more savage every day," said the barber. "Where's it all goin' to end, Bo?"

"We'll all lose," said the Texan at the door. "The killing's gone too far."

They rode slowly out of the little town on the white stallion. The young Texan seemed in no hurry, as if out to show he couldn't be scared. A few minutes after they had disappeared into the hills, the Union officer rode up to the barbershop with a troop of cavalry. They wanted to know which way the Texan had gone. The barber pointed in the wrong direction past the damaged church. The Union cavalry thundered off in a cloud of dust. The barber went back to cutting the hair of a local customer. Ordinary life had to go on, as far as possible.

* * *

The Texan rode back to the farmhouse in silence. His tanned face was sombre as if he could see what lay ahead and he didn't like it.

The incident in the barbershop had intrigued Kath, made him even more attractive to her, and now riding with him, she felt very close to him. And not only physically. His untamed spirit appealed to her. He seemed to embody all the strange qualities of this vast new country. Sitting straight and easy, perfectly relaxed, he didn't give a damn for anybody or anything. He was free—freer than anybody she'd ever known. He wasn't much older than she was, but he'd experienced much more. Perhaps that was why he seemed such a mystery, so different from the people she'd grown up with.

She tried to get him to talk about himself as they rode through the darkening Virginia hills.

"I've never seen guns like yours before."

He didn't answer.

"What's your name?"

No reply.

"The barber called you Bo."

He grinned then.

"You keep at it, I'll give you that. My name's Monroe Jack if you must know, but they call me Bo Jack."

"Who gave you that name?"

He didn't reply. He'd told her enough. But she felt him against her thigh and she wondered why he had suddenly become excited.

But he didn't share anything more with her.

Not even where his name had come from.

Bo Jack. . . .

14

A woman in Fort Worth had first given him the name Bo, though she had meant Beau, the French word for handsome. That was when he was fifteen and already over six feet.

What had drawn young Bo's attention to her was a public lynching. A young black man was strung up in the town square. Bo asked his father what the man had done.

"They claim he tried to have sex with a woman . . . a white woman."

"But don't lots of men do that?"

"Yeah, but you see, son, he wasn't a free man."

That gave Bo a picture of what freedom was—if you were free, you could chase women without getting strung up for it. Someone pointed out the woman who had caused the lynching. She was a gambler's wife and people said he'd won her in a poker game, which was their way of saying she was a whore.

One evening her husband came home earlier than usual from the local saloon and found young Bo in bed with her. Bo didn't carry a gun and, as he was reaching for his pants, the husband shot him intending to kill him, but the man was half-drunk and his aim was off. Bo was hit high in the chest and lived.

Bo's father, Ben Jack, was a captain in the legendary Texas Rangers. Known to the Mexicans as *Los Tejanos Diablos* or the Texas devils, the Rangers were the only real law along the savage Texas frontier. They hunted cattle rustlers and bank

141

robbers and fought Indian tribes when they weren't attacking Mexican troops. Captain Jack had already lost an eye (he wore a black eye patch), and his lean, tanned body was well marked with the scars of old bullet, knife and arrow wounds. At the time Bo was wounded, he was pursuing a band of pillaging Comanches who came from a village near the Canadian River in Oklahoma.

"Son," said Captain Jack when he returned home a week later to find Bo in the hospital, "It's about time you packed a pistol."

He wrote to his friend Sam Colt, who had a gun factory in New Jersey, asking for the pistol of the future for his young son, one that wouldn't be out-of-date in Bo's lifetime.

Two months later a bulky package arrived by stagecoach— two new model six-shooters Sam Colt planned to call The Peacemaker. They were the first experimental pair and he asked Bo to test them for him. For the first time, ball and powder and percussion cap were incorporated in one metallic cartridge capable of killing a man over a great distance. The guns had beautiful ivory handles.

Bo, who had never given much time to school, willingly gave hours to practicising with the guns, drawing in one fast movement and firing with deadly accuracy at increasingly distant targets. A local blacksmith made him a special cutaway holster to hang low on his thigh. Soon he could outdraw and outshoot even his father. Captain Jack was delighted. The boy had a natural talent rare even in Texas, with the instinct, eye, handspeed, and reflexes of a great gunfighter.

When Bo judged himself ready, he went over to the saloon. The gambler was on a winning streak in a poker game. Bo let him play on until he started to lose, then he walked over to the table.

"I've come to repay you."

"You're only a kid," sneered the gambler.

"That didn't stop you, but now I got an equaliser." Bo was as calm and unhurried as if he were a veteran gunfighter instead of being involved in his first gunfight. He had the confidence of great talent even then.

"Come back when you're growed up," the gambler said, feeling for his guns under the table.

Bo kicked aside the table. Both men went for their guns at exactly the same moment, but Bo's roared while the gambler was still drawing his. The gambler went over backwards and was dead before he hit the floor.

Everyone in the saloon made way respectfully for Bo as he made for the swing doors. No one tried to stop him. They knew a great gunfighter when they saw one.

Bo went straight to the sheriff's office to report what he'd done. He didn't want to hurt his father's reputation as a lawman. He was glad his mother wasn't alive. She wouldn't have understood. He was jailed to stand trial.

"Why did you kill him?" the sheriff asked. "Why didn't you just wing him?"

"It'd only have happened all over again. We was fightin' for his woman."

The jury was out for twenty minutes and then returned all smiles with a verdict of not guilty. That night Bo moved in with the widow. For the next few days, he never had his clothes on, but then his money ran out so he got a job as a guard at a bank.

One lunch break he came home unexpectedly to find her in bed with a young ranchhand. The man's gunbelt was on the back of a chair. Bo gave him time to reach for it and then outdrew him. As he was about to blast the big young man standing there with nothing on, he suddenly realised it was the same situation he'd been in with the gambler.

He froze.

He stared at her in the bed and ripped back the soiled, sweaty sheet, exposing her plump, big-breasted body that he knew so well.

"I made a mistake killin' your husband," he told her. "You weren't worth it." He remembered the young black man who'd been lynched because of her and suddenly he was very angry. "If I ever see you again, I'll kill you."

He collected his few belongings and left Fort Worth that night. He didn't even leave his father a message where he was going. He didn't know. He just had to get away. He experienced a great restlessness, but he needed a destination. His guns gave him an idea. He was dissatisfied with their range. The six-inch barrel was too short and reduced the power and accuracy. He decided to go to see the only man who knew the guns better than he did—their maker, Sam Colt. If he'd known how far it was to New Jersey, he'd probably have thought again, but once he set out, he kept going.

Mostly he rode the railroads free of charge, becoming expert at outwitting the guards. He was surprised how much less open some of the other states were and also how different their ways of life were. Some states had no black slaves even. The weather changed as he went northwards and became cooler and wetter. But above all he became aware of the sheer size of the country. He had thought Texas was vast, and that was only part of America.

Sam Colt was ill in bed but agreed to see him. Weary-looking with a straggly greying beard and shrewd eyes, he received Bo politely and asked with an eagerness matching Bo's own about the guns. He agreed to lengthen the barrel. "This is the last gun I'll make," he said softly, "and I want it to be my masterpiece, my gift to posterity. I made only two pairs—this one you've got and another pair I gave to a young professional gunman in Missouri. If you ever meet a man with guns like yours, never fight him. Treat him like a brother."

Sam Colt provided Bo with a room and meals for two weeks until he was satisfied with the improvements. The new design added more than two inches to the barrel and almost doubled the range.

It was a great day for them both when Bo tested the guns in Sam Colt's large back garden. All Colt's estimates proved correct. Pale and wasted, the ailing gunmaker told Bo, "My Peacemaker is finished. Be worthy of it."

The war had already started. His father had claimed it wasn't about slavery or secession but about "whether we let those damn fools in Washington tell us how to live our lives." Bo didn't want anyone telling him what to do. Instead of returning to Texas, he set out for the front line in Virginia. He made for Richmond to join the Confederate army.

On the way, he came within a few miles of the northern capital and had to hide from Union soldiers. Washington was only about a hundred miles from Richmond, but between the two capitals lay four great rivers and the ground was swampy and muddy and covered in dense woods. Bo went up into the hills to examine the country where the war would be fought. The great valley between the mountains was a gift for a swiftly moving army. Why hadn't the southern army come down the valley already and struck at Washington?

He learned the answer as soon as he reached Richmond. The whole town seemed to be playing at soldiers. There were more military parades and soldiers in bemedalled uniforms being photographed than if victory had already been won. The army recruiting office was already closed for the day.

Bo had no money for a hotel and the local jail was already crowded. He rode slowly through the center of the town looking for somewhere to sleep. The buildings were older and more solidly constructed than those out west. He felt like a foreigner.

A man came out of a bank ahead of him and watched him approach, a tall middle-aged man in a black suit. He looked like a businessman.

"Where'd you get those, young fella?" the man asked, staring admiringly at Bo's guns. "Never seen any like 'em."

"They're a new kind of Colt."

"You want to sell 'em, young man?" He had a strange, flat accent. When he put a friendly hand on Bo's shoulder, Bo saw he had two fingers missing. "I need me a good gun for protection now we're in a war. I'll give you . . . oh, fifteen dollars for the pair. With the holsters and ammunition of course."

"No, thanks, mister."

"Twenty dollars!"

"Wouldn't sell 'em for a hundred dollars. They're not for sale."

The man winked.

"You come to fight the war with them guns?"

"I'm joinin' the army."

"They'll give you guns."

"Not like these."

The man shrugged as if dismissing the guns.

"Where you stayin'?"

"No place."

"The town's crowded already. Full to burstin'. Everybody's come to fight or to talk about fightin'. Southerners love to talk." The man studied Bo. "You won't get in a hotel."

"Got no money anyway."

"You want to sleep in my workshop?"

"Where's that, mister?"

"Follow me."

"What kind of workshop you got?"

Over his shoulder, the man said, "Until I saw the war coming, I was in real estate. Property. Land. That's where the money is in peace time. But it's no good in wartime. Nobody respects land ownership in a war. Values go all to hell. The armies can take over anywhere for a battleground. No compensation. You got to go into a business that's suited to the new conditions. Guns, supplying uniforms, or. . . . Here we are, young fella."

Past a small wooden church was a cobbled yard full of timber in neat piles. It might have been a carpenter's or a builder's. The man pushed open a door. Immediately there was a strange, stale smell.

"Come in. Don't be shy, young fella."

It was a funeral parlor. Several plain wooden coffins were on the floor against the walls, all empty except one in which lay the body of a young man in a gray uniform. A bullet hole in the forehead had been plugged with wax and the face had been made-up, the lips tinted a bright red.

"Prettied up for the family. Very costly. He's to be buried tomorrow, the poor fella. Killed yesterday afternoon. Still reasonably fresh. Gun went off by mistake." The man pulled one of the empty coffins into the middle of the floor. "This is about your size. You can sleep comfortably in that. It's even got padded sides. I'll give you a blanket." He patted Bo's shoulder. "This is the business to be in during a war. Once they go into battle, I'll probably have to take on extra staff."

"Well, I don't know, mister, maybe I should walk around—"

"Don't be foolish, young fella. You'll be comfortable here. The dead won't bother you."

Bo didn't argue, but when the man left him, he pushed the empty coffin out into the yard. It smelled fresher there. He went to sleep at once, but something woke him in the middle of the night. He opened his eyes to see the man bending over his clothes where he'd piled them on a heap of timber.

"These what you're lookin' for?" Bo held up his guns, which he'd kept in the coffin with him.

The man winked.

"I was a little nervous someone might come in the yard and steal 'em."

"I'm a light sleeper."

"I can see that. Good night again, young fella."

The man began to walk away, swinging his arms innocently. Bo noticed his missing fingers again.

"Mister, did you lose your fingers in a battle?"

The man stopped.

"Cut off, they were," he said, flexing the hand so the stumps showed in the moonlight.

"How? By a sword? A sabre? In the war?"

The man ignored the questions. "Ache still in cold weather, they do. The nerves, you know. The ends missin'. You never appreciate your fingers until you lose 'em. Now you go to sleep, young fella. Get a good rest."

He disappeared into the workshop. The door closed. The lights went out. Silence.

Bo dressed quickly. He wasn't taking any chances. He no longer trusted the man. He walked quickly across the cobbled yard, past the small wooden church, and tried to remember his way in the darkness back to the center of town.

When he reached the army recruiting office, it was dawn. Still too early, but already someone was ahead of him. A bearded figure was asleep on the steps leading to the office. Bo sat down on the bottom step. He didn't yet know it, but this was to be his first meeting with the Reverend.

"What you waitin' for?" a voice growled.

"To fight for the South."

"You'll wait a long time. Everybody's too busy posturin' to do any fightin'." The bearded figure stretched and began to wake up. He was a good ten years older than Bo, maybe much more. "Here—have some." He held out a bottle of whisky. Half empty.

Bo took a drink. "Thanks. I needed that."

"Where you from?"

"Texas. And you?"

"Reverend Claymore from Carolina."

"*Reverend?* And you're joinin' the army?"

"Shoot, boy, it's a just cause, ain't it? God's on our side agin those devils up north. Men of God fight in the Bible, don't they?" He took a drink and wiped his lips with a big hairy hand. "Only thing is nobody's doin' any fightin', just posturin' and talkin'."

"They oughta head down the valley right now and take Washington by surprise. They're supposed to be rebels."

"That's like askin' a chess player to play poker. They do it by their rules and regulations. Army officers are as stupid as the police. None of 'em are free. That's what they don't understand about the Good Lord. *He's* free. Yes, dammit, freer'n anybody. Only they try to imprison Him in their rules and regulations and church buildings. He's in the sky, God Almighty. He don't need a roof and four walls and neither do we!"

"You sound like a preacher," Bo said.

Reverend Claymore stood up, suddenly angry.

"What you mean? You not like preachers? You a sinner, boy?"

Bo noted the Reverend's single six-shooter.

"I guess I sinned some."

"You don't seem sorry none. I'll make you sorry, boy."

Reverend Claymore's right hand streaked for his gun, but Bo's was out first, pointing at his chest.

"Careful. I wouldn't like to shoot a preacher."

Reverend Claymore threw back his head and laughed, his mood friendly again.

"Here, have another drink. Anybody who can outdraw me I gotta like!"

They both drank. Reverend Claymore was already half drunk and Bo began to feel the whisky taking over his tired body.

"Two good men like us spoilin' for a fight," said the Reverend. "We shouldn't be sittin' waitin' on these gentlemen army fellas who are more interested in lookin' heroic for the folks back home."

"That's right," Bo said.

"If they won't move, dammit, boy, we should move on our own without them. You just proved your guns can talk good. What are we waitin' for? We gotta get goin', boy, ourselves. Go ahead and capture the city of Washington and end the war. Yes, sirree, that makes sense. Are you with me?"

"All the way, Reverend."

So, shortly after dawn, two swaying drunken figures rode out of Richmond towards the enemy lines.

They didn't capture Washington, but they did capture an enemy general—and his horse, a white Arab, that Bo kept for himself. There was great confusion in the northern lines. Bo and the Reverend in their rough casual clothes were mistaken for northern scouts. They rode to within twenty miles of Washington. Entering a house in darkness, they discovered a northern general in bed, snoring. They woke him and took him prisoner. They also narrowly missed another commanding officer—Custer. He lived in the same house, but had been called that day to Washington. His daily letter to his wife still lay on a table half-finished. "Dear Standby. . . ." Bo drew a large Confederate flag at the top of the letter. When Custer returned the next day, he was enraged not only by the drawing but by the realisation that one of the enemy had read a private, intimate love letter to his wife and seen his nickname for her. It helped to explain Custer's savagery against southern guerrillas during the later part of the war, and especially his fanatical pursuit of Mosby and his men.

Knowing the country now, Bo and the Reverend rode back through woods and up in the hills where the northern troops hadn't yet organised regular patrols. The general rode between them on Bo's horse, his hands tied. Bo rode on the general's white Arab. He and the Reverend were both sobering up fast through the excitement, the sense of danger and the cold early morning air in the hills.

The army recruiting office in Richmond was just opening as the three horsemen rode up. Bo and the Reverend presented their prisoner to the highest ranking officer available—a green lieutenant only a year or two older than Bo. They expected to be treated like heroes, but instead they were met by disbelief and suspicion. If their prisoner was a general, said the young lieutenant, how had they managed to penetrate northern lines when the army hadn't yet done so? "They haven't tried," Bo replied, which only made it worse. Perhaps they were northern spies, the young lieutenant suggested to his colonel, and this was a plot to win confidence and infiltrate into the Confederate army. The result was that Bo and the Reverend were temporarily jailed pending an army investigation.

They were kept in jail for five days. Then they were released but without any apology. Bo even found it difficult to get his guns back and had to go directly to the young lieutenant who, though green, had a high code of honesty regarding other people's property and ordered the prison sergeant to release the guns. But before he got them, Bo had to listen to a lecture from the lieutenant. "What this army needs is not two crazy moondancers going their own way," said the lieutenant, "but men who will obey orders and carry out battle plans together—as a team. The very qualities that make a citizen successful in peacetime make him a good soldier. Loyalty, industry, obedience. . . ." Bo pretended to listen, waiting patiently for his guns.

"You sure love those guns," said the Reverend as Bo finally came out, strapping on his gun belt.

"They's the best in the world. You's the only one who hasn't tried to steal 'em."

"Give me a chance and just see me try." But the Reverend laughed to show Bo he was joking. They didn't know each other that well yet.

When they reached the main streets, they saw lines of gray-uniformed troops moving out. Several thousand men were pushing down the valley and their casualties had already started arriving back in Richmond. Bo saw the undertaker he'd met ride by several times with a wagon load of new coffins. He waved to Bo and gave him a big smile.

"Business is lookin' up," he said, winking.

The Reverend spat on the street.

"Coffin maker's about as lowdown as a hangman. Makin' money out of death."

"Somebody's got to do it, friend."

"You ain't no friend of mine."

The undertaker put a hand on the Reverend's shoulder, showing his missing two fingers. "Don't be like that. Live and let die."

"You better move on, Mr. Death Man, unless you want to be one of your own customers."

The undertaker flushed angrily. He nodded to Bo. "You better be careful of the company you keep in this town, young fella," and he moved on quickly before the Reverend could respond.

"Friend of yours?" the Reverend grunted.

Bo shook his head. "Tried to take my guns."

The Reverend laughed. "His kind would. Anythin' for a dollar." He took a bottle of whisky out of his pocket and began drinking. "You still joinin' that fool army?"

"Are you?"

"Hell, no."

"I don't blame you," said a voice behind them.

They swung round. Facing them was a short wiry man in a gray jacket and a hunter's wide-brimmed felt hat with an ostrich plume. Bo was annoyed he hadn't heard the man come up behind them. You could lose your life that way. He checked the man's feet. He wore moccasins, like an Indian, so he made no noise.

"Who are you?" demanded the Reverend, equally annoyed at his own carelessness.

"John Singleton Mosby."

"You in the army?"

"I'm forming my own army to work behind the enemy lines. A few men can hold down a whole army. I admired your exploit in capturing the general—"

"You're about the only one who did," grunted the Reverend.

"You showed up the army. You don't expect them to be pleased, do you? You've shamed them into making a stupid frontal attack. God knows how many have been killed already."

"So what do you want with us?" asked the Reverend sourly and he took another drink.

"You're the kind of men I want. Come and join me."

Bo said quietly, "Sorry, mister. After this, the army ain't for me. Rules and no action. Who needs it?"

"We don't have many rules," said Mosby. "Join me and I promise you your freedom. Any time what we do doesn't make sense to you, you can get up and leave. There's no such offense as desertion in my army. A man must serve voluntarily of his own free will. We don't depend on massed troops but on the daring of a few individuals like yourself. What do you say? Will you join me?"

Bo and the Reverend exchanged thoughtful looks.

"How about givin' it a try?" the Reverend said.

"I'm willin'," Bo replied. He stared into Mosby's sharp eyes. "But I'll hold you to what you said. Any time it don't make sense to me, Mister Mosby, sir, I can get up and leave and no hard feelings. That right?"

"That's right," said Mosby. "Shake hands on it like gentlemen."

Bo and the Reverend hesitated, then shook hands with him, finding Mosby's grip as hard as theirs.

* * *

That had been over two years ago. Mosby's men were soon called crazy by outsiders on both sides, but within the Mosby camp, Bo and the Reverend quickly showed such reckless courage that they were regarded as the real crazy ones by the rest. Even Mosby had little control over them. At first he didn't care, he encouraged them, but with the coming of success—after he was made a Colonel and was given full recognition by the Confederate government—Mosby became less carefree, more like the regular army in his thinking. He wanted more discipline, he introduced rules; there were more orders, more talk of obedience, until veterans like Bo and the Reverend were criticised for doing too much on their own and not working as part of the group. Mosby tried more and more to establish a chain of command like the army. He surrounded himself with young lieutenants he could dominate. But he had no respect for them. He was impatient with Bo's and the Reverend's independence, but he always treated them warily with respect.

The Reverend, too, had changed. The more he fought and

killed, the more he seemed to want to. It had become a Holy War to him, and that saved thinking, which he didn't want to do for some reason. Bo wondered what bad memories lay back in the Reverend's past.

Bo also worried about how he might have changed himself. The war had marked everyone. Brother killed brother—the hangings by Custer had brought that home to him more than the shootings which he'd lived with all his life. It had brought back the lynching he'd witnessed as a kid. The waste of it all.

But what worried him most was the effect on the Colonel. Mosby was tired after several years behind the enemy lines and he had taken the hangings very badly. Everything inside him seemed to have come to the boil. Bo hoped he wouldn't do anything crazy.

He returned to the farmhouse with Kath, full of foreboding.

15

Ram had kept busy in spite of the tense atmosphere. He washed one of Horatio Thomas's white suits and suspended a rope between two trees and hung the suit up to dry.

Horatio Thomas tried to talk to some of Mosby's men as they were playing cards, found nobody talkative, and so sat beneath a tree to read some more de Tocqueville.

One of the young Frenchman's reflections might have been written about the two sides in the civil war, Thomas thought. de Tocqueville had noted: "An aristocratic nation, which, in a contest with a democratic people, does not succeed in ruining the latter at the outset of the war, always runs a great risk of being conquered by it."

The South with its great plantations and black slaves was an "aristocratic nation" compared with the democratic melting pot of the North. The South had failed in its bid for a quick victory and now was losing the protracted war.

"What are you reading, Mr. Thomas?"

It was Mosby standing above him, stern-faced but more friendly.

Horatio Thomas held up the book.

"Ah, de Tocqueville, the Frenchman. You think he's still accurate, Mr. Thomas?"

"I haven't been here long enough to judge, Colonel."

"Did you read what he had to say about the tyranny of the

majority? This war is a good example of it. The North is trying to impose its will on the South."

Horatio Thomas had no intention of getting into an argument about the war with the irascible Colonel.

"I find de Tocqueville and Charles Darwin together a good guide to America," he said.

"Darwin?" Mosby grunted. "You believe we're all descended from monkeys? Don't you think the human race is unique because we have souls?"

"I find Darwin's natural selection easier to understand in America. Just consider how the African slaves adapted themselves to this totally different environment to survive."

"You Europeans always bring up the slavery question. I set free my slaves long ago, so did General Lee. Many southerners feel as we do. That's not why we are fighting the war, whatever Lincoln says."

"But do you think the slaves have got souls, Colonel?"

"I don't believe they're the same as we are. Lincoln doesn't either. They have different physiques, different intelligences. They're deficient in education. They're at an earlier stage of evolution than we are, to put it in Darwin's terms."

"De Tocqueville would say southern society was a good example of the tyranny of the majority."

"No, no, Mr. Thomas," Mosby said impatiently, "We have established a culture here, a civilization. Virginia was the site of the first English colony. The first immigrants arrived nearly 260 years ago. They were greedy seekers after gold, adventurers who believed in the fatal delusion that gold is the basis of life. They established slavery, which dishonors labor and encourages ignorance and false pride. They allowed themselves to be corrupted by the opportunities of the New World. Thank God they were followed by honest craftsmen and agricultural workers, who brought a more moral and orderly approach to life. Gradually we developed a more spiritual view with more civilized values. The most highly developed citizens knew slavery was corrupting, even though they were convinced the slaves were far behind them in the evolutionary process. For that matter, Mr. Thomas, they also considered themselves far ahead of the mass of the lower class European immigrants who have flooded the North and are now being trained to fight us."

"That sounds like an aristocratic point of view, Colonel. Would you call the South an aristocratic nation in de Tocqueville's sense?"

"Possibly, and I'm not ashamed of it."

"You know de Tocqueville believed an aristocratic nation like the South ran a great risk of losing a protracted war against a democratic nation like the North—"

"Yes," Mosby snapped, "and I know what you're suggesting. That we're losing this war. I agree victory would have been easier for us early on. The longer the war lasts the better the chance the North has. Its factories can mass produce. That's why we must bleed them wherever we can. We can't afford mercy now. We mustn't allow them to take any advantage. Whatever they do, we must match it—however ruthless or bloody it may be."

The Reverend came up behind them.

"May I have a word with you, Colonel?"

He whispered something Thomas couldn't hear. Mosby asked several questions. The Reverend hurried away.

Mosby, grim-faced, told Thomas, "You will be the only reporter to witness what is going to happen. Your Washington colleague has escaped. He bribed a young man named Louis Powell who was here trying to persuade me to let him join us. I had made it clear to him I didn't want him. He was a violent, unreliable young man. I suppose he did this to get back at me. When the others went into town, he went, too, with the journalist. The guards didn't suspect anything. I'd let the young woman go with Bo. But Powell and the journalist have headed for the Northern lines. We'll have to leave here by tomorrow in case they tell the Union army where we are. But by then our work will be done here. I want you to witness it, Mr. Thomas, and tell Washington what happened."

"What is going to happen, Colonel?"

"Wait and see," was the grim reply. "You won't have to wait long now."

Mosby went back into the farmhouse. Horatio Thomas watched the men playing cards. They smoked or drank, but seldom spoke. There was a growing anger about them, a feeling of hatred taking over these usually carefree men. One of those who had been with Mosby had given a full account of the hangings to a large group, and his audience had become loud with talk of revenge. In the time since, they had quietened, smouldering over their cards, but as Thomas watched and they drank more and more heavily, they pushed the cards away and started arguing about what should be done. It was an ugly scene.

Horatio Thomas was relieved to see Bo and Kath return. The young Texan seemed to be a steadying influence. He went straight into the farmhouse to talk to the Colonel. Thomas went over to Kath, who already sensed the threatening atmosphere.

"Welcome back," he said quietly. "This is like waiting for a volcano to erupt."

Kath could see what he meant. People were assembling as if for some big occasion—a wedding or a funeral. Kath wondered what had been decided in the farmhouse. The men had reached such a level of anger that they needed an outlet. The prospect scared her. They seemed foreign people to her now, capable of anything. For the first time, she was fully aware of how far from home she was and also of the danger, the uncertainty, the violence, of the war.

Dear God, Kath thought, don't let anything happen that will stop me. I need to get away from these wild people and carry on with my search. But she knew the time was not right yet. Mosby wasn't in the mood to help her. She couldn't even discuss it with the farmer's widow. The woman was inside the farmhouse with Mosby, and meanwhile Kath was left outside to listen to all the hate and anger. Some of the men were cleaning their guns as if getting ready for action. Nobody was talking casually or laughing. The card players had stopped. There was an eve-of-battle oppressive atmosphere.

She was pleased when she saw Frank and Ram. The young Sikh was no more friendly than usual, his dusky face was blank, but Frank seemed changed—less aggressive with her, less possessive, as if his mind was on the others, too. He stared round at the angry faces and rolled his eyes. "A mob feeling," he said. "Let's get out of here." But it was impossible. The

horses were well guarded, and on foot they would get nowhere. The flattened landscape meant you'd be seen for miles,
there was nowhere to hide until you passed through the ruined
wood into the hills.

"We've got to wait for the right moment," Frank said.

He was an ally while they faced possible danger together. A
temporary truce. Time enough to sort out their personal relationship when they left Mosby's camp. She could then escape
from him, too.

Horatio Thomas joined them. He said comfortingly, "Mosby
told me he wants me to witness what's going to happen, then
he'll no doubt let us all go. There'll be no more reason to hold
us. Don't worry."

"But what is going to happen?" Kath asked anxiously, staring at the silent groups of Mosby men. "Whatever it is, it's
building up. You can feel it. It can't be long now or they'll
explode right here against each other."

"At least we know it's not directed against us," Thomas said.
"We're not involved."

"Those young soldiers are. It's them I'm afraid for."

"They're prisoners-of-war," Thomas said briskly. "They
have their rights, and Mosby's an old-fashioned southern gentleman at heart." He said to Ram, "I want to do a story on
Mosby as soon as we get away. We may have to hire a messenger to take it to Washington. After our experience coming
here, a train's too risky."

Ram nodded impatiently. Thomas was interfering again.
"When report is ready, trust me."

"Very well, Ram. I was just giving you advance warning."
His eyes were on the Mosby men. "We haven't got long to wait
now."

Frank strolled over to one group who were arguing over
some dice. Soon he was gambling with them, rubbing the dice
on his thigh before he threw. He began to win.

"That's not wise," Thomas said. "In their present mood,
they're just spoiling for a fight. If Frank goes on winning, he'll
have one."

"Gambling's part of his nature," Kath said. "Sometimes he
acts like he won me at cards."

They watched Frank with concern. If he started a fight, they might be drawn in, too. Mosby wouldn't let them leave then. Frank won again, and some of the Mosby men obviously didn't like it. One of them examined the dice suspiciously. Then Frank began to lose. The Mosby men relaxed.

Horatio Thomas chuckled. "Like all good gamblers, Frank knows when to lose."

"You think he's losing deliberately?"

Thomas nodded. "Frank reads the atmosphere like we do. It isn't safe to win. They want to explode over something and let off steam."

When Frank had lost about as much as he had won, he dropped out of the game and strolled over to Kath.

"You played for safety very wisely," Horatio Thomas told him.

"It was like taking money from babies. No fun. Their minds weren't on the game, but on what's about to happen. I wish they'd get it over with, whatever it is. They can think of nothing else."

Thomas said quietly, "I'd like to speak privately with you." They walked away towards the barn.

"On the train," Thomas said, "You seemed to think—"

"I was mistaken," Frank told him. "You're not her type."

Horatio Thomas was irritated at being dismissed so easily.

"What makes you think *you* are? From what I've seen, I'd say you're the opposite of her type. She holds a lot against you. She wants to be free of you—"

"She *knows* that's impossible. She's running from the inevitable. Our lives are destined to come together. Ever since I saved her life. . . ."

And even before that, Frank thought. His mind went back to their first meeting in the wood at Heaton Hall when he'd nearly had her. He'd been trying ever since to get back to that moment.

"I think you're kidding yourself, Frank," Horatio Thomas said. "Her whole mind's on finding her father. That's all that interests her. Everything else has to wait."

"I'm damn well sick of hearing about her father. She's a

grown woman, not a little girl. She'll never be able to love a man until she forgets her damn Dad."

"She isn't interested in you."

"Are you a betting man?" Frank asked angrily.

"A little wager sometimes—"

"I'll wager you that in . . . well, within a year from now, she and I'll be together."

"Done. Fifty pounds."

"I mean a *real* bet. A thousand."

Horatio Thomas hesitated. "You mean a thousand pounds that you and she are married by this time next year—Spring, 1866?"

"Right."

Thomas reflected. Would a bet provide Frank with even more of an incentive to pursue her? Or would it make him pay for his foolishness? Anyway Thomas felt he couldn't back down. He had gone too far.

"You're afraid," Frank gibed.

"I'm afraid of nothing! But I'm not a millionaire. I'll bet this valuable ring," and Thomas took a small silver ring with a ruby stone off the middle finger of his right hand. "This belonged to an Indian rajah. It must be worth a thousand at least. Probably much more."

Frank examined the ring, holding it close to his eyes. "Done."

"Have you got a thousand pounds?" Thomas asked.

"No, but I've got a great stallion, part Arab, back in England. I'll wager him against your ring—"

"That the wedding bells ring for you both within a year—"

"Right."

They solemnly shook hands on it.

"What was that all about?" Kath asked curiously when they returned to her. Both men looked embarrassed.

Suddenly the farmhouse door slammed and Bo strode out, his usually calm face dark with anger. He looked dangerous. He walked his white stallion to the barn without speaking to anyone. The Reverend ran after him and tried to joke with him. "You went to town for a haircut. What happened—he cut off a curl and call it a day? Your golden locks look just as long to me, Bo." The young Texan ignored him and disappeared inside the barn. "What's eatin' him?" the Reverend demanded, staring at the others.

No one spoke.

The tension increased closer to the breaking point.

Kath spoke up to try to relax the men a little. She told the Reverend in a voice loud enough for the others to hear about the incident in the barbershop.

"So he didn't get a haircut," the Reverend roared. "Bo'd enjoy having fun with the Yankees. That's not what upset the old hell-raiser. It was something in the house, some of the Devil's work. I'm goin' to find out. Bo don't get mad very often, but when he do, it means trouble." The Reverend hurried into the farmhouse and they all waited. He was gone a long time. When he reappeared, he had a solemn, confused expression. The Mosby men gathered round him. He gesticulated toward the farmhouse and the barn, very excited. The men, too, became excited. Everyone began to talk at once.

The Reverend walked over to Kath and Horatio Thomas.

"You better know what's happened along with the rest of us. Bo and the Colonel had a big argument, a regular shoutin' match. I never recall that ever happenin' before. Bo's got a high respect for the Colonel. It means big trouble. Oh, yes."

"What was their argument about?" Thomas asked.

"About the Colonel's answer to those Custer hangings. I don't know what's in his mind. He won't talk about it to me. But Bo don't like it."

The Reverend's usual ebullience had gone. Discipline might be relaxed among the Mosby Rangers, but no one was allowed to disagree with the Colonel when he was in this kind of stormy mood. The Texan must have been really worked up and that was unlike him. Bo's angry face as he went into the barn didn't suggest he'd change his mind. He was absolutely opposed to the Colonel's plan, whatever it was. Whose side should the Reverend take—and the rest of the men? Everyone was unsettled even more.

One of Mosby's lieutenants, a short, broad-chested man with a hard face, came out of the farmhouse, rounded up a few chosen men, all hard-faced fanatical types like himself, and took them to the back of the farmhouse, where the remains of several old oak trees still towered like crippled giants.

Soon there was the noise of men at work, hammering and shouting, but no one could identify what they were doing. Other men began to stroll round to watch. The Reverend went eventually, so did Thomas and Frank and Ram, but Bo didn't come out of the barn. He didn't need to. He knew what was planned.

At first Kath stayed away, too. The grimness of the men worried her. She felt relieved not to witness it, to be on her own. She mustn't get involved in anything that might delay her longer. Let the others get involved if they wanted, she must stay out of whatever it was. She tried to enjoy the calm weather, the fresh, bracing air, her isolation, but all the time she was aware of the hammering, and waiting for someone to come back and tell her what was happening. When no one did, curiosity at last drew her there.

The men were working under the huge, ruined oaks with ropes and horses. They seemed to be testing the strength of the remaining branches. One of them threw a rope over a branch. It dangled down. . . .

Oh, no, she thought, it *can't* be. They wouldn't.

"What are they doing?" Ram asked innocently.

"Looks to me," said Horatio Thomas grimly, "like an old-fashioned American necktie-party."

"Can't I get away from it even here?" Frank murmured incredulously. "They're building a gallows. There's going to be a hanging."

"Who's going to be hanged?" Ram asked anxiously.

No one replied.

They all guessed, but didn't want to say it aloud.

* * *

Everyone was assembled under the oak trees and then at last Mosby came out of the farmhouse.

He had smartened up his appearance and put on a gray army jacket to stress his rank and the formality of the occasion. Gone was the old world, civilized man familiar with Ram's ancient culture. This was the ruthless guerrilla leader.

Horatio Thomas watched with a sense of powerlessness, a

feeling he was used to as a reporter. Mosby obviously had two sides in conflict, the cultured man quoting Byron and the ruthless warrior, and they must sometimes drive him to extremes like this to prove how tough he was. It probably accounted for some of his most successful raids, but also for this grim gathering.

Horatio Thomas watched the short, wiry guerrilla leader with the slight, scholarly stoop march forward to face the men massed under the trees. All eyes were focussed on him. He had total control of his audience at that moment.

"Bring out the prisoners," he instructed three of his lieutenants in a clipped, cold voice.

The young soldiers taken off the train had been kept locked up in the cellars of the farmhouse like prisoners of war. They were now marched out in single file. Kath recognised one of the boys she had talked with who resembled her brother Harold. He was very pale and his eyes blinked in the light after the gloom of the cellars. They were all lined up in front of Mosby.

The Colonel eyed each one in turn. It reminded Horatio Thomas strangely of a farmer selecting the animal to be killed for his dinner. Then Mosby told the young soldiers in a stern, biting, almost inhuman tone: "Your army has just hanged three of my men. They have no legal right to do so. We are not an outlaw rabble like Quantrill and his gang in Missouri. We are officially attached to the Army of Northern Virginia as guerrillas. I have the rank of Colonel and I am recognised as such by the lawful Confederate government of President Jefferson Davis. My men therefore have legal status as fighting men—as soldiers! Yet they were hanged like criminals by your side, the armies of the North." Mosby gazed for a moment at the pale young faces listening anxiously to his every word. "To stop any repetition of these murders, I have decided we must take the same action. It is the only way the barbarians of the North will understand the meaning of their savagery." He sucked in his breath and roared out: "Three of you will be hanged by the neck until you are dead."

There were cries of shock from several of the young soldiers. The Mosby men stirred uneasily, their faces grim masks.

Mosby turned to one of his older lieutenants and said formally: "Bring the hat."

It was like an old ritual they had rehearsed. A big wide-brimmed hat was held out. Mosby told the young soldiers: "There are six of you. There are six folded slips of paper in this hat. Three are marked with a cross. Whoever draws the marked slips will be hanged at once." His voice rose angrily: "You will then be given a decent Christian burial. We are not barbarians like your army who left my men to dangle for hours at the end of a rope!"

The young soldiers stared at him as if he were mad. It made their position seem even more hopeless. You couldn't reason with a madman. One of them tried to say something, but Mosby snapped, "This is not a trial. You are hostages of war."

Kath saw the one like Harold bite his lip and try to control himself. She felt her anger rise against Mosby. The man was being inhuman, ruthless. This was murder in cold blood.

One of Mosby's lieutenants took the hat to each soldier in turn. There was a loud gasp of relief from the first soldier when he drew a blank slip. The next soldier drew a slip and then stared at it with a blank face, rigidly at attention. His slip had a cross. He went on staring at it as if he couldn't believe it.

The soldier next to him was lucky—his slip was blank and he gave a nervous half-smile.

Then came the soldier like Harold. Kath watched closely as the hat moved to him and he slowly put in a hand that was almost too nervous to pick up a slip.

"Take one," the Mosby lieutenant said impatiently.

Kath felt furious. It was degrading this gambling with people's lives. She glared at the Colonel. He stood watching, his face impassive.

"I said take one," the Mosby lieutenant snapped.

The boy's hand came out with a folded slip. He held it for a moment, hesitated as if saying a prayer, and then slowly unfolded it. Kath felt the strain almost as if she were going through it herself. It was unbearable. He looked down at what he had unfolded.

And gave a cry. Audible yards away.

He had a marked slip.

Kath remembered his boyish fun on the train. Just like Harold. Trying to be so masculine, so rough, but no harm in him. A shy boy really. Now he was pale and scared.

The hat had passed on and another soldier had a marked slip.

"Step forward, the three men with crosses," snapped Mosby in a tone that further infuriated Kath.

The three young soldiers moved forward.

"You three are sentenced to be hanged by the neck until you are dead," cried Mosby.

The soldiers' faces were ashen.

"Take them away."

Kath watched as the three soldiers were marched to a marked place beneath the great ruined oaks. She knew just how they felt from her own experience. For a moment, she was back that morning in Manchester Prison, walking out to the gallows. The long walk and then the endless wait.

Her hand went up to her neck. But at least she had done something—she had committed a crime in society's eyes. What had these boys done? *Nothing.* Her fist clenched. She had to do something. She couldn't let it happen.

Three horses were brought and each one was stationed under an oak tree. The horses waited patiently, not part of the human scene. Then ropes were slung over the stoutest branches. The feet of each young soldier were tied, also their hands. The one like Harold couldn't control his desperation. Kath could hear his strong white teeth chattering with fright and the sound seemed to cut to the heart of her. She remembered how she had felt when she faced the hangman and the noose was put around her neck. God, it was the worse feeling in the world. Enough to turn your will to jelly. No hope—and the searing pain.

Her neck ached with the memory of it.

The young soldiers were lifted on to the horses. The nooses were slowly suspended and were about to be placed round their necks when Kath's anger surged up and she lost control of herself. She *had* to do something even if it ruined all her own plans and made her an enemy of Mosby's. She couldn't just stand there and watch these boys being strung up. She had to try to stop it, to save the boy who reminded her so much of her brother.

She pushed through the men in front of her and rushed across the sparse grass to the Colonel, not caring what she did or said, her face as fiery-looking as her red hair, which was beginning to grow long again.

"You men don't know what you're doing!" she cried, as out of control as that time in front of Edward. "These boys haven't done anything to you. You *can't* hang them." She stood in front of Mosby, her clenched fists gesturing at him furiously. He looked astonished. "You don't know what hanging's like, none of you. If you did, you wouldn't do it. Look"—she ripped off the scarf round her neck, revealing the deep scar—"I've been through it. I know what it's like. It's something you shouldn't do to another human being. You can't put these young boys through that—"

Everyone had moved forward to stare at her neck. Mosby himself had been shocked into silence, but now he recovered and gestured for his lieutenants to grab her and silence her. Hands took her from behind, holding her arms and covering her mouth. Kath struggled, kicking and biting, but she couldn't break away.

"How did you get that mark on your neck?" Mosby cried in a terrible voice.

The hand over Kath's mouth relaxed to let her reply.

"From a hangman's rope."

"Nobody survives a hanging," the Colonel snapped.

"I did."

Frank stepped forward.

"I can testify to the truth of what she says."

"Who are you?"

"I was the hangman."

A low chuckle came from some of Mosby's men.

"Where?" snapped the Colonel.

"In the North of England—in Manchester."

"You couldn't have been much of a hangman."

More chuckles.

"I was the best." Frank was angry now and gave Mosby a look of defiance. "I saved her deliberately. It happens"—he grinned sardonically—"even with the best hangmen." Frank realised he had Mosby's full attention and made the most of it.

"If you're going to hang these young men, you better do it efficiently, Colonel. The way you've got it set up now, it won't be a hanging, it'll be strangulation. They'll slowly throttle to death unless the rope snaps first under their weight. These boys' muscles are young. You need to allow for that and for their total weight in calculating the drop. Take my advice, Colonel. I know what I'm talking about from experience. But of course, if you want to *torture* these men to death, go ahead."

Mosby walked over to him. "Very well, you can supervise these hangings and make sure they are humane and efficient for us. We're not expert executioners, except with Colt pistols."

Frank shook his head. "Sorry, Colonel. I've retired from the execution business. I'm your prisoner. I'm not in your army. Hanging's a very serious matter, not a game for soldiers to play. What you've set up here is amateurish, cruel and pointless, and I don't want any part of it. I'm a professional." He looked at Kath. "You should follow what that young lady told you."

Mosby flushed angrily. "Take them both away," he snapped in a cold voice, "and let's get on with it."

Horatio Thomas stepped forward, an imposing figure in his white suit. His instinct as a reporter was to remain the impersonal observer, but he felt impelled to support Kath and Frank. Ram stepped forward with him.

"Colonel," Thomas said loudly, "these young soldiers are prisoners of war. They have their rights as human beings."

"Mr. Thomas," Mosby snapped, his eyes flashing, "What rights did my men have when they were hanged?"

"Two wrongs, Colonel—"

"Mr. Thomas, you are a reporter, not a judge advocate." He gestured angrily. "Take them all away and let's continue." The whole business was clearly becoming distasteful to him.

As Kath, Frank, Thomas and Ram were marched into the farmhouse, Mosby called over one of his older lieutenants and told him: "You're in charge from now on. Finish it off as fast as you can. No unnecessary suffering."

The Colonel had had enough and was leaving the scene, walking away to the farmhouse while behind him a final check was made on the ropes and the horses. The Reverend began to pray. "In the midst of life we are in death. We offer up the lives of these our enemies to Thee Our God in sacrifice for our final victory over the northern Devil. They have taken the lives of three of our boys by a ruthless act and we hereby take our revenge. As Thou Our Lord says in the Good Book, 'An eye for an eye, a tooth for a tooth'. . . ."

One of the young soldiers couldn't control his sphincter muscle any longer and a sour smell reached those watching. Everyone now had Mosby's mood. They wanted to end it—and forget it.

The lieutenant's hand was rising to signal the release of the horses. Mosby, his back to it all, had almost reached the farmhouse door. The lieutenant's hand fell, the horses were hit with switches and rushed forward, leaving the three young soldiers about to be left dangling from the end of the ropes when there were suddenly three gunshots, so close together that the three sounded almost like one shot. The soldiers fell to the ground.

All eyes turned in the direction of the shots.

Bo had come out of the barn on his white stallion. He had a revolver in each hand, an expression of disgust on his tanned face. He swept back his long fair hair and rode towards the three soldiers lying squirming on the ground. Everyone looked to the Colonel to see what he would do.

Mosby had turned at the sound of the shooting. When he saw Bo, his look of anger was mixed with some other emotion hard to read—was it anguish or confusion? Nobody was sure. They watched his hands go for his guns almost reluctantly.

One of Bo's Colts cracked again and the Colonel's ostrich plume flew off his hat.

"Keep your guns where they are, Colonel."

Mosby cried furiously, "This is high treason."

"No, Colonel Mosby, sir," Bo drawled as he came closer, "it's my resignation." He glanced slowly round at everyone there. "I came here to fight a war, not to hang kids!"

"They hanged our friends!" Mosby cried.

"These kids didn't." Bo stared sadly at his chief. He told about the incident in the barbershop and the message he had given the Union officer. "Looks like I was wrong, Colonel. We've become as bad as they are." He seemed to feel he had to say something more, that he owed it to the Colonel. "When

I was a boy, I saw a hanging. The fella hadn't done nuthin' any more'n these fellas here. A man wasn't born to die that way."

He swung easily off his white stallion and quickly cut the ropes tying the three soldiers' hands and feet. While he was doing so, one of Mosby's lieutenants tried to draw his gun. Bo's revolver flashed and the man's hat flew off. "What I told the Colonel goes for everybody else, too," he said.

He swung back on his horse and looked down at the scared young soldiers who were trying to rub some life back into their limbs. "Get yourself a horse. I'll take you three and the other three blindfolded back to your own army outside Richmond. That way nobody can come back here and trouble the Colonel." He told Mosby, "I'll take the other prisoners, too. There's no reason to hold 'em."

Kath and Frank were brought out of the farmhouse. Kath stared admiringly at Bo. He had achieved what she had failed to do. Horatio Thomas and Ram joined them.

The Reverend, who had been drinking, stepped forward, very confused. "You're leavin' the Colonel, Bo?"

"That's right, Reverend. After I've taken these six kids in uniform back to their own lines, I'm goin' home myself—back out west."

"Why you leavin'?"

"A diff'rence of opinion."

The Reverend thought about it.

"And you're givin' up for that?"

"Not givin' up, Reverend. Goin' on."

The Reverend thought some more and came to a decision. "Then we gotta part, Bo, old buddy. The war's not ended yet and there's some holy killin' to do. These are the only family I got left now. You go and change your mind and stay with me." Bo shook his head. "Well . . . I gotta stay."

Bo nodded. He seemed to suppress a feeling of disappointment. "Good luck, Reverend," he murmured. He sat tall in the saddle and faced Mosby and the others. "I fought with you for a couple of years. Now it's over for me. Good luck to you all."

Mosby, still angry, stepped forward close to the white stallion. "You don't understand war. To win, you have to be ruthless." He shouted, "You also have to be loyal—to obey orders."

"The trouble with that, Colonel," replied the young Texan, "is we ain't goin' to win. Nobody is. And I ain't goin' to obey orders blind. That's what we're supposed to be fightin' about, ain't it—the right to go our own way and not be told what to do by any government?" That was what he'd learned from his father.

The six young soldiers had all found horses and he signalled for them to leave. Horatio Thomas and Ram shared a horse, Frank rode alone. Bo lifted Kath up beside him. He waited until the others were well down the road heading for the ruined wood, then he formally saluted Mosby for the last time— "Good luck at all times, Colonel Mosby, sir"—and he started to follow, slowly, in no hurry. He was paying Mosby and his old comrades the ultimate compliment of trusting them not to shoot him in the back.

Nobody even made a move. They all watched him until he caught up with the others. They saw him blindfold each soldier and then take the lead through the half-ruined wood and into the hills beyond. They watched until he disappeared, and then they slowly dispersed in silence. Mosby walked back into the farmhouse, weary-looking, his stoop more pronounced than ever.

16

Bo rode fast, leading them deep into the hills. He remained silent, not even speaking to Kath. His wide-brimmed soft hat was pulled low, hiding his expression. The others, assuming he was brooding about the break with Mosby, left him alone. But Bo wasn't a brooder. Once something was over, he left it behind. His mind was on the woman close to him—Kath. He could feel and smell her. He wanted her, but there wasn't much time.

His white Arab stallion seemed to find the hidden trails instinctively, breathing heavily as it climbed through wild Virginia country. The higher it went, the farther away the war seemed. The grass grew high and the branches of the trees were big and leafy, untouched by cannon blasts, gunshots, or sabre slashes. It was a rare, peaceful scene from another time—an escape from all the bloodshed.

They stayed the night in a farmhouse friendly to Mosby in a wooded valley. The grey-haired farmer and his buxom wife—their two sons were away in the Confederate army—welcomed them, fed them, found them somewhere to sleep, but didn't ask any questions. The young soldiers were locked in a barn with the horses. Bo told Frank to take the first watch. Frank was immediately suspicious.

"Why me? Why not them?" *Them* was Horatio Thomas and Ram. "Or you?"

"Somebody's gotta be first," Bo drawled. He was the boss until they passed out of this wild hill country and Frank knew it.

"I'll be outside if you need me," Frank told Kath, who was slowly combing her long red hair. She had washed the dust out of it, and it had recovered its old luster. She didn't answer Frank. The truce between them was over as far as she was concerned. Frank went outside, slamming the door.

With Frank out of the way, Bo's attitude changed and became more open. He lounged against the kitchen table, drinking a beer and staring at her. His hard muscles stood out under the tight cloth of his blue denim work shirt and his faded blue dungarees. She met his eyes and quickly looked away. He grinned, showing his even white teeth like a pleased boy.

Horatio Thomas came into the kitchen just as the young Texan was getting another beer. He swaggered past Kath like a damned tomcat, thought the English journalist uneasily. That meant there were two aroused young men with Kath in the middle—it could mean trouble if Frank came back in. War would break out at last in this idyllic setting. Thomas tried to ease the tension by asking Kath how she planned to get into the besieged Richmond. "Grant's army hasn't managed it yet."

"Let's get there first," Kath said.

More silence. Bo was staring at Kath with a mocking smile.

"Have you ever been to Richmond?" Thomas asked him.

Eyes still on Kath, Bo told him, "Once—to join the army." He grinned. "Instead I captured a general, took his horse a prisoner, and met an undertaker with two missing fingers."

"Two missing fingers?" Kath was suddenly tense. "Which hand?"

Bo thought back. "The left."

Her eyes widened with excitement. "My Dad lost two fingers from his left hand in a factory accident. It could be him."

Bo gave her a strange look, but she didn't notice, she was too preoccupied.

"Did he have an English accent?"

"How would I know? Everybody outside Texas talks strange to me. Some folk in the northern army talk foreign languages I don't understand."

"Did he have a warm, friendly personality? Everyone loved my Dad. He kept everybody laughing at his funny stories in the beer-house in Stockport."

"This man I met was a real mean bastard," Bo said. "Mean and greedy. He'd do anything for a dollar."

"That doesn't sound like my Dad."

"He even tried to steal my guns."

Kath sighed. "Then it couldn't have been my Dad."

"A lot of people probably lost two fingers in this war," Horatio Thomas said.

"Do you know the undertaker's name?" Kath asked Bo.

"I never heard it." Bo smiled at her disappointed face. "Don't feel badly. You don't want a man like that for your Pa."

"Where was his workshop?"

"I can draw you a map." He sketched on some wrapping paper. "That should be enough to find it. Richmond's not a huge place. It's just off a main street."

"I'll go there and check. It's the only clue I've got."

Horatio Thomas stood up. He couldn't stay on to chaperone her any longer. He had his own work to do.

"I'm going up to bed," he told them. "I must write a long report before I fall asleep." Perhaps it would inspire her to go up, too, and get away from the cowboy.

"You better get your rest," Bo yelled after him. "We'll be movin' on soon after dawn."

The bedroom that Thomas had been assigned had a big four-poster bed and a hand-carved armchair made out of a tree trunk. Thomas sat in the armchair to work on his Mosby story. He hoped it would convey to English readers how the war was being fought—with increasing bloodshed and ruthlessness and also with new, unconventional methods. Mosby was of special interest because of his guerrilla work behind enemy lines and also as a pioneer with the Colt. Bo, from his father's experience in fighting Indians and Mexicans, had shown the Colonel how much more effective a pistol was in cavalry warfare than a sabre or even a musket.

At first Horatio Thomas listened for Kath coming up to bed, then he forgot all about the tension downstairs in trying to describe Mosby. The Colonel was a good example of Charles

Darwin's natural selection, the survival of the fittest. He adapted himself to his environment. The flexible Mosbys would survive more than the rigid Custers. . . .

When he had finished, his mind was still too active to sleep so he read some de Tocqueville on "Of Individualism in Democratic Countries." De Tocqueville had lamented thirty years ago that "as the conditions of men become equal amongst a people, individuals seem of less, and society, of greater importance." The young Frenchman had concluded that "in that immense crowd which throngs the avenues to power in the United States, I found very few men who displayed that manly candor and masculine independence of opinion which frequently distinguished the Americans in former times and which constitutes the leading feature in distinguished characters wheresoever they may be found."

Was de Tocqueville right, Horatio Thomas wondered sleepily, or had he been misled by a few bad experiences in America? Certainly thirty years later the Frenchman seemed to be wrong. Lincoln, Grant, Mosby, so many of the young soldiers, the cowboy downstairs, especially the cowboy, displayed that "manly candor and masculine independence of opinion." Perhaps it had needed a civil war to test American society and bring out the qualities hidden thirty years ago from visitors like De Tocqueville. Now any fool could see. . . .

He heard Kath come up and go in the next bedroom. She had escaped from the cowboy at last. Wise girl. He imagined her getting undressed. That body of hers was full and round in all the right places. Oh, yes. He tried to concentrate on De Tocqueville again, but he was too tired now. He was reaching for his ear-plugs when he heard voices in the next room—too low to understand what they were saying. At once sleep was forgotten. He stood close to the thick old wall, trying to hear more clearly. One voice was a man's. The cowboy must have crept up after her and was bothering her, maybe intending to rape her if she resisted. It wasn't called the *Wild* West for nothing. Thomas determined to rescue her as he had on the steamship.

He crept into the passage. The farmhouse was dark and still. He grasped her door handle, listening. He could hear more distinctly through the door. Suddenly Kath chuckled and the fourposter creaked. He heard enough of what she was saying to realise she was welcoming the cowboy—she was encouraging him!

He was shocked, angry, jealous. If this cowboy was an example of American individualism, then perhaps De Toqueville was right. Creeping up to a woman's damned bedroom in the middle of the night was hardly an example of "manly candor". . . .

* * *

Bo had checked first that Frank was safely out of the way before going upstairs.

Clouds completely covered the moon and there was little light in the valley, but Bo had moved surefootedly under the dark leafy trees as if he had cat's eyes. He felt good from the beer and showed it by his buoyant manner and quick step, though he was also annoyed he'd let a woman become so important to him—a woman as independent as he was. Once he'd checked Frank was obeying orders, he'd go upstairs and have it out with her.

The night was so still that the click of a revolver under a nearby oak tree sounded like an explosion. Bo's hands raced for his Colts.

"That you?" came Frank's voice.

"Yeah," Bo told him. "Bad luck for you if it's not me. You gave away where you are."

Bo didn't immediately replace his guns, but waited until he saw the hangman lower his pistol. He didn't trust Frank—not with a woman between them.

"You left me to freeze," Frank grunted. "I was just coming back in. To hell with you."

"You got time to do yet," Bo said. "I'm just checkin' on you." His sharp eyes searched the dark landscape. They could easily be trapped in this valley. But there were no sounds, not even any bird or animal cries.

"What've you been doing all this time?" Frank demanded suspiciously.

"Drinkin' beer."

"You better not trouble her."

Bo grinned.

"What's funny?"

"You followed her all this way," Bo said, "and you still don't know her. She can look after herself. She's a real tough woman."

"She's a child," Frank said. "She nearly got herself hanged. She'll get in trouble again without me to look out for her."

Bo shrugged. The poor fool didn't understand women. "Look," he said casually, "have it your way. Just keep watch until I finish my beer and then I'll take over and you can get yourself some sleep."

"That all you going to do—drink beer?"

"Sure."

"You better be sure."

"Don't threaten me, Mr. Englishman."

"Just stay away from her."

"Keep your mind on what you're doin'. Make sure nobody jumps us or I'll have your scalp."

Bo was gone before Frank could reply. Frank listened for sounds of him in the undergrowth. He thought he heard a twig snap, that was all, then the farmhouse door clicked shut. The cowboy was as quiet as an animal. Frank stared up at her window. It was covered by a light cotton curtain. Her oil-lamp was still lit. She must still be awake. He felt that he was guarding *her*—nobody but her. He had to stick with her until she found her father or gave up the search. Then she would be ready to be his woman—his alone. All he had to do was wait.

The moon came out from behind the clouds, a full moon that bathed the valley in a soft light. Frank moved farther under the leafy branches to remain hidden and leaned back against a crooked tree trunk.

Time seemed to drag. That cowboy better hurry up.

He glanced up at her lighted window again and immediately straightened up. There was a shadow behind her curtain—a man's shadow.

Frank ran to the farmhouse like a mad bull.

* * *

Kath had felt strongly attracted to Bo, more than to any man she had ever met, but she was determined not to show it. They

were separating in a few hours. In this, her second life, she
wanted to save herself for marriage, something solid with a
lasting future. A man like the young Texan would never settle
down for long. And anyway she wasn't free until she found her
father.

It would have worked out as she had planned if he hadn't
come upstairs after her. She could have handled her own emotions alone. But a man like him with sharp instincts knew when
a woman was interested. Your eyes gave it away. He'd walked
boldly into the bedroom while she was undressing. He didn't
even apologize, but swaggered over to her in his tight, faded
dungarees, reminding her more than ever of an oldtime cava-
lier.

"Look," she had told him, trying to sound angry, "I'm grateful for what you did for us, getting us out of Mosby's camp. But
I've just got one thing on my mind—finding my father. I can't
afford to get involved with *anybody*. Do you understand that?
Even if I wanted to, I *can't*—"

"You're talkin' too much," he said roughly, putting his
hands on her shoulders and gently pushing her down on the big
bed. She didn't struggle but kept her hands on her neck, covering the rope burns. He pulled away her hands. He didn't even
blink.

"Why hide it?"

"It's not pretty."

"Scars show you've not played it safe."

He opened his shirt and showed the scar on his chest.

"How'd you get that?"

"From a jealous husband."

"What happened?"

"He died."

He caressed her swelling breasts and she let him. He became
as excited as a boy and leaned down to kiss her nipples. She
pushed his head back.

"No, Bo. No—"

"Yes," he said. "We haven't much time."

He stood up, casting his shadow across the window, and
unfastened his gun belt and put it on the floor and unbuttoned
his tight dungarees. She watched him without moving. She

could no longer resist him, this young American cowboy who was freer than any man she'd ever seen. He leaned over the bed towards her.

There was a rush of boots up the stairs and the door burst open.

"I warned you, cowboy," Frank roared and grabbed his gun.

There was a loud shot and Frank staggered back against the wall. His gun thudded to the floor.

Bo had leaned down to his gun belt on the floor and drawn a Colt and shot in one swift movement. But even in his great speed, he had been careful where he shot. Blood seeped from high on Frank's shoulder.

"Frank!" Kath cried, running to him. "Are you all right?"

"It's only a flesh wound," Bo grunted. As he watched Kath tenderly examining Frank's shoulder, he felt angry at losing his chance with her. "I should have killed him. He's nuthin' but a dumb troublemaker."

"You were raping her!" Frank cried.

"You're not dumb, you're stupid, you know that?" Bo's anger grew as he watched Kath gently undoing Frank's shirt. He told her, "It'll just be painful and a little stiff. The slug didn't even stay in." He pointed to a bullet hole in the wall above Frank's head.

Someone knocked at the door.

It was Horatio Thomas.

"I thought I heard a shot."

"Come in," Bo told him, "and join the shootin' party." Ram and the farmer were behind the English journalist. "The more the merrier." Bo pushed past them and stamped loudly downstairs and outside into the moonlight. As well as getting shot, that fool had left them without a look-out. Women sure are trouble, he told himself as he checked on the night scene.

* * *

Bo woke them shortly after dawn. Kath wanted Frank to stay at the farmhouse, but he refused. "You're not leaving me behind," he told her. "When I'm not with you, you aren't safe." She didn't argue with him. She treated him with more tenderness than ever before, as if she blamed herself for his wound. Now it was over, she wasn't sorry he'd interrupted them; it would have been so much harder to leave Bo if they had made love. It had worked out for the best. She gently replaced Frank's bandage and smiled at him.

Bo watched with growing anger. "Time to go," he said gruffly as she made a sling for Frank's arm.

"I better ride with him," she told Bo.

Bo, tight-lipped, said nothing. He had wanted her close to him.

The sunlight was still sifting through the overhanging trees as they rode swiftly out of the valley. Frank, more white-faced than ever, felt a surge of pain at every jolt as they climbed steadily up hill, but he didn't speak. Nobody did. Bo's mood dominated them all. They rode for several hours in silence until the northern lines were spread out below. The lights of Richmond were in the far distance across the river.

Bo took the blindfolds off the young soldiers' faces. They were blinded still for a few moments by the sudden sunlight. They blinked and rubbed their eyes. The soldier who reminded Kath of her brother smiled warmly at Bo.

"Thanks for what you did."

"No thanks needed, soldier. Just stay alive."

"We'll do our best."

The young soldiers waved and rode off down the hill, free at last. None of them was comfortable on a horse. They were northern city boys. Crossing a field at an uneasy gallop, they were challenged by a northern patrol and they at once slowed to a walk, taking no chances. They were inspected before being allowed past the front-line soldiers in dusty blue uniforms, then they were home. Or as close to home as they would get for a long time.

"Richmond doesn't look very far away," Kath said, her hand shielding her eyes as she peered into the far distance.

"Lincoln's pass should get you through the northern lines," Bo told her. "Then you're on your own." He patted his fine white Arab stallion as he stared at her, grinning to hide his feelings in front of the pale, glowering Frank. "I can understand a daughter being in love with her Pa when she's a kid. But you're a grown woman. You got your own life to live!"

"I don't expect anyone to understand," Kath replied softly,

"but it means everything to me to find him. It's as if my life depends on it, as if I can't start living my own life until I know what's happened to him. We were very close when I was a kid. He's all I have." She remembered what she had learned when she was in the Stockport jail. "I never knew my mother. When I find my father, I want to ask him about her."

"What if you don't find him?"

"That's her business, Mister Cowboy," Frank snapped.

"I'll find him," Kath said. "I'll follow him to hell if I have to."

"Richmond's hell on earth now—cut off, short of food, a target for northern cannons. You should stay out of there," Bo told her.

"I can't, Bo. I must get into Richmond. He's still there. I *feel* it."

"Don't talk to him," Frank snapped. He eyed Bo savagely, clenching his fist. "I'll get you for this shoulder, Cowboy."

Bo eyed him back bleakly. "I knew I should've killed you."

Frank punched at him and started his wound bleeding again. He fell back, groaning.

"How can I find you?" Kath whispered to Bo.

"Through my father in Fort Worth, Texas. He's a Texas Ranger, well known, easy to find. He'll tell you where I am." Bo swept back his mane of fair hair. "Take care of yourself, Kath."

He touched her cheek for a moment and then he moved swiftly away on the magnificent white stallion. Kath's eyes followed him—his wide shoulders, the straight muscular back tapering to a narrow waist, the easy way he sat in the saddle. He receded slowly into the hills like a dream disappearing, a dream of what might have been.

Frank grasped her shoulder.

"Why are you looking so sad? What was between you and that cowboy?"

She pushed away his hand, still staring at Bo, now a speck on the horizon.

"Do you hear what I say to you—what's between you and that cowboy? Answer me."

Horatio Thomas came to her rescue. He rode up to her and

peered at the distant Bo with her. "That young cowboy's the real American I've come to find," he cried enthusiastically. "That's what's meant by American democracy—a free spirit, untamed, worthy of this wild unknown country." He patted his restive mare and smiled sympathetically at Kath. "But I, like you, must let him go. The war will end here in Virginia, not in the Wild West. The peace will be made here. That's the big news story I must cover right now. Otherwise I'd be following that young cowboy as far as he's going." Thomas laughed. "If I could keep up with him."

Kath nodded but didn't speak, continuing to stare into the hills where Bo had now disappeared. The English journalist felt as shut out of her thoughts as Frank was. What *had* happened between her and the young cowboy? he wondered with slight annoyance. Surely I'm not jealous—or am I beginning to fall in love with her myself?

He smoothed the creases in his white trousers and straightened his wide-brimmed hat. It was starting to rain and they had a long way to go.

"Now, my dear," he said firmly to bring her back and claim her attention, "how are we going to get into Richmond?"

The Reverend, too, had changed. The more he fought and

17

The Union soldiers grouped along the muddy banks of the James River had a weary appearance. Many of them were sleeping, not even bothering to unbutton their dusty, ragged, often ill-fitting uniforms. Their weapons were in high stacks, and most of the guns needed a good clean. They had overcome the town of Petersburg, then isolated Richmond, in a series of bloody battles, and now they were recuperating for the final assault on Richmond that could end the war.

Just beyond the army lines were the tents of the army followers, the travelling brothels that trailed the soldiers from battleground to battleground. The army's battle fatigue, the general exhaustion that was visible everywhere, had been bad for business, and, as Kath and the others rode past, some of the women could be seen using the free time to hang out their washing to dry.

Most of the soldiers who weren't sleeping were content to sit outside their tents talking and playing cards, reminding Kath of Mosby's men. The two sides in this war were so much alike—as alike as Cain and Abel, brothers sworn to kill each other. But when she mentioned this to Thomas, the English journalist disagreed. "These soldiers are a mixed European lot with a sprinkling of Jews and Africans," he said. "Look at their faces! They're like a stew compared with the faces on the Confederate side, even in Mosby's bunch. The southern soldiers are all

white Anglo-Saxon Protestants. You'll see the difference if we
ever succeed in getting into Richmond."

"We'll get in," Kath said.

Front-line guards ordered them all to dismount. Frank was
treated with special respect because the guards assumed his
wound had been inflicted by the enemy. They were led through
the mud past the rows of white tents. Heads turned as Kath
went by, stepping carefully round the pools of mud. She even
turned the heads of these weary soldiers, Horatio Thomas
thought admiringly, slowly following her, trying to keep the
mud off his white suit. He and Ram, who was wearing a new
white turban, were exotic figures to the soldiers who rarely saw
anyone out of uniform.

The Presidential pass and *Guardian* credentials impressed a
young lieutenant. He fussed over them and asked them politely
to wait in a large clean tent reserved for officers. They waited
a long time. Ram watched Thomas as his impatience grew. Any
moment there would be an eruption. At last the English journalist strode outside and was immediately stopped by an armed
sentry.

"Take me to your commanding officer."

"My orders are to keep you here."

"For how long?"

"Until the lieutenant returns."

"How long will that be?"

The young soldier shrugged.

"We're prisoners," Kath said indignantly.

"It's a misunderstanding," Thomas said calmly. Ram listened
to him with astonishment. The Englishman's mood had
changed with the speed of light. Because the girl was upset,
now he was calm. Amazing! She must have cast a spell on him.
"Just be patient, my dear," Thomas told her with a reassuring
smile. "We won't be detained for long. They daren't disobey
the President's instructions. He's their commander-in-chief."

"I hope you're right," Kath said. "I've got no more time to
waste."

The pounding of horses' hooves came from the distance,
growing steadily louder. The horses seemed to stop near the
tent. There was some clicking of heels and saluting outside. The

tent flaps were held back by nervous young soldiers and a familiar figure pushed his way in—George Armstrong Custer, golden-haired with oiled mustaches, and resplendent in a fur-lined cape and an elegant wide-brimmed hat with a plume. His hands sparkled with rings, and he wore gray spats to protect his fine leather boots from the mud. His red-rimmed eyes were hard and unfriendly as he spoke to Horatio Thomas, ignoring the rest of them.

"I'm told you have been in Mosby's camp, Thomas. Why didn't you report directly to me?"

"I didn't know you were here in the front line," Thomas replied coolly. "I'm also not one of your scouts. I'm an objective observer."

"You're either a friend or a foe," Custer snapped. "There isn't a no-man's-land in this war. Where was Mosby hiding?"

"In a remote farmhouse. But he'll have moved on by now. He never stays anywhere long."

"I'll burn the farmhouse and take the farmer as a hostage. You must lead me there."

"I don't know where the farmhouse is situated. We rode for hours in the hills in darkness. I don't know Virginia. I couldn't find my way back there."

"You lie!" Custer was suddenly in a rage. "You reporters are all the same—traitors, thieves, informers, all of you help the enemy. They don't need spies when they can read your reports. All you care about is your newspaper. You don't care about the country. General Grant is too easy on you all. If I had my way, I'd imprison the lot of you for the duration of the war, and we'd win all the sooner. You refuse to tell me where Mosby is?"

"I can't. I don't know."

Custer's face flushed. He shouted: "I order you, Thomas! Tell me where Mosby is hiding!"

The young lieutenant came into the tent. He said nervously, "General Grant wishes to see Mr. Thomas. He has instructed me to take Mr. Thomas to him at the hospital."

Custer mastered his anger with difficulty. "To hell with you, Thomas! You English are all on the Confederate side. None of you are to be trusted. But I don't need you. A Washington journalist tells me he can lead me to Mosby's camp. He'll be here in an hour and then I'll hunt Mosby down. I'll punish him and his collaborators. I'll take hostages. I'll hang all prisoners. I'll wipe Mosby out." He was trembling with anger. Mosby was really getting to him. You'll never catch the Colonel in that mood, Thomas thought. You'll have to be as coldly calculating as he is.

"Take him to the General," Custer told the lieutenant icily.

"We better come, too," Kath told Thomas. "I want a new bandage for Frank's wound."

Grant was visiting wounded soldiers in an old school that had been converted into a rough front-line hospital. Thomas found him walking slowly between two lines of cots, most of the soldiers half-hidden in bloody bandages and only half-conscious, not caring who had come to see them. Grant was still untidy, his uniform unbuttoned at the neck, his whiskers wilder, a hurt expression in his eyes. He looked as weary as his troops.

A young soldier who had had his right leg amputated died as Grant approached his cot. Grant stared down at the very dead young face. The hurt look in the General's eyes deepened, and he abruptly turned away from everyone and walked rapidly down the lane of cots and past the new stretcher cases that had just arrived.

"General!" cried the young lieutenant, who had brought Thomas. Grant didn't stop, he acted as if he hadn't heard, and hurried out to his horse.

"General Grant doesn't like to visit the wounded," the young lieutenant explained to Thomas apologetically. "He goes to hospitals only when he has to and never stays long. He won't even eat meat because he doesn't like to see animals killed."

"Yet it doesn't stop him being a successful war leader," Thomas replied. He'd heard about this strange conflict in Grant's character. A sensitive man, whose past was littered with failures until the war, he didn't hesitate to give orders for the most ruthless violence and had become a successful general in one of the bloodiest wars in history. He reminded Thomas of Mosby. The two men had much in common. Mosby could quote Byron's poetry and then order some kids to be hanged.

Grant could weep over the wounded, but then send soldiers to their death.

"We better follow the General," the lieutenant said.

They galloped down a rough dirt road slippery with mud where army wagons had churned up the soft Virginia earth. They found Grant arguing with a teamster whose wagon was stuck in a swampy stretch. The horses strained but couldn't pull the wagon out. The teamster was beating them brutally with the butt-end of his whip and cursing both them and Grant. He obviously didn't recognise Grant or his rank. Grant hated profanity and loved horses so by the time Thomas and the lieutenant arrived, he was as angry as the teamster. He didn't have any aides with him. No wonder the man didn't appreciate who Grant was.

"Who's drivin' this team, me or you?" the teamster roared at Grant as he struck one of the horses a great blow.

"Stop that at once, you brute!" Grant shouted back.

The lieutenant was aghast.

"Do you know who you're talking to?" he cried.

"A stupid fool," the teamster replied.

A group of Grant's aides, very flustered, their uniforms mud-spattered, rode up. They had heard the General was in some kind of trouble.

"I told you to take your rest," Grant snapped, not at all pleased to see them. "You'll need your energy for the final assault on Richmond. But now you're here, arrest this man." He gestured with contempt at the scowling teamster. "Have him tied to a tree for six hours as a punishment for his brutality."

The teamster began to realise he'd made a mistake, but he didn't try to placate the angry General. He allowed the aides to lead him away in sullen silence. Grant patted the bruised horses with great tenderness.

"Unforgivable brutality," he said to Thomas, his face still an angry red. "A man who will be cruel to horses is capable of anything." He mounted his own horse again, surprisingly agile. "I'm told you've been with the enemy, Mr. Thomas. How was their morale?"

"I was with Mosby's Rangers, General. His guerrilla group

probably isn't typical of the Confederate army as a whole. His men maintain a high morale as you probably know, but they are tired and under great pressure. There was disagreement among them. Mosby is enraged by the hanging of his men."

"Good," said the General coolly. "That's when an enemy makes mistakes."

"He intends to hang some of your men in return."

Horatio Thomas expected Grant to become angry, but he replied calmly, "We'll outlast and outkill him just as we'll outlast and outkill the Army of Northern Virginia as a whole until it's on its knees. The war is now in its final act, Mr. Thomas. There is no time for mercy."

Grant hardly seemed like the same man who had argued over the horses. This was the brisk, ruthless commander-in-chief. The hurt look in his eyes had faded. Grant was another of those men—like Abraham Lincoln—who could only rise to the top in a society like this one, Thomas thought. In England, with his lowly background, Grant would have been lucky to make sergeant. Thomas was reminded of something De Tocqueville had observed thirty years before: "A long war produces upon a democratic army the same effects that a revolution produces upon a people; it breaks through regulations, and allows extraordinary men to rise above the common level." Damn, Thomas told himself, that young French aristocrat had become like a ghost by his side—almost like his conscience in America.

"Where are you going now, Mr. Thomas? Back to Washington?" Grant asked as he lit a thin cigar.

"I'm hoping to get into Richmond, General."

"Impossible." Grant smiled. "My spies can't even get into Richmond any more. It's a fortress until we crush its defenses and force our way in. And we will! Very soon now! We'll send Lee's army with its tail between its legs running away from Richmond and then the war will be over." He puffed on his cigar. "Is there anything I can do for you, Mr. Thomas? The President told me to give the special correspondent of the *Manchester Guardian* every assistance."

"I want to get a report to Washington as soon as possible so it can be despatched to England. Could it go in your army mail?"

"I can do better than that. It can go with my despatches by special messenger."

When Thomas told Ram of this good luck, the young Sikh was very off-hand.

"Is the messenger reliable?"

"The general would hardly entrust his despatches to a dummy."

Ram shrugged. Thomas was interfering again in his side of the operation.

Kath and Frank, with a clean bandage on his shoulder, arrived from the hospital.

"General Grant says it's impossible to get into Richmond," Thomas told her.

"Let's get as close as we can," Kath said.

It was raining as they began to walk through the mud, and most of the army was sheltering. They walked past the front trenches. Nothing separated them from Richmond. The outskirts of the town were clearly visible. There was a lull even here within range of the enemy's cannons. Only occasional bursts of firing disturbed the peace. The southern defenses lay ahead. They ran the risk of being shot down by enemy snipers. The gunboats on the river caught Kath's attention. Was there a safer way into the city along the river? She stared up at the observation balloons hovering far above their heads. Or there?

Horatio Thomas noticed her interest in the balloons. "That's the real way to see Richmond," he said enthusiastically. "A bird's eye view out of range of the enemy. It'll make a good addition to my story about the new military methods used in this war." He walked over to the soldiers sheltering in a trench below the nearest observation balloon. The balloon was floating about two hundred feet up, anchored to a tree with long ropes. One man was in the basket below the balloon. He was peering through a short telescope at the enemy lines in front of Richmond. Thomas waited patiently for him to finish his work and signal for the soldiers below to run out of the trench and untie the ropes and bring him down. He was a short, unmilitary-looking man with a trim beard.

"Who's that?" Thomas asked one of the soldiers as the balloon slowly descended.

"That's Professor Shawe," the soldier replied, working on the ropes. "He's an expert in aerial observation from Washington."

"Splendid," said Thomas. "Go to the top—that's the way to get something done."

He studied the professor carefully as the short, bearded man stepped neatly out of the basket. He then announced himself in a loud, confident voice. "Professor Shawe," Kath heard him say, "I'm Horatio Thomas, special correspondent of *The Manchester Guardian* of England, here to cover the civil war as well as humanly possible. . . ." The professor said something, Kath couldn't hear what, then there was a brisk friendly exchange with the English journalist doing most of the talking. She saw the professor nod in agreement, smile, and go over to the soldiers and give them some brief instructions. Then he shook hands with Thomas and walked away in the rain between the trenches.

"I won't be up long," Thomas called to Kath and Ram. The soldiers began to help him into the basket.

Kath hurried to him. "You're going up?"

"The professor gave me his permission. It's probably as close as any of us will get to Richmond."

"I'm going up with you," Kath said.

"No, my dear, you stay on the ground—good old *terra firma*. These balloons can be quite temperamental, the professor warned me."

Kath began to climb in. A young soldier gallantly helped her. Ram and Frank rushed over.

"You're risking your neck in that thing?" Frank demanded. Kath was in the basket by then. "Very well, I'm coming, too," and Frank clambered in, trying not to disturb his wound.

That left Ram. As he moved towards the basket, a soldier barred his way. "Better not. It takes two officially and you've already got three in it. You don't want to get everybody killed."

Thomas leaned out. "You stay there, Ram. We won't be up for long." As the young Sikh looked very disappointed, Thomas added jovially, "If anything happens, then you'll be alive to tell the tale—and send the *Guardian* a story." This only seemed to depress Ram. "I'm only joking. We're as safe as a bird." Thomas cried, staring up as if the balloon exhilarated him. "Let's go," he told the soldiers.

The ropes were released and the balloon slowly rose, the basket with it. The air buffeted them, the rain lashing their faces. "Hang on," Thomas told the other two. "The weather'll improve up there." At about two hundred feet, with no improvement, the soldiers below began to tie the ropes to a tree. Through the rain, the three observers, just out of range of enemy guns, could see the shape of Richmond—the street intersections and the tops of the buildings, the lines of trenches, and the soldiers like ants. Thomas waved down to Ram and then concentrated on Richmond. Much of the city had been destroyed by northern guns. . . .

The basket suddenly gave a great lurch, throwing him back against the side. Kath was leaning out slashing at the ropes with her crude old poaching knife.

"What the hell are you doing?" Thomas shouted. She went on slashing. Frank overbalanced and clutched his wound, blood seeping through the bandage. Thomas tried to grab Kath, but he couldn't keep his balance and fell to the floor of the basket. Her red hair streaming in the wind, Kath slashed at the last of the ropes.

"Good God," Thomas cried, "We'll drift for miles."

"The wind is blowing towards Richmond," Kath cried back, as if that explained everything.

Horatio Thomas lurched towards her and pulled her back, but he was too late. The last strands of the rope parted and the big balloon was free. At once the wind caught it and blew it—and them—over the desolate no man's land between the two armies and towards the outskirts of Richmond.

They heard the soldiers shout below and saw Ram's stricken face. Thomas leaned out and yelled down to the young Sikh, "Wait for me at Willard's Hotel in Washington," but he couldn't tell if Ram heard because the balloon was caught in a great surge of air and the northern lines were soon far behind them.

Richmond came closer and closer. The balloon was strongly buffeted by the driving wind and rain, and bobbed up and down in the air currents, and they needed all their strength just to hold on. Frank groaned as the basket tilted. The balloon continued steadily across the Confederate lines. Now they could see the gray uniforms below and the curious faces in the Richmond streets staring up as the balloon floated across the trenches towards the city. They saw muskets rise and point up at them. Soon the firing would start at this aerial invasion.

"They can't miss," Thomas shouted. "We're too big a target. We must land before they shoot us out of the sky. Hold on as tightly as you can!"

He drew his double-barrelled pistol, steadied himself, aimed upwards at the balloon, and gave it both barrels. The shots were muffled by the rushing air and the beating rain. They all gripped the sides of the basket as the balloon slowly sagged. The holes made by the pistol were small and the balloon emptied gradually and their descent at first was slow. The basket rocked and tilted, but they were able to remain upright. They began to fall more rapidly. No guns were pointed up at them now. Crowds were gathering to watch the falling balloon.

The air howled past them, seeming to drag them with it into the embrace of gravity. The basket staggered and tilted even more as it rushed to earth. They grasped the sides, holding on, all now tilting with the basket, forced to their knees.

Rain lashed their faces, the air screeched, and the ground—streets, fields, buildings—seemed to be rushing up to collide with them at a great speed. A hard landing seemed certain and they all braced themselves for the shock. But suddenly their rush to earth slowed and then abruptly stopped. The remains of the balloon sagging now beneath the basket had caught on the top of a towering oak tree and checked the basket's descent, leaving them hanging a few feet from the muddy ground. They were shocked and shaken and lay sprawled on the floor of the basket, gasping for air. Soldiers appeared below, aiming muskets at them. They were prisoners of war.

"What do we tell 'em?" Frank grunted, holding his shoulder.

"The truth," Horatio Thomas panted, trying to stand up.

The soldiers brought a long ladder and Thomas, then Frank, and finally Kath climbed down to the ground. The soldiers in gray covered them with muskets. They were expecting some kind of surprise attack. What lay behind this invasion from the air?

"Who are you?" a young lieutenant demanded.

"I'm an English journalist," Horatio Thomas said loudly. "Take me to your commanding officer."

His firm, self-confident manner impressed the young lieutenant. Never mind that he had stepped out of an enemy observation balloon in a bizarre white suit, accompanied by a suspicious couple, a beautiful red-haired woman and a man with a wounded shoulder. The man obviously was Somebody and therefore had to be interrogated at the command level.

They were soon being marched through the streets of the besieged city followed by a growing crowd. The soldiers and the people were much more poorly dressed and less healthy looking with lean bodies and hollow eyes than those on the northern side a few hundred yards away.

"Look at these soldiers' faces," Thomas whispered as they walked along. Kath was amazed by the English journalist's energy and curiosity. Their perilous descent might never have taken place as far as he was concerned. He was examining the soldiers' faces close by. "You see the difference?" Kath tried to concentrate on what he was saying. "These faces might all have come from England." That's true, Kath thought, studying the bony, white-faced young soldiers at their sides. "They're Anglo-Saxons used to a safe, settled environment. Compare them to the many nationalities and mixed looks of the northern side that we've just seen. The North and the South are at different stages of evolution, as Charles Darwin would say. The South is still an aristocratic, essentially rural society, whereas the North is already at the next stage—the industrial melting pot ready to people the big cities and man the factories of mass-production."

"Is that an improvement?" Kath asked, remembering how much she'd hated the factory.

"That depends on whether you believe in progress or think the human race has already passed its peak."

"Oh, I believe in progress," Kath said firmly. "I wouldn't have left Stockport if I didn't."

"Then you must believe the North has progressed farther

than the South towards whatever the end of democracy is going to be. That's why this war is so unequal. In terms of evolution, it's like a struggle between Man at his latest stage of development and one of his remote ancestors—a monkey, say." Thomas laughed at her with huge enjoyment. "Don't tell these southerners that."

"You don't believe we come from monkeys, do you?" Kath asked, trying to keep up with him.

"In wartime, I find it easy to believe," Thomas said gloomily as they passed a row of ruined houses, the victims of an enemy barrage.

"Wait here," said the lieutenant. Thomas examined his thin face with its fair mustache—a face at home on a plantation but not in a factory. In terms of evolution, he was behind, an unlikely survivor.

They were interviewed by a colonel and then a general. It was hard to say what impressed these gallant southern officers more—Kath's insistence on finding her father or Horatio Thomas's *Guardian* credentials. The South still had lingering hopes that England would enter the war on its side, and Thomas's arrival seemed to support this idea. He immediately became an important visitor.

They were all taken to the rear of the city out of range of enemy guns and given a hearty dinner in the company of high ranking army officers. But the devastation in Richmond was great even there. Almost every building was marked and many were in ruins. Halls, churches, and large houses had been converted into hospitals. All the able-bodied men were in the front line; at the rear almost every man who could walk had a limb missing. Hospital wagons loaded with wounded thundered through the rubble-strewn streets. There was a smell of uncollected garbage everywhere. The northern soldiers had been weary, but it was a fatigue that a long rest would put right; here there was an air of exhaustion and hopelessness—it confirmed Thomas's suspicion that the war was already lost.

Kath sat impatiently through the long dinner, responding politely but distantly to the gallant attentions of the young southern officers. They tried to outdo each other in flowery compliments and in heroic tales of Richmond's resistance in which they figured prominently. But Kath was so clearly only humoring them that at last she was given what she wanted—permission to seek out that funeral parlor that Bo had seen. She had a map he had drawn and the young officers found an old man who knew where it was. She asked to be taken there immediately. She couldn't wait any longer. Perhaps this was the end of her search. . . .

"That part of the city was hit pretty bad," said the old man. He guided them past lines of ruined houses and stores that were missing roofs and walls. "Here it is," the old man told them, and it was another ruin. The walls had been hit by enemy guns and the whole roof had caved in. The remains of coffins littered the yard.

"The undertaker," Kath asked the old man, "what happened to him?"

The old man shrugged.

"Do you know his name?"

"No, ma'am, but he did much of his work for the hospitals. Someone there might know about him."

He took her to the nearest hospital. Kath went to the mortuary. The bodies of young soldiers were piled up. She stared at the young dead faces, aghast.

"Look at them all," she whispered to Frank. "Hundreds, thousands of them, dead—killed—and they made such a fuss when I killed just one man in self-defense."

"That's war," Frank said sardonically. "It's like getting a licence to shoot game for the duration—only it's human game. Or at least men. Not many women get killed in a war. Except women taking foolish chances looking for their Dads."

Kath ignored him. She talked to one of the mortuary attendants. He didn't know anything. "Try the head nurse," he told her. She was directed to the main ward in an old Baptist church. It was crowded with wounded soldiers. There was a strong smell of rotting flesh. There were few beds. Many of the soldiers lay on top of wooden packing cases. Their bandages were bloody and dirty. Death seemed to be in all their eyes. Kath tried not to be aware of them, but to keep her mind rigidly on her search.

She asked a doctor for the head nurse and he pointed impatiently to the altar. Kath walked down what once had been the aisle. Men lay on all the church benches and on the stone floor. Behind the altar was the operating room. A row of soldiers lay waiting to have their arms or legs amputated. A bottle of whisky was being passed round. There was no chloroform left. Or opium. Only whisky and not much of that.

Several soldiers were shaking uncontrollably. "They're shell-shocked," Horatio Thomas whispered to Kath. "I saw cases like that in the Crimea. The guns ruined their nerves. This is a new kind of warfare. People get wounded in new ways."

Ahead of them a colonel with a chestful of medals was trying to raise the soldiers' morale. He laughed at his own remarks; few of the wounded did. He stopped in front of a handsome, dark-haired young soldier with a pale, haunted expression. A doctor whispered to the colonel. "You are a hero!" cried the colonel to the young soldier. "You gave more than your life for the Confederacy. You gave your manhood." The young soldier didn't respond; his eyes seemed to be looking through and beyond the colonel.

"Every army has its fools," Thomas commented as the colonel, chest out, strode to the next cot.

"What's wrong with him?" Kath asked, staring at the handsome young soldier.

"Probably got hit between the legs," Thomas whispered.

"No more love," Frank said behind her.

"There's more to love than that," she snapped back at him.

A tired-looking middle-aged woman in a gray uniform came over to Kath.

"I'm the head nurse," she said wearily. "You're looking for me?"

"Oh, yes," Kath said eagerly, forgetting the young soldier, and she explained about the undertaker.

The head nurse pondered, taking her mind off her work unwillingly.

"Show me the map where his workshop was."

Kath produced Bo's neat map.

The head nurse thought some more. She was so weary that thinking was difficult for her. Her eyes ran over the wounded in the cots, wanting to get back to them.

"And you say he had two missing fingers?"

Kath nodded quickly.

Memory suddenly broke through her tiredness. "Oh, that would be Joe."

Kath's heart missed a beat. *Joe.* . . .

"You remember the rest of his name?"

The head nurse rubbed her red-rimmed eyes. A soldier began to scream nearby and her eyes went to him.

"Joe must have buried thousands for us. He came here every day through the early years of the war. He was Irish, I remember."

"*What was his full name?*"

Kath's urgent tone shocked her into remembering.

"Tracy. Joseph Tracy. Yes, that was it."

"I found him at last!" Kath cried. "Where is he now?"

The head nurse shook her head. "I can't tell you. I lost touch with him months ago. He went to work for the army. He never came back to the hospital. You'll have to ask the army what happened to him."

Horatio Thomas used his high army contacts. At first he drew a blank everywhere. No one had heard of Joseph Tracy. But Thomas persisted and at last a general put him in touch with the Secret Service. Thomas was taken to a back street in downtown Richmond, to an old private house where he was introduced to a middle-aged civilian in a black suit.

"Why do you want to find this Joseph Tracy?" asked the man bleakly.

Thomas explained.

The man asked to see his *Guardian* credentials.

Thomas produced them.

The man examined them carefully, then returned the papers to Thomas, and sat tapping his fingers, making a decision.

At last he said, "I have authority to tell you this much, Mr. Thomas. Tracy was hired as part of a secret mission for President Jefferson Davis himself. Just before the city was cut off, President Davis wished to get something out—something valuable. It was put in a coffin and we organised a funeral. Tracy, as one of the city's legitimate undertakers, was hired to conduct the funeral. He was supposed to be taking a young colonel's body out of the city for burial in his home town. There was a route still open to the south. Two Secret Service agents were disguised as assistant undertakers. Once out of Richmond, they were to take the contents of the coffin out west for safekeeping —to Kansas."

"And that's where they are now?"

"We don't know. We haven't heard from them since they left here. That was nearly six months ago. President Davis has sent a troop of scouts after them."

"The contents of that coffin must be pretty valuable."

The man hesitated, then snapped: "It was a shipment of gold. Worth half a million dollars."

* * *

Horatio Thomas expected this news to depress Kath, but she remained surprisingly cheerful.

"Can't you see," she told him, "I know he's still alive? That's what matters. *He's still alive.* I know I'll find him now, even if I have to go all the way to Kansas. It'll just take a little longer."

And cost a little more, she thought.

You didn't need much money in wartime, but if she had to go out west to find her father, she'd need far more than she had now, which was nothing. These American distances were so great. Going west was like crossing the Atlantic. And she couldn't depend on either Frank or Horatio Thomas. She'd have to pay eventually one way or another for any help from them. She had to find the financial means to carry on herself. And in this war-ruined southern city of Richmond where mere survival preoccupied everybody. The front-line would yield nothing. Everyone there was too busy repelling the enemy to help her. The best bet was the hospital—all those wounded bed-ridden men yearning for love and sympathy, for somebody to listen, to care. Some of them must have money, some of them might even be *rich.* Perhaps they could make a fair exchange.

The first person she saw in the hospital was the handsome young soldier who had the groin wound. He was lying with his eyes open, listless, without interest in the bustle round him. His face seemed bloodless beneath his dark hair. He was waiting his turn for an operation. His right leg had become infected and the doctors said it would have to be amputated above the knee.

One of the doctors came out of the operating room behind the alter as Kath stood by the young soldier's bedside. The doctor was about thirty, burly, loud, and half drunk. His arms were red with blood up to the elbows and his hand holding a sharp curved knife was trembling slightly as he waited for nurses to carry in the young soldier. A pile of severed limbs lay on the floor behind him. His only cure for anything seemed to be to amputate and most of those who lost limbs also soon lost their lives. The nurses were carrying in the young soldier to almost certain death, but his blank, expressionless eyes didn't care what happened to him.

Kath revolted against the sight. She had to do something to fight the hopelessness. He had suffered enough.

"Don't let them amputate," she whispered to him. "Keep your leg. My father had two fingers cut off and he was never the same man again. Fight for your leg. I'll help you."

She awakened some life in him—enough for him to refuse his permission for the operation and, without it, the doctor couldn't amputate. The doctor took another drink and cursed both of them. She stood firm. The young soldier watched the angry exchange wide-eyed. The doctor at last relented.

"Go away and die then," he growled. "Next!"

Kath washed the young soldier's swollen infected right leg. There was a heavy, sickly smell. He was shy about letting her see his ugly wound, but she insisted. Hot shrapnel had torn the flesh in his groin, partially castrating him. There was no sexual feeling, no possibility that he could become erect. He screamed when she washed the wound. "My life's over," he panted. "I'm finished." And he fainted. She came back two hours later. He was awake, lying with a hand over his eyes. She washed the wound again and renewed the bandage. She did it again in the evening and several times the next day. And the next. The head nurse didn't see the point of such cleanliness, it was a waste of precious bandages. The doctors in the civil war didn't appreciate the dangers of dirt, but Kath did from her factory experience. "If dirt can rot cotton, it can rot flesh," she told the head nurse.

Soon the nauseous smell of rotting flesh faded from the infected leg and the wound showed marked signs of improvement. She talked at length with the young soldier, trying to stimulate a greater interest in life and strengthen his will to fight.

"What's your name? What do your friends call you?"

"Paul—Paul Blake."

"Sounds English."

"My great-grandfather came from Yorkshire."

"That's just the other side of the Pennine Mountains from where I come from. We're from the same part of England—the North. Where's your home in America?"

"My parents have a ranch in Kansas."

A ranch.

"It's a large cattle ranch. Alpine's the nearest town. Just my folks and me. My Ma didn't want me to go to the war. My Pa needed some help on the ranch. We have a foreman and a team of cowpunchers to manage."

"You must be rich," Kath said lightly.

"I don't want for nuthin'," he replied with a grin—the first grin she'd seen from him. His wound was healing now and he'd begun to put on weight. His eyes had lost their blank look. "You've got me well," he stammered gratefully.

"You're on the way to recovery, but you're not there yet. You must work hard at getting well."

He seized her hand and raised it to his lips.

Horatio Thomas appeared at the bedside. The English journalist was much quieter than his usual style, his expression grave, his voice low.

"Kath, can I speak to you in private?"

They walked to the side of the altar where rows of wounded soldiers lay. The operating room was still busy.

"Kath, brace yourself for some bad news."

Her wide eyes stared steadily back at him.

"What is it? Something about my Dad?"

"The army investigators have reported back. The coffin has been found outside a little Kansas town called Way Cross. It was empty. All the gold was missing. And—"

"And my Dad?"

"There were dead bodies beside the coffin. Shot in the back."

Her head turned away from him. Her face was hidden.

"I'm sorry, Kath. I know how you must feel after coming so far. . . ."

Her shoulders began to shake. Horatio Thomas put a gentle arm around her.

"Has he been positively identified?" she murmured.

"Not yet. They're awaiting a fuller report."

She steeled herself and turned to face him with a proud, obstinate look.

"I'll never believe he's gone until there's real proof. If my Dad really was dead, I'd know it. I'd feel it in my heart. And I feel nothing. One thing I do know. Fate hasn't saved me from hanging and brought me to America for nothing."

"Life is full of accidents, Kath. It has no purpose. There are no happy endings."

"You may believe that if you like. I don't. My search is no accident of life, it's a test of me. A test I mean to pass."

She left Horatio Thomas and went back to the young soldier. He could see she had received bad news and asked what it was. "Don't tell me if you don't want to."

"It's about my Dad." She explained briefly.

"You're right not to give up hope," he said comfortingly. "But what can I do now?"

"Hire the Pinkerton National Detective Agency. They'll find out more than the army will. We'll search for him together. You helped me and I'm going to help you."

She eyed him carefully. He was still pale and wasted, his nerves as permanently ruined as the buildings of Richmond. He would make no big demands on any woman. Not like the hangman or the English journalist. His war wound made sure of that.

She stayed with him all that day. His nerves were bad whenever the enemy guns roared in the distance. She held his hand and talked soothingly to him. That was what the wounded, especially the dying, needed as much as medical treatment—someone to talk to. Even the nurses didn't understand that. They laughed at a big graying stretcher-bearer who sat at the young soldiers' bedsides and caressed their brows until they died. The nurses said the big graying man derived enjoyment from touching the bodies of the young soldiers; he also wrote poetry, which confirmed their worst suspicions about him. But what did it matter, Kath thought, if it helped the young men to die? They had no family there to give them love and you needed love above all when you were dying. Any kind of love.

But she had to help Paul to *live*.

She needed him.

She stayed with him all that day, and by nighttime, when death was all around them, he put it to her.

"Do you think I could ever marry?"

"Yes, of course."

"I could never make children. I could never . . . oh, you know what I mean."

"There's more to marriage than that."

"The physical side's a big part of marriage."

"You can . . . make love. There are just certain things you can't do."

"Things a woman needs. Have you ever been married, Kath?"

"No," she said reluctantly, "but I've been with a man."

"Who was the man?"

"Someone in England. He's . . . dead now. There was no love, just . . . just something physical. It meant nothing to me. I was glad when it was over."

He was embarrassed. "You're certainly a straight talker, Kath!"

The next day he said he had something to ask her. He was sitting on the edge of the army cot. He was able to walk a little now. He held her hand and seemed very shy. "You won't laugh?"

"No, why should I?"

"Wait till you hear it." He blushed. "I hardly dare to ask you." He gulped.

"Out with it," she told him, smiling.

"Kath. . . ." He squeezed her hand. "Will you marry me, Kath? Will you share my life?" He added quickly, "I'll help you to search for your father. I've got money here I brought with me from the ranch—not in Confederate banknotes that may soon be useless, but in gold. I'll spend it all on finding your father. Then he can come back with us to the ranch. There's ample room for everybody. The ranch is *huge*. You can't appreciate what land is like here in the east or where you come from in England. It's like owning all the way to the horizon. Share it with me, Kath. You'll like my parents. And if being with me doesn't . . . satisfy you . . . I mean on account of my wound . . . then I won't try to hold you. What do you say, Kath?"

She sat, thinking. Was this the next stage of her journey?

"Don't answer now. Tell me tomorrow. I can hope until then." He held both her hands. "Please give it a lot of thought before you decide. It's not just me—what's left of me. It's a new life, away from all this." His eyes took in a dying soldier in the next bed. "Life's just beginning out there. It can be what you make it. You and your father can start all over again. We have thousands of acres in the middle of nowhere, far from the nearest town . . . a little place called Alpine."

"Is that near a town called Way Cross?"

"A few hundred miles. That's not far out there."

"That's where my Dad's trail ends."

"Then you'll be close to him."

She leaned over to kiss his forehead. He was sweating with the effort of asking her. "Thank you for the offer, Paul. I will wait until tomorrow. But don't worry. I'll decide what's best— for both of us."

She left him then to be alone. But he called to her as she reached the door and he came limping between the rows of cots. "Don't decide too quickly," he whispered, staring eagerly at her.

"That's why I'm waiting until tomorrow."

"We can't . . . do . . . everything together, but, Kath, I can love you. Really love you. It's not just an animal attraction, a physical lust you'll get from many men. That doesn't last."

She put her fingers over his lips. "I know about those kind of men. You haven't lost what matters—the ability to *feel*. That's what counts. There are many ways to love a woman. That's what a lot of men don't understand. I just need a little time to be on my own and decide what's best for us."

"I'll be waiting for you tomorrow."

"I'll see you after breakfast," Kath said and hurried out. She went straight to an army tent. She didn't want to see anyone. She lay awake most of the night thinking about it.

If she said yes, would it be because her father was last seen out there and the ranch—the money—would provide the means to follow and find him? Or would yes mean she was sorry for Paul and she'd marry him in name only because he wouldn't make any demands on her?

Marriage wasn't in her plans at present, and yet this was an opportunity to get the help she needed and perhaps to establish an American home. She would be mistress, not of Heaton Hall as she had once dreamed, but of a huge ranch with thousands of acres and great herds of cattle.

And she liked him.

He was kind, sensitive, generous.

And he needed her.

He would give her anything she wanted.

And if she didn't take this opportunity, what *was* she going to do?

She tossed and turned, trying to decide.

If she said yes, what would Frank do?

Well, she couldn't worry about him. He'd interfered enough with her life.

But she did worry about him.

He was quite capable of killing anyone she married—like a gambler protecting his winnings.

Kath brooded about the pros and cons until dawn filtered through the tent, then she got up and persuaded a soldier outside to share his coffee with her. The tents looked ghostly in the faint early morning light.

"Have some of my bread," the soldier said, his face wasted and hollow-eyed. The army was very short of food, even for the front-line men.

"No, the coffee's all I need," she told him. "But thanks." The soldier was too weary to talk. She left him and walked to the hospital. The morning sky was clear, the start of a fine Spring day, and the mud was starting to dry.

The hospital was already awake. The soldiers who had died during the night were being carried out on stretchers. That was the kind of work her Dad had done as an undertaker, so different from the factory. He had become his own boss in America. Why hadn't he sent for her then? Perhaps he had wanted the war to end first.

The wounded who could sit up were eating their meagre breakfast. Paul was sitting on the side of the bed and spotted her as soon as she walked in. He had been waiting impatiently for her. His face immediately lost its melancholy and lit up. He tried to read her expression. He seemed afraid to ask her. "Have you . . . have you decided, Kath?"

She leaned down and kissed him on the mouth.

"What . . . what did you decide?" he said nervously when she didn't speak.

She slowly smiled.

"I think we should get married as soon as possible."

Tears welled up in his eyes.

"Oh, Kath, you make me so happy." He clutched her hand. He wanted body contact to convey his feelings. "And I'll make you happy, Mrs. Paul Blake-to-be. Whatever it takes." He pulled her down to sit beside him on the army cot. "I feel like shouting aloud, letting everybody know." He glanced at the bandaged faces near him. "I better not follow my feelings in here. Wait till I get outside. Perhaps one of the army chaplains resting from the trenches could marry us immediately, Kath. I don't want to wait."

"No," she said, "we must wait until we get out of Richmond. There's too much death and destruction here. Too many people dying." She didn't want to frighten him about Frank. "A marriage is supposed to be a happy occasion, even a wartime one. We should get out of Richmond while we can. I don't want my husband to be a prisoner of war."

"We mustn't wait until we get to the ranch. I want it soon, Kath, the sooner the better."

"I know someone who would do it," she told him. "Someone in Virginia . . . not too far away. But first we've got to get out of Richmond."

"Is that possible?" His eyes were downcast, uncertain.

"Well," Kath said, "I got into Richmond, so I suppose we can get out."

"Oh, Kath, you make everything sound possible. You give me such a feeling of confidence." His eyes brightened.

Kath began to appreciate what she had taken on. She was going to have to carry him for a long time, perhaps all the way out west. It was more like having a child than a husband.

18

Fort Gregg and Fort Whitworth had fallen to the Yankees. That opened the way into Richmond. The Confederate archives were already being moved out. President Jefferson Davis and his Cabinet members were said to have fled southwards. Rumor had Grant and the Army of the Potomac marching through the outskirts of the city. But the northern cannons continued to thunder, softening up Richmond for the final assault. Trenches caved in and more houses collapsed as explosions swept the streets and scattered pieces of hot metal like confetti, ripping holes in the army tents along the river banks.

Horatio Thomas, calmly writing his latest *Guardian* report in a rear tent, felt a lump of hot metal thud on the ground close to his handmade English leather shoes. He hardly blinked. The Crimean War had conditioned him to thunderous bombardments and made him fatalistic. If a cannon ball had your name on it, there was little you could do, but otherwise you were fairly safe.

The distant cannons roared again, but he wrote on. He was describing life in the besieged city. "Richmond citizens, gaunt, half-starved, shell-shocked, are at their breaking-point. . . ." English readers had never suffered a bombardment of one of their cities so it would be hard for them to identify with this. It had to be as graphic, as convincing, as possible, so *Guardian* readers would feel almost as if Manchester were being besieged. . . .

He missed Ram. The young Sikh would have known how to get the story out of Richmond and across the front line and onto a train for New York. He would have to hold on to the story until he reached Washington. He hoped Ram would be waiting for him at Willard's Hotel.

"Mr. Thomas."

He recognised the low sexual tone even before he looked up. Kath was standing before him with a respectful expression. It meant she wanted something. He studied her. Kath's face never failed to give him pleasure, like a great work of art. Some accident of nature had given her a blend of features that was intensely provocative. No one man would ever hold her or satisfy her. Before her life was over, she'd drive dozens of men as crazy as she had the hangman. But not me, Thomas thought with satisfaction. I refuse to be reduced to servitude by any female of the species, as Charles Darwin would call her.

"What can I do for you?" he asked patiently as he put down his quill pen.

She replied hesitantly, "You've always been kind to me. I want you to be the first to hear my news."

News?

"You're giving up and going back to England?"

"Oh, no." She smiled. "I'm going to be married."

"What!" He nearly fell off his canvas stool. "Who's the lucky man?" Could she possibly have surrendered to the hangman at last?

"Paul Blake—the soldier I've been nursing while I've been waiting for news of my father."

"But isn't he . . . I mean, his wound. . . ." Horatio Thomas found himself embarrassed for one of the few times in his life.

"Oh, yes, but it doesn't matter."

"It may not matter now, but later, after you're married. . . ." Thomas was disconcerted by her steady gaze. "I knew a soldier who was wounded the same way in the Crimean War. When he came home, he and his wife separated after three months."

"We won't be like that."

"Are you sure it's what you want?"

"Yes, I'm sure." She smiled at his serious expression. "Are you jealous?"

"Of course I am. I've known you for much longer. You've only known this young soldier for five minutes."

"You journalists are married to your job," she said playfully.

"Well, Kath," he told her with an effort, "I wish you all the luck in the world. Have you told Frank?"

"That's why I've come to you. Frank'll never accept it. He'll try to stop us. I can't get married here in Richmond. We must leave before he knows about it. I thought you might know a way out of the city."

"I'll consult the army officers I've met. But getting out may be even harder than getting in." He listened to the distant cannons. "They're closing in. Does this mean you're giving up your search for your father?"

"Oh, no," she said. "Paul's going to help me to find out the truth. He's going to employ the Pinkerton National Detective Agency. My Dad was last heard of in Kansas and that's where Paul's home is—near a little town called Alpine. It'll be easier to trace my Dad from there. . . ."

Oh, Horatio Thomas thought, now I think I understand.

* * *

Frank had sensed something was wrong. Kath was spending far too much time at the army hospital. But his own wound had become infected and he had spent several days recovering in an army tent. There wasn't room for him in the hospital. But Kath came to wash him, change his bandage, and feed him. When he inquired what she was doing with the rest of her time, she said she was helping to nurse a young soldier in the hospital. Frank asked about him suspiciously. She was very innocent-looking and aloof. That didn't make him any more suspicious. That was her usual manner with him. He wasn't well enough to check on her, but he didn't worry about the soldier she was nursing—what danger was a man with a wound in the groin? And as Frank's wound began to heal again, news got around that he liked to gamble and soldiers came by the tent with cards and dice. Frank was soon too preoccupied to worry much about Kath. He began to win.

But when at last he was able to get up, he went immediately to the hospital. She hadn't been that day to see him. She wasn't anywhere in the hospital. He searched down the rows of wounded men for the young soldier. He was gone, too. That was when Frank *knew*.

He ran to Horatio Thomas's tent.

"Where is she?"

He glared at the English journalist, suspecting he might be involved.

Thomas produced a bottle of cognac he had obtained from a friendly general.

"Have a drink, Frank," he said sympathetically.

"Where's she gone?"

Thomas poured out a full glass of cognac and held it out.

"Drink that, Frank, and then we'll talk."

Frank gulped the cognac and felt the liquor burn its way down through his body.

Thomas found a canvas stool for him. As the distant cannons blasted away, they sat drinking the cognac, feeling warm and friendly. When Thomas decided Frank was relaxed enough, he told him.

"She's getting married—to the soldier."

That sobered up Frank in an instant. "You're joking!"

"No, Frank, I'm serious. She told me herself."

Frank laughed unbelievingly. "She can't marry anybody but me. She knows that. That soldier's got no balls anyway."

"She's convinced herself she's fond of him and he's got money—a big ranch in Kansas. He's going to help her find the truth about her father. He'll fund the search."

"She knows she could have what's left of my money. And I could win some more with the dice. He doesn't know her. Wait till he learns she killed someone."

"That won't change him. That castrated young soldier won't believe anything against the divine Kath even if it comes from the Almighty Himself. Murder isn't a very good argument in wartime. He's probably killed a few Yankee soldiers himself."

"Where are they now?" Frank demanded gruffly, swaying slightly, his face dark with anger.

Thomas shrugged. "I've no idea, Frank."

"They must be somewhere in the city—trapped here like we are."

But that was where Frank soon discovered he was wrong.

The latest enemy attack and the impossibility of defending Richmond much longer had decided the southern commander-in-chief, the legendary Robert E. Lee, to abandon the city at last. The Army of Northern Virginia was holding an escape route for the garrison. The defending soldiers were slowly being withdrawn from the front line. The break-out would come that night. Until then, the ruined city was chaotic, taken over by a constant stream of soldiers and heavy army equipment and citizens with all their life's belongings in a few suitcases and old family trunks. The great retreat was ready to begin. But with everyone in the streets and no one home, it was impossible to find anyone.

Frank searched everywhere for her. He went back to the hospital in the church. Only the dying and a few nurses were left. Anybody who could walk had left already. He tried other hospitals—the same result. He walked the streets, looking desperately for her in the lines of army wagons ready to leave. The surging mass of people and horses and gun carriages made any kind of movement very difficult. Frank kept being held up by an immovable mass, forced simply to go with the stream for block after block. He examined every face with longing. She couldn't have left yet. Nobody had left. They were all waiting for the army to open the way. Kath was *somewhere* in this defeated capital and he would find her.

The atmosphere of defeat didn't help him. Everyone was as desperate as he was—desperate to save themselves in the general disaster. This was the real end of the war. It might drag on farther south for a few months, but once Richmond was gone, the whole Confederacy couldn't last long.

But the war wasn't important to Frank, it existed only as a background hindrance to his attempts to find her. Nothing could have been more different than his and Horatio Thomas's attitude when they met in the center of the city. The great events had completely taken over the English journalist; he had no thought now for Kath or her whereabouts.

Frank found him standing at a main street corner, surrounded by soldiers in ragged uniforms and family carriages waiting to get through. Buildings were burning through the city filling the air with clouds of dark smoke and sparks like gigantic firecrackers. Now when rain was needed, the sky was clear, and there was even a slight breeze from the river to fan the flames. It was a desperate, noisy scene, but Horatio Thomas was as calm as if he was in a theatre audience observing a play. Frank grabbed his elbow to get his attention.

"Have you seen her?" He had to shout above the noise.

- Thomas clasped his shoulder. "Frank, old fellow, where did you spring from?"

"I'm looking for her. She's disappeared." The English journalist's calmness irritated him. "Kath—she's gone. Have you seen her?"

Thomas, watching a line of wounded soldiers hobble past, said quietly, "I haven't been looking for her, old fellow. I'm doing something more important."

"What the hell do you mean?"

Horatio Thomas said patiently, "Can't you see you're at one of the great turning points of history? This is the end of the Civil War. The North has won. So has the Industrial Revolution. Lincoln and the Yankees have triumphed with the machine and its factories, my friend. So has this American experiment in democracy. Slavery's over. Conditions will change now even in England because of what's happening here today. We're witnessing one of the great historic scenes." He added in an excited tone, his eyes on the passing crowds, "What a story! I wish Ram was here to get it out."

Frank was shocked.

"You don't care what's happened to her. You've lost all interest in her because of your damned story. What a cold-blooded bastard you are, Thomas!"

The English journalist didn't take his eyes off what was happening in front of him, carefully noting graphic details, as he snapped, "Face it, man, you've lost her."

"*You* might have, Mister Reporter. But I haven't. I'll find her if I have to tear down what's left of this city."

"The city's already panicking. Soon there'll be an almighty rush to get out and it'll be everyone for himself—or herself. It'll be as mad a scramble as Napoleon Bonaparte's retreat from Moscow fifty years ago. My God, Frank, this is history you're living through. Don't you see that? I wish I was a photographer and could record all these faces and the burning buildings behind them. Once the evacuation begins in earnest, it'll be the survival of the fittest. Darwin should be here." He put a hand on Frank's shoulder to calm him. "Think of yourself now, Frank. You're a gambler—and you've got to face the fact now that you've lost. Take it from me. You don't figure in her plans."

But Frank wasn't listening. "When the streets are clearer, I'll see her. She can't hide from me." He flexed his shoulder. "My gunshot wound's as good as healed. She thinks I don't need her now. I'll show her she's wrong."

"Stop kidding yourself, Frank. Get out of Richmond. Go back to England. Get on with your own life. You're still a young man. Let's forget that bet we made." The bet had been a big mistake. Frank was still trying to win. A gambler's urge was spurring him on. "You don't need to give me your stallion. Forget all about that bet, Frank. Just go home."

"You still don't understand, do you?" Frank said softly. "I'm not doing this for any damned bet. I don't care about your ring. Kath is *mine*. I saved her life. When you hang someone, everything belongs to you—the body, the clothes, everything."

"But she survived and you've lost her, Frank. You gambled, you fool, and you lost."

"A man like you doesn't understand what love is." Frank glared. "The bet's still on—and I'll win. I've got plenty of time left. She'll get tired of running. Just keep that ring polished for me, Thomas."

Frank pushed past the English journalist in disgust and rushed into the sea of frightened faces stretching as far ahead as he could see. Soldiers were keeping people in some rough order, but when the army left that night, mobs would take over the streets. Horatio Thomas watched Frank elbowing a way through the crowd, peering at every woman's face. Suddenly Thomas decided he had to tell him. He went after Frank into the crowd and caught up with him on the other side of the main street.

"Frank," he panted, "you're wasting your time. She's left Richmond already. I happen to know she went out with the first army units. They should be outside the city already on the main route south."

"You sure of this, Thomas?" Frank snapped.

"Yes, I saw her go."

"Was she alone?" Horatio Thomas didn't answer. "Was that soldier with her?" Still no answer. "Where were they heading?"

Thomas felt he had to end Frank's hopes with some positive information. "They went to Mosby's camp. She wants the Reverend to marry them."

Frank didn't explode with rage as Thomas had expected. He received the news in silence, dangerously quiet.

"She's halfway there by now, Frank. No good trying to follow her. This means you've lost our bet. You better give me the address in Stockport where I can collect your Arab stallion."

"I haven't lost yet, Thomas. I'll stop her. She won't get away with it. Enjoy your ring until I come to collect it."

Frank left abruptly, forcing his way through the crowd toward the army wagons in the lead. Thomas's last view of him was of his black head plunging forward like a battering ram, opening up a short cut to the other side of the street. Frank was determined to get out of Richmond—on her trail.

He associated Frank's passion with gambling. All or nothing. Well, that was all right if you were winning. Frank had lost, but he wouldn't accept it. A good gambler had to be more realistic. Yet Thomas still felt sympathetic because Kath had made a strong impression on him, too, and he understood Frank's obsession about her, even if he couldn't altogether share it. I'm saved by my newspaper work, he reflected. That comes first with me, whereas with Frank, the woman comes before anything—even his gambling. Or his work as a hangman.

Then he put Frank out of his mind as he began to make notes for the opening of his story on the fall of Richmond. What would bring this desperate scene home to English readers thousands of miles away in their safe, peaceful homes? Burning embers shot past the English journalist, scattering red hot ash, singeing his white suit. He brushed off the burning ash absent-mindedly as he concentrated on his story:

* * *

Richmond, Virginia, April 4, 1865—The spring sky above the ancient Confederate capital was red with the flames of burning buildings as the tattered remnants of Lee's once mighty army fled southwards in the face of Grant's pounding cannons. It was the sunset of the Confederacy. . . .

* * *

In the darkness south of Richmond, long lines of army wagons were already rolling down the dusty roads. Lying in a corner of one wagon, beside a greasy pile of muskets, were Kath and Paul Blake. They were staring back at the half-abandoned city, glowing in the night sky like a giant bonfire. In a leather bag between Kath's breasts were the gold pieces Paul Blake had brought when he came east to join the Confederate army. Until then he had kept the gold in his army boots. He had insisted Kath carry it as if to prove how much he trusted her.

"Where are we heading?" he whispered drowsily.

"Fairfax county," she replied softly. She didn't want to wake the wounded soldiers sleeping at the back of the wagon, though she suspected one man lying very still was dead. "This minister's with the Mosby Rangers."

"Mosby's behind enemy lines."

"I know how to reach them. Through a barbershop I went to once. The barber'll know where the Reverend is. But it's a long way from here. I looked it up on a map Mr. Thomas had."

She remembered the Reverend's bewhiskered face and his loud voice and warlike manner. Their wedding would be safe with him. He was a friend of Bo's. He'd encouraged her to go on looking for her Dad. And he had offered to help her. She wanted a religious ceremony even though, ever since killing Edward, she had felt out of touch with God. Perhaps it was the knowledge that the Reverend had also killed that made her want him to perform the ceremony. Hadn't he once volunteered? "I wasn't volunteerin' as a husband," he'd told her. "I mean performin' your weddin' ceremony." It was a personal connection, and in a strange country, you needed that.

And she also had another use for him.

He'd know how they could get safely to Washington—to see the Pinkerton National Detective Agency.

19

Reverend Claymore wasn't from Carolina as he'd once told Bo. His name wasn't even Claymore. He didn't know what it was.

Until his twelfth birthday, he'd been called Henry Thorsen and had lived in Chicago, Illinois. The man he thought was his father, George Thorsen, was a bank manager. That Christmas Eve when the boy was twelve, George Thorsen had too many drinks at the bank's Christmas party, and when he came home, he was in a very aggressive mood. He and his wife, Pauline, were soon in the middle of a slambang row. When the young Reverend tried to separate them, George Thorsen cursed him out, too, making it clear to the boy that he wasn't their real son, only adopted, and he could take a walk any time he wanted. The boy was gone before they could stop him.

The Thorsens sat up all night waiting for him to return, then they called in the Chicago police. The police did what they could but they never found him. He had disappeared from their life forever.

He survived somehow on his own the way a stray dog gets by. Both men and women he met were kind to him, but he was always gone before there were any emotional entanglements. He completely wrote off his Chicago past and invented a new personal history as different as possible. He had learned from the angry, drunken George Thorsen that his real parents were unknown except that they were a seventeen-year-old couple with no means to bring up a baby, and so he was free to be anyone he wanted. He chose the name Claymore because he liked the word when he came across it in a story about Scottish clans, and it was a fighting word. The Reverend was already a fighting man. You had to be a fighter to survive as a bum, especially when you were also very young.

The Reverend was added to his name later. He didn't bother with a first name unless people insisted, and then he said he was called Moses from his Bible reading. Because the Thorsens were northerners, he claimed to be from the South and he chose Carolina because it was a woman's name. When the Civil War broke out, it was the final break with his past in Chicago. He believed he was fighting against the past he'd rejected, the society that had robbed him of his birthright, the settled treacherous society of George Thorsen—and of those unknown parents who had rejected him. Only with victory for the South would he be completely free.

He had drifted into preaching to give him an identity other than a vagrant as he wandered from state to state. His religion was based on the Old Testament and was at its most intense when he was drinking; then the Civil War became an extension of the great Biblical battles. Mosby's group was about the only organised army he could have fitted into. His vagrant habits from the age of twelve made any kind of tight discipline impossible. Mosby and his men were the nearest to a family he'd ever allowed himself, but even that seemed to encroach on his freedom. His feelings about Mosby and the war had begun to change after Bo left, though it took him some time to realise it. He came gradually to regret not leaving with Bo. The young Texan had represented complete independence and his staying behind had been a compromise—a moment of weakness. The thought made him angry and he welcomed any mission for Mosby, the wilder the better, because violence was an outlet for his anger. And the more the violence the more he gave it a religious meaning as a holy war against the northern infidels. But his uncertainty and his general dissatisfaction grew.

News came from the barber in the nearest town in Fairfax County that someone was looking for him—a woman. The

Reverend was immediately cautious. He'd been involved with several local women and he didn't want any trouble.

"What'd she look like? Was she purty?"

The barber whistled in admiration. "You can certainly pick 'em, Reverend. She's a beauty. Most pretty redhead I ever saw. And she wants to see *you.* Urgent."

"A redhead?" He hadn't been with any redheads. It was safe then to check her out. He rode back with the barber.

She was waiting patiently at the barbershop. It was the young English redhead Bo had captured from the train. He recognised her at once. Nobody would ever forget that face or that figure. But what did she want with him? He couldn't tell her where Bo was, if that was what she wanted. With her was a lean, hollow-eyed, black-haired young man with the shakes. He needed a drink bad to steady his nerves. There were a lot like him in this war. It was the cannons that did it to them.

"Reverend Claymore," she said in that soft English voice, "thank you for coming." She was perfectly self-possessed. Her big eyes were untroubled. She was some woman.

"Yes, ma'am?"

"I want you to do me a service." She smiled at the young man beside her. "Us, I mean."

The Reverend grew cautious again. Beautiful women could be a damn nuisance. They were always asking you to do something for them as if you were their damn slave. That was why he didn't go for beautiful women. Homely ones were better— they knew they had to oblige a man to get his attention and keep it.

"A service, ma'am?" he said gruffly. "What kind of service?"

"We want you to marry us."

The Reverend stared at her. She was serious, too.

"I ain't married anybody since the war started," he said. "Buried plenty, but married none. It mightn't even be legal, ma'am."

"We want to be married in the eyes of God. We can make it legal later."

The Reverend eyed her man. He seemed a weak choice for such a fine woman. He'd never satisfy her. The marriage wouldn't last five minutes unless she was scheming. Strong women sometimes married weak men to have their way.

"Will you do it for us?" she persisted.

He could see he was caught. She was the kind who got her way with most men. Well, he wasn't going to make it easy for her. He'd have some fun. Maybe he could ditch her man by giving him some liquor and get a piece himself.

"Can't perform no wedding ceremony here in town. Not safe. You'll have to come back to camp."

"Couldn't we just go in the back room of the barbershop?"

"Commercial premises ain't the house of God, ma'am. And the town is probably loaded with Custer's spies."

She and her man followed him reluctantly. He took them the long way through the ruined woods. She stood up all right to the long ride, that woman would endure anything to get what she wanted, but her man was worn out by the time they reached the latest farm where Mosby was hiding.

Along the way was a grim sight—three young soldiers in blue uniforms were hanging from some oak trees, their dead faces swollen, their boots gently turning. Mosby had done it after all with the next prisoners he captured. The Reverend said the dead bodies were to be delivered to Custer's headquarters later that day. "It's the Colonel's final warning to Killer Custer and Butcher Grant," cried the Reverend as they rode past the swinging figures under the overhanging branches. "The Colonel's only regretful he can't participate himself. He's recovering from a wound!"

Kath tried to hide her horror at the sight of the bodies and instinctively her hand went to her neck. Her face tightened and became masklike as she fought for self-control. The Reverend gave her an admiring look. She certainly had a tough stomach for a woman.

"So the Colonel turned hangman anyway," she said.

"Had to," replied the Reverend. "Custer hanged more of our men—Bert Winchester, Walt Mason—and burned the local farms that had helped us. He also took some of the farmers hostage. The Colonel had no choice but to hit back." He stared triumphantly up at the dead, swollen faces. "An eye for an eye!

Sacrificial lambs to the slaughter as in the Bible! The sons of Abraham!''

Her man began to shake uncontrollably and she put a hand on his arm to steady him.

"The war's in its last bitter stages," she said. "Anything goes. We just came from Richmond," she added to the Reverend. "People scrambled like rats leaving a sinking ship. Half the city—the half that was left—was on fire. The North won't win much."

"We ain't lost yet," said the Reverend angrily. "The Lord's on our side."

"You lost when you hanged those boys."

"You talk that way and I won't marry you two."

She stopped her horse.

"I don't think I want to be married here. It has the smell of death about it now."

The Reverend drew his pistol.

"You don't leave here so easy. You need the Colonel's permission to leave."

He left two men guarding them and went in the large white farmhouse to consult Mosby. Five minutes later he called through an upstairs window for the guards to bring them up.

Mosby was lying in a big four-poster bed. He had been wounded in the chest. He had grown older and greyer even in the short time since Kath had seen him last. There was a faraway seer's look in his normally sharp eyes.

"They nearly caught him this time," the Reverend whispered. "They shot him, but they didn't recognise him. The Colonel pretended to be one of Custer's men and managed to get away on his horse. He's lost a lot of blood. But the doctor says he'll be all right. The old man's tough as a chestnut."

Mosby half sat up, a feverish flush to his cheeks.

"You've just come from Richmond?"

"We escaped during the night."

"The city's fallen to Grant?"

"It will have fallen by now, Colonel."

Mosby clutched the bedclothes. "Now is the time for maximum ruthlessness." He pulled back the bedclothes and put his bare feet on the floor. He was very thin, almost frail. "We have to hit the enemy hard to offset the loss of Richmond. No prisoners must be taken. Let the fields turn red with their blood. Hit their supply wagons, their trains—starve them. The northern army is a pack of green kids led by fanatics like George Custer. Hit them *hard* and they will crumble. No mercy must be shown. Take no prisoners! Scare them into surrender. Victory will be ours." He tried to stand up, tottered, and fell back on the bed.

The Reverend pulled the bedclothes over him.

"Lie quiet, Colonel. The doctor said you mustn't excite yourself. Give your wound a chance to heal." He whispered over his shoulder to the others, "The man's lost a lot of blood. He's very weak."

"Remember," Mosby muttered in a feverish tone, his eyes glittering with a faraway look. "Show them no mercy. This is total war now. Turn the grass red with their blood. No prisoners, no mercy, total war . . ." He repeated the words several times like an incantation and then lay back staring blankly up at the oak ceiling.

The Reverend led them out in silence. In the distance against the clear sky, they could see the bodies of the young soldiers hanging from the trees. The sight made Kath suddenly very angry. Her throat throbbed.

"I don't want to stay here," she said quietly.

"He's delirious," the Reverend told her as if he thought she was responding to the meeting with Mosby. "His mind's affected. You saw how weak he is. The Colonel's not himself. He's become another person. It's the fever. The doctor said it'll last a day or two." The Reverend seemed worried by the impression Mosby had made. He kept trying to explain. "The Colonel's mind is confused. . . ."

Nothing in the surrounding landscape had been untouched by the war. Once there had been a dense wood on the south side of the farmhouse. Two armies had fought in the darkness of the wood. The few remaining trees had been pitted and scarred by musketry fire. The underbrush, normally reddened by the sun, had been cut down by bullets or destroyed by shells. The beautiful land had been ravaged almost beyond recognition, transformed from a scene of intense varied natural life into a setting of destruction and death.

Kath shuddered. The ravaged land was like a nightmare, impossible to escape.

"I want to get away from here," she told Paul. "There's nothing but death here now. It's like a plague. It spreads and spreads until everybody catches it eventually."

Paul seemed to come awake then. "The west, Kath—it's still largely untouched by the war. The plague hasn't reached there. You'll be happy out west, Kath. You'll love the ranch. Nature's largely unspoiled out there." He began to shake again with the effort of talking.

The Reverend took out his silver hip flask. Normally he never shared it with anyone, but he couldn't stand the young man's nervous spasms any more.

"It's brandy. Take some. Warm you up."

Paul glanced at Kath as if for approval.

"Go on," the Reverend said, "you two ain't married yet."

"Take it if you want it," Kath said impatiently.

Paul grabbed the flask and took a long swallow.

My God, the Reverend thought, there'll be none left.

It seemed to steady Paul. The shaking eased and he held Kath's hand.

"Let's get married now—this minute—while we have a minister, Kath. We've put it off long enough." He clearly thought her reaction to the setting was merely an excuse.

"We should have some life about us," she said. Her eyes went back to the hanging bodies, seeing herself with them.

"Come," the Reverend told them, taking charge.

He led them towards a barn. A few trees had escaped destruction at the back. Cattle and horses nibbled at the sparse ground. The sun was appearing from behind grey clouds.

"I'll marry you here," the Reverend said, turning his bewhiskered, whisky-red face to the warming sun. He positioned Kath so that her back was to the hanging bodies. "Ready?"

"Very well," Kath said reluctantly.

"First give me your names."

"Kathleen Tracy."

"Of what parish?"

"Stockport, England."

"And you, sir?"

"Paul Blake . . . of Alpine, Kansas."

The Reverend made a sweeping sign of the cross, blessing them both.

"Those who we are about to join together. . . ."

Suddenly there were gunshots in the distance.

"Good God," said the Reverend, "it must be the Yankees."

A horseman was galloping towards them.

Just one man.

The Reverend relaxed. He could deal with one man, whoever he was.

There were puffs of gunsmoke in the air behind the hurrying rider. He wasn't shooting at them, but into the air to attract their attention.

"Stop!" yelled the rider as he came closer.

Kath recognised the voice and stared incredulously.

"Oh, no," she murmured, "it can't be. . . ."

It was Frank.

In dark, dusty clothes, very weary, and wild-eyed.

His horse, panting for air and lathered with sweat, pulled up in front of them in a cloud of dust.

"I come to stop you, Minister," Frank cried, confronting the Reverend. "This woman can't marry."

"And why not?" demanded the Reverend, half angry, half amused. He recognised Frank.

"She's wanted by the law. She killed a man."

Kath cried hotly, "Don't listen to him. He's trying to ruin my life."

The Reverend bellowed with laughter.

"Most of the men in this camp have killed a man. We're in a war, my friend. There's no Law here except Colonel Mosby. You're living in a romantic dreamland. This lady has the qualifications for matrimony. She's of age. That's all that matters. Get out of my way and let me perform the ceremony."

Frank didn't move. "You're on her side. I've ridden through the night to stop you." He glowered at Paul and his hand dropped to his gun. "If there's no bridegroom, there's no marriage, right, Reverend?"

The Reverend's huge hand closed on Frank's wrist, stopping him from drawing his pistol. "We'll have no killings today," he roared. "This wedding *will* take place. I gave the little lady my promise on that."

The Reverend signalled to two of Mosby's men, who had come out of the farmhouse on hearing the gunfire.

"Hold this fool," he told them.

They knew Frank. They had gambled with him. They tried now to reason with him. Frank wouldn't listen. His strong, muscular body wrestled both men to the ground. Kath, watching fearfully, found herself strangely confused. She wanted Frank out of the way and yet not hurt. Part of her sided with him in the fight, wanting him to win. Yet she also wanted him restrained so the wedding could continue. She watched anxiously as Frank punched one of the men and elbowed the other in the face. Frank's black shirt was ripped, revealing his hairy chest, which, like his shoulders, showed the benefit of the weights he used to exercise with in his Stockport cottage. He held one man with his left hand and hit him with his right. The man went down. The Reverend came up quickly behind Frank and struck him on the back of his head with the butt of a pistol. Frank fell forward, unconscious.

"Now I'll proceed," said the Reverend, putting away his pistol.

"Is he all right?" Kath asked anxiously.

"The man's made of iron," roared the Reverend. "We'll be lucky if he's out long enough for us to get you married."

"I wouldn't want him hurt," Kath said.

"What does he mean to you?" Paul asked. "Was he telling the truth?"

She grasped Paul's trembling hand. "He's crazy. I knew him in England," she whispered, "but there was never anything between us—except in his mind." She wouldn't tell Paul about the hanging now. She would explain about it later.

The wedding ceremony was brief. The Reverend said a quick prayer in his most dramatic style and then asked Kath if she'd take Paul Blake for her husband. "I will," Kath replied in a strong, firm voice.

A low moan came from Frank.

"He's coming round," one of the men warned the Reverend.

"Keep him in the barn until we're through."

The two men half-carried Frank into the barn, his boots dragging through the sparse grass.

"I pronounce you man and wife," cried the Reverend, blessing them with a sweeping sign of the cross. He pulled Kath to him. She could smell the stale liquor and tobacco and male sweat. "Now give me a kiss!" The Reverend's wet lips smacked against hers. "Don't worry," he told her. "We'll keep that crazy Black Irishman locked up in the barn until you're far away. Where's the honeymoon goin' to be?"

"Paul's family have a ranch in Alpine, Kansas. We're going there to live. But on the way, I want to stop in Washington—"

"That's the Devil's capital!"

"I must go there on my father's business. Can you tell us the safest route at the present time, Reverend?"

"A man of God always knows the way to hell, little lady. Go to Washington if you must, but don't linger there. Heaven's where you're goin' to stay—out West." He noticed Paul standing shyly behind them. "Here, give your husband a kiss," and he pushed Paul into her arms.

Kath saw the hurt look in Paul's eyes . . . in her *husband's* eyes. She was married! She'd need some time to get used to it. She smiled tenderly at Paul. She'd neglected him since Frank's arrival. She kissed him gently and whispered, "Our turn will come when we're alone together, just the two of us. Let's get away from here and start on our journey." She was impatient to get away from Frank. But she couldn't share her worries, her fears, with Paul. She must be a buffer between him and the world until he was stronger.

She walked Paul slowly over to the horses. His movements were awkward, as if his wound still pained him. They'd have to rest overnight in Washington before leaving on the long journey to Kansas.

The Reverend came up behind them. "I'll ride with you part of the way. I gotta protect you newlyweds from those damn Yankees." He slowly swung his great heavy body onto a sturdy mare. "We'll go on the Shenandoah side. A short cut across the valley and through the woods. The Yankees won't have moved in there yet. Once across the river, you'll be all right. That pass you got from Abe Lincoln'll see you through the enemy lines." The Reverend grinned, revealing a row of broken, stained teeth, and took a bottle out of his hip pocket. "Let me toast the bride." He took a big drink and wiped his mouth with his hand. "You two want some?"

"It's time to leave, Reverend," Kath said, trying to hide her impatience. If he went on drinking, they'd never get away.

"You're the boss today, lady, on account it's your weddin' day. Let me just say howdy to the boys and then I'm ready." He walked his horse over to the barn. The two Mosby men joked him that he'd fall off. Kath heard something about Kansas and the Reverend say, "Hold him till I get back," and then she saw his huge hand slap his horse's rump, and they were off, galloping past the farmhouse toward the Virginia hills—and Washington.

As Kath rode down the dirt road, she was sure she heard Frank's deep voice bellow from the barn as if he could see them leaving. He stayed in her thoughts as they reached the hills; she felt his presence almost like another rider with them. She was scared—not for herself, but for Paul. Frank had stared so murderously at him. Frank had become a desperate, lost man here in America, pursuing her because she reminded him of home where he'd been rooted and safe. He was like a gambler who wouldn't quit until he'd won or lost everything. Yet there was something about Frank that she couldn't ever forget, a feeling he gave her—a feeling she didn't quite understand. It was almost as if they were related. But she knew she could have no peace with both Frank and Paul in her life. She and Paul had to get as far away from Frank as possible. Surely they'd be safe out West.

* * *

The men in the barn tied Frank's feet together with rope, but left his hands free—for cards. Frank let them win, hoping to relax them enough to escape.

"No hard feelings, Frank," one of the men said. "When a woman's wed, you gotta give her up."

Frank, scowling, kept his eyes on his cards.

"It wasn't our fault, Frank," said the other man sympathetically. "The Reverend agreed to marry her before she and her husband went off to Kansas."

Frank looked up.

"Kansas? Where's that?"

"I keep forgettin' you're English, Frank. Kansas is a western state. The Reverend says her husband's rich out there. His family's got a ranch at a place called Alpine."

"That's in Kansas state?"

"Yeah, a little cowboy town."

So that was where she'd gone—*Alpine, Kansas*. Frank began calculating how much money he had left to cover the expenses of a long journey. It was to a different part of America, across the continent—in English terms, it was like crossing Europe. His money might run out. He needed to win some, but it wasn't safe to take much from his captors or they'd never release him until they had won it back.

He tried to explain his situation in a way they'd understand. "I got a bet on winning her—my stallion back in England against a ruby ring worth a fortune."

The men grinned knowingly.

"That makes more sense, Frank," said one. "I follow better now the crazy way you've been actin'."

"Then give me a chance of winning." Frank picked up the cards and shuffled them slowly in an amateurish way that wouldn't worry the other two men. "What d'you say we play a little more and then you let me get going?"

20

A gunboat blew up on the river James. The huge fiery explosion shook the ground where Horatio Thomas was standing in the center of Richmond. Then an arsenal went up in flames and exploded with a great thunderous roar. The English journalist was staggered by the blast.

Much of the abandoned city was on fire. Heavy clouds of smoke shut out the clear blue sky and the bright spring sunshine. Sparks showered the streets and gardens. The few remaining windows soon shattered and sprayed the sidewalks with glass. Tall chimneys cracked and tumbled like forest trees cut down.

This scene of destruction was the Union Army's reward for months of siege. As the weary lines of blue-uniformed soldiers moved into Richmond, they had little sense of victory. In place of fighting the enemy, they now had to put out the fires. There was no rest for the victors—and little left to plunder.

The front line was now far away. Horatio Thomas had to find it to be in at the kill. He asked a middle-aged colonel to take him to General Grant's headquarters. But the colonel was the wrong man to ask. He was an old army man, a veteran of the war, and he hated journalists, regarding them as informers helpful to the enemy. He ignored Thomas's request and restricted him to the main streets. It meant he couldn't leave Richmond.

The second day, security precautions were greatly increased. The streets were flooded with Union soldiers and army wagons. Somebody important was arriving from Washington to inspect the captured prize. Horatio Thomas hoped it was General Grant, but that was unlikely—Grant would be in hot pursuit of Lee's army.

The visitor came by the river. Thomas wasn't allowed near the docks. But a high black silk hat was soon visible above the crowd of army generals and politicians. It was Abraham Lincoln.

The tall, bearded President wanted to see as much of Richmond as possible. He strode through the still-smoking center with a sorrowful expression, ignoring the security arrangements. This made it easier for Thomas to get close to him. He recognized Thomas at once.

"The fall of Richmond is good news for my friends in Manchester," Lincoln said, shaking Thomas's hand. He looked much older. His face was now deeply lined and more sallow. There was also a weariness in the eyes that hadn't been there before.

"Is the war over, Mr. President?" Thomas asked.

"Very nearly," Lincoln replied sombrely, "unless there is a last-minute breakdown in the negotiations. General Grant at this moment is in touch with General Lee to discuss surrender terms for the Army of Northern Virginia. I hope General Lee has the power to speak for all combatants."

The President put a long, bony arm round Thomas's shoulders and walked him away from the waiting group of army officers and politicians. Thomas was above average height, but Lincoln towered above him.

"I understand you have met the famous Colonel Mosby, Mr. Thomas. Was it your impression that General Lee can speak for him? Or is Colonel Mosby completely beyond army discipline by this time?" Lincoln patted his tall hat thoughtfully. "Too much freedom can corrupt as easily as too much power. My fear is that Mosby and the other guerrilla groups will ignore whatever agreement General Grant and General Lee come to and go on fighting and the war will drag on in pockets of resistance across the nation."

"Not Mosby, Mr. President. He's still a lawyer at heart. He personally might want to continue fighting, but if a peace is negotiated, then he will abide by its terms. His lawyer side wouldn't let him do otherwise."

"If he's a lawyer like me, then we have a lot in common. We lawyers don't need to fight. We have the law on our side all the time." Lincoln's tired, lined face and wide, generous mouth creased into a grin. "Colonel Mosby once sent me a message—that he would raid Washington and get a lock of my hair. I'm still waiting."

"Don't challenge him even this late, Mr. President. He has men fighting with him who would accept any challenge. Real moondancers. But Mosby himself is a realist. He'll recognise the end when it comes."

"The freedom he has known can be as heady as good champagne," Lincoln said sombrely. "Most human beings talk a lot about wanting complete freedom, but they don't really. They want security, a refuge from their fears. They want the government to run their lives. The war has brought us more freedom than we have ever known. Perhaps we have gone too far, too fast. The test now will be to see what we do with it."

"You sound worried we may fail the test, Mr. President."

"Frankly I am, Mr. Thomas. We've held the union together at the cost of thousands of lives, we've freed the slaves, but we haven't freed men's minds. It'll take time—a lot of time, maybe more than we've got. I just hope the Good Lord will grant us enough time to digest all the changes. Fear can make people give up their freedom, even when they have fought so hard for it."

A loud cheer went up close by. A group of black workers clearing the debris in the streets had recognised Lincoln. He waved to them.

"Where are General Grant and General Lee meeting, Mr. President?"

"At a little place called Appomattox. I'm told it's about eighty miles away from here, near Lynchburg." Lincoln straightened his hat. It looked new and he seemed unsure of it.

"I'd like to cover the end of the war, Mr. President, but the army is making it difficult for me to leave Richmond."

The President smiled. "You journalists are no more loved than us politicians." He turned to the generals standing behind him. "Please see that Mr. Thomas, the special correspondent of the *Manchester Guardian* of England, is given every assistance in reaching Appomattox. We owe it to the working people of Manchester to make sure they receive an eyewitness account of the peacemaking." He shook Thomas's hand warmly. His sombre mood seemed to have passed. "Come to see me when you return to Washington, Mr. Thomas."

A soldier brought a fine black horse for the President to ride. His long legs that seemed to be permanently bent at the knees dangled over the horse's sides, and as he had no straps, his trousers gradually worked up above his ankles. His black clothes were soon covered in dust. Lincoln looked out of place among the uniformed soldiers surrounding him, all professional cavalrymen, but no one showed anything but awe of him as he rode past. Like many men brought up in the west—Lincoln was a Kentuckian by birth—he was a good horseman and was clearly enjoying his ride. For all the marks of the war, the deepening lines and sadness, he was still a strong-looking man. He sat on the horse very erectly, and his great height made him always visible above the security guards—a perfect target. And now the North had won, he would be hated by thousands of people. His life was definitely in danger, Horatio Thomas thought as he watched Abraham Lincoln slowly ride away.

* * *

Lincoln's instructions worked like magic. The journalist-hating colonel no longer detained him. But a horse wasn't easy to obtain and there was no other way of reaching Appomattox in a hurry. The horses that hadn't been eaten during the siege or ridden away during the overnight retreat had been commandeered by the Union Army. Eventually Horatio Thomas had to bribe a Union soldier to steal him one—a lean, bony nag with a mean temper.

It was a long, uncomfortable, muddy ride. The Confederate army had fought several savage rearguard actions and churned up the landscape. Thomas saw the waiting armies resting in crude tents constructed round their rifles and bayonets while a few miles away their commanders negotiated the terms of the peace.

Grant rode past Thomas looking very weary and dusty— Grant might have been the loser and Lee, who passed a few moments later, erect and shining on his great horse Traveller, might have been the victor. But it was a matter of appearance only. They were coming away from their meeting. Lee had formally surrendered. It was all over. But, Thomas thought uneasily, the peace was just beginning.

* * *

Horatio Thomas headed then for Washington. He had to get the story of the end of the war to England as fast as possible. He wanted the *Guardian* to be the first to break the news in England.

He arrived at Willard's Hotel, worried that Ram might not be there, though his calm, confident manner gave no hint of his concern as he strode into the crowded lobby.

He stared round.

Half the people sitting there were drunk. Washington was celebrating the end of the civil war.

But no Ram.

He must still be somewhere in Virginia.

A frown appeared on the English journalist's smooth face, like the first tremor of an earthquake. Several choice English, French and Indian curses were uttered silently. His plans were being upset. Ram, the vital link, was missing.

But, as he continued to survey the vast crowded lobby a couple suddenly moved towards the main doors, revealing behind them, sitting patiently waiting in a padded armchair— Ram! Thomas hurried over, showing no sign of his relief. The young Sikh's dusky face beamed with delight beneath his white turban as soon as he saw Thomas.

"I know nothing has happened to you," he cried, standing up respectfully and shaking Thomas's hand. He examined Thomas's clothes. "Need new suit."

Thomas interrupted him briskly. "Ram, we must send a rush story about the ending of the war. We must beat the London *Times*. I want a summary to go on the first steamship to Ireland. Your man there can telegraph it and save at least a day. Then the full story, the whole gory description, must go on the first steamship for Liverpool for collection by the *Guardian*. I think you should take them yourself as far as New York to make sure that there's no possible mistake or time lost."

"When will you have the reports ready?" Ram asked, businesslike.

"They're in my bag, ready to go."

Before Ram left for New York, Horatio Thomas went over to the War Department to check that there had been no late news. He was shown into the Secretary of War's office immediately. Edwin McMasters Stanton was short and paunchy with gold-rimmed spectacles and gray, scented whiskers. His appearance was deceptive. Secretary Stanton was a tough, merciless politician, reputed to be the most powerful man in the government after Lincoln. He had no news Thomas hadn't already heard, but while he was expressing concern the Confederate guerrilla groups wouldn't accept the peace terms, a familiar, short, stocky, gray-bearded army officer, as untidily dressed as ever, came in. It was Grant. The government wished to reduce its immense wartime budget as soon as possible and Grant had rushed to Washington to show how the army's expenses could be cut. But that wasn't what he had come to discuss with Stanton. He had just received an invitation to go to the theater with President and Mrs. Lincoln. He wondered if he dared refuse.

"Certainly," Stanton told him. "The President invited me, too, and I sent him my regrets. The Cabinet has warned the President many times about these public appearances. They are too dangerous at the present time. Washington is a nest of southern sympathisers and wild plots. Now the war's over and people can travel more freely, this city will be like a magnet for every madman in the country. The President should stay home. Turn down the invitation, General, and persuade the President not to go himself. The trouble is that Mrs. Lincoln doesn't seem to understand the danger and keeps coming up with these fool ideas for showing him off in public."

Thomas asked Grant which theater the President planned to visit.

"Ford's on Tenth Street," said Grant.

"When, General?"

"Tomorrow night—April the fourteenth."

Thomas's eyes widened.

"That's Good Friday."

It was an eerie coincidence.

* * *

Ram left for New York as soon as Horatio Thomas returned to the hotel. The English journalist hadn't slept much since he'd left Richmond so he had a leisurely dinner with a bottle of French red wine and then went to bed. A dream woke him close to dawn—he had been witnessing the Crucifixion, that was all he remembered. Good Friday had been on his mind when he lay down, the day of Lincoln's visit to Ford's theater. But perhaps the President wouldn't go if Grant turned down his invitation.

Willard's was at Fourteenth and E Streets. When Thomas went out for an early breakfast, people were already on their way to one of the capital's many churches. It was a solemn day for them, Good Friday, the day of Christ's death. But downtown the mood was different. Washington was a southern city in character and habits celebrating a northern victory. The whole war was being refought in bars—Gettysburg and Shiloh and Vicksburg and Bull Run and all the rest. Drunks seemed to be everywhere—and fights. The city was like a barrel of gunpowder, and the more the drinking went on, the more likely it was to explode. Everyone seemed to have a handgun or a musket; the war had made them an essential feature of American life, and even though the war was over, the guns remained, ready to go off. Peace wouldn't be achieved just by an agreement at Appomattox; it would have to be fought for. The next evolutionary stage, Thomas thought uneasily.

Boys ran through the cobbled streets passing out handbills. Thomas took one. The handbill's big black print announced that that evening's performance of *Our American Cousin* at Ford's Theater "will be honored by the presence of President Lincoln." So Lincoln was going as planned. Perhaps Grant had changed his mind and agreed to accompany the President and Mrs. Lincoln. Thomas hoped so. He found Grant a reassuring figure. Lincoln alone was more vulnerable. Thomas decided to attend the performance, too.

Black coachmen waited with parked carriages along both sides of Tenth Street. A few soldiers on leave stood waiting to see the President arrive. Thomas waited with them. The play had already started. At last the President's carriage drew up. Grant wasn't with him and Thomas's sense of concern grew. Lincoln seemed very unprotected, far too close to the people, like a democratic leader in some idealistic romance. Thomas remembered the scenes of simmering violence downtown. Lincoln was an obvious target for all of that. Thomas watched the tall, angular, bearded man help his rather dumpy wife out of the presidential carriage. His face was more lined and sad-looking, his mouth as generous, and Thomas found himself moved by the sight of this homely figure more than he had been by all the monarchs and dictators he had seen in Europe and the East. Abraham Lincoln was a wise, kindly man, yet shrewd enough to deal with all the politicians and financiers seeking to profit from the peace.

Thomas watched the President and his wife hurry into the theater and then he rushed in to find his own seat. The Lincolns were in Box 7. From his seat downstairs, Thomas could just see the top of the President's head. As they entered the box, the action stopped on the stage and the actors applauded along with the audience. It was a full house. The band played "Hail to the Chief." Then everyone settled down and the play went on. It was a comedy and the audience was soon rocking with laughter. The second act came to an end. Thomas, along with everyone else, kept peering upwards, but the President in his rocking chair was rarely visible. Good, Thomas thought, he doesn't present a target.

The third act began.

"Wal," one of the actors cracked, "I guess I know enough to turn you inside out, you sockdologizing old mantrap!"

There was loud laughter. Thomas thought he heard a sharp cracking sound above the laughter, but he couldn't be sure. He glanced up at the presidential box. The sound seemed to come from up there.

Heads bobbed up and down. There was unusual activity in the presidential box. A man stood up close to where Lincoln was sitting and shouted, "Revenge for the South!"

The actors on stage faltered and stared up at the box. The attention of the audience moved from the stage to the box. There was a buzz of intense curiosity, a growing feeling that something was wrong up there.

A man climbed out of the box and dropped to the stage. He fell heavily and limped across the stage and disappeared into the wings. It all happened too quickly for any of the actors to stop him. The audience was unsure whether this was part of the play, but then a loud scream came from Box 7. A loud, chilling woman's scream. Something *was* wrong, terribly wrong.

Thomas ran across the aisle and dashed up the already crowded stairs. He elbowed his way down the corridor to the door leading to Box 7. Everything was confusion, noise, panic. Thomas caught a glimpse of the President, his head on his chest, his eyes closed. The English journalist knew from his war experience what it meant—Abraham Lincoln had been shot in the head. Nobody recovered from a wound like that. A man pushed past Thomas, saying, "I'm a doctor." Thomas made way for him. The English journalist felt more personally affected than on any other story he had covered. Lincoln, with his human warmth and modest homeliness, seemed the one person who could steer the country through an uneasy peace. Power was safe in his hands. But now. . . .

* * *

It was a night of rumors.

The man who had jumped to the stage from Lincoln's box was identified as an actor—John Wilkes Booth. He was already being hunted. But he hadn't worked alone. It was a conspiracy. Not only President Lincoln had been attacked that night, but also Secretary of State Seward as he lay ill at his home.

The cry of Lincoln's assassin, "Revenge for the South!," began the rumors that swept Washington. It suggested a wholesale attempt to destroy the Federal government and reassert the power of the Confederacy. It couldn't win on the battlefield; was it trying to win another way, through assassins' bullets? The name most commonly mentioned as the leader of the conspiracy was—Mosby. Horatio Thomas didn't take this seriously at first. It wasn't Mosby's style to play the assassin.

What mattered that first night—Good Friday night—was not who had done it but what they had done.

If Abraham Lincoln died, his successor would be Vice-President Andrew Johnson. The Republican radicals, men who hated the South and wanted to see it punished for the war, would be in full control. The white South would lose its freedom and in turn would blame not only the North but its former slaves, the black South. The peace would be a bad one. Hatred would grow, a desire for revenge, a wish to turn back the clock to pre-war days when the white South's prosperity was measured by its black slaves.

All this hung on a single life.

Lincoln hadn't recovered consciousness.

Doctors hadn't dared to take him the long ride back to the White House. He had been carried to a private house near Ford's Theater. Still unconscious, he lay in a room rented by a soldier on leave. His wife and son were there and members of his Cabinet. Vice-President Johnson came for a short time and stared down at the body that was too big for the bed and barely seemed to be breathing.

Horatio Thomas in the street outside watched the continual traffic in and out of the little house all night and waited for news. Lines of soldiers were on guard in the street, reflecting the fear that now gripped the government. Secretary of War Stanton seemed to be temporarily in charge. Thomas watched him come out of the house shortly before eight o'clock in the morning. Stanton's moon face looked tired and grim. Thomas waved to attract his attention, not expecting that Stanton would bother to talk to him. But when Stanton saw him, he had the soldiers clear a way for him.

"Get in my carriage, Mr. Thomas. Ride with me to the War Department."

Stanton didn't say any more, but stared out of the carriage window at the waiting crowd. More than half the people in the streets were black. Uncle Abe was their hero, perhaps the only white leader they trusted. Stanton sat back so he couldn't be seen.

"How is the President?" Thomas asked at last.

Stanton didn't look at him but continued to stare out of the window. His hands gripped his knees. Normally a decisive, dogmatic man, he seemed almost frightened. "Abraham Lincoln now belongs to history," he said slowly. "The President breathed his last a few minutes ago."

Thomas sat back, stunned. He had expected the news, but it still shocked him. Lincoln had been a victim of the plague of violence that had swept the country for four years. He could have controlled the wild hatreds that had divided the states. His death released people from reason. They were free to go wild. . . .

I'm not making sense, Thomas thought, still shaken. I better clear my head before I write anything. The problem would be to convey to faraway English readers what the death of Abraham Lincoln meant—how he was irreplaceable in this divided democracy. Perhaps he should address his report to the working people of Manchester as Lincoln had done. "Washington—April 15, 1865. President Abraham Lincoln died this morning at. . . ."

He said to Stanton, "Do you know the exact time the President died?"

"Twenty-two minutes after seven." Stanton turned away from the window. "I asked you to ride with me," he said, "because the President told me you know Colonel Mosby."

"I stayed at his camp."

Stanton eyed Thomas. He seemed unusually tense. It was more than the President's death. He seemed scared. Perhaps he expected to be next.

Stanton said abruptly, "I'm convinced the murder of the President is just the beginning, Thomas. The whole of official Washington is in danger. The South is making a last desperate effort to reverse the situation. The aim of its complex plot is to put the Federal government out of action and to terrorise Washington." Stanton rubbed his tired eyes with a trembling hand. "An actor has been identified as the President's assassin. He had some amateur help. We'll get them all. We've closed every escape route out of the city. All vessels on the Potomac are being stopped. We're sealing off Virginia as far as Harpers Ferry and Leesburg. We'll get him and his gang. But the far-ranging plot I have outlined couldn't be the work of a mere crazed actor and a few amateur accomplices." Stanton shook his head to stress his conclusion. "It needed a professional strategist respected by the Confederate leaders, a mastermind skilled in terrorist raids, at getting in and out of Washington. There seems to be one obvious choice—John Singleton Mosby. His history is full of daring guerrilla attacks. He has raided Washington several times and kept a large army tied down." Stanton leaned forward, careful not to be close to the carriage window. "What do you think, Thomas? Is Mosby capable of it?"

Thomas said hesitantly, "He's capable of it, he's got the means and the ability, but an assassin's bullet isn't his style."

"Why not? He's obviously extremely ruthless. He recently hanged several of Custer's men."

"After Custer hanged some of his men." Thomas had read about it in the Washington papers. Mosby had been determined to do it.

"You sound as if you're defending him," Stanton said. "You don't understand the mind of the American South. You English never have done. They'll do *anything* to avoid humiliation and defeat, to save face. They're great when they're winning, full of noble, chivalrous sentiments, but when they're losing—beware! They'll stop at nothing to beat you."

Horatio Thomas still didn't take Stanton's theory seriously until the government captured several of the assassins. The actor, John Wilkes Booth, was reported to have been cornered in a Virginia barn and shot down like a dog, though there were rumors the wrong man had been killed and Booth had escaped. Among the captured accomplices was the man who had attacked Secretary of State Seward—a strong, silent young giant named Lewis Paine.

Stanton in triumph called Thomas to his office at the War Department. Stanton had recovered all his old confidence.

"You were wrong, Thomas," he declared flatly. "This Lewis Paine once served with Mosby. He's the Mosby connection I've been looking for."

"There was no Lewis Paine at Mosby's camp when I was there," Horatio Thomas said thoughtfully.

"He was probably already in Washington working undercover for Mosby," Stanton said impatiently. "Mosby was the mastermind behind the President's assassination, I'm certain of it now. He must be hunted down, brought to trial and hanged in front of the White House as a lesson to all southerners—to all traitors to the Union."

21

Paul's wound made him grimace with pain as he rode with Kath. He needed to ride alone, sidesaddle. They stopped at a farm where two lean mares were grazing in a field. Perhaps the farmer would sell one of them.

The farmer, a fat, balding Dutchman, refused. The mares were all he had left. Retreating Confederate soldiers had taken his other horses and all his cattle. Then he saw Paul's gold pieces and he changed his mind. Kath chose the stronger-looking mare. The Reverend also bought some corn liquor.

As soon as Kath was in the saddle, the mare sat down. Kath smacked its rump as she'd seen the Reverend do to his horse. The mare slowly got up and allowed Kath to guide it down the road. She struggled to master it over the next few miles. It was good practice for out West where they lived on a horse.

The real problem wasn't the mare, but the Reverend. He was a fairly reliable guide until the corn liquor took him over, then he missed several short cuts in the hills and led them for miles out of their way. When he fell off his horse, Kath had a hard time getting him back on. A farmer mending a stone wall showed them how to find the right trail.

It was a great relief to Kath to sight the tall northern army forts guarding the approaches to the city and leave the Reverend behind. In his drunken, drowsy state, he wasn't aware of her annoyance, but bade her and Paul an emotional farewell, watched them ride off with tears in his eyes and waved vigorously until he could no longer see them.

They were well received at the leading fort as soon as Kath produced Lincoln's note. It was even more effective than before. Young Union soldiers held the worn parchment in their calloused hands and stared reverently at the dead President's signature as if it were the relic of a saint.

It was the day the President's body was to leave Washington. As Kath and Paul reached the outskirts of the capital, silent, grieving crowds were already gathering to watch the coffin go by on its way to the railway depot, where a nine-car funeral train was waiting to take the dead President home to Springfield, Illinois.

Church bells tolled a mournful beat and cannons boomed a steady, deathly chant. Kath and Paul tried to find a clear view of the approaching cortege, but they were quickly trapped in the middle of the crowd and pressed up against a group of black workers, who were openly weeping and praying aloud for the man they knew affectionately as Uncle Abe. Kath, too, felt a personal sense of loss, a feeling she had never experienced before for a public figure. Prime Minister Palmerston or Queen Victoria had always seemed remote from her own life. But Abraham Lincoln hadn't been remote; he'd even told jokes like her Dad.

A heavily built bearded man, who reminded Kath of the Reverend, broke out of the front of the crowd and ran across the cobbled street before the police could stop him to lay a sprig of lilac on top of the passing coffin. Two policemen grabbed him and pushed him back into the crowd near Kath.

"What's your name?" growled one of the policemen.

"Walter Whitman, Junior," said the bearded man proudly. "Unemployed poet."

Kath could see the lilac's heart-shaped leaves, so similar to the lavender sprigs she used to break off from the bushes at Heaton Hall in the early spring, about this time of year. The strong lilac fragrance came back to her then, evoking all those happy days of childhood, and she found the tears rolling down her face. For the first time, she feared her Dad might be dead and she wouldn't succeed in finding him. But her depression lasted only a moment or two, until the funeral procession had gone by, Then she wiped away her tears and felt foolish to have considered failure even for a moment. She blamed her weakness on the draining experiences of the last few days, on all the worries that she had tried not to think about and that had suddenly come down on her at the sight of President Lincoln's coffin—and the sprig of lilac.

Washington was so crowded that all the hotels they tried were full. She had intended to stay away from Willard's Hotel, where Frank had found her before, but she knew the manager and perhaps one night there would be safe. They had a suite vacant and Paul insisted on taking it, even though it cost a fortune. "It's our wedding night," he said shyly. There was a big bedroom, a sitting-room, a kitchen with a dining-table, and a bathroom—great luxury after Richmond.

Before going to bed, they went out to dinner. The capital was a changed place since her last visit. The war machine was running down rapidly, and Washington was adapting itself to the pervading spirit of peace and reconstruction. As they enjoyed a leisurely three-course dinner at the George Washington Dining Rooms, a wonderful change from Richmond's starvation diet, they listened to the loud talk around them. After the grim austerity of the war years, people wanted to get back as fast as possible to developing the interior of the continent—that was where the future fortunes lay. The huge northern army would be employed not only to occupy the defeated South and suppress any pockets of resistance, but to subdue the Wild West. Kath leaned forward as a group of businessmen at the next table discussed how the frontier was to be pushed farther into the wilderness. The Indians and Mexicans were to be "crushed" like the South. According to these loud-talking businessmen, the Federal government, having held the Union together, must now try to centralise the running of the whole country. The next big step was to improve national communications with a transcontinental railroad linking the East and West coasts. Then the Wild West could be tamed!

Kath listened avidly to all this talk about the West, soon to be her new home. Paul was annoyed when the businessmen at the next table took a superior attitude, as if the West—his

West—really was wild and the cowboys were as dangerous and uncivilised as jungle beasts. His annoyance reminded her of how irritated she had been at the way people in the south of England talked about the north—the wild north. She laughed to calm him down. "What do they know? Have they ever been out West? Most of them probably know far more about Europe."

"I'm just tired of hearing these dude Easterners talk that dumb way," Paul grumbled. It was the first time he'd become worked up since they left Richmond. "Easterners think they're the only ones who're civilised, but all they do is imitate Europe and its fancy ways. The people out West are the real Americans. You'll soon see that for yourself, Kath. If America succeeds in becoming a New World for people from everywhere, it'll be out there. We've the wide, open spaces and the chance to start from the beginning, to learn to live together in peace whoever we are, wherever we come from." He held her hand across the table. "Just wait until you see it, Kath."

She was pleased to watch him so animated, and she kept him talking about the West. Her big fear was that people who had fought each other in Europe would do the same in America. But Paul thought the American environment would change them and blend them together peacefully. "It might take a little time to become one nation, but it'll happen. . . ."

They went up to bed late. Kath tried to make their first night in bed together as easy for him as possible. He stayed an age in the bathroom as if afraid to come out. She didn't try to hurry him, but sat at the window staring out at the shadowy, unfinished Washington skyline, at the huge, incomplete public buildings and monuments—another monument would probably be built now for Lincoln. When at last Paul came back into the bedroom, he was obviously relieved to see her over by the window instead of lying in wait for him on the big double bed. He quickly joined her and they chatted about the view. He wanted to do some sight-seeing before they left if they had time. "Who knows when I'll ever get to Washington again?" he said with a shy grin. When they climbed into bed, he was much more relaxed. He kissed her on the mouth, then he lay back.

"That's as far as I go," he murmured in a dead voice. "Oh, Kath, I've done you wrong in marrying you. I'm lifeless down there. I've no feeling, nothing."

His face was very boyish and vulnerable. She felt so much older, so much stronger. She held him to her breasts and rocked him like a baby.

"Put your hand here," she said.

He didn't move.

She took his hand and drew his fingers down between her legs, and she moved up in the bed. But he didn't respond. His hand lay where she'd placed it against her thighs.

"Paul," she whispered, "there's more than one way to make love." She felt a need for him then, a womanly passion that she longed for him to satisfy. "Let me help you. Move down in the bed. . . ."

He went so far and then he stopped. His hand froze. His head moved back to the pillow.

"It's no good, Kath. I can't do anything. You're just trying to be kind. But I don't want that from my wife."

"Your trouble, Paul, is that you don't know much about how to make love." She lay back, suppressing her own feelings. "What do you men do out West? Treat your women like slaves? Perhaps it's true what those Easterners say about you. Maybe you need more of our fancy European ways to relax and enjoy yourself."

He laughed.

That was a start.

"Look at me." She held the bedside oil-lamp close to her bare neck. "See that scar—that rope burn?"

"Hell, how'd you get that?"

"I was nearly . . . hanged. I was saved just in time." She'd explain some day, but not now. And he was too worried about himself to ask her about it. "I nearly died . . . like you with your wound. You can recover completely, Paul, like I did."

But it was going to take time, she thought. One night in Washington wouldn't do it. Perhaps, back home, he'd feel secure enough for his memories of the war to dim, and he'd relax more with her. She wouldn't feel safe about their marriage until it worked in bed for him. They *could* be happy together. It was true she'd married an impotent young rancher, but he was a warm, sensitive man, he had money and a place of his own, and she needed to belong, even while she searched for her Dad. She wanted the ranch to be her first real home, and then if her father was in any kind of trouble, he'd have a refuge.

Paul slept with his head on her breasts, murmuring several times in his sleep, but he didn't wake. He sounded as if he were replaying a battle scene from the war, perhaps the time he received his wound.

In the morning, she had him up early and out in the streets for breakfast. He tried with an embarrassed grin to talk about what had happened in bed, but she was brisk and businesslike. They were there for one purpose only: to find the Pinkerton National Detective Agency.

She took the Lincoln note to the Washington police. It won quick action with them, too. After a short wait, she was told to contact Major E.J. Allen at the War Department. She and Paul went there immediately. At the mention of Major Allen, they were taken to a back office on the second floor. A young lieutenant asked suspiciously why they wanted to see Major Allen.

"You must understand," he said, "that since the President's assassination, everyone requires a security clearance to see senior staff."

"My business is with the Pinkerton National Detective Agency," Kath told him.

"Follow me," he said at once and led them down more corridors to an office at the front of the building. "This is *not* part of the War Department," he told them. On a glass door was a large eye and the motto, *We Never Sleep.* The lieutenant knocked and a gruff voice growled, "Come in."

A big, bearded man in a plain dark suit was sitting at a wooden desk. Behind him was a wall map of the whole country marked with little flags on which wére depicted the same all-seeing eye that Kath had noticed on the glass door.

"Major Allen?" she asked.

The man shook his head.

"Now the war's over, I'm back to being myself—Allan Pinkerton at your service. The War Department allows me to rent this office until I've completed my work for the government. Major Allen was one of my many aliases during the war when I was setting up a secret service spy network for the Union Army. Are you from England?"

"From Stockport," Kath told him. When he frowned in ignorance, she explained quickly, "That's on the border of Lancashire and Cheshire. Near Manchester."

"I thought I recognized your accent. I was born in Scotland myself and came over here twenty years ago."

Kath was familiar with Scots. Many Scottish workers had come across the border in search of jobs in the Lancashire factories. They were usually trustworthy people, according to her Dad, though not quite in the class of the Irish.

"This is my husband, Mr. Pinkerton. He's an American."

Pinkerton eyed Paul, who was standing in the background, leaving Kath in charge.

"You look like a war veteran," Pinkerton observed.

Paul nodded without speaking. He didn't want the northerner to learn he had served with the Confederate Army. Pinkerton didn't press him, but said to Kath cheerfully, "Now what can I do for you, young lady?"

"I want you to find my father."

The detective patted a pile of letters on his desk.

"Half of these are requests to find missing persons. The war has displaced thousands of people. Many families don't know if their sons are alive or dead, and if they're alive, where they are. The army records are far from perfect. Somebody could be rotting in some obscure front-line hospital and no one would know. I've more than a hundred requests here and I'm only just starting to get back to my agency work. I'm sorry, young lady, but I can't take on another case just now."

"Oh, *please,* Mr. Pinkerton," Kath said earnestly, "I'm counting on you. I've lost touch with my father since he left England."

"Then, my dear young lady, it'll be like looking for a needle in a haystack. Even worse—a drop in the ocean. This is a huge country and it's getting bigger every day as we discover more of it. You could fit the whole of England into the state of Texas and have a big piece left over."

"But I have several clues. Let me tell you about them."
Swiftly, without waiting for Pinkerton's agreement, Kath described how her father had left home and she had come over in search of him, and how, in Richmond, she had discovered he had gone with a consignment of Confederate gold out West, together with two Confederate agents. The coffin had been found—and dead bodies.

"Your father then may be dead," Pinkerton said when she had finished.

"I want proof. I'm certain I haven't come all this way for nothing."

"And if your father is still alive, he may not want to see you."

"Why do you say that, Mr. Pinkerton?"

"He hasn't got in touch with you all these years."

"He was probably waiting until he was well placed and the war was over."

"That's possible, but it doesn't seem probable to me." He considered her eager, determined face. "I'll tell you what I'll do. I'll telegraph my representatives in Kansas and ask them to check immediately on what happened to the coffin shipment of gold and the men with it."

"How long will it take?" Kath asked anxiously. "We can't stay long in Washington."

Pinkerton pointed with a smile to the motto on the glass door. *We Never Sleep,* remember. I should have an answer for you by tomorrow."

* * *

When they returned the next day, Allan Pinkerton had a telegraph message in front of him. "I have news," he told Kath, "but not necessarily the news you want. The coffin was empty. That has been established. There were three men with it—your father the undertaker, and two agents. Only two bodies were found. I told my inquiry agents to check whether the bodies had any fingers missing. Neither had."

Kath smiled with relief. "That means he's alive!" She turned to Paul. "What did I tell you?"

Pinkerton, who was nicknamed "The Eye" or "The Private Eye" after his agency's symbol on the door, told her sharply, "There's a further conclusion that could be made."

"I don't see what," Kath replied. "If his body's not been found, he *must* be alive."

"I'm not arguing about whether he's alive, but he may have disappeared with the gold."

"You mean—you're trying to suggest—that my Dad took the gold?"

"It's a possibility. Half a million dollars is a big temptation for anybody. It seems certain that someone took it."

"Not my Dad. You don't know him."

"That's true," Allan Pinkerton said gently, "but he's bound to be suspected."

"Mr. Pinkerton, I want you to find my father for me. That means finding out the truth. I've come all this way to Washington to ask you. We—my husband and I—are willing to pay your full fee with expenses. Reasonable expenses. And if you find the gold, you can keep it."

"The gold belongs to the United States Government now."

"Then you can have the reward, if any." Kath sat forward, her bosom touching his desk. "Will you help me, Mr. Pinkerton?" The detective eyed her swelling breasts. "I appeal to you as a Scot, a fellow Briton—as someone who knows what it's like to be far from home."

Pinkerton felt cornered. This forceful young woman would never take no for an answer. It wasn't a very rewarding case, but it intrigued him. What *had* happened to this Stockport factory worker and the coffin full of gold?

"Very well, Mrs. Blake," he said, "I'll put one of my best western agents on the inquiry. He'll report directly to you at your husband's ranch in Kansas. But I must warn you that it may not necessarily be *good* news, Mrs. Blake."

"What do you mean, Mr. Pinkerton?"

"It's a long time since you last saw your father. You don't know what's happened to him—how he may have changed. . . ."

22

Kath was unusually quiet on the way back to Willard's Hotel. The sun was out, a pale, watery spring sun, and she wanted to walk. She remained silent for block after block. At last Paul said, "What's worrying you?"

Her eyes flashed indignantly. "What Mr. Pinkerton said. He doesn't even know my father."

"Detectives are suspicious of everybody. That's their job. You should feel pleased. He'll find your father if anyone can."

If anyone can . . . .

"Look," Paul said to distract her. Across F Street was a bay window with a large notice announcing: LATEST PARIS FASHIONS. "Let's take a look, Kath. You need a new wardrobe. You've worn your clothes long enough."

Her mood changed at the sight of the fine silk dresses in the window.

"Oh, Paul, they're so pretty."

"Go in and inspect them."

"Come in with me, *please*. Just for a minute."

With a resigned expression, Paul followed her into the store. A bell tinkled as the door opened and a small, portly man in a yellow suit came to greet them. He stared disapprovingly at their worn clothes.

"*Bonjour, Monsieur et Madame,*" he said cautiously.

"What did he say?" Kath whispered.

"I don't know," Paul told her awkwardly.

"Can I help you?" the man asked slowly in a foreign accent.

Kath hesitated. "I'd like to see some travelling clothes. The latest fashions." She gazed at his yellow suit. "This must be where Mr. Thomas gets his suits," she whispered to Paul with a giggle. She was excited. This was the first time she'd ever been in a high class women's shop—a shop for *ladies*. "Clothes must be very expensive in a shop like this. Can we afford it?"

"Oh, sure," Paul said. "It'll give me pleasure to buy you something."

"I'd love to wear some new clothes," Kath said, letting her red shawl fall back on her shoulders. "But I'm always going to keep this shawl to remind me of where I've come from."

The man in the yellow suit studied her long hair admiringly. It was as luxuriant now as it had ever been. "Ah, yes, let us try blue, the right shade of course for your hair. *Oui?*" He brought out several fine blue silk dresses and Kath wanted them all. She settled for the most expensive with a low neckline.

"You look ready for the opera!" Paul said. "But it won't be much good on the ranch."

"Oh, please, Paul, just one for Sunday best, for when we have a party."

"Très belle!" cried the man in the yellow suit when she came out of the changing room. He pranced round her, examining the dress and her in it from every angle, and then he had her walk up and down like a model. "That is the one for you, madam. It shows off your beauty perfectly." He wanted her to buy only low-cut dresses after that, but the other clothes she chose were all simple, useful, durable attire suitable for open-air ranch life out West. She also persuaded Paul to buy two fancy suitcases, one for each of them. Then she waited nervously while the man added up the bill. It came to $87. It seemed a huge sum to her, but Paul paid it without blinking.

The man in the yellow suit escorted them to the door. *"Au revoir,"* he told them, half bowing.

"Excuse me," Kath said to him. "But what does that mean?"

" 'Good-bye until we meet again,' " and he kissed her hand. He made her feel important. It was almost as good as the feeling the new clothes gave her.

"Oh, thank you," she told Paul outside, holding up the pretty packages. "I'm ready now for the West—whatever awaits me."

"Happiness awaits you," he said, smiling at her, enjoying her girlish enthusiasm, so different from her gloomy mood earlier.

They went back to Willard's Hotel to pay their bill. They were ready to leave Washington. And not a moment too soon, Kath told herself nervously as she inspected the crowded hotel, fearing that Frank might pop out from behind every pillar. There was no sign of Frank, but talking to a short bearded man in a straw hat was a familiar figure in a white suit—Horatio Thomas.

"Mr. Thomas! I was just talking about you. How wonderful to see you!" Kath meant every word of it. She had grown fond of the English journalist and missed his reassuring presence. "Meet my husband, Paul Blake. The Reverend married us."

"Congratulations to you both," said Horatio Thomas, doffing his wide-brimmed hat. "You're a very lucky man, Mr. Blake." Thomas turned to the bearded man with him. "What do you say, Brady? Give a professional appraisal."

The bearded man regarded Kath with narrowed eyes, like an artist studying a model. "Yes, Mr. Blake is a *very* lucky man."

Kath laughed. "This is my day for compliments."

"This is one worth having," Horatio Thomas said. "My friend here is Mr. Mathew Brady, the great American photographer, pioneering historian of the camera. Let me show you some of his work." Thomas opened a large envelope, "Look at these great Brady pictures of the Civil War—the dead and dying on the battlefields, the ruined woods, the wounded in the hospitals—Brady's caught it just as we saw it ourselves in Virginia."

He passed the photographs one by one to Kath. She was astonished by their stark beauty. She had missed it when she observed these scenes of death and destruction herself. It needed an artist's eye. She passed the photographs to Paul, but he only pretended to look at them. His memories of the war were still too painful; he wanted no reminders.

"Here's one of General Grant . . . and here's your masterpiece, Brady." It was of Abraham Lincoln looking much the way Kath remembered him.

"The President's son, Robert, liked that one," Mathew Brady said modestly.

"It's a wonderful portrait, Mr. Brady," Kath said, admiring the photograph at arms' length as Thomas had done. "Can we buy a print of it? I'd like to put it in a family picture album when we get to Kansas to remind me always of my meeting with President Lincoln."

"Accept it as a gift, Mrs. Blake, but in return I'd like you to pose for me." He gave Kath's face another close examination. "You have such an extraordinarily beautiful English-Irish bone structure that I'd like to add your portrait to my gallery."

Kath blushed. "I'm afraid we're leaving today, Mr. Brady, for Kansas."

"It needn't take long. My studio is quite near."

"Oh, please, Paul, can we?" Kath said, showing her husband respect in front of the other two men. "Mr. Brady could take our first picture together. The last time I had my picture taken, I was only ten years-old. I loved that picture so, it was the first time in my life I felt like Somebody. I gave it to my father to remember me by the day he left for America."

"My picture will also make you feel like Somebody," Mathew Brady said, gallantly tipping his straw hat.

"Come," Horatio Thomas told Kath, "you can't miss this opportunity. Brady will make you more than a Somebody—he'll make you *famous*. Posterity will want to know all about this beautiful Brady model—you! I'm sending the *Guardian* a few Bradys in the hope the editor can reproduce them to illustrate my stories. Ram's taken them with my Lincoln story personally to New York. I must beat the *Times* with the news of Lincoln's assassination."

Soon they were all in a coach rattling through the Washington streets to Mathew Brady's photographic studio.

"Any news of your father?" Thomas asked Kath.

"Only two bodies have been discovered. My Dad's missing. He's alive, I know—I hope still in Kansas. We've hired Pinkerton's National Detective Agency to find him. Wouldn't it be wonderful if we finally met again out there! You must come to visit us, Mr. Thomas."

Horatio Thomas patted her cheek. "I certainly will, Kath. The Wild West is next on my agenda."

The Brady studio was in the loft of an old mansion and was as untidy as Kath expected an artist's workroom to be. Mathew Brady replaced his jacket with a white smock, but left his straw hat on. He posed her and Paul on a platform against a simple black cotton cloth. Kath combed Paul's hair and tried to get him to relax and smile. Brady kept changing their position and then disappearing behind a big box camera on stilts to study how they looked.

"Don't be so formal. Relax! Thomas, please engage them in chitchat, keep them talking. Interview them." Brady disappeared again behind his camera.

"When the Reverend married you," Thomas said thoughtfully, "was Colonel Mosby there?"

"He was recovering from a wound. He hanged three other Union soldiers after we left, you know. I think the war's affected his mind."

"You may be right," Thomas said casually. "He's suspected of being involved in Lincoln's assassination."

This so surprised Kath that she forgot she was posing and sat forward. "He's been affected by the war, but not that much, Mr. Thomas. The Colonel's still a gentleman at heart."

Mathew Brady appeared from behind his camera.

"Life, animation, talking, yes, but not perpetual motion. You must sit *still,* Mrs. Blake, or you will spoil the picture. Your face will be nothing but a blur—what good is that? Even a Mathew Brady blur is still a blur."

"Sorry, Mr. Brady. It won't happen again." She went back to her original pose.

"Hold that! Your beauty responds to the camera like a flower to the sun. Don't move!" Brady disappeared again.

"Mr. Thomas," Kath said thoughtfully, careful not to move, "Do you think experience—extreme experience—a war, killing someone, struggling for existence in a strange country—can completely change a person's character?"

"There's no easy answer to that," Horatio Thomas replied

carefully. "We human beings are made up of inheritance, environment, and experience, Kath. I don't know if experience can radically change what we inherit. I expect Charles Darwin would say it can. Who are you thinking of—yourself, your father perhaps?"

"No," she said quickly, "I mean Colonel Mosby. He's too much of a gentleman to be an assassin. Could life—his experiences in the war—turn him into one?"

"You better ask him." But Thomas felt she had more in mind than just Mosby.

"Why don't *you* ask him, Mr. Thomas? You don't want to have a story without an ending for your newspaper. Do you know how to find him?"

"Do you?"

"Yes."

"Very still now!" Mathew Brady shouted from behind his camera.

Kath froze, with Paul standing like a statue on her right. They reminded Horatio Thomas of a picture he had once seen of the young Queen Victoria with her husband, the Prince Consort. They certainly made a handsome couple, with no sign on their smiling faces of all that they had been through. Even a Brady photograph could lie.

* * *

Horatio Thomas left Washington later that day. He crossed the Potomac River with help from the War Department and easily followed Kath's directions to the barbershop in Fairfax county.

When he produced his *Guardian* credentials, the barber said, "I heard about you from Bo and the Reverend. I'll close the shop and take you to the Colonel immediately."

The Virginia countryside had never appeared lovelier. It was as if nature realised the war was over. Green buds were already appearing in the ruined woods and wild birds were singing on the higher branches. Long grass and drooping leaves and thick undergrowth would soon cover the surface destruction of the war. Brady's pictures of the ruined woods would then become part of history, but it would take much longer for that to happen to the human victims of the war he had photographed.

Mosby was staying at a remote farmhouse near the village of Salem. As Horatio Thomas and the barber approached along a dirt road, two men on horseback came out of a wood, pistols in hand. The war wasn't over here yet. They recognised the barber and dropped their pistols back in their holsters.

The Colonel was still recovering from his wound, but he was much more active. He came out of the farmhouse to greet Thomas, pale but very alert.

"You heard about Lincoln's assassination, Colonel?" Horatio Thomas said, watching Mosby's face closely.

"I did, indeed," Mosby replied gravely.

"You know you're among the suspects?"

Mosby's face flushed angrily. "I thought it was a joke when I heard. But I should have known better. People like Stanton have no sense of humor. If they can't get us one way in open warfare, they try to get us this underhand way."

"They claim to have traced Lewis Paine, the man who attacked Seward, to the Mosby Rangers. Do you know him?"

Thomas expected Mosby to deny it, but the Colonel nodded. "Yes, I know him, but not under that name. His real name as far as I know is Louis Thornton Powell. He changed his name to Lewis Paine when he went to Washington."

"And he was one of your men?"

"No," Mosby snapped, "Louis Powell was never one of my men, Mr. Thomas. He wanted to join us, but we didn't want him. It was easy to see he was mentally unbalanced. The other men wouldn't ride with him. But that was some time ago. I haven't seen him since."

Louis Powell . . . Horatio Thomas had heard that name before. He thought back. He remembered the Washington journalist who had been captured on the train with the rest of them. Someone had helped the journalist to escape from Mosby's camp. Mosby had told him the man's name. "Wasn't it Louis Powell who helped that Washington journalist to escape, Colonel?"

"That's right, Mr. Thomas."

"I remember, Colonel, you said then that he was 'violent' and 'unreliable.' It doesn't seem as if Stanton has much of a case against you, but he's convinced you're the mastermind behind the assassination, the South's last stand."

"Stanton's a fool. He's even against parole for my men. Most of them want to go on fighting."

"You can't fight a war on your own, Colonel."

"We *could*. We've done pretty well so far without much help. But I believe the time's come to stop—"

"Dinner!" yelled a voice from the farmhouse.

The farmer had killed a hog. Everybody ate and drank well, but nobody seemed talkative; the dinner had the melancholy air of a last supper. Afterwards Thomas sat with Mosby on the porch, smoking a cigar. It was dark on the ground, but the sky was clear with a full moon.

Thomas said gently, "Lincoln told me he hoped you wouldn't prolong the war, Colonel."

Mosby gestured impatiently with his cigar. "I respected Abraham Lincoln as an individual. The man had many fine personal qualities, but our attitude towards the civil war, the war between the states, was very different. Abraham Lincoln represented the paradox of this new modern world—the all-powerful Federal government and the individual's yearning to be free. By refusing the South's request to leave the Union, he suppressed individual rights. His government was acting as much like a dictator as Napoleon Buonaparte. Yet at the same time—and here's where the paradox arises—Lincoln also condemned slavery and asserted the individual's right to be free."

"You could make the same argument about the South in reverse, Colonel," said Horatio Thomas. "The South upheld slavery and yet demanded the individual's right to break away from the Union."

"That's probably why we lost and why Abraham Lincoln was killed. We were both divided in our hearts. That confuses people."

Mosby brooded over his cigar. Only when it glowed brightly was his face visible. The darkness encouraged him to share his thoughts. He was also aware that in confiding in the English journalist, he was speaking for the record in case anything happened to silence him.

"If I don't continue fighting, Mr. Thomas," he said slowly,

"It won't be because I support General Lee's surrender or because I think our cause is hopeless. It'll be an individual decision. I notice in myself a big change that worries me. At the start of the war, Mr. Thomas, it was a sport, a game in defense of the Old South I'd grown up in. There were rules of conduct to observe. Nobody was killed if you could avoid it." The cigar glowed for a moment, showing his bright, haunted eyes. "But over the years, the rules relaxed. Killing became almost routine. I've noticed the changed attitude in myself. I want to try to retrace my steps, to find myself again—the self that was appalled by killing of any kind, whoever it was. Tomorrow morning in the little village of Salem, where we have gathered so many times before a raid, I'm going to disband my men."

"May I attend, Colonel?"

Mosby's cigar glowed so that Thomas could see him shake his head.

"This isn't for the world's eyes. Not even for the readers of the *Manchester Guardian.* It'll only take a few minutes. There'll be no ceremony. Just an offhand farewell in the best tradition of the Mosby Rangers. No southern grandiloquence. I just want to release my men to make their own decisions. I've made mine. The war is over for me. I don't want to deteriorate into Mosby the Outlaw with a price on my head, dead or alive. I'll ride away from Salem on my own to give myself up and, I hope, to be paroled."

"Don't count on it if Stanton's still running the government, Colonel."

"I count on nothing, Mr. Thomas, in times like these. But I'm happy with the decision I've made. Now, if you'll excuse me, I must circulate a little. . . ."

He walked stiffly across the grass, chatting casually with his men as he came to them in the darkness. The Colonel was talking individually to his Rangers for the last time. Tomorrow was the formal farewell, but this was the real good-bye—the real end of the war.

How right Kath had been about Mosby, thought Horatio Thomas as he watched the Colonel talking in the moonlight to the Reverend. She had insisted that Mosby had been changed by the war, but not out of character. She was right. Mosby had drawn back in time from the abyss. But perhaps Kath had also had her own father in mind, the extent to which he had been changed by the New World. It reminded Thomas of a passage in Charles Darwin's *The Origin of Species:* "When a plant or animal is placed in a new country amongst new competitors, though the climate may be exactly the same as in its former home, yet the conditions of its life will generally be changed in an essential manner. . . ."

Was this true of Kath's father?

The answer seemed to be out West.

23

"It's not the best time to travel west," warned the railway ticket clerk, a tall, solemn-faced man with greying sidewhiskers, when Kath and Paul arrived at the Washington depot with their two new suitcases. "The war disrupted all rail connections with that part of the country. Gangs of guerrillas blew up miles of track and stopped work on all the new railroads crossing the west. It'll take months to repair the damage and start things moving again." He studied maps and timetables and the latest communiques. "About the surest way is to get as far as St. Louis by way of Chicago, and then from St. Louis, you'll be safer going by stagecoach."

So that was the way they set off.

It took two trains and over a day to reach Chicago. They stayed overnight at a hotel near the depot and then, early in the morning, boarded another train for St. Louis. Kath felt the way she had when the steamship left Liverpool and crossed the immense Atlantic ocean. For the first time in her life, a journey by land had to be measured in time rather than miles. The thirty miles to Liverpool had seemed a great journey; thirty miles here was nothing, just a drop in the immense ocean of flat, barely inhabited land. A journey was so many days or even weeks long. The land stretched on and on, leaving cities behind, then towns and villages, and finally even lonely farmhouses became rare in the vast, open landscape stretching west-wards.

They were going west still unsure of their marriage (though Kath had been careful to make it legal in Washington, not trusting the Reverend's authority below the spiritual level). A night in Willard's Hotel and another in Chicago hadn't been enough to bring Paul out of his tense, defensive shell. She wondered how much of his trouble was physical now, how much the mental reaction. Nothing could bring back his missing glands, but his skin had healed well over the wound. He had little pain now, he was putting on weight, and his face was a much healthier color. Yet something had been destroyed in Paul's spirit, something in the way he saw himself as a man. His face in repose often looked so melancholy that she felt a rush of tenderness for him. She hoped he would recover this lost sense of his manhood in the calm, healthy surroundings of the ranch he'd grown up in; she'd do what she could for him.

As the train roared down through Illinois, Kath noticed a change not only in the landscape but in the air they breathed. There was a desert dryness that gave them both a sore throat and discouraged them from doing much talking. They gazed silently through the train window for hour after hour, mile after mile. But such isolation wasn't possible when they reached St. Louis and changed to the more intimate, confined travelling conditions of a stagecoach, where they were brought together much more closely with other people.

The stagecoach was like a giant rocking cradle, drawn by six strong, fast horses that were changed at regular stops about every twenty miles. It carried twenty-seven hundred pounds of mail and five passengers when it set off, though some of them got off and were replaced at stops in Missouri. They were people who had come originally from Europe, foreign to each other, but committed to the American belief in friendliness to strangers while travelling. They exchanged life stories, some-times in broken English, to pass the long days and nights, sharing intimate secrets like a family with people they would never see again. Many of them regarded Paul's short answers and unwillingness to gossip about himself as a sign of an un-American arrogance. It seemed to Kath that Americans would forgive any failing sooner than being stuck-up. She found herself making excuses for Paul and talking non-stop herself to compensate for his reticence.

Close to one dawn in the middle of a desert scene with hills like huge sculptures, the stagecoach gently rocking, Kath found herself sharing her worries about her father with a motherly older woman from Georgia, who had lost her home in the civil war and was going west to start again, all her belongings packed in a trunk on top of the stagecoach. It was a help to Kath to talk about where her father might be or what trouble he could be in with someone she'd never see again. The woman listened sympathetically and then told Kath, "Remember, fathers are human. Whatever you find out, bear that in mind, my dear. And whatever happens, you have to go on. You're beautiful, you'll never be in need. Men will always want you." The woman said that as if it solved everything. I could do with men not wanting me, Kath told herself, remembering Frank. But the woman with her plain, drained, grieving face was talking of herself more than Kath. She had lost her man in the war.

Antelopes and prairie dogs followed the stagecoach for miles. Kath saw elk, wolves, and bears watching them rattle by. Life was becoming more open, less safe; nature here made England seem as orderly as a well-kept garden. As they approached the Kansas border, herds of buffaloes could be seen in the far distance. With heads down and tails up, the magnificent, burly horned animals galloped over to inspect the stagecoach. There was a shot from above and one of the buffalos staggered, bleeding from the side.

Paul stuck his head out of the window. "Stop that shooting! They won't attack us!" But as he was shouting up at the driver, another blast came from above and the wounded buffalo went down and rolled over. The other buffalos gathered round the dead body. The driver shot again, wounding another, and then they began to run, stampeding back to where they had been peacefully grazing.

"The fool!" Paul said, slumping back in his seat. "That's bad luck. Every dumb gunman shoots at them—they're such a big target, you can't miss. They'll all soon be gone in the West."

The land slowly began to change. Trees, vegetation of all

kinds, thinned out into a desertlike plain, roasted by the sun. Everyone in the stagecoach developed a great thirst and water had to be rationed. The horses seemed to slacken with weariness. The stagecoach bumped over a long stretch of stony ground and then rolled smoothly again as the earth turned sandy.

At the last stop before the Kansas border, an extra armed guard joined them. Kath saw him, shotgun in hand, climb up to join the driver. The others saw him, too, but said nothing.

"Is he just coming for the ride?" Kath asked, suddenly concerned.

Nobody answered.

She stared at the faces opposite. "Do they expect trouble?"

A gray-haired man, a former store-owner in Montgomery, Alabama, told her reluctantly, "We're passing through Quantrill territory." Kath's face showed she didn't understand. "He's one of the worst of the border outlaws."

The man's wife added: "At the start of the war, Quantrill was a guerrilla behind Yankee lines in Missouri."

"Like Colonel Mosby in Virginia?" Kath asked.

"No, ma'am, Mosby's an honorable man," the former store-owner replied. "This Quantrill's a criminal. There's an insane streak in the man. He and his gang have killed, looted, and burned people's houses without caring who they were, friend or enemy—it's all the same to Quantrill. He once asked for a colonel's commission from the Confederacy. They turned him down flat. So he went over to the Yankee side, but they wouldn't have him. The Yankee commander told his men to shoot Quantrill on sight—or hang him. So Quantrill broke with both sides and now claims to fight under an outlaw's flag, loyal to nobody but himself. He's raided and plundered across the Missouri–Kansas border for years."

"You seem to know a lot about him," Kath said.

"He killed my cousin in Lawrence, a small town across the Kansas border. He and his men massacred altogether 142 people there. They shot my cousin in front of his wife and family. Quantrill's completely ruthless. That's why we've got two guards instead of one, ma'am. We're starting to cross his territory now. I hope to God we don't get stopped by him. The mail we're carrying will be an attraction." The man smiled grimly at Kath. "I bet you're sorry you asked, young lady."

"No, I like to know the reason for things," Kath told him. There was silence then; they were all alone with their fears. Two guards didn't seem like much protection against a whole gang in that wilderness.

Paul suddenly said, "You shouldn't talk that way in front of the ladies. It's upset them all."

"It was my fault," Kath said, "I asked."

"Even so," he insisted obstinately, "Men should keep some things to themselves."

Hostility flared up in their little group; faces scowled at Paul, who had taken no part in the earlier get-acquainted talk and now was laying down the law. Kath said quickly, "We don't want to talk him up—Quantrill, I mean. Speak of the Devil and he sometimes appears."

One of the other passengers was a youngish woman, heavily made-up, her clothes cheap and colorful. The men seemed afraid of talking to her, at least in front of the other women. She addressed her remarks to Kath, as if she felt Kath was the only one who didn't disapprove of her. She explained that she had a job as a singer in a saloon in Abilene, a small Kansas town. She laughed at the crudity of life out West compared to New Jersey where she'd grown up. "Some of those cowboys go crazy on a few drinks. They're like nothing but big, rough boys. Always wanting to fight or gamble or chase after one of us. Someone as pretty as you will have to fight 'em off."

"I'm safe," Kath said, smiling. "I'm married. This is my husband."

The woman gave Paul a quick glance and was clearly not impressed.

"Being married ain't no protection out west. There's a big shortage of women in those little cow towns. That's why we free travelling girls are important. Help 'em cool off before they explode and cause trouble for you married people."

"You'll be giving my wife a depressing view of the West before she gets there to see for herself," Paul said nervously.

"She ought to be prepared for what she'll find. It ain't England, honey."

"Virginia was different, too," Kath said. "The war affected everybody."

"It's a different kind of war out west."

"The war's over."

"Not out west. Those gunfighters know only one way to live. Fight for what's yours or somebody else's. There's no real law in a lot of places. Who shoots fastest—that's the law."

"That's not true," Paul said. "Most towns have a sheriff."

"When were you home last?"

"Two years ago."

"I think you'll find a great many changes. The good guys went to war, the bad guys stayed home. They took over."

An uneasy silence greeted this speech. The woman, seeing Paul's growing anger, gave up. Nobody else wanted to talk. There was great uneasiness as the stagecoach rattled deeper into Quantrill territory. Everyone felt very exposed. At night sleep was elusive in the cramped seats. It was cool in the darkness and they huddled closer together. Paul rested his head on Kath's shoulder. She couldn't tell whether he was asleep or not. She stared out at the stars so bright in the clear western sky. There was an unbelievably yellow full moon, and it made the pale desert scene look stark and lifeless as if suspended in space. Kath tried to sleep, but she was too tense; the closer she came to Kansas the tenser she felt, waiting for something to happen. She draped her old red shawl over her shoulders, partly for its warmth and partly to remind her of how far she had come.

As the sun rose across the desert, the trail cut through a valley between high sandstone hills. Walls on all sides dwarfed the stagecoach. It wasn't a safe place to get trapped in.

The former store-owner was gently snoring, and at first Kath assumed a faint explosion she heard came from him, merely a slightly louder snore. Then she heard a bump above like a body falling across the roof. There was a slithering sound as if somebody was tumbling off the stagecoach. The pace momentarily slowed and then, as the driver saw the danger they were in, the team of weary horses were whipped into a mad rush for the exit to the valley.

A gun cracked above them. It was one of the guards firing his rifle.

Everyone was awake in the stagecoach now. They sat forward, exchanging horrified glances, staring upwards and listening. Kath put a hand on Paul's. He was trembling. She wondered what memories the guns had brought back.

One of the windows shattered and a bullet lodged in the wall above the former store-owner. They all slid to the floor.

There were several gunshots and a heavy fall above them. The horses seemed to go out of control. The stagecoach's wheels rattled and bumped over rocks. The other window shattered, scattering glass over them on the floor.

Kath clutched Paul's hand, trying to give him some reassurance and strength. Somebody—a woman—was whimpering with fear. Everyone now had the same thought: Quantrill.

A back wheel loosened and the bumping and rattling increased. They were rocked into a mass of arms and legs on the floor, thrown this way and that. Suddenly the stagecoach began to slow down. Someone was in control of the horses again. There were a few more bumps over rocks and then the stagecoach screeched to a stop. They all lay winded and scared—waiting.

One of the doors was flung open.

"Get out!" a hard voice roared.

A heavy, numbing fear gripped them. They clambered off the floor of the stagecoach and slowly stepped to the ground, blinking nervously in the early morning sunlight. They faced a semi-circle of grim-faced gunmen on horseback, dressed in a mixture of rough cowboy clothes and old Confederate gray uniforms. Only one was dressed neatly, all in black, and he was obviously the leader. He stared at them with a strange, cold, secretive look from heavy-lidded eyes. From the scared expressions of the other passengers, Kath guessed this was Quantrill.

"Line up," this man snapped.

Two of the other outlaws began to throw the bags of mail and the trunks off the top of the stagecoach. The trunks fell heavily and split open. The driver was sprawled across his seat and looked dead. There was no sign of the two guards.

"Empty your pockets," snapped Quantrill, and two of the outlaws helped them do it. They stopped in front of the saloon singer. One of them put a hand on her bosom. The woman paled beneath her make-up, but stayed calm.

"Can we take her with us, Boss?" one of the men asked with a leer.

"You crazy? A woman'd slow us up."

They reached Kath.

"What about this one?"

"A redhead's poison," said Quantrill. He noticed Paul next to Kath. "What's troublin' you? Come here." Paul hesitated. Quantrill drew a pistol. "I said come here, fool."

Kath stepped forward.

"What do you want with us?"

"Can't he talk or is he yeller?"

"He's a war veteran—"

"Let him speak for himself. Hear me?" He shot at Paul's boots, making him jump. "Dance like a woman, that's it." His eyes were wild under his heavy lids.

Kath flushed, her anger rising.

"Leave him alone."

"You talkin' to me, bitch?" He sounded surprised. "What's this fool to you?"

"He's my husband."

Quantrill stared at her and then laughed evilly.

"That's what you call a marriage made in heaven."

A yell came from high above them on the rock face.

"Horsemen approach!"

Immediately Quantrill and the others lost interest in the stagecoach and its passengers.

"Who are they?"

Brief pause, then the voice above shouted: "Troops. Union troops. Looks like cavalry."

"Let's go," Quantrill shouted.

A desperate urge to prove himself seemed to overcome Paul and he grabbed Quantrill's reins. The outlaw clubbed him with his pistol and Paul went down, his face covered in blood. Kath screamed and ran to him. Quantrill hesitated, pistol in hand, pointing at Kath, a tall, defiant figure in a red shawl.

Kath stared back at him, daring him to shoot, thinking *Is this how it's all going to end?*, but then the voice above yelled,

"They're coming into the valley," and this broke Quantrill's concentration on her, and he must have decided time was running out for him. His horse reared up at his command and galloped away. Soon all the outlaws were hidden in a dust cloud down the valley.

Kath knelt and wiped away the blood from her husband's face. He was unconscious and twitching nervously. Even when he did something, she told herself, it was foolish; he might have been killed. But then she thought, *That's unfair, Kathleen Tracy. What he did was brave—more than anybody else did. Give him some credit. . . ..*

A line of horsemen entered the valley from the other end. As they thundered closer, the former store-owner from Alabama had a dazed expression. "They're all black," he said incredulously. He couldn't have been more surprised if rain had begun to fall on the dry, sun-baked valley.

"It's the Buffalo Soldiers," said the saloon singer.

"Who are they?" Kath asked, wondering if the newcomers were to be any more trusted in this wilderness than the outlaws.

"An all-black regiment in the Union Army," the woman replied, watching closely as the black faces under the blue caps became clearly visible.

"The women better get in the stagecoach," said the former store-owner. "Nigruhs ain't to be trusted around white women."

"Stay calm, little man," murmured the saloon singer. "They couldn't be no worse than Quantrill."

There were about twenty soldiers, all black. They stopped a short distance away and a young lieutenant came over to them. He touched his cap respectfully, smiling reassuringly at them.

"Lieutenant Washington Greene at your service. Was that Quantrill and his outlaw gang?"

"It certainly was, lieutenant," said the saloon singer, giving him a warm, professional smile.

He gave a quick order to his men, and about a dozen galloped after the outlaws.

"Haven't you men got a white officer?" asked the former store-owner.

The black lieutenant examined him politely. "Our captain's

been wounded. I'm in command." He smiled understandingly at the Alabamian. "Don't be alarmed, sir. We've only come to help you"—he glanced up at the dead driver—"though, I guess, we've arrived a little late to help him. Your guards were shot, too?" He told one of his men, "Check back on the trail that they're dead."

The lieutenant leaned over Paul, who was slowly recovering consciousness. "He all right, ma'am?"

"He was only knocked out, thank you, Lieutenant Greene," Kath told him gratefully.

"Give him a good rest, ma'am, on your lap." Lieutenant Greene took off his cap and mopped his brow. "We'll help you to complete your journey." He assigned a man to drive the stagecoach and left two more as guards. "*Bon voyage* to you all. Now I must catch up with my men—and with Quantrill. We keep gettin' close. We'll get him one day." And then he was gone, kicking up more dust, before anyone could speak.

They all helped to repack the trunks and replace them and the remaining bags of mail on top of the stagecoach, then they climbed back inside. A whip cracked above and the horses were off. Everybody relaxed except the former store-owner. He still seemed to be amazed at being rescued by black soldiers.

"He's lived with slavery all his life in Alabama," whispered the saloon singer to Kath. "He's not caught up with the changes that the war's brought."

Kath remembered the buffalo that the driver had shot. Paul had said it was bad luck and now the driver was dead. Being rescued by the Buffalo Soldiers had been good luck. Was there any connection between the soldiers and the animals? "Why are they called Buffalo Soldiers?"

"They've fought some of their greatest battles against the Indians," the saloon singer said softly. "The Indians respect a brave enemy. So they called the soldiers after the buffalo, an animal they consider sacred."

The former store-owner, who had overheard, leaned over. "I heard the Indians thought the nigruhs' kinky hair was like the buffalo's shaggy coat," he said sourly.

"You got it wrong," said the saloon singer, annoyed.

"Why do the Buffalo Soldiers hate Quantrill?" Kath asked.

The former store-owner's superior racial attitude reminded her of upper class people in England. They looked down on factory workers like her Dad as slaves.

The saloon singer whispered, snubbing the Alabamian, "The Buffalo Soldiers have a vendetta against Quantrill. He helped black slaves in Missouri escape to Kansas, then he rounded them up and sold them back to their masters in Missouri, making money both ways. Many of the slaves were killed. The Buffalo Soldiers want revenge."

"They certainly saved us," said Kath. "I was sure Quantrill was going to kill Paul."

"You risked your life, honey, speaking up like that. I thought he was going to shoot you."

"We could all have been shot—or raped," said the former store-owner's wife. She sounded almost disappointed.

The saloon singer laughed. "They wanted your money, honey. Rape wasn't on their minds."

Paul groaned and half sat up, holding his head. Kath squeezed his hand. "You'll soon be home now," she told him.

* * *

Welcome to Alpine!

The faded, hand-painted sign by the roadside made Paul laugh out loud with the pleasure of homecoming.

"Look, Kath," he cried, his face to the window.

Kath caught a glimpse of a dirt road and a row of wooden shacks, and her heart missed a beat. Was this *all?*

The horses slowed to a dusty stop, the stagecoach rattling and rocking on worn springs.

"If you ever get to Abilene, honey," said the saloon singer, "Ask for Galina at the Diamond Saloon."

"The same likewise if you ever make Bitter Creek," the former store-owner told Kath. "We'll be at the Roxy Hotel— Mr. and Mrs. Herbert J. Wallace, Junior. You'll always be welcome."

Kath gave them both the ranch's address.

One of the Buffalo Soldiers lifted down their suitcases.

"Thanks for looking after us," Kath told him, and she waved to the other soldier above in the driver's seat. They were both very young, but tall and sturdy, their white teeth flashing in their black faces as they urged the horses into action once more.

Kath was sorry to see the stagecoach leave. After days of being enclosed with the others, she and Paul were suddenly left alone on a dirt road with a few shacks. Beyond was the prairie, an ocean of land with a vast, cloudless sky, and not a mountain or tree in sight. They were two lonely figures in a great expanse of nothingness. She had never felt so far away from England, her England where nature was tamed and factory chimneys filled the sky with smoke. Yet this was home to Paul—Alpine, a little frontier town with no frills. There was one main street, a few plain shacks in different bright colors, a few stores, a church, a school, and a saloon. It reminded Kath of the little towns in Virginia except that this was cruder and far more lonely. Yet to Paul, as a boy, it had been as exciting as the town of Stockport had been to her.

He stood staring now at the familiar sights, noting the differences since he'd been there last, and he seemed different himself, warmer and more sure of himself now he was back among the people and places he knew.

"There's the saloon," he told her, pointing to a pair of black-and-white swing doors that badly needed another coat of paint. "I used to wait outside there for my Pa."

"Like I used to wait outside the beer-house in Stockport for my Dad."

"I bet you didn't have gunfights in the beer-house."

"I remember one fist fight between two of the men from the factory."

"People have been killed in that saloon, over gambling or women. Let me introduce you to my pal, Hal, the blacksmith. I used to watch him shoeing horses when I was a kid."

He walked her over the dirt and sparse grass to a fenced-off yard near the saloon. Several horses were waiting. A big, muscular man, his shirt sleeves rolled up, was examining a horseshoe on a black mare's back foot. He stared curiously at Kath and Paul, but especially at her. It was plain he didn't know Paul.

"Where's Hal?" Paul asked eagerly.

The man put the horse's foot down.

"You new in town?"

"Just got back from the war."

The man examined Paul again as if to find out which side he fought on.

"Hal's dead."

Paul's face paled.

"How'd he die?"

"Shot." The blacksmith spat out some tobacco juice. "An argument in the saloon."

"Who with?"

"A guy from the Western Cattle Expansion Company."

"Never heard of them."

"They're new in these parts since the war, but they're mighty powerful now."

"What was the argument about? Hal was a peaceful guy."

The blacksmith hesitated. "Can't rightly say."

"Dr. Bennett will know. Come, Kath, I'll introduce you to the doctor—"

"Dr. Bennett's retired," said the blacksmith. "Went back to California."

"There must be somebody I know that's still here."

"The war's changed the town a lot."

"How about Mr. Harrison, the teacher?"

The blacksmith shook his head. "You'll find him in the graveyard, too. Someone shot him through the schoolhouse window. Never did find out who. He was a man that liked to speak his mind. Some people don't care for that."

Paul's enthusiasm for being home died. He said quietly to Kath, "No reason for staying any longer in town. We better get out to the ranch."

"You from these parts?" asked the blacksmith.

"Yeah, the Silver Star Ranch."

The blacksmith frowned. "I heard they had some kind of trouble there, too."

"At the Silver Star?" Paul blinked nervously. "What kind of trouble?"

"I can't rightly tell you, mister. It's best to keep your mouth shut and your eyes, too, in this town since the war come."

Paul said anxiously, "We better get out to the ranch as fast as possible, Kath." He asked the blacksmith, "Can we buy two horses from you?"

"You can take your pick from them horses over there."

Paul walked round and round the waiting horses and finally selected two mares that seemed to be well trained and gentle. They were black and sorrel. Kath chose the sorrel and walked the mare up and down the yard, patting and talking to it until she felt she knew the horse well enough to ride it. She wasn't experienced enough yet to trust a strange horse, and there was a long ride ahead. Before they left, Paul bought enough food and water for a day's journey from a little general store. The store-owner he had known had also retired and left town. He asked the new store-owner, a thin, taciturn man from Kentucky, if he had heard about any trouble at the Silver Star Ranch. The store-owner shook his head. This seemed to relieve Paul, but Kath sensed the man knew something, his eyes were so evasive as he talked.

"People don't come in to gossip like they used to."

"Alpine's certainly changed a lot since I was here last," Paul said.

"Yeah," replied the store-owner, his eyes watchful. "It used to be real different. People had their own homes. So many folk have sold up and moved on. Now most of the town's owned by one company."

"What company's that?"

The storeowner hesitated; he'd said too much.

"The Western Cattle Expansion Company."

* * *

They left just after dawn so they could reach the Silver Star Ranch before dark. They rode along a rough trail out of the town. The dirt had been flattened by horses' hooves and carriage wheels. But this soon led into grassland that covered the trail, and then this changed to more desert, flat, sun-baked land stretching never-endingly to the horizon.

They were completely alone except for a few birds wheeling overhead like vultures.

The immensity of the landscape made Kath feel dwarfed, a midget under the huge clear blue sky. Her self-confidence faltered. Had she come too far from home, like a swimmer out of her depths? But she suppressed these fears. She had travelled all this way with a purpose. Her life had *not* been saved for nothing. She was being tested again.

"What happens if we get lost?" she asked nervously, eyeing the birds circling above.

"Don't worry, Kath. I know the route from here backwards. I rode into Alpine every Saturday when I was a boy." He was silent while his horse stepped carefully between high rocks and then he said casually, "Alpine really has changed. It's no longer the place I knew. . . ."

Kath could tell he was seeking reassurance. She had to keep his spirits high. He mustn't falter now they were so close. She said lightly, "Several years is a long time to be away. I haven't been away from Stockport nearly as long, but if I went back now, I'd see a lot of changes." She felt a surge of homesickness. This open prairie landscape was so alien to her. She said quickly, as much in need of reassurance as he was, "I'm looking forward very much to meeting your parents."

"You'll like them both, Kath," he said enthusiastically, trying to forget the changes in the town. "Pa's a quiet kind of guy like me, but Mom talks all the time to make up for him—and for me, too, when I'm home. Then there's Aunt Martha, who keeps us all in order like an army sergeant. But you'll like her. She's a real pioneering type of person." He tried to shed the bad effects of the town; he was ready for a happy reunion with his family and for introducing them to his young wife. "Just hold on tight and follow close behind me. I want to get home fast. I just hope that blacksmith's wrong about trouble. . . ."

The prairie sun baked them and their water supply dwindled. Talking became too much of an effort with dry throats and they rode on mile after mile in silence. Paul maintained a fast pace; she could tell how worried he was by the way he drove the horse in the heat. She soon had a feeling of foreboding herself, caught from him or the town. Alpine had been strange, its atmosphere all wrong, as if preparing them.

They passed a rock marked with a big silver star.

"Home—the ranch—begins here," he murmured huskily.

"It always gives me a thrill to see that silver star and know from here on it's ours, all ours."

They rode on more happily, with less urgency. Kath began to lose her bad feeling. There was no sign of trouble. Just land, endless land. It was far bigger than the grounds of Heaton Hall, as big as the royal estates in the south of England she had read about. And it was theirs, all theirs. She wanted to stop and rub her hand in the red earth.

They went on for miles before they glimpsed fences and then a ranch-house in the far distance.

Paul, his face puzzled, stared round in all directions. Land, land, nothing but land. He was looking for something that was no longer there.

At last he said, "Where's all the cattle? When I left for the war, there were thousands of cattle spread right across the whole landscape. You could hardly see the earth for cows. Now I can't see any. Pa can't have sold 'em all. Where's all our cattle gone?"

It was the first sign of trouble—a marked change as in the town. Many of the fences were broken or even torn up as if by a stampede. Paul noted them and rode on more quickly. Kath watched his face, pale and frowning. If there was any trouble, he wasn't in any shape to handle it. She'd have to cope. Yet the feeling that all wasn't well didn't spoil her pleasure at the first close-up view of the ranch. That all this land was theirs was still unbelievable, beyond her dreams. It didn't matter if her Dad hadn't made it in America; she had. They could be happy here.

Paul suddenly began to gallop towards the ranch-house as if he'd seen something that alarmed him.

The ranch-house was even bigger than Heaton Hall—big enough for a castle. It was built in oak to last forever. There were two floors in the main section and three floors in adjoining wings. But there was no sign of life. No one came out to greet them. There was no one at work in the corrals. And no horses.

Kath began to notice the signs of destruction that Paul had already seen—the broken fences, the burned barn, the smashed windows. It reminded her of the war—the ruined woods in Virginia, the sense of desolation.

Paul left his horse and ran for the main door. Kath followed him. She heard his feet clump on an oak floor.

"Anyone home?" Paul shouted.

His voice echoed.

No reply.

The signs of destruction were in the house, too. Furniture smashed, family portraits torn down from the walls, mirrors shattered.

Paul stared round in horror.

"My God, what's happened?"

This had been his *home*.

"Whoever you are, mister, put up your hands and do it quick."

The voice came from the stairs and the barrel of a shotgun pointed down at them over the bannisters. The hoarse voice could have belonged to a man or a woman.

"I said put up your hands, mister. Next time I'm shootin'."

Paul slowly put up his hands.

"Aunt Martha, it's me—Paul."

The shotgun wavered.

"You ain't Paul."

He stepped nearer so her old eyes could see him better.

"No closer, mister."

"Look at me. I lost weight in the war. I was wounded bad, Aunt Martha."

An old woman's lined, tanned face showed over the bannisters.

"Don't move a lick till I get a good look at you."

The shotgun relaxed, but never shifted its aim. A grizzled, tough old woman in worn dungarees and cowboy boots stood up. She peered at Paul. Then she slowly smiled.

"Yeah, I guess you're Paulie all right, though you look mighty different from my boy who went off to war." She lowered the shotgun. "Come and give me a hug."

Paul ran to her. She put down the shotgun carefully and wrapped her arms round him.

"You're so little, Paulie. That war done you no good. This ain't our family's lucky time."

He broke away from her hug. "Aunt Martha, tell me . . . what's happened?"

She didn't answer.

"Where is everybody? Where's Ma and Pa? Where's all the cattle?"

"All . . . gone, Paul." She sat down on the stairs, drawing him down to sit beside her. "It's bad, Paul. I wish to God I didn't have to tell you. Your Pa and Ma—" Her hoarse voice broke and she couldn't continue.

"Pa and Ma—what's happened to them?" His voice rose emotionally. "Why aren't they here?" He shook the old woman. "Martha, answer me. What's happened to Ma and Pa?"

"Paulie. . . ." The old woman clenched her false teeth. "They're . . . both of 'em . . . both . . . *dead*. Paulie, it's true! They were both . . . *shot*. They died. . . ."

He put his hands to his face and his shoulders shook. Kath put an arm round him, feeling his sobs shaking his thin body. He broke away from her and walked blindly out of the ranch-house. Kath began to follow him. The old woman stopped her.

"Leave him alone," she said harshly. "He needs to be on his own for a little time. The land, the ranch—they will bring back memories, and the past will help him to accept what has happened. We can't help him. A man likes to weep alone."

"He was so looking forward to being home, to seeing you all again after so long," Kath said, standing in the doorway and watching Paul walk so slowly over the grass, his head down, his shoulders shaking.

"Who are you?" the woman asked. "A friend of Paulie's?"

"I'm his wife. We were married in Virginia."

The old woman smiled. "I'm glad. He won't be alone." She noted Kath's determined chin and proud bearing. "You can give him strength." She stroked Kath's luxuriant red hair falling over the red shawl. "You have such beautiful hair. Red is for fire. You have much fire in you. You'll be good for Paulie in these hard times. What's your name?"

"Kathleen. Most people call me Kath."

"I'm Aunt Martha Tyler Blake. I make up my mind about people when I first see 'em, the way you have to decide about cattle or horses. You, Kath, I like. Paulie chose well. He was always a shy boy, and I can see the war ain't done him no good. You'll be able to give him some of your strength."

"Who shot his parents, Aunt Martha?"

"Forces out there, Kath. Strangers who want the Silver Star." The old woman suddenly looked her age and very weary. "Some people come wantin' to buy the ranch. Paulie's Pa turned 'em down. Then a gang of rustlers come, killed Hank Turner and some of the other ranch-hands, and drove away all the cattle. Then those people come back and made another offer for the ranch. Paulie's Pa again told 'em nuthin' doin', he wouldn't be pushed off his land. He was expectin' Paulie back from the war. He was keepin' the ranch for him. So next day more rustlers come. They shot Paulie's Pa before he could even defend hisself. Then Paulie's Ma run to him and they shot her, too. I hid in the fields until they left. They smashed up the house like you see and took the bodies of Paulie's Ma and Pa away with 'em, so there's no proof they've been killed."

"But the police—"

"We ain't got no Law, Kath. Sheriff Watson was shot down in the main street in Alpine by persons unknown and the man goin' round with his badge on now is a sheriff in name only. He's somebody's dummy, the somebody that runs the town. There's no Law in these parts any more. It's not like before the war come. The man with the fastest gun is the Law and that's the truth. These folks that come to buy the Silver Star had an army of gunmen with 'em. They was their own Law."

"Who are they? Why do they want the ranch so bad?"

"They said they come from some company."

Kath tensed.

"What's the company's name?"

"A long name—somethin' like the Cattle Expansion Company, I think."

"The same company that's bought up most of the town," Kath said thoughtfully. "Why do they also want the ranch?"

"That company's the Law here now. You and Paulie better stay in Alpine until all this is over." The old woman picked up her shot-gun. "I'm too old to move, but you and Paulie have a lot of life to live yet, Kath. You better not stay here. It ain't safe. They'll be back."

"This is Paul's home, Aunt Martha, and now it's mine. We can't give it up."

"Enough people have been killed, Kath. I don't want to see you and Paulie hurt. Look, you must be hungry. I'll cook you both somethin'. You go out and see how he's doin'."

Paul was standing near the burnt barn. Two walls were still intact, though charred and blackened.

"We used to picnic here when I was a kid." Tears were rolling down his face. "Who could have done it . . . killed Ma and Pa?"

Kath held his hands and looked into his reddened eyes.

"Are you ready to hear about it?"

He brushed his tears away and made an effort at self-control. "Tell me who did it."

Kath repeated what Aunt Martha had told her. Paul listened with increasing bewilderment.

"It's like the war all over again. And Aunt Martha thinks these rustlers and this Western Cattle Expansion Company are connected?"

"They must be."

"But why did they kill Ma and Pa?" A sob burst from him and he put his hands to his face. His shoulders shook.

"Paul. . . ." Kath gripped his hand tightly, imagining the strength flowing from her to him. "I'm with you, Paul. We're together."

He nodded, trying to smile. "Maybe we should sell and move somewhere else, Kath, somewhere we can be happy with no killin'."

"No, Paul, we must stay here. You can't be driven out of your own home. Don't you see if you give up here, it's like you fought the war for nothing? It'll be like your parents died in vain. Your Pa refused to run. He wanted you to have the ranch. It's yours. You've got to fight for it. The people who killed your mother and father must be punished, Paul."

"Kath," he said slowly, "This isn't England. It's not even the East—or Washington. You heard what Aunt Martha said. Whoever has the most guns is the Law, they can get what they want."

"You told me the West was the real America, Paul, that this is where you want to live. Well, fight for it. Don't give it up so easily." She struggled to stiffen his will to fight. "You can't run away or you'll never have anything of your own."

"You don't know what it's like here, Kath. You're not facing up to the facts. We're outnumbered. There are too many for us."

"I can shoot. So can you. Aunt Martha's got her shotgun—"

"Three of us against a gang of rustlers that's backed by a big, powerful company. Three of us against an army. You should know from the war what that's like. They'll mow us down the way Grant's army mowed our troops down in front of Richmond."

Kath stared across the land at the immense open horizon, so full of hope and promise for the future. It was almost sunset time. The yellow and blue sky was already streaked with crimson. The ranch-house in the dusk looked even more isolated, more vulnerable and hard to defend. Paul was right. The three of them couldn't hold the ranch on their own. They needed help. But where was help to come from? What people did she know who could deal with these gunmen?

She thought of Bo.

She remembered the young Texan's rescue of the Union soldiers—alone against all the Mosby men—and how he drew with lightning speed against Frank . . . Yes, Bo could outshoot these gunmen, but would he come?

Horatio Thomas. The English journalist had shot the sailor on the Atlantic steamship to save her. He was a strong, capable man. His newspaper connections might also scare the Western Cattle Expansion Company. But, even if she could get a message to him, would he come?

Bo, Horatio Thomas . . . who else?

The Reverend. For all of his drinking, he was a warrior, scared of nothing. Hadn't he offered to help her if she ever needed him? Well, she needed him now. But would he come so far?

And Frank Butler. He would certainly come. He would probably like to get his hands on her and Paul, and she'd be willing to risk it. He was a good shot and they needed all the guns they could get. But she had no idea where Frank was.

She kissed Paul on the cheek reassuringly.

"Don't worry. I'll try to get us some help. We must go into town to the telegraph office. I'll ask some of my friends to come. You've met Mr. Thomas and the Reverend. There's also a Texan cowboy I met—"

"Kath, you can't expect people to come all this way and risk their lives. You're fooling yourself."

Kath hesitated. Was Paul right? If they had been people in Stockport going to a job at the factory each day, she might have agreed. But Bo, Horatio Thomas, the Reverend . . . they were different from any people she had ever known. She told herself, *They also like me . . . more than like me . . . have a real feeling for me . . .* But would that be enough to bring them?

Perhaps she *was* asking too much.

It was one chance in a million, but she had to take it. She had no choice.

Dear God, let them care enough to come.

24

Kath and Paul left soon after daybreak. The ranch was very cool and pretty at that hour, but they hadn't ridden many miles before the sun was burning down on them, and Kath had to shade her face with her shawl. They passed only one other rider all the way into town. You could die out here and nobody would know about it, Kath thought uneasily. But she didn't say anything to Paul. He was withdrawn and nervous enough already.

As they came down the dusty main street, the town was very quiet except for the noise from the saloon. Only two men, both unknown to Paul, were to be seen outside the general store. They watched Kath and Paul go into the telegraph office. A young clerk took Kath's messages, and she waited while he sent them out. She was taking no chances in this town.

Next stop was the sheriff's office. They found the sheriff playing cards with a deputy. He was a hard-eyed, plump little man named Baxter, who wore his guns too high as if he never expected to use them. Paul asked for his help. Sheriff Baxter was immediately hostile.

"You suggestin' these rustlers were hired by the Western Cattle Expansion Company, Mr. Blake? That's a pretty big accusation, ain't it? The Company's important to this town. It has a fine, upstanding reputation."

"They come one day wanting to buy our ranch, my Pa turns

them down, and then the rustlers come. All I'm saying, Sheriff," Paul said hesitantly, "is that—"

"Exactly what are you sayin', Mr. Blake?" the sheriff said aggressively.

Kath moved forward. "We're saying his parents have been killed and his cattle's been stolen, Sheriff Baxter."

The hard eyes examined Kath. "You're a stranger to these parts, young lady, ain't you? Maybe you ain't aware of how we do things out here in Kansas. We don't make serious accusations against established citizens or institutions in our community without the evidence to back 'em up. If your parents have been killed, Mr. Blake, where's the proof—the bodies?"

"They took the bodies."

"So it's just hearsay, ain't that what you're tellin' me? You also claim your cattle's gone. Is that hearsay, too? Where's the proof of any rustlers? Have you any more evidence than the word of an old woman who's three-parts senile?"

Paul began to back down. Kath became furious. They didn't get anywhere. Sheriff Baxter wasn't willing to do anything for them.

"He's a company man," Kath said angrily as they hurried back to the horses.

They left Alpine immediately. They wanted to reach the ranch before sundown. They knew now for sure that Aunt Martha was right. They were on their own—until help arrived. Kath hoped the telegraph operator could be trusted more than the sheriff.

* * *

A big collection of Colts, shotguns, and rifles was laid out on a table in the vast ranch-house kitchen. The well-oiled weapons were as shiny as kitchen cutlery. Aunt Martha fondled them proudly as she showed them to Kath one by one.

"This was Paulie's Pa's . . . This was Paulie's first gun . . . Take any you like, Kath."

Kath carefully tested each gun. Some didn't shoot straight, but swung a little; you had to make allowances. She finally chose two Colts and went outside to practice with the strange guns in the clear prairie air. You had to learn a gun the same way you had to learn a horse. But it was easier to be accurate in this clear air than in the polluted, smoky air of Stockport. She was still awed by the sense of endless space. The flat land stretched on and on like England must have been hundreds of years ago. She used a handkerchief on a broken fence as a target. Each shot hit the handkerchief and the fifth knocked it off the fence; the sixth pierced it before it reached the ground.

Paul watched her in amazement. He didn't know the Colt needed much less skill than her old poaching gun.

"Where'd you learn to shoot so good?" he asked her, examining the holes in the handkerchief.

"My Dad taught me in England," she said proudly. She wished her Dad was with them now. He'd know what to do. The old woman wouldn't be much help. She sat rocking on the back porch, content to let them take over. She'd endured enough.

Kath worked hard clearing up the mess in the house. She wanted to make a home of it again. She took out Mathew Brady's photograph of her and Paul from her suitcase. Aunt Martha was delighted with it. But when Kath showed her the portrait of Abraham Lincoln and wanted to hang it on one of the downstairs walls, the old woman protested. "I don't want that man in the house."

"President Lincoln was a good man," Kath protested. "He was very kind to me."

"Jefferson Davis was my President," the old woman snapped. "You're English, Kath. You don't understand about the war."

It was no good arguing. Kath put the Lincoln portrait back in her suitcase. She'd get her way later. She also showed the old woman her blue dress she'd bought in Washington. Aunt Martha loved it. She hadn't seen the new fashions before.

"My, what a low neckline! Is it legal, Kath? The men ain't goin' to take their eyes off you when you wear that dress. Let's pray there's good times on the way so you can wear it at a party and show off!"

The old woman insisted on doing the cooking still. Her meals were simple and monotonous. Beans with everything. Kath waited to buy other vegetables until she had another reason for the long ride into Alpine. So they were stuck with the dull diet. There were sacks of beans in the kitchen, enough to last for months.

They soon had their first visitor. A carriage with a plain top to keep off the blazing sun rattled up to the ranch-house. They retired behind the shutters until they identified who had arrived.

"Anybody home?"

It was a youngish, friendly looking man with a small, neat brown mustache. He had no guns that were visible.

Kath stepped outside, her hands on her hips, a Colt stuck in her belt.

"Mrs. Blake?"

"That's right. Who are you?"

"Charles Fogarty from the Pinkerton Agency. Mr. Pinkerton asked me to report directly to you."

"Oh, come in, come in," Kath said eagerly. "Will you have some food with us?"

"My horse would like a drink."

Kath couldn't hold back any longer. "Have you found my father for me?"

The Pinkerton man shook his head. "Not yet, Mrs. Blake. We've carried out a thorough investigation. Two bodies were found outside the town of Way Cross a few hundred miles from here. They were identified as Confederate Secret Service Agents. This, I think, you already know—"

"Yes, but what happened to my Dad?"

"A third man known as Joseph Tracy was traced as far as a little place called Abilene—"

"He's alive?"

"A man answering his description was positively identified by a rancher who sold him a horse. He had two fingers missing from his left hand."

"That's my Dad!"

"He hasn't been seen since, Mrs. Blake. We checked the whole Abilene area—there's a great deal of new development going on there. People are being attracted to Abilene like bears to honey. But no one I talked with had seen any man like your father's description. That's about as far as we can go, ma'am. The expenses are becoming excessive. Mr. Pinkerton regrets you haven't got more for your money, but he wanted me to report personally to you before he bills you."

"Thank you, Mr. Fogarty, for what you've done. But that can't be the end of it, not now we're so close. I don't want you to stop until you've found him for me. Isn't that right, Paul?"

"That's right," Paul assured the detective. "It's my wedding gift to my wife. Please search for her father, Joseph Tracy, until you know where he is, however long it takes and however much it costs."

"There's something else you can help us with," Kath said quickly. "Have you heard of the Western Cattle Expansion Company?"

"Yes, indeed, ma'am, that company's pretty well known in this part of Kansas. It's bought an interest in Abilene. It's behind some pretty big land deals there."

"We think they're behind the killing of my husband's parents and some of the ranch-hands." Kath explained what had happened. "We believe they're trying to force us out."

"I heard some rumors about the company's methods," the detective said slowly. "Towards the end of the war, while everybody was still busy fighting, they grabbed land and cattle throughout the state!"

"They're still doing it. They'll be coming back here any time. Will you wait with us to receive them?"

"I'd like to, Mrs. Blake, but this isn't my only case. I can help you best in Abilene. Maybe I can stop them coming back—"

"Be very careful, Mr. Fogarty," Kath said. "These are very dangerous people." He was unarmed as far as she could see.

"Don't worry about me, ma'am." The detective grinned. "We're trained at Pinkerton's to look after ourselves in any situation."

* * *

The news that the Pinkerton detective had brought made Kath feel much more cheerful. She was close to her father now. They were in the same American state. She could feel his nearness. She had wanted to set off for Abilene herself—she'd find him if he was there—but she couldn't leave the ranch, not yet.

The days dragged by. They all kept close to the ranch-house, waiting for another visit from their unknown enemies.

It soon came—with no more warning than puffs of dust on the horizon.

The old woman sat with her shotgun behind heavy shutters on the first floor at the front. Kath was doubtful the old woman could see well enough to shoot far with accuracy. And as for Paul, his hand shook too much as he stood on the front porch beside her. They both wore gunbelts with two Colts. Kath caressed the butts for comfort as she watched about a dozen horsemen approaching. If there was trouble, this would be the first time she'd ever shot at a person. She wondered if it was much harder than shooting at a hare or a pheasant. But then, she told herself, I've already killed a man. A knife isn't that much different from a gun; shooting someone is more remote so it should be easier. Her morale was high, but not Paul's; his hand was shaking too much to press a trigger.

"They won't attack us," she told him reassuringly. "They've just come to repeat their offer to you. They'll have learned in Alpine that you're home."

"And when we refuse, what are they going to do?"

"We've got to stall them, Paul. We've got to buy some time until my friends arrive. Sweet-talk them. Lie."

The prospect made Paul even more nervous. His hand shook violently as the horsemen approached the ranch-house and spread out. In the lead was a bearded man in a gray suit and big leather cowboy boots. His wide, toothy smile was intended to be friendly, and he raised his tall gray hat when he looked at Kath. His eyes widened when he saw her guns, slung low down at a professional angle. Kath guessed he was a lawyer. The other men were different—cruder, paid gunmen. They formed in a half circle behind him but all within pistol range of the porch.

"Good day to you both," said the gray-suited man. The shutters hid the old woman, whose shotgun was pointing down at him. "I'm Howard Wright, Attorney-at-Law, representing the Western Cattle Expansion Company. And whom do I have the pleasure of addressing?"

Paul, in a low, uncertain voice, introduced himself and Kath.

"Glad to meet you at last, Mr. Blake. I was told you were away fighting for the Confederacy." It was impossible to guess from the lawyer's voice which side he'd been on in the civil war. "You'll know that the Company I've the honor to represent has made a handsome offer for this ranch, the Silver Star—the property, land, everything." He stared round pointedly at the damage. "My, the ranch doesn't appear to be in as good condition as when the Company first made its offer. There's been a marked depreciation." He smiled comfortingly. "I'm sure, however, that that won't cause any reduction in the very generous offer. But I must tell you, Mr. Blake"—and here his voice hardened—"this is the last time the offer will be made. Now I await your answer. My principals have no more time to waste. Do you accept their offer or not?"

Paul was silent, unsure how to reply. Kath said quickly, "Can you tell us why the Company wants the ranch so badly?"

The lawyer touched his hat politely. "I'm sure the answer's obvious, young lady. This here's a fine ranch—or it was." He turned back to Paul and said briskly, "Now, Mr. Blake, what d' you say? What's your answer?"

Paul glanced back at Kath for help.

"We've only just arrived, Mr. Wright," Kath said firmly. "We are interested in what we've heard, but we'd like . . . a little more . . . time. We want to talk it over with . . . with a lawyer of our own in town. We haven't been back long enough to do that. There has been a family tragedy. I'm sure you know about it." She stared hard at the bearded lawyer. He didn't give anything away; his expression remained hard and businesslike. "You know my husband's parents have been killed, Mr. Wright?"

He still didn't respond; it was impossible to read his reaction.

"My husband has to go through the family papers. We need a little more time."

He didn't like it—or her defiant attitude.

"My clients are getting impatient," he said curtly.

"We want to do it right. I'm sure you understand that, Mr. Wright." Kath's confidence grew as she talked. "We have to check the deeds to the ranch and the cattle are in order. You probably know the cattle's been stolen. . . ."

She waited for him to answer; he kept silent, hard-eyed as ever.

"It'll take some weeks to go through all the papers, Mr. Wright. My husband's parents' last will and testament . . . Isn't that so, Paul? It'll take some time."

"Yes," Paul mumbled, "Weeks."

The lawyer glanced back at the gunmen, lounging on their horses like vultures. It was a clear warning.

"My clients want this land," he said bleakly. "They like the . . . location. But their patience is running out. They can't wait forever." Suddenly his mood changed. He smiled, showing gold teeth that flashed in the hot sun. Kath was reminded of a picture of a snake's eyes, shining but without feeling, she had once seen in a schoolbook. "But we appreciate you young people have just arrived back from the war and need time. Very well, to show our generosity, we'll come for your answer on the first day of next month. But that'll be your last chance."

He tipped his hat and spurred his horse into action, followed by the gunmen.

Kath sighed with relief. The start of next month. It was longer than she'd hoped for—surely long enough for help to arrive. They must be on their way now, she thought. They *must.* . . .

25

Kath's message to Bo went to Fort Worth care of his father in the Texas Rangers—that was the address the young Texan had given her. But Bo wasn't there when the message arrived. He was away in Mexico.

In the months since he'd parted with Kath outside Richmond, Bo had never stopped travelling for long. He had returned slowly across the states to Texas, earning food money as a stagecoach guard. His plan was to settle in Fort Worth and spend some time with his father until he became restless again. But when at last he reached Fort Worth, his father wasn't away with the Texas Rangers as he'd expected, but was in a local hospital recovering from a serious bullet wound that had left an entry hole in his back the size of a fist and severed a portion of intestine, narrowly missing his spine. He was still only semi-conscious. Bo learned from a nurse that the Texas Rangers had been disbanded at the start of the civil war and his father, Captain Ben Jack, had then served with the Buffalo Soldiers along the Kansas–Missouri border. That was where he'd been shot.

"Who did it?" Bo asked his father, who was lying with his good eye closed, the other hidden as usual by his black eye-patch. Bo put his ear to his father's lips to hear his reply.

"A young outlaw from Clay County, Missouri."

"What's his name?"

"James . . . Jesse Woodson James. Known as Jesse. A real wild kid, full of hate."

"Where was he last seen?"

"He joined Quantrill's gang . . . But don't you worry, son." His father rested for a moment. "I'll track him down as soon as I get out of here."

"I'll get him for you."

Bo left that same day for Missouri. He caught up with the Buffalo Soldiers on the Kansas side of the border. They were celebrating. Quantrill had been killed and many of his gang had surrendered. Lieutenant Washington Greene told Bo happily, "The War's over here, too."

"What happened to one of the gang named Jesse Woodson James?"

"There was a mix-up. He was going to surrender at Lexington, but the Union Cavalry opened fire on him and he disappeared. His mother's been banned from Missouri for her outspoken Confederate sympathies and she's gone to live in Nebraska. He may have joined her there."

Bo went to Nebraska, but by then James had returned to Missouri, so Bo followed him. The men were back from the war and trying to start farming again. But southern sympathisers had lost their farming equipment, their horses and mules and plows, and they weren't allowed to own guns to hunt wild game. They couldn't meet their mortgages and Yankee farmers bought up their land cheap. Hatred and desperation were so much a part of everyday life that it seemed as if the war would be fought all over again. Former guerrillas kept their weapons hidden and well-oiled. The tricks they had learned in the war might be turned to earning a living in peacetime. Just as they had raided Union Army trains, they could rob banks. Several banks in Missouri were robbed by a gang that was said to include Jesse James. Six militiamen had gone to his family home in Kearney, and he had fought them off with a revolver in each hand.

Bo learned that James had gone to hide out in Mexico. He tracked him down to Matamoros during a local fiesta. The first person Bo met in the Mexican town was Lieutenant Washington Greene of the Buffalo Soldiers.

"I follow him, too," said the black soldier.

"I want him," Bo said. "He shot my father. Luckily the old guy's so tough, he's comin' round."

"Quantrill's men killed my brother."

"Then we hunt him together, but he's mine. A father rates above a brother."

"Your father's still livin'. My brother ain't."

"I still want him."

So the fair-haired young cowboy and the black soldier combed the Mexican town together. They heard of a young American who had had a fight in a Mexican dance-hall and shot two Mexicans. He had been stabbed in the arm with a stiletto.

"How did he look?" Bo asked the bouncer at the dance-hall, who had narrowly missed being shot himself.

"Early twenties, señor. Slender and sallow, about four inches under six feet tall. I'd say he weighed a hundred and forty pounds before he got cut."

"That's our man," said Lt. Greene.

"Well, he bled a lot. He should be easy to find, señor."

They checked with the local doctors and eventually tracked him down to a back-street hotel. Bo listened at the door. He heard a man say, "I got a job in Abilene, come with me," and then a woman said something, too low for Bo to hear. He signalled to Lieutenant Greene and together they burst into the room. They found the young outlaw in bed with a Mexican woman, swarthy and big-busted. His left arm was bandaged and inconvenienced his love-making; he had to lie on his right side. He turned over, grimacing with pain, and his right hand went for his pistol under the pillow, but Bo put his Peacemaker to the young outlaw's face. "Leave it there. The doctor says your arm'll be healed in a week," Bo told him. "Then I'm goin' to kill you."

"I could outshoot you with one hand," the young outlaw said fiercely. "I'll kill you, then I'll kill him," and he glared at the black lieutenant. "I hate Yankee troops. They put my mother in jail and tortured my stepfather by hangin' him up. I'll kill you both."

"The war's over," said Lieutenant Greene.

"Not for me, it ain't," shouted the young outlaw, and he grabbed for his gun under the pillow again.

Bo gripped his wrist.

"Don't get smart. I'll meet you when you're ready. You shot my father in the back—Cap'n Ben Jack of the Texas Rangers. I'll shoot you face-to-face, a better chance'n you gave him."

"I hate the Texas Rangers and I hate you. I'll kill you the way I killed your Pa."

"He ain't dead."

"Then he's goin' to miss you."

Bo laughed. "I'll wait for you. I want you to die healthy."

"You should've killed him then," Lieutenant Greene grunted as they left the hotel.

"I was once shot in bed when I was with a woman. That ain't my style, Wash."

Bo waited until the bandage was off the young outlaw's arm and the doctor was satisfied the wound had healed. Then he went back to the hotel.

"Meet me down in the street at noon," Bo told him.

The young outlaw's woman screamed Mexican abuse at Bo; she was about to lose her meal ticket. Bo was careful not to turn his back on her.

The downstairs door of the hotel opened promptly at noon. The young outlaw walked toward Bo with great confidence, his hands hanging close to his guns. Bo took a quick, professional look at the guns, checking what the young outlaw used. The guns had beautiful ivory handles like his own. Bo looked more closely. They were Colts—Peacemakers! They were the same as his. The other pair. He remembered what Sam Colt had told him.

If you ever meet a man with guns like yours, do not fight him. Treat him like a brother.

Damnation, Bo thought. He felt suddenly pulled two ways at a time when his mind should have been concentrating. A simple revenge had become complicated. His great respect for Sam Colt made him hesitate. Sam Colt had created these guns and should have a say in what was done with them.

He shouted angrily, "You get your guns from Sam Colt?"

"Yeah," the young outlaw answered suspiciously, his hands hovering over his gun butts. "Why'd you ask?"

"He gave us twins."

The young outlaw's eyes flashed down to Bo's guns. "We got equalisers. Don't be yeller, Texas."

Bo made a quick decision. "I can't fight you. Get out of here. But don't cross my way again."

"What's wrong with you?" demanded Lieutenant Greene. "That man shot your father. I gave you first chance."

"Sam Colt made our guns. He told us not to fight."

"That's crazy superstition. Well, I don't share the same guns. He killed my brother and I'm goin' to kill him."

Lieutenant Greene strode into the middle of the dusty Mexican street, facing the young outlaw. "Go for your guns."

"Your guns ain't a match for a Peacemaker," Bo shouted. "He can outshoot you—"

But it was too late. Lieutenant Greene went for his standard model Colt. It had hardly cleared his holster when the young outlaw's ivory handled Peacemaker roared and the black lieutenant went over backwards. The young outlaw stretched his arm full length as if he were sighting for another shot.

"To hell with Sam Colt!" cried Bo, and in one swift movement, too fast for the eye, one of his Peacemakers came out and roared. The young outlaw staggered back, dropping his gun and clutching his side.

Bo walked slowly over to him, Peacemaker in hand. The young outlaw glared, expecting another shot. Bo put his pistol slowly back in his holster.

"You been lucky this time. Next time I'll kill you."

"You got it wrong, Texas. Next time I'll get you." He spat in the dust, blood on his lips, and nearly fell.

Bo called over to the Mexican woman, who was watching from the hotel steps. "Get your man to a doctor." The woman came running. Bo, careful not to have his back to her, walked over to Lieutenant Greene, who was half sitting up, holding his shoulder.

"You shoulda killed him. He'll only go on killin' until someone gets him. You could've saved a few lives."

Bo examined his wound.

"He hit you too high. It's just a flesh wound. I'll patch you up."

Bo did more than that. He pressed Wash Greene to accompany him back to Texas. The lieutenant had already resigned from the army, but wasn't sure what he wanted to do.

"Come to Fort Worth and have a good time. You can meet my Pa."

"You're only askin' me along because I got shot," Wash Greene told him. "You don't need to feel guilty."

"Hell, I don't! Get yourself a better gun and learn to shoot!"

"I could've taken him but for all that crazy superstitious stuff about your damned Peacemakers."

"I just hope it ain't bad luck."

"Bad luck? You ain't got shot, you just turned soft, that's all. Maybe I better go to Texas and take care of you until your Pappy's well enough to do it."

So Wash Greene went back to Fort Worth with Bo.

They first visited the hospital. Captain Ben Jack was sitting up, supported by a pile of pillows. With his black eye-patch, he resembled a pirate. His good eye lit up when he saw Bo. "You got him?"

Bo sat by the bedside and explained. "I just hope it ain't bad luck goin' against Sam Colt's last words."

"You did right, son," said Captain Ben. "Some code's gotta be obeyed even in killin'. Sam Colt made those Peacemakers. He was an artist, they got an ideal view. Life ain't like that. You gotta take care of yourself." Captain Ben winked his good eye. "Been waitin' for you, son. An urgent message came for you by telegraph. From a lady. I've kept it here by my bedside."

Bo took the telegraph message and read:

* * *

NEED HELP DESPERATELY STOP PLEASE COME IMMEDI-
ATELY SILVER STAR RANCH ALPINE KANSAS—KATH-
LEEN TRACY

* * *

Bo read it over twice, wondering who "Kathleen Tracy" was. Then he remembered—it was Kath, the beautiful, red-headed English girl who set off to get into Richmond during the siege. How the hell had she ended up in Kansas? His loins stirred at the thought of her. She was still very much alive to him even if he hadn't remembered her name. Names like brands didn't mean much to Bo. But how had she known where to reach him? Then he remembered he'd told her his father lived in Fort Worth and was a Texas Ranger—that was enough to find Captain Ben Jack anywhere, even in a hospital. He gave the message to his father. "Read that."

"I already did. I hope she's a good looker."

Bo grinned. He showed the message to Lieutenant Greene. "What're you goin' to do about it?" asked the black lieutenant.

"She's tough." His voice thickened at the thought of her and his father grinned at him. "She'd only ask for help if she really needed it." There was more to it than that, but he couldn't tell them. There was something unfinished between him and that redhead. "I guess I better go," he said, thinking of her as he'd last seen her. "Want to see Kansas, Wash?"

"Not got nuthin' better to do."

"You young bucks have all the luck," said Captain Ben. "If I was movin' around, I'd come with you. But before you leave, get me some liquor for these long nights."

"You ain't supposed to have liquor."

"When did a doctor make the rules for a Texas Ranger?"

Bo brought him a pint of whisky hidden in a pair of socks. The captain took a quick swig.

"What've you got there, Captain Ben?" demanded a passing nurse.

"Just wishin' my son *bon voyage*," said the captain with a guilty grin. "He's goin' to Kansas to have hisself some fun. Come and join us, nurse."

She came, but to take away the bottle. "You know what the doctor said, Captain," she told him reprovingly. Captain Ben waited for her to depart, then cursed long and loudly.

Bo grinned. The old man was getting better. He and Wash Greene could leave immediately.

By sundown, they were on their way.

*   *   *

When Kath's message for Horatio Thomas arrived at Willard's Hotel in Washington, the English journalist was at the

War Department. He had already tried to convince Secretary Stanton that Mosby wasn't involved in Lincoln's assassination. Stanton had rejected his arguments. So Thomas, who didn't give up easily, had now approached General Grant. The General was basically fair-minded and admired Mosby as an opponent, even though guerrilla warfare was against the old soldier's code.

Thomas—or rather Ram—had delivered a lengthy memorandum to Grant at the War Department. Then Thomas followed it up with a personal meeting. He had to wait for Grant to return from a visit to the White House. Several powerful businessmen already wanted Grant to run for President. Grant hadn't said no.

At last Grant arrived. He appeared a little smarter out of uniform. His plain, dark suit suggested he might be preparing for a political career. He even seemed to be drinking less.

Grant had Thomas's memo in his hand. "I asked the Secret Service and Pinkerton to check out Colonel Mosby for me, Mr. Thomas. Their findings agree with your assessment," he said cordially, smouldering cigar in hand. "Mosby's an able man and thoroughly honest. I've told Stanton there's no evidence against him regarding the assassination of the President that would stand up in a court of law. All we'll succeed in doing is to turn him into an outlaw, and we'd be damn fools to do that. We need men like him and Robert E. Lee in the South and we need them on our side or at least not against us. I've told Stanton I want Mosby left alone!"

"I'm sure you won't regret it, General," Thomas said as Grant walked with him to the outer door of his office. In place of the Custers and other army men who used to be around Grant, now businessmen sat waiting to talk to him. Shrewd, calculating eyes examined Thomas as he said good-bye to Grant. The General seemed like an innocent among these skilled manipulators and bargainers. They had flocked to Washington during the war, profiting in any way they could from supplying the army, but now the capital seemed to be filled with additional swarms of adventurers and confidence men from all over the country, seeking to gain any advantage they could from the new period of peace and reconstruction. Men sat in smoke-filled back rooms in every leading hotel, making deals about new industries and railroads not yet built and land and cattle and oil—America was seen as a great goldmine up for grabs.

All the financiers wanted Grant as President because of his easy-going attitude, Horatio Thomas thought. Grant had stated publicly that all the big industrial and financial people were doing great things for the country by making it more prosperous and more important in the world's eyes. What was good for financiers like Jay Gould or great projects like the Union Pacific Railroad, Grant had said, was good for America. Grant, Thomas thought, sounded like an incurable sucker.

He asked the General if he wanted to be President.

"Frankly, no, Mr. Thomas, but I owe my honors and opportunities to the Republican Party, and if my name can aid it, I'm bound to accept."

Thomas didn't follow this reasoning. Grant wasn't indispensable. Sounded as if they were playing on his ego and his patriotism to make him a patsy.

He left feeling depressed. The country at this post-war time of great expansion needed an Abraham Lincoln capable of handling the politicians, the financiers, the con-men. They would manipulate Grant as they wished. That was why a Lincoln got himself killed and generals like Grant died in bed of old age. Grant was a good man, but that wasn't enough; a lot of people would lose more of their freedom and their dreams because of his innocence. Greed was in the air in Washington. America was rebuilding, changing, expanding. Riches and power were there to be fought over. It needed a strong, shrewd man in the White House to control all the special interests. Ulysses S. Grant couldn't do it. The army wasn't the right training. You couldn't give orders to politicians and businessmen and financiers; you had to outwit them, Thomas thought. It had helped Lincoln being a lawyer.

Ram met him in the hotel lobby. The young Sikh handed him Kath's message. The wording was the same as the one to Bo:

* * *

NEED HELP DESPERATELY STOP PLEASE COME IMMEDI-

ATELY SILVERSTAR RANCH ALPINE KANSAS—KATH-
LEEN TRACY.

* * *

Horatio Thomas's first reaction was impatience. It was typical
of a woman to get into trouble, probably with some man, and
then expect everybody she knew to rescue her, as if you had
nothing better to do than rush half way across this huge country
to her aid.

Women!

They always played the poor, defenseless innocent when
really they were tougher than any man, capable of endurance
far beyond any masculine urge to survive.

Hadn't he helped her on the steamship coming over and then
in Washington and then later in Richmond? What more did she
want from him?

"What's your reaction to her appeal?" he asked Ram sourly.

"She made her own bed. Let her lie on it." The young Sikh's
face burned with indignation. "No bed of roses, whose fault is
that? Hers! You busy. You plan to go South to Atlanta and
Montgomery for big important series of articles. No time to
help damsel in distress."

Ram's strong adverse reaction weakened Thomas' own. Ram
didn't like her, he was prejudiced against her. But, thought
Thomas, perhaps this is just what I need—to get away from
Washington and its politicians and sample the real frontier
America. Perhaps that made more sense than going South to
look at the beaten Confederacy. He said gently to Ram, "I want
to write about the West, you know. That's where everybody's
looking now the war's over. All the big deals will come to
fruition there. The next war will be fought out West. This
might be a good chance to get an inside look." Horatio Thomas
read the message again. "She says 'desperately.' That sounds
bad—"

"Female exaggeration to win male sympathy!" exploded
Ram. "The Black Irishman has probably caught up with her
again. You cannot help there. They are destined for each other.
Ram sees it! Their *karma* show it. They know each other from
previous life. They have to work out their destiny now. You
cannot help, however 'desperate' female is."

"I'm sure it's not just Frank again. It must be real trouble. She's no clinging violet. She's a tough woman. You remember how she got into Richmond in that damn balloon? Nothing could have stopped her. She's crossed half the known world to find that father of hers. If she says she needs help, I believe her, Ram. I think we should go."

The young Sikh sighed.

"No argument possible. Your mind made up. Very well. When?"

"We should get there as soon as possible. You better work out the fastest route. We'll leave late today—after I've finished my story about General Grant and how he's going to be the next President, God help America."

* * *

The Reverend was the last to receive Kath's message.

He had attended Mosby's brief farewell gathering on the village green at Salem. The Colonel's men had come on horseback, dressed in their best Confederate gray with their pistols polished. They were lined up and then they sat in their saddles and waited for Mosby. He, too, was unusually smart, his boots gleaming in the noon sunshine. He gave no orders and there was no roll call. He simply rode down the line, meeting the eyes of each man in a silent farewell ritual. Then he rode to the front and told them: "Soldiers, I have summoned you together for the last time. The vision we cherished of a free and independent country has vanished, and that country is now the spoil of a conqueror. I disband your organisation in preference to surrendering to our enemies. . . ."

Tight-lipped, the Colonel had ridden off, leaving everyone to go his own way.

The Reverend had nowhere in particular to go. He was angry at the Colonel for not going on fighting. Holy wars for freedom against the armies of the Devil didn't end until they were won. It also left the Reverend alone with his thoughts and he didn't want that. Action to him meant escape—like liquor and the role he played. The sensitive man, still an orphan at heart, was always hidden by the blustering, aggressive "Reverend."

He stayed in Salem and became very drunk. He lay on the

village green with a bottle of whisky and no one dared bother him.

He drank for a week and the village green was soon littered with empty bottles. He had several fights over the war. Finally he was jailed in Millwood to sleep it off. It was only when he was jailed that Kath's message caught up with him. It had been sent to the barbershop and the barber had taken several days to find him.

* * *

NEED HELP DESPERATELY STOP PLEASE COME IMMEDIATE SILVERSTAR RANCH ALPINE KANSAS—KATHLEEN TRACY

* * *

That damned redhead!

Trouble certainly followed her around.

But what the hell did she mean bothering him?

The Reverend held his aching head and tried to think about it.

She wasn't a crybaby. It *must* be a bad situation. And that husband of hers wouldn't be much help.

The Reverend tried to stand up and shake off the effects of a week's hangover.

He staggered, but remained upright.

His head felt like someone was pounding it with a hammer.

He needed something to do to stop drinking—some *action*.

He re-read her message.

The West attracted him.

You could go on fighting the war there.

Why not help her out?

She had a ranch, she might reward him.

He had no better ideas.

"Jailer," he yelled, "let me outta here. I'm late already."

26

The first of the month crept closer.

Kath made a rough calendar and crossed off each day before she went to bed.

June 16, 1865 . . . .

June 17 . . . .

June 18 . . . .

"Doesn't look as though your friends are comin'," Paul said, putting her own thoughts into words.

"Oh, they'll come. They've not had enough time yet." Paul's attitude irritated her. He was feeling down and he wanted to drag her down, too.

He talked about the past like an old man. "You ought to have seen Kansas before the war, Kath. Things went bad when Kansas joined the Union four years ago. Most people in Alpine were on the Confederacy's side. Aunt Martha says when I was away fighting in Virginia, outsiders came in from the East—greedy, violent immigrants tryin' to take over. Kansas turned bad—"

"Kansas still has a lot worth fighting for," Kath said, annoyed with him and with herself, impatient with the waiting. She disliked being dependent on other people, she liked to be free to be herself.

She worked hard at repairing the ranch-house and then the barn to make the waiting more bearable. But a hundred times a day, her eyes looked to the horizon. It was time for them to come. Surely they wouldn't let her down. Not all of them. Surely Bo would come. Surely Horatio Thomas would . . . and the Reverend. *Oh God, please let them all come—and come quickly.*

Her thoughts also kept returning to Frank Butler. It was almost as if she sensed he was close by.

Frank, in fact, had reached Kansas ahead of the others. He had no idea how far away Kansas was when he set out from Virginia. He sold his horse and boarded a train and then a stagecoach. Then he bought another horse and crossed Missouri. When that horse collapsed, he bought another. He stayed occasionally in cheap rooming-houses when he couldn't find a haystack. It used up his money. By the time he crossed the Kansas border, he was nearly broke. With what he had left, he decided to try his luck at cards.

Late that afternoon he stopped at a small town called Pine Bluff. People out shopping stared as the tall, handsome young man in dusty black clothes rode past. Frank had a black wide-brimmed hat pulled low over his eyes, a black silk shirt unbuttoned down to his navel, and black pants tucked into black cowboy boots.

He tied up his weary horse outside the saloon. It was half-empty. He bought a few drinks for strangers and that way eased his way into a card game. He lost enough to give the others confidence, then he started to win and went on winning. When he had amassed well over a hundred dollars, someone brought in the sheriff.

"Where you from, son?" asked the sheriff, a lean, balding man with a flat stomach and a six-shooter in his hand.

He claimed that Frank resembled a cattle rustler he was looking for. He said he'd have to hold Frank in the jail until someone who could identify the rustler came to see him. It was an old trick for breaking up card games in which the sheriff's friends were losing. Frank didn't know that. He was anxious he shouldn't be mistaken for the rustler. Rustlers were hanged. His best defense was the truth, to be honest about himself. Frank Butler of Stockport, England, couldn't be a Kansas rustler. He'd only just arrived.

"What's your work in England?" asked the sheriff through the cell bars.

"I was the northern hangman."

"You're kiddin'. You were the official executioner?"

"That's right. My father was the hangman before me."

The sheriff grinned, more friendly. "You lookin' for a job, Frank? Judge Drake wants a hangman."

"I need to make some money, but not by hanging. I gave all that up when I came to America."

"But say it's your only way of gettin' out? What then, Frank?"

"Then I'd have to think about it."

The jail food was half-cooked and Frank had to share a little cell with four other men. The sheriff seemed to be trying to make the outside as attractive as possible.

Then Judge Drake came to see him—a portly, middle-aged man with a great, smooth, bald head and penetrating dark eyes.

"Solve this problem, Butler. The condemned is male, aged twenty-four, five feet six inches tall, and weighs 160 pounds in his clothes. What should the drop be?"

Frank calculated quickly.

"Six feet eleven inches, Judge."

"Why so much?"

"Because of his young age and the strength of his muscles at that age. There's more resistance, more expansion. You want death to be immediate, don't you?"

"Of course." The judge looked pleased. "That was the work of a true professional, Frank. The job's yours."

"I don't want to be a hangman, Judge. I've retired."

"Come out of retirement," said the Judge. "It's a profession with a lot of opportunities in Kansas at present. I need a good man to carry out my sentences. I don't want any amateurs. I'll pay you top money, Frank—$200 a month and all found."

"I'm sorry, Judge, but I've done enough hanging."

The sheriff outside the cell spoke up.

"Take the job, Frank, and you get out now—today. Turn it down and you stay in jail and I throw away the key."

Frank realised he was trapped.

"I'll take the job."

* * *

On the outskirts of Pine Bluff, the Judge's closed carriage passed the bodies of two men left dangling from towering pine trees. A hand-written notice beneath them stated: SO DIE ALL RUSTLERS.

"That's what the Governor wants me to stop," said Judge Drake, mopping his great bald head. "Vigilante justice, they call it. There's still no Law in much of the state, Frank, and the Vigilantes take over. But it's no substitute for the real thing. They often hang the wrong men. Hang first and talk afterwards is their motto. The Governor wants to break their power before they become a political force. You and I have got to get busy to make the Law visible. A few legal hangings will do it. I'll try 'em, Frank, and you hang 'em. We'll make a real show of it. Get a big crowd. That way the news'll spread throughout the whole state. The Law's coming back! I'll give you a free hand, Frank. You're a professional, I can see that. I have great admiration for English craftsmen." The judge pulled back his jacket to show the butt of a small pistol sticking out of his inside pocket. "Always carry a gun, Frank. I'm setting up my main court in Abilene and that's a wild town. We'll have our first hanging there in two days' time."

27

June 20 . . . June 21 . . . .

The first of the month was looming ahead.

And still no one came.

Kath found a new way to distract herself, to soothe her nerves—take a bath.

The tin bath-tub was like the one at home in Stockport, only bigger. It held more water and you could lie full length in it. Kath had to make ten trips with a bucket to the well outside before the tub was full. The great sun blazing down on the ranch made the sweat trickle like tears down her face. She lost pounds. When she jumped into the tub, displacing a wave onto the kitchen floor, the water was warm. She lay back and let her breasts float on the surface. She was relaxing under the soothing caresses of the warm water—her first bath since Washington— when Paul shouted from the front porch, "Someone's coming."

Immediately water, tub, bath were forgotten.

Kath leapt out, sending another great wave across the kitchen floor. She hurriedly dried herself, put her clothes on with lightning speed, and rushed outside.

It must be *them*—the first of them. It *must*.

An old stagecoach, drawn by four frisky horses, was rushing towards the ranch-house. A cloud of dust hid the driver. Kath stared, open-mouthed. Who could it be? The stagecoach, with squealing brakes, rocked to a standstill, the sweat-soaked horses heaving with weariness. Kath rushed over, anxious to see who had arrived, fearing a disappointment.

"My dear Kathleen," cried a very clear, precise voice from the driver's seat above, "What have you here—the Promised Land?," and a familiar figure in a white suit stood up, smiling and waving.

Kath almost cried with relief. *They were no longer alone.* She had hoped it would be Bo, but Horatio Thomas was very welcome. The sight of him always gave Kath a feeling of confidence, a sense that life for all its dangers was perfectly manageable. And now Thomas was here, perhaps the others weren't far behind.

"It's wonderful to see you," she cried up at him, tears of pleasure in her eyes. She felt so grateful to him for caring enough to come all the way from Washington.

The English journalist stepped down briskly. His white suit, usually spotless, was slightly soiled, a sign of how far he had travelled. "You look fine, Kath. The West really suits you," he said, embracing her. He was so matter-of-fact he might have come for a vacation. He shook hands vigorously with Paul. "You haven't got a home here, Mr. Blake," he told Paul cheerfully. "You've got an empire."

As Horatio Thomas was speaking, Ram appeared from inside the stagecoach, already at work lifting down several large trunks that Thomas had bought—and filled—in Washington.

"Welcome, Ram," Kath said when the young Sikh made no attempt to greet her. "It's great to see you again. Let me help you with that luggage." Ram unwillingly let her lift one end of a trunk. "You must be tired after such a long journey. Where did you get this wonderful old stagecoach?"

"Mr. Thomas buy it in St. Louis from man going bankrupt."

How like Horatio Thomas to have his own stagecoach! she thought, giving the English journalist an affectionate look.

Thomas stood surveying the land, talking to Paul, while Ram and Kath struggled inside the ranch-house with the trunk. Paul was smiling proudly, more cheerful now with the arrival of allies. "Ah, Mr. Blake," Thomas told him enthusiastically. "You have to see the West to believe it. It reminds me of something De Tocqueville observed thirty years ago. God himself, wrote the young Frenchman, gave Americans 'the means of remaining equal and free by placing them upon a boundless continent.' One has to be here in Kansas at the Silver Star Ranch to understand fully what De Tocqueville meant. It also makes me more sympathetic to those wily financiers setting up their deals in Washington. It needs a gambler, a prophet, or a fool to think of taming this boundless frontier."

"Come and see the house," Kath called through a window.

"I want to see everything," Thomas said, striding indoors. He put his arm round Kath's shoulders. "You have your own home at last. I'm so happy for you, Kathleen."

The ranch-house was neat again and well repaired. Aunt Martha came out of the kitchen to be introduced. Thomas was extraordinarily gallant with her and she was clearly very impressed.

"You've come all the way from England to help us, Mr. Thomas?"

"By way of Washington," he replied. "Ram here has come even farther—from India," and he introduced the young Sikh, who was very respectful toward the old woman.

She dished up some food for them—a large plate piled high with beans. Horatio Thomas stared disapprovingly. It definitely wasn't his kind of food.

"Tell me what the trouble is," he said to Kath as he picked at the beans.

She told him very briefly.

Thomas became increasingly thoughtful. "You don't know for sure the rustlers and this company are connected," he said when she had finished.

"They must be."

"It all happened so close together," the old woman said. "The people offer to buy, we turn them down, then the rustlers come."

"You should have seen the company's lawyer," Kath told him. "There was a veiled threat in everything he said to us. He had some gunmen backing him up. They looked *ugly*. We had to sell—or else. That was the lawyer's message."

"You should check out the company," Horatio Thomas said.

"Go to the top. You might stop it there. Confront the head of the company and see what he says. Maybe he'll call off the gunmen."

"I've hired a Pinkerton man to investigate. I'm waiting for his report."

Thomas pushed his plate aside, leaving half the beans.

The old woman said with concern, "You're not hungry, Mr. Thomas? Beans are good for you and you look too thin. Eat a few more."

He reluctantly picked up his fork again. Kath watched him, hoping her story hadn't made him regret coming. He realised what she was thinking and told her cheerfully, "It really sounds like the Wild West and that's what I've come to see! Those con-men in Washington know what they're doing. Perhaps Grant does, too. Only people willing to take great risks should come out here to develop the country. If you want a safe, ordered existence, you better stay in the East. The problem is to control the varied, sometimes opposing forces let loose in these vast prairies. It *is* like being back in the Garden of Eden, tempted by the forbidden fruit. Greed's the danger, and perhaps you're the victims of it. But we mustn't just sit waiting for trouble. We must do something about it." He put down his fork and told the old woman firmly, "I really don't have much appetite." He brushed the soiled lapel of his white suit. "I'll change my clothes and then Ram and I will get some pistol practice."

When he and Ram went outside later with their pistols and a box of ammunition, Horatio Thomas muttered irritably to the young Sikh, "If we're going to stay here long, you've got to organise some other kind of food. I can't live on those damn beans."

*   *   *

Bo and the Lieutenant arrived next.

Kath's heart rose as she recognised the tall, fair-haired cowboy. Horatio Thomas was an eccentric out West, a transplanted European and city man, and would be however long he stayed, but Bo was a part of this way of life, at home in it, as familiar with gunfighting as the English journalist was with the game of cricket. Bo was her best hope.

All her old feeling for him awakened as she watched him sitting on his white horse, moving easily with the horse's rhythm, as if he belonged in that wild western landscape as much as the birds circling overhead.

He came up to the ranch-house with easy casualness, but his eyes, hidden by the wide brim of his dark hat, missed nothing. He took in Kath, Paul, Thomas, Ram, and the old woman, and he noted the location of the ranch-house and its advantages and disadvantages in the case of an attack.

Kath was careful not to show her feelings. But Bo had no such inhibitions. "Kath!" he shouted, dismounting quickly and swaggering over to her. His eyes roved down her body. "You ain't changed," he said with satisfaction and held her head and kissed her. Kath had to struggle to control her feelings then. The hardness of Bo's body was against hers and she wanted to respond. But Paul had come out of the ranch-house. She tried to push Bo away.

"I want you," she said quickly as he tried to kiss her again, "to meet my husband."

Bo stood still. "You got married?"

"Yes, this is Paul." She tried not to meet Bo's eyes. "We met in Richmond."

Bo frowned, obviously not welcoming the news, though he never took husbands very seriously. He shook hands politely with Paul.

"I met Bo at Colonel Mosby's," Kath explained quietly to Paul, who nodded curtly as if he sensed the feeling between Kath and the handsome young cowboy, and he didn't like it.

Bo introduced Lieutenant Greene.

"We've met before," Kath said. "Aren't you a Buffalo Soldier, Lieutenant?"

"I was, ma'am. I've left the army except for the final paperwork for the records." He was amazed that Kath remembered him from the Quantrill encounter. "I didn't think you'd recognise me out of uniform."

"I never forget a face. You rescued us and now you're doing it again." The Lieutenant was a bonus she hadn't expected; a seasoned soldier like him was very welcome.

"We need some sleep and a bath," Bo said. "We got time for that? When does the trouble start?"

"The first of the month. . . ."

Just a few days, but it was no longer hanging over her like some inescapable disaster. She was beginning to hope again. Thomas and now Bo had greatly boosted her confidence. Her prayer had been answered. They had come . . . all but the Reverend. . . .

* * *

The Reverend had stopped for a drink in Alpine and nearly didn't make it any farther. The little town was tense. Every stranger was a potential threat. The Reverend was followed by hundreds of eyes hidden behind wooden shutters as he came riding in looking for the saloon.

When he pushed his aggressive way through the swing doors, the first person he saw was a tall young black man leaning easily against the bar with a bottle of whisky in front of him. He wore the faded remains of an old Union Army jacket over dungarees.

"What are you doin' here, Yankee?" the Reverend demanded.

The young black face glanced up with a sleepy, amiable expression. The other people at the bar backed away.

"You talkin' to me?" asked the young black man pleasantly.

"You're damn right I am! The war's not over yet for you and me, nigruh! Go for your guns and let's find out how yeller you is."

The black man stood a little straighter and turned to face the Reverend, his hands close to his guns.

"You make a lot of noise," he told the Reverend. "You look like you rode a long ways. Maybe you need a drink to cool down." The black man pushed his whisky bottle down the bar.

"I don't drink with no Yankees." The Reverend pushed back the whisky bottle, spilling some. "Now go for your guns, Yankee, if you ain't yeller."

"The trouble with you preachers," drawled a voice behind him, "you get carried away by your own eloquence."

The Reverend's hand froze on his guns.

He knew that voice. Bo! He grinned with delight and swung round, completely forgetting the black man.

"Bo, you old Texan renegade, what brings you to this primitive place?"

"Same as you, Reverend," drawled the tall, fair-haired young cowboy. He smiled over at Washington Greene. "This is an old buddy of mine, Wash. Thanks for goin' easy on him. His heart's in the right place, even if his head ain't. He gets crazy like a lotta preachers."

"I'm sorry to see you mixin' with the Yankee enemy, my boy!" roared the Reverend, giving the top of the bar a great slap and rattling the glasses. "Bring us some whisky," he snapped at the frightened barman.

"You got yourself into that war way of thinkin', Reverend, and you can't get out. See every man for hisself now the war's over. The lieutenant here's a buddy of mine. Think yourself lucky he didn't get angry at you."

The Reverend beamed at the young black man.

"Any buddy of Bo Jack's a buddy of mine."

"I feel likewise," said Wash Greene, relaxing and leaning against the bar.

The saloon doors opened with a clatter. All three men swung round, ready for action. It was Ram.

"Mr. Thomas ready to go now."

"That English dandy's here, too?" said the Reverend. "All we need is Colonel Mosby."

"And the rest of the boys," Bo said grimly.

"That bad, huh?" grunted the Reverend.

"Look at this town—you can smell trouble."

The young Sikh came down the bar, telling Bo impatiently, "Mr. Thomas, he ready to go now."

The young cowboy sighed and emptied his glass. "Then we better get goin'. He's been buyin' food supplies and I promised Kath we'd travel back together. She's expectin' trouble on the first of the month," he told the Reverend.

"What's the trouble—her rent overdue?" the Reverend said, beaming. Nobody smiled. "Well, I've come to help her if I can. I guess that's why we're all here. That little lady's built mighty persuasive." He leaned over the bar to order a drink. A nervous young barman came over to him.

"Do your drinkin' at the ranch," Bo told him. "I'm takin' some liquor back. You look like you could do with some food and sleep and," he added, sniffing at the Reverend, "a good hot bath."

Horatio Thomas was outside with the stagecoach, the horses ready to go. Boxes of food and liquor lay on the seats inside. Thomas and the Reverend greeted each other coolly, the Reverend half drunk as he had been throughout the journey from Virginia, the English journalist completely sober.

"An English dandy like him ain't goin' to be much help," the Reverend muttered to Bo.

"There you go misreadin' people. He's all right, that Englishman. There's steel beneath the silk, you watch."

"What's troublin' the little lady that she had us all come?" Bo told him.

The Reverend whistled, hiding his concern. "The war's still goin' on out here." Rustlers, a big company—he had a sense of powerful forces against them. The Reverend reacted the usual way he hid his feelings—with noise. "Those money-grabbin', land-hungry Yankees have let all the evil spirits loose. America needs a good exorcist, Bo, my boy!"

"We'll have to do the exorcisin', Reverend," drawled Bo, patting his Peacemakers.

"Suits me, old buddy. Lead me to 'em. I feel like some action."

The afternoon heat beat down on the dusty street. The heat made the Reverend's head reel. The town moved under his feet. He clumsily tied his horse to the back of the stagecoach and climbed slowly up on top to join the others. He held his head until the main street of Alpine stopped moving.

Horatio Thomas whipped the horses into action. "Where'd he learn to do that?" muttered the Reverend as Thomas expertly controlled the frisky horses rushing down the trail out of town.

"I said you misread him." Bo grinned at Horatio Thomas. "What'll you do, Mr. Thomas, if the old woman refuses to cook all this new stuff you've bought? You'll have to eat beans and like 'em.''

"Ram can cook," Thomas said.

"First you gotta capture the kitchen from her. That's the old woman's fortress."

"I'll expect your help if you want to eat well."

"Not me. I'd sooner shoot it out alone with an army of gunmen than try to get that old woman outta her kitchen," Bo said, chuckling. He enjoyed teasing the English journalist.

"Beans," mumbled the Reverend. "Hate 'em. My foster mother used to cook beans."

"You better get used to 'em. An old woman does the cookin' here," Bo explained, chuckling, "and her meals are sorta basic —the kind an old woman cooks for herself alone." The stage-coach rattled past the big rock with the silver star. "This is where the ranch begins, Reverend."

The Reverend whistled in amazement. "My God, this is like ownin' your own state. This is what I call temptation, Bo, my friend. Get someone with the greed of the devil and he'll want all this. Those gunmen are thirstin' for this the way the Union devils were wantin' the South." He sat back, watching the endless land flash by. "A man could be happy here. . . ."

As they neared the ranch-house, a lone rider was ahead of them. A man. On a black horse. Moving slowly as if overcome by the heat. Then they saw that the rider was slumped over the horse's neck.

"He must be really exhausted," Horatio Thomas said.

"He's not exhausted," Bo muttered, "he's been shot," and he sat up straighter and his hands moved to his thighs, close to his guns.

The stagecoach drew level with the horse.

"He looks bad," Bo said and he jumped to the ground as the stagecoach stopped.

When the others caught up, Bo had stopped the horse and lifted the man to the ground. He was youngish, with a small brown mustache. He had been shot in the side of the head near the left ear. He was still alive, but only just.

"Exactly where President Lincoln was shot," Thomas said, kneeling beside the man.

"What are you goin' to do—write a newspaper story about it?" snapped the Reverend. He took a small whisky bottle from his hip pocket and thrust it at the man's lips.

"No," Bo said, "he might choke."

But the drunken Reverend didn't understand and pushed the bottle in the man's mouth and uptilted it.

The man coughed, choking on the whisky.

Bo thrust the Reverend roughly aside, opened the man's mouth and pushed his fingers inside and pulled at the base of the man's tongue. In a few moments, the man's breathing resumed and his bloodshot eyes flickered half open. He stared mistily at Bo and tried to say something.

Bo put his ear closer to the man's mouth.

"Black . . . gloves."

The man fell forward. Bo felt for his heart and shook his head.

"What did he say?" Thomas asked.

"Sounded like 'black gloves,' " Bo said. "There was a pause between the words, but maybe he was just waitin' for the strength to finish."

" 'Black gloves,' " roared the Reverend. "The devil wears black gloves."

"We better take him to the house," Bo said.

Kath came out to meet them.

"We found him down the road," Bo told her. "He was headin' here."

"Who is he?"

"No idea. All he said before he died was 'black gloves.' That don't tell nuthin' unless you know who's in the gloves."

" 'Black gloves'?" Kath repeated, suddenly feeling a deep uneasiness, a dread, she couldn't explain. "Let me look at him."

"You don't have to."

Kath walked over to the body laid out in the stagecoach. She didn't need to lift up the head; the side face was enough.

"I know him," she said. "His name's Charles Fogarty. He's a Pinkerton detective."

28

The shock rocked Kath. Her world reeled, momentarily out of control. *My God,* she thought, *if they can kill a Pinkerton detective, then nobody's safe.* Her grim fears had now been proved real—as real as the murdered man stretched out before her. These people would stop at nothing to get the ranch. Human life had no importance to them. Fogarty must have been killed as a warning of what to expect. Perhaps Paul had been right—they should sell and run.

Pale and trembling, Paul was staring at her to find out how she had taken it. She steeled herself. The effort was gut-wrenching. But she couldn't break down or Paul would collapse. The calmness of the others helped. Bo and Horatio Thomas and the Reverend—who had arrived, she noticed thankfully—were used to violent death. They stood quietly, impassive, unafraid. More than ever she felt grateful to them for coming. No one had failed her. She didn't trust herself to speak to the Reverend. She squeezed one of his big, rough hands and he half-grinned at her, strangely shy.

Kath tightened her jaw and her face became masklike. She told herself, *You've survived worse. This is just another trial to get through.* But what had made the shock harder to bear was the sense that once more, as she drew close to her father, something had happened to keep them apart. Fogarty had traced him as far as Abilene and now Fogarty was dead and couldn't help any more. But she mustn't lose her father this time the way she had in Richmond.

"We must telegraph Mr. Pinkerton in Washington," she said as calmly as she could. "Mr. Fogarty may have a wife and family back East. Mr. Pinkerton must also assign another detective to the case—to investigate Mr. Fogarty's murder and to find my Dad."

"Ram and I'll go into Alpine and send a message," said Horatio Thomas. "We'll also inform the sheriff."

"That's a waste of time," Kath said. "The sheriff's against us. He's a company man."

"You better keep it legal on your side," Thomas told her.

Bo said thoughtfully, "Fogarty must have found out somethin' and was comin' to tell you, Kath. They shot him to stop his mouth. But he nearly made it. That man had guts. But what does *black gloves* mean?"

"Maybe he was out of his mind," said Lieutenant Greene.

"No, you only had to see his eyes. He was tryin' to tell us somethin' before he died. *Black gloves* was his way of tellin' us fast. He had no time for more. But what does it mean?"

Late that day, the hard-eyed, plump little sheriff and a tall, laconic deputy came back with Thomas and Ram to inspect the body. Sheriff Baxter seemed more worried by the presence of strangers at the ranch than by the murder.

"You got visitors, Mr. Blake?"

Paul hesitated, so Kath said quickly, "We telegraphed for our friends to come. We felt we needed protection."

"You men come a long way?"

"Why'd you ask?" grunted the Reverend.

"I like to know when there are strangers in my territory."

"I wish you were as interested in the men who killed my husband's parents," Kath said fiercely.

Sheriff Baxter knelt by the body. "You say you know this man?"

"He was a Pinkerton detective we hired to find my father—and investigate the Western Cattle Expansion Company. He must've found out something important about the company and they killed him."

The sheriff stood up abruptly. "That's a very serious allegation, young lady," he snapped. "It's more likely he got into a quarrel with somebody in a local saloon. Pinkerton men often ain't popular out here. They're seen as interferin' Eastern snoopers."

"But, Sheriff, he was shot *in the back* of the head," Bo drawled quietly. "Whoever did it came up behind him."

"Maybe he got in a fight and started runnin'. What's your name, son?"

Bo had been lounging easily against the front porch, a hand in a pocket of his faded dungarees; at the sheriff's hostile question, he straightened up, his hands by his sides.

"I ain't nobody's 'son,' Sheriff, except Cap'n Ben Jack's, formerly of the Texas Rangers. You'll be callin' my friend here"—and he slapped Wash Greene's shoulder—" 'boy' next and we'd have some objection to that as you're a stranger to us both."

Sheriff Baxter was clearly not used to being addressed that way, and he was about to make an aggressive reply when he saw the expression in Bo's cold blue eyes. He remained silent. Kath saw him exchanging warning glances with his deputy, who loosened his gun belt. Kath hoped he wouldn't be foolish enough to try to take on Bo.

She said quickly, "Does *black gloves* mean anything to you, Sheriff?"

He watched her uneasily.

"Why do you ask, Mrs. Blake?"

"That's what Mr. Fogarty said just before he died. *Black gloves. . . .*"

The sheriff grew even more nervous. Did it mean something to him? Kath wasn't sure, but she thought it did.

He got back on his horse.

"If any information pertainin' to this man's death comes to my office, Mr. Blake," he told Paul, ignoring the others, "I'll let you know. You better get him buried by sundown before the heat makes him start to decompose."

"And bury the evidence?" Bo asked mockingly.

"The body won't help find who shot him."

"We already know *black gloves* did it," said Bo with a challenging look.

Sheriff Baxter seemed to pale beneath his tan and he quickly galloped away.

* * *

The next day, when Ram went into Alpine to learn the stagecoach routes and times for sending Horatio Thomas's stories eastwards, he found a new man in the telegraph office—a company man from Abilene.

"I made a mistake telling the sheriff I telegraphed you all," Kath said.

"Don't count on getting any more messages out," Thomas told her grimly.

* * *

Fogarty's murder, the sheriff's hostile visit, and now the change in the telegraph office . . . Kath was reminded of the slow tightening of a noose. Her hand went instinctively to her neck. *We mustn't wait like condemned prisoners,* she thought. *We must act.* The first of the month was four days away. There was still time . . . .

She brooded over what to do while she fried some steaks for dinner. Aunt Martha had given up the kitchen without much of a fight when she learned she'd have to cook for five more men.

Paul approached his steak apprehensively, stuck his fork in it expecting it to be tough, tried a piece, then munched happily. "Wherever did you learn to cook?" he asked, pleased by his wife's new found skill.

"I've been cooking since I was a kid. My stepmother went out to work so I had to cook for the whole family."

"You sure know how to do steak good," said Bo, his mouth full, grinning at her. Even though he was careful in front of Paul, he couldn't resist a slight swagger occasionally or a provocative grin. Kath tried never to be alone with him. She was sure Paul sensed something. He seldom spoke to Bo and then in a resentful, surly way. To her surprise, Paul and the Reverend had become friendly. The Reverend was trying to drink less so his appetite was enormous. He chided Paul about the Wild West, but Paul, who grew more western every day, especially in his way of speaking, only laughed. On the surface, the two men—one so loud and aggressive, the other so quiet—

had little in common, but at heart they were very alike, Kath thought. They were both very vulnerable men. The Reverend was just better at hiding his feelings.

"You know who we need out here, Bo?" he was roaring boisterously down the table. "That undertaker in Richmond. He'd make a fortune out of all these gunfights. A customer every time—"

"You knew an undertaker in Richmond?" Kath said in an excited tone.

"Yeah, Bo and I met this rascal—"

Bo kicked the Reverend's foot under the kitchen table.

"What do you mean—rascal?" Kath cried indignantly. "That was my Dad."

Glancing at Bo, the Reverend said uncomfortably, "Oh, forgive me. I didn't know. I only saw him for a moment, he—"

The entrance of Horatio Thomas, clean-shaven in a spotless white suit, saved him. The steaks could be cooked only three at a time so not everybody could eat at once. Thomas had volunteered to be last so he could take a bath in his room. Ram had laboured up the stairs with the water. The bath seemed to have put the English journalist in a good mood.

"This is *really* Charles Darwin country," Thomas cried enthusiastically. "Everything I've seen is an example of the survival of the fittest. Even our situation here—"

"Darwin?" the Reverend shouted at him, seeking an escape in loud argument. "The man's a liar—"

"The man's a distinguished naturalist," retorted Horatio Thomas. "Darwin's provided scientific data to back his view that man evolved from creatures of lower order—"

"I'm no monkey!" snorted the Reverend, joyfully playing his noisy, aggressive role. "Man came into existence suddenly and fully formed as the Bible tells us."

Horatio Thomas and the Reverend glared at each other across the table. It showed the strain of waiting was beginning to tell on everyone, Kath thought, watching them anxiously. That lawyer had thought himself very shrewd to give them so much time. Waiting was weakening them. They needed to *do* something.

"Let's have a council of war," she said loudly, sitting down facing the Reverend. Everyone reluctantly took a seat, including Aunt Martha, who had been washing the dishes. "We have four days left. We should use the time." She had their attention then. "I suggest we take up an idea of Mr. Thomas's. When he first got here, he suggested we go to Abilene to the offices of this company and see the bosses."

"At the top level," Thomas said. "They often don't know what's happening in the front line." He eyed Paul and then Bo and Wash Greene. "Didn't you see that in the war?" They nodded. "Well, these ruthless methods may not have the company's approval. The bosses may be willing to call off the lawyer and his hired guns. It's certainly worth a try."

"And leave the ranch unguarded?" Paul asked, worried.

"It won't matter if we're successful," Kath told him.

"What if we fail? They can occupy the ranch while we're gone. Possession's nine-tenths of the law out here."

"We'll have to risk it," Kath said impatiently. Paul was trying to talk her out of doing *anything*. He had acted strangely since Bo's arrival. Even in bed at night, he had been different, trying to make more of an effort as if to show she was his and nobody else's. But there was no real feeling behind it. He caressed her more out of anger than love.

"Why not split up?" Bo said quietly. "Some of us go to Abilene and the rest stay here on guard."

"We should all stay together," Kath insisted.

"Bo's right," put in the Reverend loudly. "Why don't you and your husband go to Abilene and we'll stay here as the welcomin' committee?"

"That way your ranch'll be protected," Horatio Thomas told Paul.

"Maybe you should go, too," Bo told Thomas. "Your newspaper credentials could help. If the company thinks its dirty work's goin' to be made public—"

"You're right," cried the Reverend. "That'll scare 'em."

Paul said obstinately, "I'm goin' to stay at my ranch. I want to be here when that lawyer comes back. I'm the legal owner. He has to talk to *me*. The rest of you have no legal authority. You go to Abilene, Kath, and talk to 'em if you want. I'm goin' to wait here with whoever wants to wait with me."

"I'll stay with you, Paulie," roared the Reverend.

"Me, too," Bo drawled.

"Count me in," said Wash Greene.

Kath didn't like this arrangement. She tried to persuade Paul to change his mind. He would be of little help in a gunfight, but as the legal owner, he might be needed in Abilene. But Paul refused to accompany her. She didn't want to leave him and the rest of them, but there was no other way she could see. Nobody had any other suggestions. In the end, after arguing back and forth across the table, she had to agree to leave them all except Horatio Thomas. He would accompany her. They would leave that night to save time. Horatio Thomas studied his map of Kansas. There were more blank spaces than occupied territory. It was already out-of-date. "Kansas is growing so fast the map changes every day," he said. "But at least distances remain the same. We're lucky it's a clear night and there's a full moon, plenty of light to follow the route. Even if we stop for a short rest, we'll be in Abilene by late afternoon."

Aunt Martha helped her to pack some food and then carried a pile of blankets out to the stagecoach. "You'll need 'em, Kath. Gets cold at night on the prairie. Kansas gets its name from its strong winds. It's an Indian word meaning 'People of the South Wind.' So keep wrapped up, darlin'."

Left alone in the kitchen, Kath made sure everywhere was clean. The table scrubbed, the floor washed down, no dirty dishes. Aunt Martha would have to go back to cooking while she was away. But no more beans! Ram could help her prepare the meat and vegetables for all the men so she wouldn't be overworked.

Suddenly Kath was grabbed from behind and whirled round to face . . . Bo.

He kissed her on the mouth, pressing hard against her. For a moment she responded eagerly, hungrily, blindly, but then she controlled herself and struggled to break free.

"Bo, please, I'm married—"

"Marriage ain't a prison. Your husband ain't your jailer. Never did like husbands." He grinned at her, leaning against the kitchen wall with one hand in his gun belt, his tight, faded dungarees making his hard muscles stand out. "I understand

your husband ain't goin' to give you what you need anyway."
He'd been talking to Horatio Thomas about Kath's marriage
and had learned about Paul's war wound. "You and me need
to spend some time together, Kath. I've been waitin' for it ever
since I came. Why d'you think I came? Now before you go
away, let's do some lovin'. Let's go lay in the barn and I'll give
you a time to remember me by."

"No, Bo, Paul—"

His mouth silenced her protests. He kissed her with surprising gentleness. All the pent-up feelings of weeks rose inside
her. She couldn't hold him off any longer. This was what she
wanted—a release for her unsatisfied emotions, a real man. This
was what she needed—someone to lean on, to draw strength
from, instead of having everyone lean on her, draining her.
Her restraints were gone, all her caution. She returned his
kisses then with just as much passion. His hands opened her
dress and he fondled her breasts with the same gentle
touch. . . .

"Kath!"

It was Paul's voice.

"Damn," Bo murmured, but he didn't let her go.

There were footsteps across the back porch, the kitchen door
slammed open.

They sprang apart. Paul stood in the doorway, glancing at
both of them. She had no idea how much he had seen. You
couldn't tell from his expression what he was thinking or feeling. She was flushed and sure she looked guilty. Bo was lounging against the wall very innocently—oh, far too innocently.
She saw one of her long red hairs on his pale blue workshirt.
Paul seemed to be staring at it, too. There was a moment of
great tension, a time when madness could strike.

"What do you want, Paul?" she asked casually, watching
him, cursing herself for being so careless.

His hurt eyes regarded her.

The tension grew. She felt Bo waiting like a cat, ready to
defend himself—and her.

Then Paul said abruptly, "I came to tell you to be sure and
take a gun and extra ammunition. Be prepared for anything."

His eyes moved from her to Bo and back—slowly, unbearably slowly. Then he walked out.

Kath watched him through the window. He was walking slowly towards the barn, with his head down. "Do you think he saw us?"

Bo shrugged. "What does it matter?"

"I don't want to hurt him."

"You did that when you married him."

"That's not true. I helped him. But for me, he wouldn't be alive now."

"What can he expect? His wife ain't stayin' like a sexless nun for the rest of her life. You're a full-blooded woman, Kath. He knows that. He knows you're goin' to lie down with somebody who can give you what you want. So let's finish what we started. That ain't goin' to hurt him any more'n he's hurt already." Bo moved closer to her, making all her feelings for him rise again.

"Are you crazy?" she said weakly, knowing she should break away, yet wanting him. She stood against him, feeling the strength of his body, aware Paul might come back at any moment.

Bo kissed her slowly, with the same gentleness that was so surprising in him.

"Kath, feel me against you. That's how much I want you. Can your husband love you that much?"

He held her against the wall. At his touch, a madness entered into her. She didn't care what happened as long as he held her, feeling the length of his hard body against hers. All the worries, fears, dangers were forgotten. She might have been back in her childhood, back when it always seemed to be spring and her desires were warm and uncomplicated by adult troubles. As he kissed her, her eyes closed, and there was a sound of thunder in her ears—the thudding of her heart. "Bo," she murmured. "Bo. . . ."

She wasn't aware at first that he'd stopped and his hands were still. The feeling went on and on. Then she opened her eyes and saw him standing back, listening.

"What is it?" she whispered.

"A shot."

Then she heard it—a shotgun outside.

Bo opened the door cautiously. He stepped carefully onto the back porch, followed by Kath. The moonlight showed up a figure near the barn, shotgun pointing. Bo's hands hovered over his Peacemakers.

"Wait," she whispered. "It's Paul."

"I know," he murmured, his hands still ready.

Kath stepped boldly off the porch.

"What are you doing, Paul?" she cried.

The shotgun pointed at her. She felt a chill down her spine. Had he gone crazy?

Then the shotgun rose and roared towards the distant moon.

"Just gettin' some target practise," Paul cried back through the darkness.

"You scared us."

Paul didn't reply, but walked away around the barn.

Bo's hands relaxed.

"Let's go back in." His white teeth flashed.

"No, Bo, that was a warning. We've got enough trouble. We don't want any fighting among ourselves."

Horatio Thomas came out and stood staring up at the clear night sky. "It's about time to leave, Kath." He walked over to the stagecoach to make a final check that Ram had packed all he needed.

Kath welcomed the thought of getting away, but she was unsure about Paul.

"Should I stay?" she asked Bo.

"Why?"

"Because of Paul."

"Don't worry. Now he's let off steam, he'll be all right." He grinned boyishly at her. "If you stay, let it be for me." The moonlight caught his fair hair. She envied him his self-confidence and his freedom at that moment. "I'll be waitin' for you, Kath," he told her.

"Bo, look after him for me."

Horatio Thomas was sitting in the driver's seat, waiting for her. She went in search of Paul. She found him in the barn. He turned his head away when she tried to kiss him good-bye.

"What does that Texan mean to you?"

"Nothing." It wasn't a time for truth.

"There's somethin' between you."

"Paul, trust me," she said. "Bo's just a friend of mine. I knew him before I met you. Oh, Paul, don't let's part like this," and she tried to kiss him again, but he pulled his head away like a moody child. She walked away slowly. It was the first time they had been parted since their marriage. She felt badly about his attitude. He seemed hurt and angry. She should have been more careful. It must be very humiliating for him. She wanted to run back and throw herself in his arms, but that wouldn't help in his present mood. Perhaps it *had* been wrong to marry him.

She climbed up beside Horatio Thomas. Ram was fussing over the horses. He was keen to accompany Thomas, but he was needed at the ranch to help Aunt Martha with all the cooking. Aunt Martha stood on the back porch and yelled at Thomas, "Mind you take good care of Kath."

"Like a daughter," he replied.

"And tell that company to stay out of our business."

Everyone gathered at the front of the ranch-house to wave—everyone except Paul. He was standing at the entrance to the barn. Kath waved to him, but he didn't respond. She saw the Reverend walk over to him and start arguing. Then the Reverend waved to her, but Paul still didn't. Her eyes sought Bo. He was very slim and straight against the clear night sky, his face hidden. Her body could still feel his hands. She wished she had never married. Was life always this complicated? Yet it was marriage that had brought her to Kansas, close to her father.

"I feel badly about leaving them" she said quietly to Horatio Thomas to stop her thoughts as he drove the horses hard across the flat dark land.

"You're doing the right thing, Kath."

"I'm sorry to leave Paul like that." She knew the observant journalist must have noticed.

"I was sure there'd be trouble as soon as I saw Bo arrive," he replied quietly.

"Why did you tell him about Paul's war wound?"

"I thought Bo should know who he can depend on in case of trouble."

"And he can't depend on Paul?"

"No, he's not a well man. He might crack."

Kath's loyalty was stung, but then, remembering Paul with the shotgun, she had to agree. He had nearly cracked then. "When you think of them all back there, they're a strange mixture of people. Paul, Bo, the Reverend, Aunt Martha. . . ."

"They all have one thing in common—they have the courage to be themselves, to act like nobody else."

"You can say that of anybody."

"No, you can't. Many of us are just sheep—even here in the West where it should be easier to be free."

Kath thought she knew what he meant. Her mind went back to Stockport and the people she had grown up with and knew best. There was great pressure to behave like everyone else—like sheep . . . or machines. She remembered the wave of people going up the hill to the factory each morning. What courage it took to be different from your neighbor! Was that one reason why her father had come to America—to be free to be himself? To be as untamed as the buffalo she had seen from the stagecoach? But the buffalo were steadily being killed off. To be free, completely free and untamed, you had to be willing to pay the price. Those men back at the ranch were willing to pay. Perhaps that's what Thomas meant. Perhaps that's what made them different. This company threatening the ranch wanted everyone to be as tamed as the townspeople in Alpine. . . .

Horatio Thomas cracked his whip over the horses. The sound in the still night air was like a series of gunshots. Kath had a sudden fear for the people back at the ranch, her friends who had come to her aid.

"Let's keep this speed up all the way," she said. "We must get there in time to stop anything happening. I'll never forgive myself if there's an attack on the ranch and I'm not there."

"Relax," Horatio Thomas told her gently, patting her knee. "There's a long ride ahead across the Great American Desert— the route of the old pioneer settlers and their wagon trains. Try to get some rest."

He cracked his whip again, sending it snaking close to the

lead horses. The stagecoach rushed through the night toward the full moon low in the sky—and Abilene.

29

People poured into Abilene from daybreak onwards. Horses, carriages, stagecoaches, every kind of transport churned up the unpaved main street until it was like a river of mud running through the town. The north side was regarded as respectable, and here were the weatherboard stores with false gaudy fronts, a cabin housing the First National Bank, a jail, and a few other public buildings. These were all closed for the day. On the south side—the wild side—the saloons and shady hotels catered to the crowds non-stop. But the center of attraction was the crude wooden gallows set up at the end of the main street facing westwards.

Early settlers had named Abilene after the "city of the plains" in the Bible. It was then little more than a village with a few log cabins. Now it was growing fast. There was an air of expectancy, the kind of feverish atmosphere that makes a boomtown, and it was never more evident than on that day of the hangings.

The condemned prisoners were brought from the crowded, stinking jail at three o'clock in the afternoon. Frank Butler had wanted the hangings held at eight AM as in England, but Judge Drake decided an afternoon matinee would attract far more attention. He was right. People had begun arriving during the night and slept beneath the scaffold to be sure of a ringside seat. Whole families had ridden as far as several hundred miles to witness Abilene's first hanging. Newspapermen had come from

Little Rock, St. Louis and Kansas City. By three o'clock, with
the sun roasting the town, more than two thousand men,
women and children were ringing the crudely constructed gallows.

It's more like a damned carnival than a hanging, thought
Frank Butler sourly as he waited, his head covered with a black
hood, for the procession ascending the thirteen steps to reach
the rough platform of wooden planks.

He had tried to be as professional as possible, but any way
you looked at it, Abilene's first public execution was crude by
English standards. There wasn't even an official doctor in atten-
dance to check that the hanged prisoners were dead. "We don't
need to waste money on doctors," Judge Drake had told him.
"You've got my complete confidence as hangman, Frank."

The noose was hemp fiber, woven by hand, obtained from
St. Louis, and to be extra careful, Frank had treated the rope
with a special pitchy oil. There would be no snaps or slips. As
in England, he'd made sure he knew nothing about the people
he had to hang except their age, weight and height until they
stood before him.

He saw now that all were men, two white and one Indian.
He found himself examining them with an unprofessional curiosity, wondering how they were reacting so close to death. One
of them twitched nervously, but the other two were impassive.
Their arms were tied, and they were led onto the platform by
four local clergymen and ten well-armed guards with sawn-off
shotguns.

Judge Drake himself, his great smooth head protected from
the burning sun by a wide-brimmed black hat, read out the
death warrants—the Indian's in both English and Cherokee—
while part of the crowd howled insults. All the three men were
being hanged for murdering local landowners. The Judge told
them in a loud dramatic voice that the crowd could hear: "The
rope of human justice is about to break your guilty necks. You
have taken the lives of distinguished local men of property and
sent souls unprepared to their Maker. May your end here today
be a warning to all other evil-doers in the state of Kansas."

Great cheers and boos came from the immense crowd, and
then prayers and hymn-singing and farewells—one of the men

had a long confession, *How I Came to the Gallows,* read out by a minister. "When I got drunk, I knew not what I was doing, and so killed my best friend. Oh, that men would leave off drinking. Let them learn from my ruin. . . ." The crowd became very restless before the end. "Get on with it," yelled a man on the front row. "Hang them!"

Frank took a noose and placed the big knot under the first prisoner's left ear in the hollow just back of his jawbone. Frank couldn't stop himself from peering into the man's eyes as he did so. He saw a wild fear, a rising panic. My God, he thought, the fellow's terrified—terrified by what I'm doing. Frank tried to control himself, to detach his own feelings from his work. But he was out of practice. Such professional detachment was hard to learn, even harder to recapture after all that he'd been through in America.

He concentrated by working slowly, methodically checking every detail. It was nearly a year since he'd hanged anyone and he had to make sure there were no errors that could cause a slow strangulation. His mind flashed back to the last hanging—Kath—for a moment, but he suppressed the thought of her. He had calculated the length of each drop the night before, but he made a final check of his measurements. Then he put hoods over the prisoners' heads, trying to avoid looking into their eyes as he did so, and he lined them up on the scaffold with their feet across the crack where the planks forming the death trap came together. One of the men began to moan, a loud, guttural sound half-muffled by the hood. Frank wanted to put his hands to his ears or cut the rope. Let the man live. Let them all live. We die soon enough. He lost his self-control for a moment. Then he steeled himself. He *had* to be detached—cold. He signalled to the Judge he was ready.

"Into the arms of your Maker we send you to repent your crimes!" cried the Judge, releasing the bolt, and the three men fell through the trapdoor. Many people in the crowd stood up, screaming hysterically.

Frank ignored the crowd reactions and the great noise and went immediately down the steps and under the platform to examine the dangling bodies. They had all been killed outright. He hadn't lost his skill. Yet, as he looked at the dead men with their swollen faces and rope-cut throats, he felt no real professional satisfaction, but was reminded again of Kath and the great scar on her neck. Was her memory haunting his work? Would he be able to achieve the old detachment only when he forgot her?

He began to put the bodies in the waiting pine coffins. An undertaker would later collect them and take them to Boot Hill, the nickname for the graveyard north of the town in a treeless bluff.

"Great job, Frank." It was the Judge. He barely glanced at the bodies. "We made some converts to law and order today. I'll have three more for you next week."

They left in the Judge's closed carriage, with armed guards on horseback, front and rear. "Look at those faces," said Judge Drake, sitting back so the crowd couldn't see him but he could observe the nearest people. "Wild, greedy, undisciplined. We've got to tame 'em, Frank, the way you tame a stallion. Make 'em respect you. Corral 'em with laws they've got to obey or hang 'em high."

The traffic was heavy now with people going home. The guards tried to clear a way for the Judge. A line of horses came past the other way. Young cowboys staying in town to have a good time. It wasn't yet dusk, a long time to go before the saloons closed.

Frank was watching the stream of traffic passing the window when an old stagecoach, covered in dust, rattled past. He caught a glimpse of a woman's face and a man in a white suit. The vision shocked him—*Kath!* Immediately he stood up. "Driver, stop!" he shouted, opening the carriage door and trying to see the stagecoach. But it was too late. The stagecoach was already disappearing in the dense, home-going crowd.

"Frank, what in hell's name are you doing?" demanded the Judge. "Don't you know that crowd's dangerous? Come back here—"

"It's a woman I know, Judge. I must see her." Frank jumped out of the carriage into the crowd. A drunken man clutched at his clothes. He felt the back of his jacket rip across the shoulders. He didn't care. The woman had definitely been Kath. He'd know that face anywhere—those eyes and that red hair.

She had been with Thomas. Those two had got together again. What had she done with her husband?

He battled his way through the crowd. Luckily no one recognised him, thanks to the hood he'd worn at the hangings. He had lost sight of the stagecoach. He was ankle-deep in mud as he rushed down the main street. Where had she gone? God knows Abilene wasn't that big, but it was still so overflowing with visitors that carriages and stagecoaches were parked everywhere, even among the rundown shacks and tents on the outskirts where the town was about to spread its borders.

He ran up to two stagecoaches and was met by hostile looks from ranchers and their families, all heavily armed. She had disappeared like a dream—like the memory of her that had come back to him during the hangings. She acted on him like powerful liquor, making him crazy enough to give up everything he was doing. He remembered the condemned prisoner's statement that was read out. "When I got drunk, I knew not what I was doing. . . ." That was her effect on him. She'd ruin him and then drive away as she had then. He couldn't let her do it. Not in this Wild West on the other side of the known world. . . .

He gradually cooled down and slowed to a walk. He'd never find her today in this town. He had to think of himself. His sudden wild departure had upset the Judge. He couldn't afford to lose that $200 a month until he had some money saved. The old feeling that hangings used to give him came back. He needed some action—drinking, gambling. . . .

In front of him was the DIAMOND SALOON. It was a combination drinking bar, dance hall, and gambling casino. Over the gambling tables—the dice and cards and spinning wheels—was a handwritten sign, "Only Legitimate Gambling Permitted." In the West, as Frank had already learned, that kind of sign wasn't intended to discourage gambling but merely to keep out anybody who might spoil the fun. Gambling was taken seriously, and there was even a ten-dollar tax on gambling operators.

Frank eyed the roulette and dice and poker games. He chose a poker game played by a group of cowboys who had just been paid. They were half drunk and wild in their bets. He waited his chance to join the game, lost for a short time until he had their confidence, then took them for a hundred and twenty dollars.

He waited then for the right time to leave, but the cowboys had soured and wanted a chance to win their money back. One of them had become too drunk to play any more, and a man in a black suit who was watching took his place. The man soon began to win. Frank could tell by his eyes and the way he handled the cards that he was a professional gambler. When he had won a hundred dollars from the cowboys and forty from Frank, one of the cowboys kicked over the table and went for his guns. But he was too slow. Long before his guns were half out of their holsters, he faced the guns of the man in the black suit. The cowboy paled, sobering up fast. But instead of shooting him, the man called over one of the bouncers. "Here's somebody that don't like losin'," he said. The bouncer grinned and threw the cowboy out.

"I'm Doc Holliday," the man told Frank, ignoring the others. "Let's quit playin'. These dumb cowboys ain't no fun." He ordered them both a 25-cent glass of whisky. "You just arrived in town?" he asked politely.

"A couple of days ago."

"Don't play poker in Abilene unless you're fast on the draw. The town's full of wild characters."

"I got a job."

"What'd you do?" The man seemed to think he had to give information to get any. "I used to be a dentist."

"I'm the . . . hangman."

The man's sharp eyes widened with surprise and then he slowly grinned.

"You did those hangings today?" Frank nodded. "Well, keep that to yourself while you're here. One of those men had relatives in this town. What took you into that line of work?" Again on the principle of fair exchange between strangers, he added: "I could never rightly make out what made me take up dentistry."

"My father was a hangman."

"In the family, huh? Your father die young? Hangmen don't usually live long out West. You married?"

"No."

"That's good. Any children?" Frank shook his head. "At least you won't leave no family."

"You're bringing my spirits down."

"Just the facts of life. You've chosen a dangerous profession."

They had several more whiskies. It was like raw alcohol burning down the throat. Frank found himself telling the Doc about Kath. He couldn't have explained why except that he needed to unload his feelings, the whisky slackened his self-control, and the Doc was a good listener. The Doc was a young man, but he had the gravity of someone much older, and a gambler's sense of how short life is, which sharpened his commonsense. He waited patiently for Frank to finish telling about his pursuit of Kath, sipping on whisky after whisky, and then he said firmly in a don't-give-a-damn manner, "Turn the bitch loose. A woman like that's poison. A man ain't free. Might as well be a damned slave. You should've hanged her when you had the chance."

Frank was astonished by the Doc's cynical attitude, but before he could argue, the Doc gestured to a big woman down the bar, and she came over and asked Frank to buy her a drink. She had a low-cut red dress and Frank couldn't keep his eyes off her plump breasts. "Want some action, handsome?" she murmured, touching his tanned cheeks and winking and rolling her big eyes.

"Go with her," the Doc said. "Galina'll give you a good time, better'n some of the young girls. And all you'll owe her will be money, not like your wench. But don't tell her who you are. Never trust a whore—or play poker with anyone called Doc." He laughed and then had a fit of coughing. "Damn," he muttered and took a quick drink. The liquor seemed to have no visible effect on him.

Frank went with the woman to a back bedroom upstairs above the saloon. She had nothing on under her red dress and her big-breasted figure excited Frank even more. She lay back with her legs up. He had her twice and then he relaxed, physically drained but with his mind beginning to think about what the Doc had said. *Turn the bitch loose.* When others had said that, he'd been angry. But that was before he came out West and got caught with no money. He had to think of himself now. He *had* to.

The woman, her head on his chest, might not have been there and she knew it. "Handsome," she whispered to get his attention, "it's good to be with a real man. I'm more used to bein' with old guys and manchildren in this cowtown. Who are you?"

The liquor was still strong in Frank. Why not tell her? he thought. He had nothing to be ashamed of. "You want to know who you're in bed with? You've heard of the hanging judge that's come to Kansas—Judge Drake? Well, I'm his hangman."

"Good God." Her head shot off his chest and her whole body moved away from him. There was a long silence in the darkened room and he thought he'd lost her. Then suddenly, close to his ear, her voice murmured, "What's it like? I mean— hangin' people, stringin' them up. What do you feel when you're doin' it?"

What did he feel? Frank thought, still confused by the whisky. *Nothing.* That's what he'd have said in England. I feel nothing. It's just a job—as cold and detached as a whore's.

"What do you feel?" he grunted.

Nothing, too, if you're honest, he thought. It was all an act. But now it was different with him. The long lay-off and his experiences in America had changed him. He was no longer detached from what he was doing. The eyes of the condemned man that afternoon came back to haunt him. The sheer terror in those eyes as he placed the noose around the man's neck still shocked him. He couldn't be detached from that. The difference now was that he *understood* what he was doing. He was administering death the way this woman beside him was selling sex. My God, he thought, I won't be able to do it if I go on feeling this way. He recalled how the memory of Kath had upset him during the hanging. Maybe the Doc was right. Turn her loose. *You should've hanged her when you had the chance. . . .*

"What I feel depends on the man. Usually nothing. What do you feel?"

"Feel?" he said. "I can't afford to feel, woman."

She had been watching him, but now she rolled over against

him, caressing his chest and his navel and dropping her face between his thighs. "Come on, handsome, I'll make you feel good and forget about everything. . . ."

And for a time, she did.

But he'd made his decision.

He'd keep the hangman's job.

He'd save his money.

He'd be *cold*.

* * *

Kath hadn't noticed Frank in the Judge's carriage, but she had sensed a nearness to someone as soon as the old stagecoach reached Abilene. It was as if the town itself was familiar in some way. She had assumed it was the effect of her father. He was *here*, in this town. It was the first time she'd had such a definite sense of his presence. She felt at that moment she could find him there simply by following her instincts like a homing pigeon, and her spirits rose with every stride the horses took along the main street. Here in Abilene was to be the fulfillment of her dreams—the long, delayed reunion with her father. In a way that she couldn't explain—but it was as sure as her feeling that her father was leaving home forever when she found him at the front door that early morning—Kath knew that this was the end of her journey that had begun in Stockport nearly a year ago.

But she had waited so long she could be patient a little longer. Saving the ranch had to come first. There was so little time left. . . .

As the weary horses struggled through the mud, both she and Horatio Thomas watched for the offices of the Western Cattle Expansion Company. Crowds often blocked their view and sometimes Thomas had difficulty in controlling the horses. The people massing along the main street reminded Kath of Richmond the day she left, but this wasn't an army retreating in defeat; it was more like an intoxicated mob, the kind that got drunk and celebrated at big sporting and political events. Kath had slept on and off during the long journey and felt refreshed, ready for battle. The sight of the crowds encouraged her, the sheer animal energy of these people. No wonder her Dad had been attracted here!

Sensing her mood, Horatio Thomas leaned forward to block the view of the gallows, but then a sudden stop to avoid a runaway horse threw him back. One quick glimpse of that wooden scaffold was enough. Her hand went to her throat. It was as if she could feel again the torture of waiting and the horror of the drop and then that agonising burning pain.

"So that's why the crowds are here," she murmured. She saw them differently now. What kind of people would take their children to watch somebody being hanged? People who lived everyday with violence!

"I wonder who they hanged?" Thomas said.

"Does it matter? It's the same for everybody."

"You don't believe in an eye for an eye, Kath?"

"Not when it means a hanging."

They had nearly reached the end of the main street when they saw the company's offices. An imposing bay window displayed a map of Kansas with a sign "Invest in the Future." Little American flags marked where the company owned land; there were a lot of flags. Kath noticed one at Alpine and another where the ranch was situated—that was certainly premature. It made her even more determined to fight them.

The office door was locked. A small handwritten notice stated: "Closed for Hanging. Open Tomorrow at 9 o'clock A.M."

"We'll lose a day," Kath said. She shook the door handle in frustration. "This is only a small town. People must know where the company bosses live." But passersby she asked were of no help. "Let's go to the local sheriff's office. They should know."

"That'll alert the whole town," Horatio Thomas warned her. "We better try to surprise them even if it means waiting until tomorrow."

"I know somebody here." Kath thought back. "Paul and I met a woman on a stagecoach crossing Missouri when we were on our way to Alpine. She works here at a place called the Diamond Saloon. She probably knows everybody in town."

The Diamond Saloon was easily found. Kath asked a barman if Galina was there.

"Who wants her?"

"I'm a friend."

A man in a black suit sitting at the bar drawled, "She's busy at present. Come back in a couple of hours."

They took two rooms in a local hotel and had a bath and a meal and then went back. Galina was sitting at the bar talking to the man in the black suit. They were saying something about a hangman and laughing.

Galina greeted Kath enthusiastically and eyed Horatio Thomas and his white suit with approval. Her opinion of Kath obviously went up seeing her with another man and someone so successful-looking so soon after meeting her with her husband. "I knew it must be you," she told Kath, "from the Doc's description. He said you were a beautiful redhead—"

"And I stand by that," said the man in the black suit. "Now I must get to work," and he strolled over to a poker game.

Galina watched him affectionately. "The Doc doesn't give a damn for anybody or anything. The only woman he ever cared about dropped him when he became sick. He's got tuberculosis, he won't do anything about it. I guess he wants to die his own way." She smiled at Kath. "Now how can I help you?"

Kath told her.

Galina said thoughtfully. "That company owns part of the town. The boss is a man named Hugo White. I don't know where he lives, but I can find out from one of the girls who knows him. He sometimes comes here through the private entrance at the back to see her. I'll go and ask her where you can find him."

She was gone a long time. Kath waited impatiently, watching the man in the black suit start to win in the poker game. Galina came back at last, full of apologies.

"Sorry, Kath, I know you're in a hurry, but I had to wait for the girl to finish with a customer. She says Hugo White has a private ranch outside Abilene. It's hard to find so she's drawn a map for you. . . ."

It was, indeed, hard to find, especially in the darkness of early evening. A private dirt road, several miles long, climbed round a hill like a switchback through gullies and blind turns that frightened the horses. Strong winds rocked the stagecoach and then at the top a wooden barrier blocked the road.

A voice yelled, "Who are you?", and they could see a man with a sawn-off shotgun.

"I'm a journalist," Horatio Thomas yelled back. "I've come to see Mister Hugo White."

"And the woman?"

"My . . . assistant."

A second man, similarly armed, appeared from behind them.

"You say you're a journalist. Can you prove it?"

Horatio Thomas produced his *Guardian* credentials.

"You from England?"

"Yes, I'm a special correspondent for the *Manchester Guardian*. I'm writing a series of articles about the development of the American West. I was recently in Washington, talking to General Grant. I want to talk to Mister Hugo White about his company and the development of Kansas, particularly his plans for Abilene."

"It's outside company hours, Mister."

"I'm well aware of that and I apologise for disturbing Mr. White in his home, but I have come a great distance and I am very short of time."

"Very well. Stay here. I'll ask him if he'll see you."

The man had a horse beyond the barrier. They heard him gallop away. They were covered by the other man's shotgun until he returned.

"Mr. White says he'll see you for a short time."

Kath squeezed Thomas's hand in triumph.

The barrier was pulled back to allow the stagecoach through. The dirt road flattened out after a short distance, and ahead lay about seven hundred acres of prime land in beautiful isolation.

The horseman led them directly to a ranch-house, an eight-room adobe home that was neat and plain on the outside but spectacularly colorful and well-furnished inside, with polished oak floors and lion skins for carpets and great cushioned armchairs and couches. Every room they glimpsed gave an impression of great wealth.

Kath and Horatio Thomas were passed on to a tall black man in a butler's formal dark suit, and he showed them into what he called "the library," though there were no books to be seen, only antique tables and chairs and valuable collections of silver goblets and china crockery in floor-to-ceiling glass cases.

"Please wait here," said the butler. "Mr. White is just completing his dinner with his family."

He half-bowed and disappeared.

Horatio Thomas chuckled. "It's hard to remember this is the Wild West. That butler would be more at home in England."

He brushed a fly off his white suit and sat down on one of the hard antique chairs, but Kath prowled restlessly round the room, inspecting everything.

"It's like an antique store," she said admiringly. "The contents of this room alone must be worth a fortune. Whoever lives in a house like this must be a gentleman. Certainly not the kind to go round shooting people. I bet he doesn't even know what happened at the ranch. . . ."

Kath had been slowly circling the room staring at the pictures on the walls as she talked to Thomas. There were paintings, drawings and photographs, all in heavy gold frames. Suddenly she stopped in front of a photograph as if unable to believe what she saw. She gave a cry of astonishment.

"My God. . . ."

"What is it, Kath?"

"Look. . . ."

She pointed and her hand was trembling.

Horatio Thomas stood up to get a better view. He saw an old photograph of a child—a young girl with long hair and a bold smile—so faded and creased he could hardly see the face.

"What's so surprising about that?"

Kath turned to him, her eyes wide with shock, her face bloodless.

"Don't you see who that is? It's *me!* That's the photograph I gave my Dad when he left home."

30

When a dream starts to come true, you daren't believe it. You try to explain away what's happening. . . .

The sight of the worn old photograph caused a surge of emotion in Kath that scared her. It seemed to unlock the past and bring everything flooding back. There she was again thrusting the photograph into her father's hands as he stood at the front door, ready to leave home forever. But how had it reached this ranch-house, the home of the enemy? Her Dad would never have given it away, not *her* picture.

There was only one explanation.

She shrank from it, but she had to face it.

He was *dead*.

They had murdered him just as they had Paul's parents.

Her eyes blurred with tears.

"I've lost him for good. . . ."

Her shoulders shook, and Horatio Thomas's long arms went round her, drawing her to him.

"Kath, don't give up until you know for sure. Be brave. . . ."

Horatio Thomas obviously thought he was dead, too. That made her feel even worse. Her tears flowed, smudging the lapels of the English journalist's white jacket. He stroked her hair and tried to comfort her.

They were both so absorbed that they didn't notice someone

enter the room until a man's deep voice said behind them, "I'm Hugo White. What do you want with me?"

Standing in the doorway was a middle-aged man, heavily built, with a tanned, clean-shaven face and dyed black hair. He was wearing a dark, formal suit that matched the antique room, but not the cattle ranch outside.

Kath wiped away her tears as Horatio Thomas faced the man and said politely, "I'm a special correspondent for the *Manchester Guardian*. My name's Horatio Thomas. I've come here, sir, to write about the west—"

He was suddenly interrupted by a loud cry from Kath. She half-pointed at the man with shocked eyes, then fell to the floor, fainting for the first time in her life.

* * *

Her head cleared in a few moments. As she struggled towards consciousness, she saw two faces bending over her.

Horatio Thomas's familiar features, full of concern, swam into view.

Then the other man's.

She clutched the man's hand.

"Is it really *you?*" she murmured, afraid she was dreaming.

The man was momentarily bewildered. "I don't understand. I'm Hugo White—"

"No, you're not," Kath said with a wide, almost ecstatic smile. "You're Joseph Tracy."

It was the man's turn to seem stunned, like someone experiencing the first spasm of a heart attack.

"Good God, it's Kathleen!" he cried.

His discovery was so unexpected that he stood gazing at her with his mouth open.

Kath was the first to recover.

She stood up, her whole body trembling with emotion.

"Dad," she murmured, "I've found you at last."

And she fell into his arms.

Horatio Thomas watched them embracing and laughing at each other. What pluck this girl had shown in chasing her dream halfway across the world—and now she had found it! They deserved time alone after all these years. The answers could come later. Thomas walked quietly out of the room.

They didn't even notice his going. At last they stood back and examined each other.

"I've dreamt about this moment," Kath said eagerly, "ever since you left home."

"Wherever did you spring from, Kath—a magic carpet?" He touched her cheek. "I never thought I'd see you again. You bring it all back—that vanished life. I can see you now, the little girl in the photograph. How did you ever find me?"

"I've been searching for you for months. I started in Richmond, the last address we had for you. I was told you'd come out here so I followed you. Oh, Dad, you look so well—and so prosperous. You're *rich!*" Her eyes took in his tanned, fleshy face, so confident-looking, and his expensive, well-cut suit and his air of belonging in these luxurious surroundings, and she tried to compare him with the man she had known in Stockport —they seemed like two different people. They even had different names. "Why do you call yourself Hugo White?"

He replied slowly. "I had to begin a new life in America, Kath. It wasn't easy to get started here. I had nothing but the few clothes I brought from England. I had to struggle for years before I got my chance. I needed a new name—a new . . . everything."

"But you're established now. Just look at this ranch, the size of it. You've got more land than Heaton Hall. You're a big success. Oh, Dad, why didn't you ever send for me? You promised you would. I waited and waited. I wouldn't have cared how hard it was."

"There was a civil war dividing the country," he said gravely. "Then out here, there's another kind of war. It's a violent way of life. Not a life for a young woman. I thought you'd be happier staying in Stockport."

"If you only knew how much I've longed for this moment— just to see you and hear your voice! You've got an American accent now, but I love it! Oh, you look so young." She touched his dyed black hair. "It suits you."

"And you," he said, gently caressing her cheeks, "you've grown into a beautiful young woman, Kath. All the young men must be after you."

"I'm married, Dad—"

"Married? My Kath? Who's the lucky fellow? Someone worthy of my girl, I hope."

"His name's Paul Blake. He was in the war and was badly wounded. I met him in a Richmond hospital when I was looking for you. He brought me back here to his family ranch." Her face grew troubled as she remembered. "That's why I came to Abilene, Dad. Your company's been trying to take over his ranch. I'm sure you know nothing about it, but his parents were killed."

"Were they now?" He drew a deep breath. "This can be a very violent country, Kath, in ways that you won't yet understand. People want to solve everything with a gun. I've been thankful a few times that I know how to use one—in self-defense, of course. But I sometimes have a hard time even controlling the people who work for me."

"I know, Dad, you're not involved. But you must stop them. They'll listen to you. There's a lawyer named Howard Wright who's backed up by gunmen. If you telegraph him—"

"We'll go into the company offices tomorrow morning and take care of it. Don't worry, Kath. Howard Wright can't be involved in the killings, but he may have exceeded his instructions. People out here are accustomed to a cruder way of doing business. They expect you to use a little muscle. But I'll straighten it out for you. You've no need to worry any more. You can relax. Now tell me," he added thoughtfully, "who's this journalist in the white suit? What's he after? Has he come all the way from Manchester just to see me? What does he know?"

Kath laughed. "Don't look so serious, Dad. You're not in some kind of trouble, are you?"

"Certainly not. I'm one of the leading citizens of Abilene. I just don't trust journalists. They're born trouble-makers!"

"Horatio Thomas is a friend. He came to America to write about the war, not about you. He's out west because I invited him. Some other friends, too. I felt I needed help against the lawyer and his gunmen."

He put an arm around her affectionately. "Any friend of yours must be all right. You wouldn't do me any harm, not my daughter Kath, the girl I used to go poaching with at the Hall!" He smiled at the memory and seemed more like his old humorous self. "But there's one confession I have to make, Kath darlin'. And let it be a secret between us. No one else must know." He winked at her the way he used to. "I've got married again in America."

"But you already have a wife!"

"In England, but not here." He explained confidingly, "I needed a wife to become established in America. An American businessman needs a solid reputation to win confidence—local roots, a settled home, a nice family. I married a woman in Richmond whose father had an undertaker's business. When he died during the war, I took over. At the start of the siege, I sent my wife away to Montgomery, Alabama, where she had a sister, but I stayed with the funeral home as long as I could. It was my real start in America."

"You were known as Joseph Tracy in Richmond."

"I changed my name when I came out west. I got *Hugo* from Victor Hugo, the author of a popular novel the Confederate soldiers were all reading. And *White*— well, in America, the superior race is white so I gave myself a superior name." He chuckled, showing several shiny gold teeth. "My wife had to become Mrs. White and keep her mouth shut about the past. She didn't like that. But, dammit, she's nothin' to complain about. I've set her up good. And moving on and starting again is much more common in America than in England, Kath. You accept anything to survive in wartime and in a violent place like Kansas. Never compare this with England. It's two different worlds."

"Why did you have to change your name? Because of that missing gold from Richmond?"

That surprised him. "So you know about that."

"Horatio Thomas learned about it in Richmond."

"That journalist. I knew he was a snooper—"

"No, Dad, he was doing it for me. I was afraid you'd been killed. What happened? Were you captured?"

He shrugged. "Well. . . ." The gold teeth flashed again. "Kath, at this rate, you'll know all my secrets. That was a terrible time, believe me. I was . . . left for dead. But I knew I'd get blamed for the missing gold. So I changed my name to be safe and I came here where no one knew me!"

"But if you were wounded, people wouldn't blame you."

He wagged a finger at her. "Kath, this isn't Stockport. People will kill their best friend here for gold. Human greed's a terrible thing."

"Who took the gold?"

"I don't know. Probably one of those Confederate generals back in Richmond. They plotted so they got the gold and I got the blame. But I was too smart for them. I got away."

"And the gold?"

"You sound like you're cross-examining me. You mustn't worry your pretty head about it. I'm safe now. Success protects you. Come, I'll introduce you to my wife, Rose. I hope you'll like her and become friends in time. But where's your journalist friend?" he asked suspiciously.

They went to look for Horatio Thomas. He was standing at the far end of a long, polished hallway, staring through a bay window at the light night sky studded with stars.

"Isn't it wonderful" Kath cried, rushing to him. "I've found my Dad at last. It's really him."

Horatio Thomas carefully eyed Kath and her father, and relaxed a little when he saw their pleased expressions. "I'm very happy for you, Kath. Your long search has been successful. You don't know what she's been through to find you, Mr. White. Nothing could discourage her, not even the civil war."

"That's my Kath. She was a determined little thing even when she was a young girl." Father and daughter linked arms affectionately. "How do you like the west, Mr. Thomas?"

"It's like turning the clock back," Horatio Thomas said. "The Industrial Revolution might never have happened out here." He stopped abruptly. It was out of character for Thomas to play a silent, retiring role, but this was Kath's show.

"We're not as backward as you think," the man now known as Hugo White said. "We're getting railroad connections through to the east coast. The Kansas Pacific Railroad, pushing westward across the great plain, is establishing a cattle shipping terminal at Abilene."

"But you haven't got the factories, the crowded industrial cities, the belching chimneys filling the skies with smoke—"

"Give us time and we'll catch up. The cattle business will

soon be very big here. You've seen Abilene. Well, we're setting up acres of stockyards, shipping-pens, and hostelries for
cattle drovers. Overnight, the town will become a center for a
great new era. The East needs beef and the West's got it. Steers
that cost next to nothing can be fattened on the range and sold
for $30 or $40 a head in the slaughterhouses of Chicago and
New York, and they'll be shipped from right here in Abilene.
The motto of Kansas is *Ad Astra Per Aspera*—Through Difficulty To The Stars. And that's where I'm going. I'm shooting
for the stars."

He chuckled and gently caressed Kath's cheek. Americans
believed in body contact, she thought. They liked hand-shak-
ing, touching you. It was part of the informality of Americans.
Her father had acquired the habit.

"Everything I've done, Kath, has been with Abilene's future
in mind. It's a once-in-a-lifetime opportunity, and if I don't grab
it with both hands, others will beat me out of it. Abilene is
going to become a boomtown and I'm going to boom with it.
I already own key areas needed for this economic expansion.
Everyone's goin' to have to buy from *me!*"

His eyes had a strange, acquisitive gleam as he talked. Listening to him, and then when he called the black butler, his attitude very much that of the Master, Kath was reminded not of
her Dad in Stockport so much as Edward—Edward giving orders at the factory, Edward bossing the servants at Heaton Hall,
and, yes, though she didn't like to think about it, Edward in the
stables, having his way with her. But the English social position
Edward inherited had given him that attitude, whereas her
father had learned it here in America. She had never expected
her Dad would have anything in common with Edward. It was
a big change in him—she'd have to get to know this strange
new side. It went with his success.

"Bring a bottle of French champagne and some glasses," he
instructed the butler in a cold, flat voice—the voice of authority
—and then, his tone warming up again, he told Kath, "We must
celebrate our reunion. Come to the sitting room and meet
Rose. But don't forget," and he put a finger to his lips, reminding her to keep quiet about his wife back in England.

He led them into another beautifully furnished room. A

blonde woman was sitting in a large blue padded armchair, the latest style in comfort, knitting what looked like a man's woollen sweater.

"Rose, I have someone very special I want you to meet."

The blonde woman put aside her knitting and stood up with a polite smile, and Kath took a good look at her. Her father's American wife was outwardly very different from his English wife—younger and smarter in appearance and more out-going —and yet Kath sensed a similar coldness from her.

"Hugo"—the woman's soft drawl reminded Kath of the way people in Richmond talked—"Why didn't you ever tell me you had a daughter in England? You never once mentioned her all these years."

It was obviously a big shock.

Hugo hastened to say Kath's mother was dead.

The woman said sympathetically, "I'm sorry, my dear," but her eyes were hard. She was clearly wondering why Kath had appeared after all this time. Was she after her father's money? Kath quickly explained that she was married to a rich rancher. That seemed to relax the woman a little.

Then, attracted by the strange voices, someone else entered the room.

A little boy.

With her father's features.

The resemblance was startling.

"This is little Joe," her father said proudly.

His son and heir!

Kath felt a pang of jealousy.

This woman and this little boy were her father's family now.

Somehow she had expected that when she found him, their relationship would be just the same as it had been before, but now she realised it could never be the same again.

She watched her father balance the little boy on his knees and she felt shut out—an outsider.

She noticed he held the boy with one hand, his left hand hidden in his pocket. He was still self-conscious about those missing fingers after all these years.

That somehow made her feel better.

Oh, she thought fondly, he can't have changed all that much. Deep down, he's still the same man he was in Stockport.

But she knew it would take time to get to know him again—and to be sure her dream really had come true.

* * *

They left for Abilene after an early breakfast served by a fat black housekeeper.

Rose pressed her to come again to the ranch—"Think of it as another home, my dear"—but her cold eyes said the opposite. Little Joe was no more friendly, as if he knew his mother's feelings. He informed Kath aloofly that he was waiting for his private tutor. *Private tutor!* Kath had a sudden memory of the damp, overcrowded stone schoolhouse with ragged books she'd attended in Stockport until she was old enough to work in the factory. My God, this boy had it easy. She wished she'd known her father in such rich, easy circumstances. They could have spent more time together. But her envy irritated her. She tried to kiss little Joe, but he turned his face away, that face so like her father's. The black butler was standing politely in the background, so she shook hands with him. He seemed surprised. As Rose walked with her to the front door, the blonde woman whispered, "Never treat servants as equals, my dear. They don't understand." The woman certainly was cold.

Outside the man she had to remember to call Hugo White was waiting with Horatio Thomas in front of a smart enclosed carriage drawn by two sleek black horses. Her father travelled in style!

"One of my men will drive your stagecoach," he told her.

"I'll drive it, Mr. White," said Horatio Thomas politely. "You and Kath can then talk privately. After all these years, you must still have a great deal to catch up on."

Hugo White—remember that's his name now! Kath kept telling herself. He seemed very relieved when Thomas walked away to the stagecoach. The English journalist's presence really did make him nervous.

Kath ran after Thomas. "Thank you for leaving us alone. I haven't had much time with Dad. His wife was always there. It'll give me a chance to ask him some questions about the Company. He says everything's going to be all right."

Horatio Thomas smiled to hide his own doubts.

"Just tell your father everything that's happened at the Silver Star Ranch. Now you've found each other, you can surely stop all the trouble. No one else need get hurt. Talk frankly!"

"I have done. But I'll talk some more on the way into town!"

As the two horses, so glossy and fresh at the start of the day, began the journey to Abilene, Kath noticed that one of the gunmen she had seen on her arrival rode behind. When she asked about him, Hugo White explained the man was his bodyguard. "A successful businessman needs bodyguards out here, Kath. Success makes enemies. People want to seize what you have. And who's to stop them? There's been no real law since the civil war. It's a wilderness compared to what you're used to. We never needed bodyguards in Stockport, did we? We had nothing to guard of any value, except our beautiful young daughter, Kathleen." He regarded her admiringly. "You've inherited your mother's beauty. That's another confession I've got to make to you. Victoria's not your mother."

"I know, Dad. I could never understand why Victoria gave the boys more love than me, then she told me the truth. She wasn't my real mother, just my stepmother, and she didn't know who my mother was. Or she said she didn't." The confrontation in the Manchester prison came back to Kath with all its bitterness. "She didn't seem to care."

"Victoria's a hard woman. She could have done well out here, but she's too narrow-minded to adapt herself. She'd merely have held me back. She couldn't have grown with me. I was better without her. But she told you the truth. She didn't know. That all happened before I met Victoria—back in Ireland when I was a youth. Your mother lived in my hometown in County Roscommon. She was going to be a nun, then she . . . I suppose people said she *sinned*. She got pregnant and died giving birth to the baby. The baby was you, Kath. She was 17 and I was 18."

"What was her name?"

"Kathleen Clare. I gave you her name. You also have her red hair and her looks. She was very beautiful. I couldn't forget her the first time I saw her at Mass in the parish church. I had to make her my own. It was hard because she was training to be a nun. But I sat near her in church every Sunday until she noticed me. Her father tried to have me arrested. When she died, he had the parish priest denounce me in the church at every service. I fled to England with you."

Kathleen Clare. . . .

"Tell me more about her—what kind of person was she?"

"You remind me of her, Kath, in your ways as well as your looks. When we used to go poaching at Heaton Hall, I felt sometimes as if I was with her again. She was innocent but she was also . . . independent . . . *free*. She had the courage to be herself, to go her own way once she made up her mind. She went against both her father and the parish priest. That wasn't easy. . . ."

Sunlight flashed on the window and he pulled down the shade. He had gradually relaxed as he talked, and his deformed left hand had come out of his pocket. Kath took a quick look at the two little hard stubs, so ugly and out of character on the self-confident, successful man he had become.

"I sometimes think your mother was the one thoroughly good person I've ever known and that my life took a wrong turn when she died—all those wasted years with Victoria in England, all those babies year after year I didn't want and couldn't feed. I felt I'd been a different man with your mother, a free man, and now I was trapped. The factory was my prison, a lifetime's imprisonment. I had to escape, even though it meant leaving you."

"You were trying to find her again in America. Someone as good as her. You were pursuing a dream."

"No, Kath, that's too romantic. I came to America to make my fortune and I've succeeded after a long, hard struggle. When I arrived in New York from Liverpool, I became just another Irish immigrant on slave wages. But then I heard how the South worshipped the English so I moved to Virginia and made the most of my English connections. At first I hated the undertaker's work, dealing with the dead, but it was very profitable as the civil war raged on. In time, you can get used to anything. In America, I've had to. Success doesn't come easy. You've got to fight for it. You have to become as hard as everyone else. Ruthless even. I don't think your mother would recognise me now, Kath." His face tightened, and his deformed left hand disappeared back into his pocket. He said gruffly, "Now let's get down to business about this ranch of yours. You say your husband's parents were killed about the time we made our offer. Who killed them? Is that known?"

"The killers were supposed to be rustlers."

"That's quite likely. Kansas is riddled with cattle thieves."

"But they came right after that lawyer had made his offer and been turned down. Then he returned and threatened me and my husband."

"You're talking about our company's attorney, Howard Wright?"

"He said that was his name."

"What else did he tell you?"

"It wasn't what he said so much as how he behaved. He had a gang of gunmen with him."

"They could have been his bodyguards, like mine back there."

"Then a Pinkerton detective named Fogarty was killed. I'm sure it's all connected."

The man known as Hugo White frowned thoughtfully as the carriage bumped over a stretch of rough ground. "Feelings are one thing, Kath, but evidence is another. People have been killed out here for pointing a finger at the wrong man. My company's not involved. I can assure you of that. We're well established here now. We're buying up cheap land all over the state ready for the time Kansas becomes a magnet for outside investors. But it's all quite legal. We're simply outsmarting the other speculators. Where is this ranch of yours?"

"Near a little town called Alpine."

His eyes narrowed. "What's the name of it?"

"The Silver Star."

He blinked rapidly. "You're involved with that?"

"My husband is sole owner now his parents are dead."

"That's special land," he said slowly, as if deciding how much to tell her. "Your husband should get a good price. It'll set you up in any business you want."

"But Paul doesn't want to sell."

"He must, Kath. That land's too important to Abilene."

"Why's it so important?"

He hesitated.

"You can trust me, Dad."

He said reluctantly, "The railroad's goin' to cross that land. Without the railroad, Abilene'll stay like it is and I'll lose the chance of a lifetime. Get your husband to sell and I'll cut you in, Kath. You'll make a lot of money."

"You don't understand, Dad. It's Paul's home. He *won't* sell. He's made up his mind he's staying—and I think he's right."

"I'll not have anybody ruinin' my plans," he snapped, his face flushing with anger. He made a great effort to control himself. For a few moments, the only sound was the bumping of the carriage over the hard, sun-baked earth. Kath felt uneasy. This was the strange new side of her father. The ranch *was* important to him. It was part of his dream for Abilene. But surely it was just a good business deal he could give up if he had to.

She urged him, "Telegraph your attorney, Dad. There's not much time left. He's due back on the first of the month—the day after tomorrow. My husband and my friends are waiting at the ranch. I don't want them harmed."

He didn't answer, but pushed up the windowshade and stared grimly out. The carriage had reached the outskirts of the town. It was obviously well known. People began to wave or touch their hats. This pleased him. He smiled at her. "Look, Kath, your father's well-respected. Some of these Americans even . . . *fear* me." This proof of his power seemed to give him great satisfaction.

On the muddy main street, the two sleek black horses slowed instinctively in approaching the Diamond Saloon, but the driver urged them on with a crack of his whip. Kath remembered what Galina had said—that Hugo White was friendly with one of the girls. Kath wondered if he was going behind his blonde wife's back with another woman, but even if he was, what did it matter? His wife was cold. The Diamond Saloon was his beer-house now. That thought pleased her. She welcomed anything that made her father seem unchanged from the old days in Stockport.

"Have you any children?" he suddenly asked.

"No, we can't have any . . . because of my husband's war wound."

"A woman should have children. A childless marriage won't last long. Do you love the man?"

Love Paul?

"He's a good man," she said hesitantly.

"But do you love him?"

Tell him the truth.

"I . . . like him."

He nodded, as if pleased with her admission. "Liking's not enough for a hot-blooded young woman. Maybe you should get yourself another man and make me some grandchildren. Don't look angry, Kathleen. I'm only being realistic. That man and his ranch might be just a heap of trouble to you."

"That's my business, Dad. I'm Paul's wife."

"And I'm your father, not his. I want the best for *you.*" He seemed to reach a decision as the horses drew up smartly in front of the Company's offices. "Very well," he said slowly, "We'll leave the Silver Star Ranch alone. I'll telegraph Howard Wright to that effect right now. He'll have the message by lunchtime. Your happiness comes first with me, Kath."

"Oh, Dad." She kissed him impulsively. "I knew I could count on you." She was thinking of Joseph Tracy, not Hugo White. "I can go back now without any worries."

"There's one condition."

"What's that?"

"You have dinner with me. I know a saloon with a restaurant for the elite that serves excellent buffalo meat. It tastes as good as the pheasant we used to poach together."

Kath smiled at her father.

"We certainly have cause for a celebration."

She had accomplished what she had come to America for.

She had found him.

She had also succeeded in her mission to Abilene.

The ranch was safe.

She began to relax.

It was time to enjoy herself.

"I accept your invitation with pleasure, Mr. Tracy . . . I mean, Mr. White."

31

The Diamond Saloon was crowded. Several noisy groups of cowboys were spending their wages. There had already been a fight at the bar, and the bouncers were being kept busy.

Galina, listening to the drunken shouts below, was pleased she wasn't available. She was in an upstairs bedroom with the young hangman and he had bought her for all night.

They had already made love, and now he was lying back, naked, with his eyes closed. She didn't know if he was asleep or just brooding—he seldom shared his thoughts with her.

Suddenly a terrific crash came from downstairs. It sounded like a chair thrown against a wall. Frank Butler's dark eyes half-opened and he leaned over, feeling for the whisky bottle on the floor.

"It's empty," she told him.

"Get me some more."

"You want more lovin', not more liquor."

"I told you what I want," Frank grunted.

Galina wondered why he sometimes turned so cold. It wasn't the coldness of a customer, who thought his money gave him the right to treat her any way he wanted. Money meant little to the young hangman. He always treated her generously and he could be very warm and loving when he wanted. But then he seemed to change and become deliberately cold. It was as if he didn't trust his feelings. She sometimes thought he was haunted by a ghost from his past, and when he made love to her, he was thinking of someone else. Perhaps it's for the best, she told herself. Otherwise I might fall in love with him.

"You want the same whisky?"

"It's the strongest they have."

Frank slept while she was gone. He dreamt of his cottage in Stockport and the black stallion, and Kath was there. She was in some kind of trouble. He awoke sweating. His hand groped for Galina, wanting to forget the dream, but she wasn't back yet. He lay there waiting, struggling against sleep. Finally she came in with a bottle. He drank thirstily. The heat out west made him drink more. The heat and the hangings.

"You been gone a long time. Been servicing another customer?"

"No, Frank, honey, I was just talkin' to some people I know. A local rich man. Ever heard of Hugo White?"

He shook his head. "Should I know him?"

"Stay long in Abilene and you will. Hugo White is a powerful man in this town. He's here with a young woman I met on the stagecoach coming here. They bought me a drink."

"So I had to wait for my drink."

"Not long."

"Long enough."

Galina had been surprised to see Kath so friendly with Hugo White. He was buying her and the man in the white suit an expensive dinner. That was surprising, too. He was known at the saloon for being tight with his money.

"Mr. White said there's going to be another hangin'."

Frank took a long drink.

"One of the men's real young," she said. "Came in here last week and it was his first time. They got him for rustlin'. His name's Chris Curtis. Seemed a nice kid."

"Shut up," Frank snapped at her. "I don't want to hear it. I never talk about it. I told you that. *Never.* Come here." He pulled her to him and kissed her on the mouth. His knee forced her thighs apart.

"Take it easy, handsome. You got all night." But he didn't listen and she knew it was her own fault. She shouldn't have mentioned the hanging. It always aroused him. . . .

* * *

"To Kath!" toasted Hugo White.

"To us!" said Kath.

"To you both!" cried Horatio Thomas, touching glasses with each of them.

They were sitting in a quiet back room at the Diamond Saloon. They had just finished eating. A waiter had brought another bottle of heavy red wine and that had set off the toasts. Until then, Horatio Thomas had sat back and let them talk about the old days. He must be thoroughly bored, Kath thought, but he's being very nice about it.

Now he stood up. "If you'll excuse me for a few minutes, I'll take a quick look at the gambling."

"Be careful," Hugo White warned him. "A lot of drunken cowboys are out there."

"I'll keep my distance," Horatio Thomas said with a smile as he departed.

"Journalists like to snoop around," said Hugo White. "But people in this town don't like snoopers. I'll get someone to watch out for him." He was gone for a few minutes. "That's taken care of your friend the journalist," he said with satisfaction on his return. "I also got you this." It was another bottle of wine.

"You'll get me drunk," Kath protested.

"I'm not reunited with my daughter every day! Stay longer, Kath. I'll show you my cattle herds and some of my land holdings. Maybe you and I can work together like in the old days."

"I must get back tomorrow, Dad. Paul needs me."

She was aware of a tension in her father. At first she had assumed it came from the revival of unpleasant memories, and perhaps even guilt about abandoning his family in England. But she had noticed his manner change after he sent the message to the attorney in Alpine. She had asked him if anything was wrong, but he had told her, "Everything's fine. There's nothing to worry about." But he had grown tense and he remained so all evening. The wine and the reminiscing didn't relax him. He had the tension of someone waiting for news.

"You left some of your buffalo meat," he said reprovingly. "Didn't you like it?"

"It was very tasty, but. . . ." She held her hands to her stomach and grimaced as if very full. How could she explain that the meat reminded her of the buffalo she'd seen shot? The man who'd done it had been shot himself later. Maybe even eating the meat was bad luck with the Indians—like spilling salt or walking under ladders in Stockport. "I must get some sleep so we can leave early."

"The night's still young," he said thickly. "Don't leave me yet, Kath."

"I have to." She stood up. "I must find Horatio Thomas. . . ."

Her father rose unsteadily, holding on to the table, and led her down a private passageway. A burly man with a green eyeshade stepped out of an office.

"Everything goin' well, Mr. White?" The man glanced at Kath as if to check she had supplied what the customer wanted, and he seemed surprised to see a strange face.

"Where's the journalist?"

"In the bar."

The man took them a private route through side rooms to avoid the gamblers. Horatio Thomas was sitting calmly at the bar talking to a lean, hard-faced cowboy, dressed all in black.

"Howdy, Mr. White," said the cowboy respectfully. "I think I got two great guns for your collection."

Hugo White nodded brusquely. "Bring them to the office in the morning."

"An interesting fellow," Horatio Thomas said as they went out to the carriage. "He says he was one of Quantrill's men."

"That murderous outlaw!" Kath said. "He and his gang raided the stagecoach Paul and I travelled on."

"There's been a general amnesty since the war," her father told her. "Quantrill's men are free to start a new life. That man back there's a gunsmith. I buy my guns from him. People collect guns here the way they do umbrellas in England."

He climbed laboriously into his carriage and didn't speak during the short ride to the hotel. Kath thought her father was drunk the way he sometimes was when he came home from the pub. But, as she leaned over to kiss him good-bye, he suddenly came awake. He seemed to shake off the effects of the heavy

red wine and, leaning close to her, he whispered, "Kath, remember . . . everything that happens will be for the best
. . . Trust me. . . ."

It was intended to reassure her, but instead filled her with
uneasiness, a tension similar to his own.

What did her father *mean?*

But he was already on his way, the carriage rattling up the
main street towards the edge of town.

"You need some rest," Horatio Thomas said, looking at her.

"I don't need rest, I need to get home. Let's leave at once."

* * *

The ranch was so quiet that Bo, cleaning his guns on the back
porch, could hear the horses moving in the barn.

He worked for a long time on the Peacemakers and then
tested them with some rapid target practise. The Colts were
perfectly balanced, every part working smoothly.

"Bo's restless," said the Reverend, watching the young
Texan through the kitchen window. "You can always tell when
he starts playin' with them guns."

"Who the hell cares if he is restless?" grunted Paul. "I didn't
ask him to come here."

"You and him should get together. If there's trouble, we'll
need each other and we'll need Bo more'n anybody."

Paul's eyes blazed with hatred.

"He wants my wife."

"A lot of men will feel that way. You betta get used to it,
Paul. But, remember, wantin's one thing and havin's another."

Bo came back inside, his tanned face unusually serious. Paul
immediately got up and went upstairs.

"Our host still don't like me."

"Give him time, Bo."

"We ain't got that much time."

"You think somethin's goin' to happen?"

Bo brushed his fair hair off his forehead. "I got a feelin',
Reverend."

"Well, you ain't no emotional woman. If you say that, it
means somethin'." The Reverend reached for his gunbelt on
the back of a chair.

"Keep it to yourself for now, Reverend."

Bo lit a thin cigar. Behind him, Ram and Wash Greene were arguing as they washed the dirty dishes from dinner. The black American thought their dark color gave them both something in common. But the young Sikh soon corrected him.

"You an American, me an Indian—Asian Indian. You belong to a young, uncivilised country, but India has an ancient culture."

"I came from Africa, the oldest country of all."

"You yourself born in America, but me, Ram, I born in Kashmir!"

The argument didn't help Bo's restlessness, and he threw away his thin cigar and went outside again, standing on the porch and staring at the horizon against the starry night sky. He could see nothing, nobody. There was another day to go before the first of the month, so why did he feel uneasy? Yet the young Texas knew himself well enough to trust his instincts.

Something was wrong.

Something was about to happen.

But *what?*

Watching him from the kitchen window, the Reverend saw him pause to light another cigar and then walk across the dry, hard-baked ground until he reached the trail.

Bo knelt and put his head down, one ear touching the ground.

He listened for a long time.

There was a far-off murmur like the sensation from a seashell. But it wasn't the sea Bo could hear, but the faint reverberation of horses' hooves.

And it wasn't the stagecoach with its four horses.

There were at least a dozen coming.

They were still a few miles off, but riding straight to the ranch, their thudding hooves sending a warning ahead of them.

They were returning a day early.

Bo didn't bother to wonder why.

He raced for the ranch-house.

He slammed open the door and everyone looked up.

"They're comin'," he said calmly. "Everyone take the positions we worked out." He touched the Peacemakers at his sides. "I'll take the barn." He looked directly at Paul. "If you have to talk to 'em, don't show yourself."

"I can take care of myself," Paul snapped.

"We all gotta take care of each other," Bo said. "It sounds like we're outnumbered."

He left them and walked quickly to the barn. From there, he might take the visitors by surprise.

There wasn't long to wait. Soon he could hear the horses' hooves without putting his ear to the ground, and a faint dust cloud in the distance grew steadily bigger. There were over a dozen riders, and they all wore neckerchiefs over their faces. As soon as Bo saw that, he opened a box of bullets. He knew he'd need them.

Most of the riders came straight to the ranch-house, though a few hung back as a rearguard.

"Paul Blake," one of them shouted, "we wanta talk to you."

There was no immediate response.

"Paul Blake," shouted the leading rider again.

Slowly the ranch-house door opened.

What's the fool doin'? Bo thought angrily.

Paul came out slowly onto the porch, looking very nervous.

"You Paul Blake?"

"That's right. What do you want with me?"

In answer, the rider raised a shotgun. Paul realised his danger then, but he seemed confused as to whether to draw his own gun or to try to get back inside. The shotgun roared. Paul was blasted back against the door and then his body fell like a rag doll.

Bo, in a deadly rage, stepped out of the barn. Even then he couldn't shoot anyone in the back.

"Here," he cried.

The riders turned, their guns out, and the Peacemakers roared this time. One, two, three, four, five shots came in rapid succession, and five riders, one after the other like so many skittles, tumbled off their horses. It was a remarkable display of marksmanship, especially as Bo had given them a chance. The other riders quickly retreated down the trail to regroup. They'd soon be back.

Bo ran to the front porch, but he knew already Paul was

beyond help. Nobody survived a shotgun blast in the chest. Bo looked angrily down at the pale, dead face. He'd warned the fool, but Paul had wanted to play a hero and he'd paid for it.

A rifle cracked and a bullet thudded into the woodwork over Bo's head. He darted into the ranch-house, leaving Paul's body on the porch. They probably had a long siege ahead, and a dead body could have a bad effect on morale.

The battle had begun. . . .

*   *   *

The lean, hard-faced cowboy brought the guns early the next morning to Hugo White's office. He had hidden them in a roll of cotton.

"These guns are special, Mr. White. I got 'em from a wounded boy who needed money for treatment. He was shot up in Mexico. He was with Quantrill's old gang with me."

All the time the cowboy was talking, he was unwrapping the guns. Now he held them out, the ivory handles glistening in the early morning sunlight through the office window. Hugo White gave a low whistle of admiration, even though he knew it would put up the price.

"I saw guns like 'em once in Richmond. Never saw any like 'em again, before or since."

"There's only one other pair. This boy didn't want to sell, but the doc wanted money in his hand before he'd treat Jesse's wound. Damn near bled to death."

"How much did you give him?"

"Two hundred in gold."

Hugo White knew he was lying. He'd added at least another fifty.

"How much do you want for 'em?"

"Three hundred to you, Mr. White. Four hundred to anybody else. In gold. I don't deal in Confederate money or any other kind of paper money. Most of it ain't worth the paper it's printed on since the war."

"Three hundred's a lot of money for a pair of guns."

"These are the finest I ever saw, Mr. White. A man's a king with guns like these. Nobody can touch him. I'd charge you less, but I gotta make a profit. I had to ride down to Mexico to see Jesse and bargain with him."

Hugo White eyed the Peacemakers. He knew he had to have them. Guns like that were power; they earned a man even more respect than a good horse.

"I'll give you two-fifty for 'em."

"Well, Mr. White, seein' as you're special, how about two-seventy-five?"

"Done."

He counted out two hundred and seventy-five dollars in gold from a leather bag he took out of his jacket pocket.

"Your daughter still here, Mr. White?"

"No, she's gone back. Rode off at daylight with the journalist. I held her as long as I could."

"But you've kept her out of trouble?" The cowboy winked.

"Sure. I'm waiting for news now. I told Wright to telegraph me as soon as it was all over."

32

Going late to bed and getting up before dawn, Kath was still sleepy as the old stagecoach left Abilene behind and rattled along the rough trail back eastwards. The flat sun-baked plain soon stretched endlessly on all sides—the great American desert!

Kath yawned, lulled by the heat and the horses' steady rhythm. Horatio Thomas, sitting erect in the driver's seat, felt her head rest against his shoulder. Dear Kath, he thought, the excitement of meeting your father has worn you out. I just wish that all your troubles were over now, but I'm afraid they're not.

Thomas pulled his wide-brimmed white hat further down over his face against the blazing sun and urged on the tiring horses with a snaking crack of his whip. After the first hour, he felt he knew the horses' backsides by heart, and to stay awake, he began to name the other parts of the horses' anatomy: mane, tail, hoof, muzzle, forelock. . . .

The horses' sweat, oozing out of their dark hides, reminded Horatio Thomas of the froth on the top of the Atlantic waves. That sent his mind back over all that had happened since his arrival in America. Like the young Frenchman, De Tocqueville, thirty years ago, he had come to seek "the image of democracy" and learn what it promised—could the American Dream come true? He thought of Kath's father. Had the American Dream come true in his case, or was Hugo White just another robber baron, like the men he had seen waiting for General Grant in Washington?

Kath suddenly moaned in her sleep against his shoulder.

He glanced down at the beautiful, troubled face.

That's my answer, he told himself. I can't see her father objectively because I'm too involved with her. I want the American Dream to come true for Kath. But that can only happen within, he thought. Was Kath ready? She had matured in America, but had she matured enough yet in this, her second chance at life, to find what she was truly looking for and not just the security the figure of her father had meant to her as a little girl? Thinking of the way she clung to her father, Thomas doubted she was ready.

She suddenly opened her eyes and, for a moment, seemed unsure where she was.

"Had a bad dream?" Thomas asked softly.

"How did you know?"

"You were moaning in your sleep."

She had dreamt she was with Edward in the stables that last time and the knife was already in her hand when . . . when Edward's face suddenly turned into the tanned, fleshy features of . . . *her father.* She remembered back in Abilene thinking that her father gave orders like Edward. That was where the dream had come from. Surely it had no more importance than that.

The draining heat and the monotony of the endless, sun-baked land strangely comforted her now. It seemed so far from the setting of her dream.

"Don't you love the west?" she murmured.

"The landscape, not the way of life. The dangers are so much greater, human life's cheaper—"

"The rewards are bigger, too. Look at my Dad."

"He's certainly done well for himself."

Kath sensed a lack of enthusiasm in the English journalist's voice. "You don't like my Dad?"

Horatio Thomas said slowly, "I must be frank with you, Kath, and please don't take offense. I built up a picture of your father from all that you'd told me about him, and the man I met was nothing like him."

"He has changed. He's become a success. That would change anybody. It gives you great self-confidence, brings out qualities you didn't know you had." She added quickly, "Life's different here. You're more on your own. Dad had no chance to prove himself in England. Here he has had the chance to show what he can do."

Kath sounded very defensive, Thomas thought. Perhaps she's beginning to doubt him herself. "I suspect your father would fit Charles Darwin's theory of the survival of the fittest perfectly," he told her gently. "Darwin says in *The Origin of Species* that each successful new species has to have 'some advantages over those with which it comes into competition,' and that it often successfully 'takes the place of other breeds in other countries.' Darwin quotes the example of shorthorn cattle, but he might just as well be referring to successful immigrants like your father."

"You're not comparing my father to shorthorn cattle?"

"Cattle or human beings . . . it's all the same to a naturalist like Darwin."

"Or to a journalist like you. You're just passing through the west as an observer—an outsider. You're not struggling to settle here and make a new home for yourself like me and my Dad. He told me how hard life was for him when he first arrived."

"Did he explain about the Confederate gold?"

"He was left for dead—and to take all the blame. That was why he changed his name. And I don't blame him!"

"What happened to the gold?"

"He didn't know." Suddenly she didn't want to be questioned about it. Journalists asked too many questions. She stared at the horizon that seemed as faraway as ever. "Can't we go any faster?"

"The horses are feeling the heat as badly as we are. I can't push them any more. What's the rush? Your father told you there'd be no trouble."

"I just want to get home."

She wanted to have a long talk with Paul.

They had to reach a better understanding.

She watched the horses and seemed to become part of their

steady rhythm—near hind hoof, off hind, near fore, off fore, all touching the hard ground in a fast, natural, four-beat gallop.

Horatio Thomas insisted on stopping briefly during the long hot afternoon to eat and drink, and twice to relieve himself, but otherwise they kept on at the same fast pace towards the ranch —towards home.

* * *

Half a dozen more raiders had arrived to replace the men Bo had shot, and sheer numbers now began to tell. The ranch was surrounded, and a steady barrage of pistols, shotguns and rifles kept everyone at bay behind the shutters, upstairs and downstairs, front and back. Wash Greene and Aunt Martha were upstairs, Bo and the Reverend and Ram were downstairs.

The first switch in tactics came with a fiery wooden stake that was hurled through the back kitchen window. It burst through the shutters and fell in a blaze of sparks on the kitchen floor.

The Reverend, who had held off several attacks with a gun in each hand, shouting "Come and get it, you devils," roaring with laughter as if having a fine time, grabbed the blazing stake, opened the kitchen door, and hurled it out. But as he did so, his huge figure was clearly outlined in the doorway, and waiting gunmen shot him several times in the chest. He went on firing himself as he went down.

"Bo," he called.

Bo came running, leaving Ram to cover the front. The Peacemakers cracked. Someone screamed outside. Bo quickly shut the kitchen door and knelt by the Reverend.

The big man, his chest covered in blood, murmured softly, "Looks like I'll be leavin' . . . before the end." The real person, shy and unfulfilled, seemed to have come out of hiding in the dying warrior's body. The Reverend's face trembled with effort as he whispered shyly, "Hope I haven't . . . let you down . . . Bo." He tried to say more, but even his great strength failed at last. And his weary, pain-wracked head sank on his shattered chest.

Bo gripped one of the huge, lifeless hands. He couldn't believe the Reverend was dead. The big man had always seemed so indestructible. It made him feel more mortal himself. For the first time in his life, Bo thought of the possibility of losing—that the raiders might win.

"You never let nobody down in your whole life, Reverend," he said aloud. "You always fought a great fight."

His face ice cold, Bo went to the broken shutters and waited for one of the raiders to show himself. He needed some kind of release for his pent-up feelings. Killing would do.

* * *

Kath and Horatio Thomas passed the rock with the silver star at dusk. Ahead of them on the trail was a lone horseman, a tall, straight figure riding slowly with great care and dignity. The horseman had already heard them, but he let the stagecoach reach him before turning coolly to examine them with one good eye, the other covered with a black eye-patch.

"I'm Captain Benjamin Jack," he said with a friendly grin.

"You must be Bo's father," Kath replied, surprised but pleased, too.

"And you must be the little lady my son came to rescue." He touched his faded old Texas Ranger cap. "My son's got good taste, ma'am."

Kath didn't know how to respond to that. She was a married woman and all her guilt feelings about Paul returned.

"Bo's at the ranch, Captain Ben," she said quickly. "We're on our way there now."

"You go ahead and I'll follow you, ma'am. I'm just out of the hospital. I gotta ride easy."

"Take your time, Captain Ben. There's no hurry. We'll ride along with you."

"Bo came expectin' trouble."

"It's all over now."

"You mean I could've stayed home?"

"Now you can pay us a visit."

Captain Ben Jack began to make a gallant reply when he suddenly stopped, listening.

"You sure the trouble's over, ma'am?"

"It was settled in Abilene. We're just coming back from there to give the others the good news."

Captain Ben went on listening. Kath could hear nothing.

"I think you're mistaken, ma'am. I hear some shootin' ahead."

Kath, her heart beating faster, listened again, but she still couldn't hear anything. She looked at Horatio Thomas. He shook his head. He could hear nothing.

"You sure?"

"I lost an eye, ma'am, but nuthin's wrong with my hearin'. There's a shootin' party a few miles on. We better get there fast."

Captain Ben forgot his need for care and dug his spurs in. His chestnut mare, restrained for so long, rushed ahead. Horatio Thomas used his whip to catch up. Soon both he and Kath could hear the crackle of gunfire.

"That's at the ranch," Kath said, all her fears returning.

She took her gunbelt out of a bag and strapped her two Colts round her waist. Horatio Thomas put his pistol on the seat beside him.

The ranch came into view.

Captain Ben yelled back at them, "Looks like real trouble."

Smoke was pouring out of the barn. There was also a fire at the back of the ranch-house. Sparks shot up over the roof.

Through the smoke, Kath saw several gunmen firing at the front of the ranch-house. Occasional answering shots came from the ranch-house, but not many.

"I thought your father said there wasn't going to be any trouble," Horatio Thomas said angrily.

What had gone wrong?

* * *

Bo coughed and his eyes smarted from the smoke coming from upstairs.

"I'm goin' to check," he called to Ram.

Aunt Martha, her head roughly bandaged, was propped up behind the shutters at an upstairs window. She was a great old warrior, Bo thought, but she couldn't take much more. She was protecting her face from the smoke with a wet towel, but her breathing was bad.

He then went to see Wash, who had covered a whole side of the ranch-house for hours and also kept the fire under control.

Wash was lying face down on the floor of a bedroom.

Bo rushed to him and gently turned him over.

Wash had been shot so many times his clothes had been torn away, exposing his smooth, black skin. One of the raiders was lying dead on the roof outside. Another was on the ground below.

Bo thought Wash was dead already, but his eyes flickered open, bloodshot and full of pain, but still glinting with amusement.

"Time to go," he murmured, trying to grin, his white teeth red with blood.

"Too soon, Wash," was all Bo could think to say to his friend. He'd got Wash into this.

"The . . . luck of the game, Bo," panted Wash.

The young black man's eyes froze, losing all their life, and his head became a dead weight against Bo's hand.

Wash was gone.

Bo slowly stood up, as close to despair as he'd ever been.

He decided not to tell Aunt Martha, but went on downstairs.

He was in time to see two gunmen coming in from the kitchen, creeping up on Ram. The Peacemakers were drawn and fired in one swift movement, but not before one of the gunmen had shot Ram. The young Sikh went over as if he were dead.

My God, Bo thought, that leaves just me and the old woman.

Another shot rang out and Bo grabbed his shoulder.

It was then he heard the yells and the shooting in the distance.

* * *

"Make as much noise as you can," Captain Ben shouted.

He fired into the air several times with both his old Colts and gave a series of loud, blood-curdling war whoops.

Kath and Horatio Thomas also fired their guns and yelled.

To the distant gunmen circling the ranch-house, ready for a final attack, it must have seemed as if the U.S. Cavalry had arrived.

Kath saw the gunmen race for their horses and gallop off round the back of the ranch-house. She counted five men, the lower parts of their faces hidden by neckerchiefs. They were soon speeding for the horizon.

Kath noticed then about a dozen bodies scattered over the ground between the ranch-house and the barn. She stared anxiously at each one, afraid she might recognise one of her friends. But the dead were all strangers. The scene reminded her of the civil war in Virginia. Death and destruction. Her father hadn't been able to stop the raid. His instructions had been ignored. They hadn't even waited until the first of the month, but had made a surprise attack a day early. What did it *mean?*

Captain Ben galloped up to the ranch-house, closely followed by the stagecoach.

The Captain got stiffly off his horse and hurried up the steps of the front porch, pistol in hand. But then he suddenly stopped and looked down.

There was another body in the doorway.

A man.

Coming behind him, Kath peered over his shoulder, dreading whom she'd see.

A thin, dark-haired face with sightless eyes.

"You know him, ma'am?" Captain Ben asked gently.

"Yes . . . he was my husband."

Paul . . . with a gaping shotgun wound in his chest.

The life had been blown out of him.

His dead face had a surprised expression.

At least death had come fast.

But she should have been here with him.

And she would have been but for her father's promise.

Now there would be no talk . . . no better understanding . . . no reconciliation.

Her spirit felt crushed. . . .

The front door of the ranch-house opened with a clatter.

Bo.

A Peacemaker in his right hand, his left arm in a bloodstained, white cotton sling.

"You got here just in time," he drawled with a weary grin. "Our bullets are all used up."

"No," Kath murmured, still staring at Paul's dead face, tears blinding her eyes, "we got here too late."

Bo, although exhausted after leading the resistance for hours, greatly weakened by his wound, gave Kath his full, sympathetic attention. He told her gently, "I did all I could. I told him to stay inside the house. When they rode up here, they called for him to come out. The fool opened the door and they gunned him down. I was in the barn to spread our fire so all I could do was step out and take five of 'em that killed him."

Captain Ben whistled admiringly, "That's pretty good shootin', son."

Bo wasn't listening; his eyes were on Kath. "Ain't nuthin' more I could have done. Seemed like that's why they come—to kill him. They called for him by name and then gunned him down without givin' him a chance to draw his gun. I done my best."

Kath still seemed to be mesmerised by Paul's dead face, remembering how they had parted . . . and then how they had met in the Richmond hospital . . . Paul's war wound . . . and all they had been through since then. Now it was over, all over. And she felt guilty about it. They had parted so badly.

"I don't understand," she murmured. "I was promised . . . If only I hadn't stayed in Abilene last night, I would have been here in time. . . ."

The front door clattered open again.

Aunt Martha, holding a shotgun, a bloody bandage round her grey head.

She grasped Kath's hand. She seemed beyond words— beyond even tears.

"And the others?" Horatio Thomas asked with sudden anxiety when no one else came out of the ranch-house. "Where's Ram?"

Bo gave him a sympathetic look. "Ram's been wounded, but he's still alive."

Horatio Thomas rushed inside. It was the first time Kath had seen the English journalist lose his iron self-control.

"Where are the Reverend and Lieutenant Greene?" Kath asked quietly.

Bo shook his head grimly.

"We lost them both. The Reverend first, then Wash. But they didn't die easy. They took several with 'em."

Kath put her hands to her face. The Reverend and Wash Greene had been so full of life—like the swashbuckling cavaliers in her old schoolbook. A wave of guilt hit her. It was all her fault. They wouldn't have been killed but for her.

But she had to face it.

She went inside the smoke-filled house to see for herself.

The living first—Ram. The young Sikh had a bad leg wound high up that needed immediate skilled medical attention or his leg might have to be amputated. Ram was lying on a couch in a front ground-floor room as far from the fire as possible. He was obviously in great pain, but he was trying to be cheerful, his white teeth flashing in his dusky face, as Horatio Thomas fussed over him. Their roles had been temporarily reversed and the young Sikh was enjoying it.

When Kath came into the room, Horatio Thomas looked up from washing Ram's wound and said in an angry tone, "Your father's got a lot of explaining to do."

Kath flushed. "Something must have gone terribly wrong. His instructions were ignored. The company men in Alpine seem to be going their own violent way."

"I don't know what the explanation is," Thomas said, "But as soon as I've got Ram to a doctor, I intend to find out."

She must get to her father first.

But not until the ranch was safe to leave.

The Reverend's body was in the kitchen near the window he had been defending.

His bewhiskered face looked relaxed, as if he had enjoyed the battle. He probably had. Death at least had solved the problem of what to do next—of how not to get bored in peacetime. Kath remembered his friendship with Paul. Two sensitive, vulnerable men, both dead now.

Wash Greene's body was upstairs beneath one of the bedroom windows. He must have been hit at least ten times, yet his expression was calm and unafraid, just the way he had looked when he was alive.

Kath gave a low, hysterical cry, close to breaking point, but immediately two bony hands like claws gripped her shoulders from behind.

"This is no time for tears, girl," snapped Aunt Martha.

"We've got things to take care of that won't wait. That young Indian needs a doctor. He fought bravely for this ranch—yours, now Paulie's gone. We've also got to put out this fire before the whole house burns down, or you'll have no ranch left and those evil men will have won. There'll be time to mourn for Paulie and the others later."

The old woman was right.

Tears were a luxury.

She was behaving like a spoiled, hysterical girl.

She grabbed a bucket and joined the others outside. With all of them bringing water from the well, the fire was soon put out. But part of the ranch-house's back wall and two back rooms were left a smouldering ruin.

As soon as the house was safe, Horatio Thomas and Captain Ben left for Alpine with Ram propped up inside the stagecoach with a pile of pillows to protect him against the bumps along the way. The people in Alpine couldn't be trusted, but the nearest competent doctor lived there. "He'll treat Ram," said Horatio Thomas, "even if I've got to put my pistol to his head."

"And get him to check my Pa's wound," Bo shouted as the stagecoach set off. "That old Texas Ranger oughta still be in the hospital."

"I gotta share the fun, son," Captain Ben yelled back.

Father and son gave each other a cheerful wave. They were more like brothers, Kath thought. That was the kind of relationship to have with your father.

Kath steeled herself to examine the bodies of the gunmen. Bo helped her to untie the neckerchiefs covering the dead faces. Several of them were familiar—men who had accompanied the lawyer on his first visit.

Bo could tell she'd recognised some of them.

"Do you know who's behind this raid?" he asked grimly.

"The Company's attorney—Howard Wright."

The lawyer was responsible, not her father.

He had ignored her father's message.

He had gone ahead with the raid.

He probably wanted to take over the company.

Perhaps her father was the next to be killed.

My God, she thought, somebody had to stop that lawyer.

Nothing could bring back Paul or the Reverend or Wash Greene, but she could save her father.

"I'm going back to Abilene tonight," she told Bo.

"And I'm comin' with you," he said.

They went to tell Aunt Martha. The old woman insisted they must travel in her sturdy, two-seater carriage. "You ain't goin' to ride your white stallion with that wounded arm," she told Bo. "Hitch him to the carriage."

"That stallion ain't gonna haul us to Abilene," Bo said. "That's work for mares."

"Tie him up behind then."

"He don't like bein' tied up."

So Bo left the stallion behind, but as the carriage sped away down the trail, he turned back to look at it, magically white in the moonlight, as if he feared he might never see it again. Bo wasn't one for sentimental farewells. It made Kath realize the dangers they faced ahead.

33

It was a mad dash through the night.

One-armed Bo was masterly with the horses, winning from them their maximum effort. He talked to them and soon had their trust and yet controlled them with an iron hand, letting Kath hold the reins only when he wanted to light another of his thin Mexican cigars.

She could barely see his face under the pale new moon until his cigar glinted and lit up his strong, tanned profile. Bo didn't talk much, but she felt the power of his presence. She marvelled at the strength of his slim wrist as he held the horses in check throughout the long journey—the strength of steel.

She moved closer so that their shoulders and thighs touched, and she felt Bo's firmness and warmth through the roughness of his work shirt and faded dungarees. She had never been more attracted by a man, but Paul weighed heavily on her mind, and Bo respected this and left her alone.

They stopped once—for food and to rest the horses—just before dawn. It was still quite dark. The light from the moon hardly touched the carriage. Bo was just a shadowy outline. She heard him unbuttoning his shirt with his one good hand and she imagined how he looked.

"Can I help you?"

"I want to take off my shirt and cool off."

She helped him slip it off and her hand touched his bare

shoulders. He appeared so slim in his clothes that his heavily muscled body always came as a surprise. His hand fumbled with his belt.

"I just want to loosen it while we're relaxin'."

Her hand touched his thigh and felt for the belt. It was hard to unfasten and her fingers struggled with it. His hand came to help and touched hers. She fought against her feelings. She had just lost a husband. She was a widow. But she hadn't loved Paul and nothing she did now could hurt him. Suddenly her feelings swept away all her restraints and she didn't care. Bo and she were alone together on the plain, and that was all that mattered.

"Oh, Bo."

"Kath, I've kept away."

"He's gone now. I can't hurt him any more. And we've got so little time. We must be in Abilene as soon as possible."

"You're not a wife any more. You're free."

She didn't feel free.

She felt a terrible urgency.

She felt afraid.

She wanted to forget it all . . . if only for a few moments.

"We must be careful of your arm."

"To hell with my arm."

His good hand found her in the darkness. In their excitement, they stood up, kissing with gentleness and then growing passion, pressing against each other. His hand began to unbutton her clothes, surely with no fumbling, and at the same time he dropped his dungarees. Their bare bodies were soon against each other, his muscle against her soft flesh. He caressed and held her with a touch that brought great comfort to her. He kissed her neck and her breasts, and she felt herself becoming unbearably excited as he moved down her body.

"Oh, Bo. Bo!"

This was what she had wanted for so long.

Oh, that it would last forever instead of a few short minutes.

Again she felt that terrible urgency.

But she tried to forget it.

"Let's lie down."

The carriage seat wasn't wide enough for them to lie side-by-side. She lay on her back looking up at his dark face, his long fair hair falling over his forehead. He gently pressed open her legs. There was a moment of difficulty with his wounded arm. He chuckled, his white teeth flashing.

"Let's lie sideways," she whispered.

That did it. Suddenly he was in her and riding her, and she had a feeling of being totally involved, an overwhelming emotion growing inside her, that she had never experienced before. It was as if she had become a part of Bo and she was rising with him. All the pain of the previous day seemed to leave her. The weight of her grief dropped away. She was free of her fears. All that mattered were these timeless moments in the desert.

Her passion, so long held back, was free at last. But his feeling matched hers. They became as close as one person. He lay in her, probing the depths of her being. He had none of the usual young man's impatience for a quick thrill, but took his time with loving care, drawing her with him even deeper until she felt there wasn't a part of her body that hadn't been touched by him. He seemed to search for the heart of darkness in her and at last he penetrated it, releasing his passion in a torrent too long held back.

"That was just the beginning," he whispered.

"You've put your brand on me."

"You're mine now, Kath."

He began again.

And then again.

By then, she knew him more deeply than any other man. The young Texan had mysterious depths of his own—a strange blend of strength and tenderness that he expressed only in making love.

"I wish we could stay all night," she whispered. "But we've got so little time."

"When all this is over, let's take a hotel room and not go out for a week. I did that once when I was a boy."

"Who was the woman?"

"Someone's wife." He didn't want to talk about her. It was bad luck to talk about one woman with another. What you did was just your business and the woman's. They all liked to think they were the only one. But he wasn't going to lie to Kath. Just tell her the truth. She was one hell of a woman in bed. "You've drained me," he drawled, "more than any woman." He grinned wickedly at her and then gently kissed her.

"I feel drained, too—of all my grief about our friends and confusion about my father."

Kath felt refreshed and renewed for all that lay ahead in Abilene, however dangerous.

Bo's strength was in her, protecting her from all her fears. She was ready at last to face the truth.

* * *

Abilene was holding another public hanging.

Not as many people came from out of town to this one, and stores and offices didn't close. Hangings were becoming routine. Judge Drake had announced he intended to hold at least two a week until Kansas became law-abiding.

Hugo White disapproved of hangings. Only crude cowboys, in his opinion, watched such public spectacles. But because one of his employees, a young ranch-hand named Chris Curtis, was to be hanged for rustling cattle, he felt obliged to attend out of respect for the young man's family.

He wore the same well-cut, expensive black clothes he kept for church on Sundays. He sat in an open carriage so he could be seen, close enough for the condemned man to know he was there, but far enough away so he wouldn't see the man's eyes or the drop.

People were continually tipping their hats to him or waving respectfully or coming up to ask for small favors for themselves or their families.

Hank Curtis, the condemned man's eldest brother, approached his carriage. A bodyguard looked for permission to let him through. Hugo White nodded. He shook hands without taking off his gloves.

"Can you do anythin' to save young Chris, Mr. White?"

"I've done all I safely can, Hank. I got him the best lawyer in town. He'll have to take his medicine now. He was a damn fool for gettin' caught."

"He was drinkin'. He's only a boy, Mr. White."

"You should have thought of that before you let him join the gang and go rustlin' with you."

"Me and the boys are thinkin' of rescuin' him when he's brought out from the jail-house."

"Then they'll hang you, too. Judge Drake has the governor and Washington behind him. The town's full of Federal marshals and army guards. If you're goin' to do anythin', don't do it in Abilene."

Hank Curtis was full of false bravado from a whisky bottle, but Hugo White told one of his bodyguards to watch the fiery-eyed cowboy just in case of trouble.

And of course nothing happened.

Judge Drake's hangman disposed of young Chris in record time and all brother Hank did was weep—and take another drink. He wanted to come back for sympathy, but Hugo White showed his contempt by shaking his head when the bodyguard looked at him.

"I'll get my revenge for my brother," Hank Curtis shouted.

Unreliable big mouth, Hugo White thought. In such times as these, men like that are dangerous.

He instructed his driver to leave. He wanted to miss the home-going crowd. It had certainly been a very efficient hanging. The whole business had only taken a few minutes—not nearly as sordid as he had feared. On the way through the crowd, his carriage passed Judge Drake's. The Judge waved to him. They had met socially several times, on the last occasion at the governor's mansion. He had talked to the Judge about his plans for Abilene. The Judge, like the governor, strongly approved. "We both have the same aim, Mr. White," he'd said. "We both want to get Kansas back on the right, law-abiding road to prosperity."

The carriage took him to the company's offices. The sight of his company's name—*his* company—never failed to give him pleasure. He imagined one day a statue of himself in Abilene, dressed in these Sunday clothes, complete with his gloves to hide his missing fingers.

"Any word from Alpine?" he asked the chief clerk curtly.

"Mr. Wright is in your office now."

The lawyer, a big bearded man in a gray suit with shiny brown leather cowboy boots, stood up as Hugo White came in.

"How did it go?"

"No problems."

"And the new owner?"

"No more." The lawyer nodded with satisfaction. "They'll sell now."

"I hope so."

The chief clerk knocked on the door and came in.

"A young woman who says she's your daughter wants to see you, Mr. White."

Hugo White was startled.

"Say I'm not here."

But it was too late.

Kath had followed the chief clerk in, with Bo close behind her.

"Dad—"

She stopped when she saw the lawyer.

He was already here.

She had arrived just in time.

But Bo was staring at her father.

At his black Sunday clothes.

At his . . . gloves.

"Black gloves," Bo cried, pointing with his one good hand.

Then suddenly Kath understood everything.

The full horror of it.

Her dream had become a nightmare.

34

"You killed the Pinkerton detective—Charles Fogarty," Kath said in an awed, horrified tone, staring at her father as if they were alone in the room together—alone in the world.

"You had Paul killed—that was why you kept me in Abilene for dinner that night and why the raid was a day early. You wanted it all to be over by the time I got back to the ranch. But the resistance was greater than you expected."

Love had made her blind, but now she saw through him with terrible clarity.

"You killed the guards with the Confederate gold. The gold gave you your start here in Kansas."

Her father might have been a stranger. Her accusing voice and appalled expression showed no love for him at all. Doubts and suspicions, long suppressed, had come together in a torrent of disgust.

"Oh, Joseph Tracy, why did you do these murderous things? Whatever has happened to you in America?"

"Kath. . . ." Her father found his voice at last. But he realized with the shrewdness of a cornered fox that there was no advantage now in denying what he had done. The angry red-haired young woman facing him wouldn't believe it. He had to win her sympathy. "Kath, don't you know even now what kind of world you're livin' in? It's us or them." He looked down at the black gloves that had given him away. "If I killed anyone, it was because I had to. That's the way things are settled here—with a gun, a duel to the death. Killin's an accepted way of gettin' what you want."

"So you killed my husband to get the ranch. He was never given a chance. He was gunned down."

"You're better off without him—a eunuch."

"Who are you to say that—God?"

"I'm your father."

"You *were* my father. I was fooling myself all those years. You never intended to send for me. I was dead as far as you were concerned."

The loathing in Kath's voice touched him. "Kath, you don't appreciate how hard this country can be for a poor immigrant. I crossed the Atlantic to find no more than I had left behind—*nothing!* A sweat-shop at a slave's wages! Can you imagine how I felt? Do you know what it's like to have your dream turn into a nightmare? That's how I felt until I started fighting for my life like everybody else. It was them or me. That Pinkerton detective was threatening to ruin everything I had struggled for. Sure, I took that gold. If I hadn't, the others would have. If I hadn't killed them, they would have killed me. I was smarter than they were. That gold bought my way to the top here in Abilene. I was a Somebody for the first time in my life. Listen, Kath, I have plans you won't believe for Abilene. There's talk already of making me mayor, and when that happens, I'm going to rename the town. Do you know what I'm going to call it? *Stockport!* Stockport, Kansas. The main street will be Mersey Road after the river in Stockport. And I'll build a Heaton Hall specially for you, Kath." His voice rose emotionally as Kath listened, wondering if he was mad. "I'll make you my partner. You'll have a third share of everything. You'll become one of the richest women in the state of Kansas—you, little Kathleen Tracy from Stockport, England. You'll be a millionairess, Kath, before you die. Think of all that money and power over people. Have you ever held half a million dollars in gold in your hands? It makes you feel like God. . . ."

Kath wanted to put her fingers over her ears. What had happened to the Joseph Tracy she had known as a child, that poor but honest man who told jokes to keep up his spirits? This man was crazy with greed. He could justify doing *anything*.

"Law and order's comin' to Kansas, Kath. Soon we won't need the gun. We'll be able to work through the law. There won't have to be any killin'. We'll get what we want legally and the losers'll go to jail or be hanged. Kath, I understand how you feel. But I had to beat out my rivals and that meant being ruthless. Everybody can't be rich. I'm worth a fortune already. I'll take you to the bank and show you my account. You can see my cattle and all my land holdings. . . ."

Kath listened in stunned silence. She didn't know what to answer. The past had blown up into a nightmare and she was still in a state of shock. After all these years, her dream was shattered. All her sacrifices had been for nothing. The truth was too terrible to accept. She stared at her father, unable to reply to him. But Bo, growing restless beside her, answered for her.

"Look, let's cut the talk and have some action." The young Texan addressed the man known as Hugo White slowly and formally. "You killed some of my friends and you gotta pay." He included the lawyer with a quick glance. "You, too. I'm goin' to turn you both over to a Federal marshal." He added apologetically to Kath, "I'm sorry. I know he's your Pa."

Kath shook her head.

He wasn't her Pa.

He was a stranger.

A stranger mad with greed.

An idol shattered into a thousand pieces.

"Come on then, you two, let's get goin'," Bo drawled, his hand on his gun.

As the young Texan was handicapped with an arm in a sling, the lawyer made the mistake of drawing his gun.

A Peacemaker appeared in Bo's good hand with lightning speed.

The sound of his rapid shot was like a cannon roar in the small office.

A bullet ripped through the front of the lawyer's white shirt. His gun dropped from his hand and he collapsed, dead before he hit the floor.

Hugo White meanwhile had drawn one of his Peacemakers

from inside his black jacket, and he grabbed Kath as a shield. She struggled to break free of his arm. But her father in his desperation was too strong.

Bo was concerned that Kath might get in the way of his shot, and then he recognised with astonishment the ivory-handled gun in Hugo White's hand. How had this man obtained the Peacemaker? Bo's memory flashed back to the gunfight in Mexico with the young Quantrill outlaw, Jesse James, who possessed the only other Peacemakers in existence. Had that fight meant bad luck? Were the guns following him?

Bo's concentration was momentarily affected. He hesitated for a brief moment, long enough for Hugo White to press the trigger. A Peacemaker roared for a second time, and Bo took the bullet just above his heart.

His face seemed to grimace with self-disgust at his lapse in concentration, and then Kath saw the brightness of his blue eyes begin to fade.

She cried out in horror and redoubled her efforts to break her father's tight grip.

The young Texan was forced down on one knee, all the time trying to aim his beloved Peacemaker. His eyes seemed to consider Kath and decide not to take the risk of hitting her.

"Shoot, Bo," she screamed.

The Peacemaker wavered.

"Shoot, Bo, shoot," she urged him frantically.

But Bo's grip on the Peacemaker slowly relaxed, and Kath would never know whether it was because of her or his failing strength.

Most people would probably have been dead already, but Bo's heart was so strong that his vitality, though ebbing fast, still struggled against the force of the bullet inside him.

Hugo White took no chances. His gun roared again. For a moment, he must have thought he was trying to kill one of the immortals. Bo didn't immediately show any reaction, though more blood slowly stained the front of his workshirt. He was quite still as if even then unwilling to die, and then he gave a great sigh and his bent knee gave way, and he slipped to the floor and rolled over as gracefully as a cat.

Kath stared at the slim, muscular figure in the faded jeans.

He might have been sleeping, his tanned face still seemed so full of life, but Kath knew he was dead by how she felt. It was as if the room had suddenly lost all its air and she couldn't breathe. Her heart felt crushed.

God, there had been too many violent deaths.

Her husband, her friends, and now . . . Bo, her moondancer.

The time together in the carriage had been a beginning—the real beginning of her life as a woman. And now here it was all over so soon.

The man she loved lay dead on the floor . . . killed by her father.

She turned in a fury, but he was no longer there. While she had been grieving over Bo, he had opened the door and escaped. The chief clerk, who had been a bewildered, terrified witness of the violent scene, said in a shocked voice, "I must go for the Sheriff" and rushed out.

Kath's eyes went back to Bo, curled up like a great cat on the floor. The young cowboy had been part of her American Dream that had turned into a nightmare. She knelt and touched his face. He was already growing cold—like marble. She remembered the marble statues of ancient Greek heroes in a schoolbook. They had had bodies like Bo's, and now his was as lifeless and cold as theirs. She recalled his feeling about leaving his white stallion behind. How right he had been! She should have taken that as a warning.

Her father was responsible.

Bo wouldn't be dead but for trying to help her.

The hatred surged up in her—as strong as her love had once been. Her father had killed Bo . . . and her dream, too. He hadn't even given Bo a chance. He hadn't cared what happened to her. It was all a lie. She had to stop him before he killed anyone else. He had gone mad. He was no longer her father.

There was only one place he would have gone . . . the ranch. She knew that as surely as if she was with him.

Bo's face was before her all the way. She could feel the hard strength of his chest, the touch of his hands with their surprising tenderness, the power of him inside her . . . and it would never be again. Her hatred grew with every mile for this man called Hugo White. She could no longer think of him as her father.

She was lucky at the wooden barrier—one of the men recognised her and let her pass.

"She's Mr. White's daughter," she heard the man explaining to someone else.

She left the stagecoach some distance from the ranch-house and walked slowly towards her father's home. A big, round moon cast a carpet of light before her. This was the end of the path of enlightenment. She knew the truth now. It was all over—ahead lay the heights of fulfillment. She could feel her father's presence in the house as if he were drawing her like a magnet.

Her boots made sharp sounds before the house, but no one appeared.

She opened the door.

There was nobody inside.

She walked through the richly furnished house, the symbol of her father's success.

She reached the library.

The door was closed.

She slowly opened it.

The antique room was the same except that her photograph was missing from the wall.

Her father was sitting behind a desk.

They stared at each other and Kath's hatred for him rose again.

"You killed Bo," she said. "You killed others . . . Why? Was it always in you? Was I blind to it?"

His hand came up holding a gun—a Peacemaker.

Kath stared at the barrel.

He was going to kill her, too.

This was how her dream was going to end.

She walked towards him.

"No nearer," he said. "I can't let you stop me now. I've triumphed over the past. Nothing, nobody, must stop me."

She grabbed for the gun across the desk.

The Peacemaker roared and she felt a heavy blow against her left shoulder.

Then she had a grip on the barrel with her other hand. They grappled over the desk. She wrestled furiously, not caring if he killed her. Hugo White tried to point the Peacemaker at her, thinking only of his own survival now, but her fury over Bo's death, over her father's betrayal, seemed to send a surge of great power through her wrists, and slowly she forced the barrel of the gun away from herself as he pressed the trigger.

The roar this time was muffled by his dark jacket. He gave a low, agonized cry, and his grip relaxed around her. His heavy body went over backwards, overturning the chair, and the Peacemaker fell on top of him.

He lay with his eyes open, blood frothing on his big, open lips.

Kath looked at him reluctantly, her hatred still so strong for this man who had crushed her dream.

"Kath," he murmured, barely audible, his face twitching with pain.

She could see he was dying.

"Kath," he murmured again, even though speaking was a great agony for him. Wracked with pain, his face had lost its hard, cruel look and reminded her more of the man she had once known . . . and loved so much.

"Kath . . . please. . . ."

He wanted to say something, the blood trickling from his mouth as he tried to speak again.

She knelt down by his side.

The change in him was even more marked. It was as if the closeness of death had driven him back to the man he used to be. Some of the black dye had faded from his hair, revealing gray patches . . . of the real man.

"Kath. . . ."

His mouth opened wide with effort. He panted for air. She wiped the blood off his lips with a handkerchief.

"Kath . . . Sorry, Kath . . . I got too big . . . for my britches. . . ."

It was an old saying she had heard a thousand times as a girl.

Suddenly all the hatred left her.

"Dad," she said, holding his already lifeless hand, "You *tried* . . . Your britches were too small for you in Stockport, that was the trouble . . . You tried to wear somebody else's britches. . . ." Was that true? Or was Hugo White the true man?

But what could she say to comfort him before he died?

Her mind was a blank.

But it didn't matter.

He was no longer listening.

His eyes seemed to light up with a faraway vision. "Come now, Kathleen Clare," he whispered, trying to smile through the blood and pain, "Meet me after morning mass. . . ."

He had gone back to his youth . . . and to her mother. Back to the happiest time in his life.

"Kathleen," he murmured, his eyes shining. "I love. . . ."

His head fell back.

Kath stared at him with dry eyes. She remained perfectly still, her emotions frozen.

It was as if she had fallen into a great well of darkness, with no light, no air, no life.

Bo . . . and now her father.

The two men she loved.

Both lost in needless, sickening violence.

What a waste it was. . . .

She heard footsteps enter the room.

A gunman covered her with a shotgun while the black butler put a hand on his employer's chest.

"Mr. White's dead," he said in a shocked tone, as if announcing it to the world.

Yes, Kath thought wearily, Hugo White is dead. But Joseph Tracy died a long time ago.

35

The shooting of Hugo White caused a sensation in Abilene, even though shootings were commonplace in the town.

A leading citizen like Hugo White, with all his prestige and protection, seemed beyond such an everyday premature fate. Spice was added to the event by the news that the killer was a beautiful young woman. At first everyone supposed that it was a young whore from the Diamond Saloon, who perhaps had expected Hugo White to marry her and had discovered he had no intention of leaving his wife—now his widow.

But then the truth began to come out.

It was learned that the killer, Kathleen Tracy, was Hugo White's daughter from England.

The murder was a family affair.

A family scandal.

The whole of Abilene was fascinated and waited eagerly for the trial to learn all the juicy details.

They didn't have long to wait.

Judge Drake moved fast. He felt he had to. Much more was at stake than a single shooting. To bring law and order back to Kansas meant that authority had to be recognised. Hugo White was one of the figures of authority—a rich rancher, a company president, one of the architects of the town's booming future. His murder struck a blow against all the people who ran Abilene. Nobody could feel safe. His murderess had to be dealt with quickly and in a way that would scare off any similar killings. Abilene's establishment had to be above the battle, secure and respected, in Judge Drake's law-and-order plan.

He had Kath before a grand jury in three days—the day after Hugo White's big public funeral. Only the bodies of well-known outlaws were usually displayed in public, but Hugo White had been such a well-respected citizen that it was felt the whole town wanted to see him and pay its last respects by filing past his body. So he was embalmed by the local undertaker— even his hair was re-dyed—and he was displayed in a silver-trimmed casket in the company's large bay window for a day. Then he was taken in an $8,000 glass-sided hearse, preceded by Abilene's brass band, to a special grave in the cemetery known as Boot Hill outside the town. The grave eventually was to have a marble top and a statue of Hugo White in his best suit. The governor and Judge Drake were among the huge crowd of mourners.

Kath heard the brass band come up the main street and pass the jail-house. Her father would have liked the presence of the band. She remembered accompanying him to the park in the summertime to listen to Stockport's brass band. Kath never thought of her father as Hugo White, the rich rancher—Hugo White had been killed and no longer existed for her. It was Joseph Tracy who lived in her thoughts. Abilene and Kath were mourning two different men.

A familiar white-suited figure came to see her late that afternoon.

The appearance of Horatio Thomas on the other side of the bars brought Kath renewed hope.

He was just as calm and confident as if they had been chatting back at the ranch, and she wasn't charged with murder.

But, as usual, his relaxed manner was deceptive.

He was very practical and realistic underneath.

He had brought with him a youngish man with a short, well-trimmed black beard and a fussy, precise manner.

"Kath, meet Herbert Trencher. He's a local lawyer I've hired for your defense. He'll get you out of here. Now tell Mr. Trencher exactly what happened—the whole truth. Hold nothing back."

The two men listened carefully and the lawyer took copious notes. Kath watched Horatio Thomas's face grow increasingly grave as she described the confrontation with her father. She felt compelled to defend him—Thomas might have represented the world. "My father wasn't a bad man," she insisted. "He did some bad things, but it was like what you told me once about the survival of the fittest. That was the way he saw life. He was a fighter, not like so many people who take the easiest way out all the time. But freedom went to his head in America. He went too far. But he wasn't *evil*. You do understand?" She wanted Horatio Thomas to agree with her, but the English journalist remained silent. He obviously saw Hugo White differently, but then he had never known Joseph Tracy in his good days.

When Kath finished, Thomas looked triumphantly at the lawyer. "What did I tell you, Trencher? A clear case of self-defense. Just tell the court what you've told us, Kath. Hide nothing. Then they'll have no choice but to release you. Don't you agree, Trencher?"

The lawyer wasn't so optimistic.

"Truth has more than one face in Abilene," he said cautiously. "Hugo White was a very powerful man in this town. The law will be on his side—to protect his memory and his investment in this town."

* * *

"Order! Order! The Honorable District Court of the United States for the Western District of Kansas, having criminal jurisdiction of Abilene and surrounding territories, is now in session," cried the portly court crier in the plain, log-cabin style courtroom above the jail-house.

"The court is ready for the first case," announced Judge Drake behind a huge cherrywood desk on a small raised platform.

"The United States versus Kathleen Tracy," called the clerk. "Charge—murder."

So her trial began. It was all rather crude compared to the ancient legal ritual of her first trial in Manchester. But Kath understood lawyer Trencher's caution as soon as the prosecution witnesses gave their accounts. She hardly recognised the "Kathleen Tracy" they portrayed.

The widow, a sympathetic blonde figure, dressed all in black and accompanied by her young son, also in black, depicted Kath as a scheming poor relation from England, who had come to take advantage of her rich father. "I warned Hugo about her," the widow said tearfully, "But he was such a generous man. He didn't see through her lowdown tricks." The widow also described Horatio Thomas as a decadent Englishman in a white suit—Thomas's clothes became proof of his decadence in her telling—who was obviously Kath's accomplice but who claimed to be a journalist. She added coldly: "Journalism, as everyone knows, is not a very respectable profession."

The Company's chief clerk told how Kath and Bo had forced their way into Hugo White's inner office, had insulted Mr. White, and then Bo had shot Howard Wright, the Company's attorney. Mr. White then had shot Bo in self-defense.

The gunman at the ranch described how Kath had shot Mr. White "in cold blood with his own gun." He denied Mr. White had drawn his gun against her.

Sheriff Baxter was brought from Alpine to give further damning evidence about Kath's disreputable associates he had seen on his visit to the ranch. He described the Reverend and Wash Greene and Ram in such a way that they seemed obvious outlaws, ex-guerrilla types that no respectable rancher would want to entertain.

Bo was made to seem the worst of the lot. He was reported to have shot down a woman's husband in a saloon when he was no more than sixteen—a teenage killer, who went from bad to worse.

Captain Ben Jack caused a sensation by standing up and saying in a loud voice that carried to the street outside: "That's a damn lie!"

Judge Drake reproved him sternly.

"I'm sorry, Your Honor," replied the Captain, "but I'm not going to sit here and listen to a pack of lies about my boy. It's bad enough that he's been killed by some murderous jackass."

Judge Drake instructed the Sheriff to take him outside.

It needed three men.

Lawyer Trencher then called Aunt Martha for the defense. Her evidence was ridiculed as merely an old woman's romantic opinion, lacking facts. How did she know Attorney Wright and the killers were connected? demanded the Judge sarcastically.

"Plain as your bald head, Judge," she replied.

"Next witness," cried the Judge.

Horatio Thomas obviously made a strong impression on the jury by his politeness and confidence, but Judge Drake kept demanding, "Facts, not impressions, Mr. Thomas. You're not writing a newspaper article, full of fictional color and romance, but giving evidence in a court of law."

"I'm fully aware of that, Your Honor," Horatio Thomas replied firmly. "But what we're dealing with here is a business conspiracy and the facts have been concealed. I'm an experienced reporter and therefore my observations have some validity."

"Not in this courtroom, Mr. Thomas," the Judge told him sharply. "Observations are apt to be prejudiced. We want facts so we can judge for ourselves. . . ."

Kath came last. She stood up slowly, feeling very alone and vulnerable. This courtroom was much cruder-looking than the one in Manchester, and the way the trial was conducted was also much cruder, just a step away from a vigilante lynching mob, in spite of the Judge's pretensions. Many of the older women in the crowd seemed to resent her good looks, as if that proved she was a Fallen Woman. Some of the older men were uneasy when they looked at her and avoided the eyes of their wives.

Kath gave her account, slowly and methodically, but Judge Drake reacted as if he didn't believe her, and he made his attitude clear to the jury.

The Judge recalled Sheriff Baxter to question him about the raid on the ranch.

"All I know is they was rustlers," said the Sheriff.

The Judge turned to Kath.

"What evidence have you they were in the employ of Mr. White's company?"

"Some of the gunmen who were shot down accompanied

Attorney Wright on his visit to the ranch when he talked to my husband and gave him a deadline for accepting the Company's offer."

"You are referring to Mr. Howard Wright, who was shot by your accomplice shortly before you shot Mr. White?"

"The lawyer—Howard Wright—yes."

"And can you prove these men were in his employ?"

Of course she couldn't.

The court tittered.

Nor was Judge Drake interested in the Confederate gold. It was all hearsay, he told her. Where was the proof?

But the most damning exchange came close to the end.

"Have you ever killed anyone before?" Judge Drake asked her.

"Objection," protested Lawyer Trencher. "The use of the word 'before' implies the charge has been proved. Our contention is that my client hasn't killed anyone. Hugo White was shot in self-defense."

"Objection accepted," replied the Judge. "Let me rephrase the question. Miss Tracy," he said politely, "have you *ever* killed anyone?"

Kath hesitated.

Horatio Thomas had told her, *Hide nothing.*

She had sworn an oath on the Holy Bible.

She had to tell the truth.

"In England."

The court gasped. The widow's cold eyes gleamed with triumph.

"Who did you kill in England?"

"A man."

"How did you kill him?"

"With a knife."

The court gave a collective sigh. Faces frowned with disapproval. Knives were regarded as more vicious than guns—almost as low class as poison.

Feeling this disapproval, Kath said quickly, "It was in self-defense. I was struggling to get away—"

Judge Drake interrupted with a sarcastic smile, "All your killings seem to be in self-defense, Miss Tracy—or so you say."

"Objection," cried Lawyer Trencher.

"Were you charged with murder for this knifing in England?" Judge Drake asked smoothly.

"Yes," Kath replied in a very low voice.

"I didn't hear your answer, Miss Tracy."

"Yes."

"What happened?"

"I was sentenced to be hanged."

"But apparently you weren't."

Kath felt trapped. What could she say?

"I escaped."

"So you're still wanted for the crime of murder in England?"

Judge Drake stared at the jury—at each face—as if to say that completes the case.

The jury took only a few minutes to reach a verdict.

A thin, grey-haired man stood up. "We, the jury, find the defendant, Kathleen Tracy, guilty of murder as charged in the written indictment."

The courtroom exploded with cheers and handclaps. It was certainly a popular verdict. Hugo White had been a home boy and had the crowd's loyalty. Kath was merely a stranger from out-of-town, one of those relatives left behind in Europe that many on the jury and in the crowd feared would one day come looking for them, too, to make a claim. They identified with Hugo White in every way.

The clerk called the court to order. The Sheriff and his deputies walked up and down the aisle silencing the noisier people.

Judge Drake, sitting behind his huge cherrywood desk, said in a solemn, formal voice: "You, Kathleen Tracy, are hereby sentenced to be hanged by the neck until dead by the public executioner of this said town of Abilene. On Friday the fourteenth day of July, A.D. 1865, pursuant to the said judgment and sentence of this said court, you will be taken from the jail-house of this town, where you will be confined until then, to some safe and convenient place within the said town of Abilene, and there, between the hours of noon and three o'clock in the afternoon of this said day, you will be hanged. . . ."

Kath's pale face was expressionless, masklike.

People in the watching crowd concluded she must be very hard-boiled not to show any emotion.

Judge Drake leaned over his huge cherrywood desk and told her angrily, "You won't escape from hanging this time, Kathleen Tracy." He called over the Sheriff. "I want round-the-clock guards and let them all be happily married men—nobody who's likely to be susceptible to a beautiful, unscrupulous young woman. I'll have your badge if you let her get away."

"She won't escape," the Sheriff promised grimly.

The Judge's sharp, penetrating eyes looked for Kath's reaction, but her face was still masklike and gave no sign she had even heard.

"Take her away," the Judge snapped.

Kath was taken back to the jail-house below down the private staircase behind the Judge's platform to keep her away from the crowd. She followed the guards as if she was hardly aware of what was happening.

Her mind was frozen on one thought: *I have been through this already.*

It is happening all over again.

My second life is ending like my first.

36

As soon as Galina heard the news—and the Diamond Saloon learned as fast as anywhere in town—she borrowed a fast brown mare from one of the other girls and rode to the wooden shack that Frank Butler had rented outside Abilene.

Frank was hard at work painting the outside of the shack when Galina came riding across the fields.

"Why are you painting it white?" she asked, dismounting near him and inspecting the two walls he had completed. "You can see it for miles. I thought you wanted a quiet life."

"I had a white cottage once," Frank told her. "I had some good times there."

Galina waited, but he said no more. He seldom talked about his past. That wasn't unusual with the people who came west. They often had something to hide. From a few of Frank's remarks, Galina gathered a woman had treated him badly. It must have been a damn fool woman to let a man like him go. He was a real man and they were rare, didn't she know? He was strong and warm under his cold hangman's front. He should give up being a hangman, she thought. It wasn't his kind of work. But when she said so once, he snapped back, "I'm the hangman for the same reason you're a whore."

"It's good money, honey, and jobs are hard to find."

"I feel just the same way," he replied.

Now he asked her, "Why aren't you working?"

"I took the day off. I wanted to tell you the news—a friend of mine's been sentenced to be hanged."

She wanted to discuss the whole Hugo White affair and Kath's involvement, but at the word "hanged," Frank's manner hardened, and he scowled at her.

"You know I don't talk about that."

"She's a friend of mine. That makes it personal."

"Not to me. I don't want to hear any more about it, Galina. I'm serious, believe me. Keep it to yourself."

"I thought you'd want to know they've sentenced a woman."

"I've hanged a woman before. Now shut up about it."

She'd touched on memories he tried to forget.

Kath. . . .

The thought of her made him angry.

She'd preferred a spineless American soldier.

She'd treated him like dirt ever since they left England.

What was it Doc Holliday had said?

You should've hanged her when you had the chance.

The Doc was damn right.

He should have done his job in England and stayed with the cottage and the black stallion. It was an easy life compared to this one.

Coming to America was a damn fool mistake.

And it was all that redhead's fault.

"What are you thinking about?" Galina asked, "You look so angry."

"Just the dead past." He certainly didn't want to talk to her about it. "Let's go inside."

She had the power to make him forget. That was why he only went with her, none of the other girls. But a whore could get a wrong idea when you treated her as someone special. Galina already looked at him with soft cow eyes. But he didn't want her love. He didn't want anybody's love.

Love was a weakness.

You could risk sex, but not love.

You had to remain cold, in complete control of your feelings. Otherwise you couldn't do your job on the gallows.

He took off his dungarees splashed with white paint and stood just in his cotton shirt. Galina felt herself growing excited

—but why did this man have that effect on her and no other? She looked down his shirt front.

"You're always ready, Frank."

"Only with you, Galina."

This woman always moved him with her big, well-shaped, soft body and her skillful, warm loving. He had known her for some time now, but he always waited eagerly for her. She didn't pretend and fuss and play teasing games like so many respectable women. She treated having sex simply and natural-ly, and he always knew if she wanted to or not because she told him. None of that damn teasing that irritated him so much with respectable women—like Kath. It was better to pay and be direct about what you wanted. And Galina always did want to do it. However many men she'd had, he always seemed to excite her. That always made him feel good. Perhaps she did love him. But he didn't want her love. He didn't want anybo-dy's. But he wished she didn't have to go with anyone else and he could keep her for himself.

He thought he heard a sound outside and he listened careful-ly, but he heard nothing more. It was probably her mare grow-ing restless. Well, the horse better be patient because it had a long wait ahead. He intended to stay in bed with her until it grew dark. No more painting of the shack today.

He slipped off his cotton shirt, and she kissed his chest and nipped his right nipple with her sharp teeth.

"Damn, that hurt."

"Love's painful."

"But not sex."

"Sex, too. Ask a woman. Men have it easy."

He didn't want to talk so his hand slipped down between her legs and opened her up. He caressed her until she was ready. He was moving into her, his mind completely involved, her head back, her legs entwined round his hips, when suddenly the shack door was thrown open.

A man was silhouetted against the bright sunlight.

He had a gun—a Colt—in his hand.

"You the hangman?" a gruff voice demanded.

Frank moved out of her carefully and stood up.

"I asked you a question," said the man, pointing his gun.

"I'm Frank Butler."

His gunbelt was hanging on the back of a chair. He estimated his chances in grabbing for it. Not good if the man could shoot.

"I'm Hank Curtis. You hanged my kid brother, Chris. I've come to repay you."

"Hanging's my job. I just do it for money. I don't choose who's hanged. Your brother meant nothing to me."

"You did it, that's enough."

Frank heard Galina stirring on the bed behind him. A whore sometimes packed a gun or a knife for protection, but Galina was naked. She couldn't help. He eyed the gunbelt again. That was his only chance.

"Say your prayers, Mr. Hangman. My brother was one hell of a nice kid and you ended his young life."

"You better argue with the court that found him guilty, Mister. I can't even tell you what he was supposed to have did."

"I saw you put the noose around his neck. You wore a hood, but people said you was Frank Butler the hangman." The man pointed his gun. His hand was shaking. He was very nervous or he'd been drinking heavily.

"It's not Frank's fault your brother died, Hank Curtis," Galina said, standing up.

The man eyed her naked body.

"You stay out of this. I ain't got no argument with you. Mr. Hangman, I sentence you to be shot dead right now."

Just as the gun roared, Galina sprang forward in front of Frank. Perhaps she hoped to spoil the man's aim. But she took the bullet under her big left breast and blood seeped over her white skin. She fell back on the bed.

Frank grabbed for his gun on the back of the chair.

Hank Curtis, shocked by what he'd done, ran out of the shack.

By the time Frank reached the door, horse's hooves were thudding away across the fields. He tried a quick shot at the distant rider, but it was just to release his rage. The man was already out of range.

Frank was tempted to leap on the waiting brown mare and gallop in pursuit, but getting Galina to a doctor was more important.

He went back in the shack.

He stood at the bedside, looking down at her.

Her eyes were closed, her face unnaturally pale—almost gray.

The only sign of life was a trickle of blood from the bullet wound across her stomach.

He put his hand on her heart.

He felt nothing.

Not even the faintest beat.

She was dead all right.

"Damn it, Galina," he said aloud, "I was ready to take that bullet. It was meant for me. Why did you get in the way?"

But he knew the answer.

She *had* loved him.

Maybe if the ghost of Kath hadn't come between them, he could have loved her.

He leaned over and kissed her lifeless lips.

* * *

Captain Ben Jack came to see Kath in the jail-house.

His one good eye regarded her tenderly through the bars.

"I know you loved my son," he said simply, "so I came to tell you where I took him. Don't feel badly about his death. What counts is not how long you're on this earth, but what you do with your time. Bo lived every minute like a free man. I'm proud of my son. I carried him back to Texas and buried him alongside his Ma. And when I die, I'll go in the same grave. You're welcome there, too, Kathleen, when you're ready."

His pirate appearance with the black eye-patch and his great masculine dignity raised Kath's spirits. She felt as if she was still in touch with Bo through him.

"What did you do with Bo's guns, Captain Ben? They meant so much to him."

"His Peacemakers were the finest pistols in the world bar none. There was one other pair—those that killed him—but they didn't have the improvements Sam Colt and Bo worked out together."

"They were like a part of Bo."

"I was tempted to keep 'em for myself. But somebody might steal 'em. Then what would have happened to 'em when I died?

So I took 'em to the Indian Lake where Bo used to fish as a kid. The Indians call it *No End* because legend has it there's no bottom to the lake in the middle. The water drops down forever, they say."

Captain Ben's eyes had a faraway look, remembering the scene. "I held the Peacemakers in each hand, whirled 'em round my head, and let 'em go as hard and as high as I could. The ivory handles flashed in the sun as they rose above the water of *No End* and then dropped somewhere in the middle with a great splash and disappeared. Then a strange thing happened. As I was lookin' where Bo's guns had gone, a little boy appeared by my side and held my hand. He reminded me of Bo at that age—the same spunk and freedom, a little hell-raiser in the makin'. 'What was that you threw in *No End* that flashed like diamonds in the sun?' he asked me. I told him it was the mightiest weapon in the world, worthy of a great king. Then the little hell-raiser said, 'When I grow bigger, I'll dive in for 'em, and if I find 'em, will I be a king?' That you will, I told him. Anyone who dives into *No End* and comes back with those Peacemakers, he'll be worthy of 'em. He'll be another Bo, Kathleen."

"There'll never be another."

"Our lives can inspire those who come after us, Kath."

"You did just right, Captain Ben. Now they're safe from useless killing by someone unworthy." Kath imagined the guns lying on the bed of the lake like sunken treasure in her old schoolbook pictures of the Spanish Main. "What are you going to do with Bo's white stallion? He loved that horse." She remembered again Bo's superstitous feeling on leaving the stallion behind and how magical it looked in the moonlight.

"I'll leave it at the ranch. I want you to have it."

Kath smiled shyly.

"It looks as if I won't be here that long. You should take him with you."

Captain Ben winked with his one good eye. "Don't give up hope, Kath." He put his face close to the bars and whispered: "You're gettin' out of here tonight. I'll come for you at nine when the guards have their supper break. Be ready."

Bo would have rescued her, so he was going to do it. He'd shoot his way out with her if necessary.

He walked back to his hotel to wait for nine o'clock. He kicked off his boots and lay on the bed with a whisky bottle for company.

The door opened and the Sheriff came in.

"I got a warrant here from Judge Drake. You're goin' to be held in custody until after Friday."

"What the hell for?"

"To make sure the hangin' takes place."

* * *

Frank rode grimly into town on the brown mare. He left the horse in front of the Diamond Saloon and asked a bouncer who owned it.

"One of the girls—Belle."

"Tell her I brought it back."

He went to the barman.

"Is Hank Curtis here?"

"Why do you want him?"

"He killed Galina."

"He's upstairs—in Room 3. The bed's on the right of the door."

Frank walked quietly up the stairs. Room 3 was facing him at the top. He listened at the door and heard nothing. He gripped his gun and flung open the door. Hank Curtis was lying on the bed. A girl was between his legs.

Frank levelled the gun at him.

"I could shoot you now like you shot her. But I'll wait outside in the street for you."

On the way out, Frank met Doc Holliday.

"I heard the news," the Doc said. "Did she suffer?"

Frank shook his head.

"I'll miss Galina," Doc Holliday said, and he had a sudden fit of coughing, the only sign of his emotional state. "If you don't kill him, I will."

"Just make sure he comes out," Frank said.

He waited in the hot, dusty street. He didn't have to wait long. The saloon door opened slowly and Hank Curtis came out. He looked scared, but he knew he had to go through with it. He was wearing two Colts slung low down. Frank wondered how good Curtis was as he stepped into the middle of the street to meet him. Passersby, recognising the ritual of a gunfight, rushed to get out of the way.

The two men walked slowly towards each other, their hands hovering over their guns.

When they were within range, both stopped.

"I'm the hangman," Frank cried. "What was it you wanted with me?"

"You hanged my brother."

"And you killed my woman."

And both men went for their guns.

There was a single shot almost immediately.

Doc Holliday, watching from the open saloon door, nodded approvingly as Hank Curtis slowly sank to the ground, his gun still only halfway out of his holster.

"Good shootin', Frank. Couldn't have done better myself."

Frank looked down at the man he'd killed. Hank Curtis still had a scared expression. He'd only been trying to avenge his kid brother, but he hit on the wrong person. He should have gone to see Judge Drake. Frank felt angry. There was no merit in killing Curtis. It wouldn't bring Galina back.

Doc Holliday clapped him on the shoulder. "I know how you feel, Frank. There's no satisfaction in it. But you gotta do it sometimes to make life worth livin'. You know the old Mexican sayin', 'Seek Death and you shall find life.'"

Frank remembered what Galina had said about Doc Holliday. "He's dying slowly of tuberculosis, so he doesn't care if he gets shot first. The Doc's seeking death. . . ." Galina had found it before him.

Next day, Judge Drake rode out to Frank's shack.

"I heard about your gunfight, Frank," he said, mopping his great bald head. "Gunfights are illegal in my territory. But I told the Sheriff to overlook it this time. At least the man you shot had killed someone. But no more gunfights. I need you. There's an important hanging on Friday—a woman. I want it done just right, Frank."

* * *

Aunt Martha came to see Kath. The old woman was very

indignant about being searched, but the guards weren't taking any chances.

"Kath," said the old woman, "You done right so you need have no fear. You were a good wife to Paulie. It wasn't easy for you. The war changed him. But you stuck by him. You fought with him for the ranch like a loyal wife." She squeezed Kath's hand through the bars. "I'm not sayin' good-bye, Kath, because God tells us that while there's life, there's hope. So I'll be prayin' for you, darlin'. . . ."

That visit helped, especially the words about Paul.

* * *

Horatio Thomas still hadn't given up.

He met with local hostility because he had been depicted during the trial as Kath's decadent accomplice, but he pressed on with trying to keep Kath's defense alive.

He persuaded lawyer Trencher to appeal to the governor. There was no immediate reply.

He telegraphed General Grant in Washington. Grant replied courteously that he had been informed such cases were outside Federal jurisdiction.

He talked with local Pinkerton detectives, who tried unsuccessfully to find evidence linking Hugo White to the murder of detective Charles Fogarty.

He requested a meeting with Judge Drake.

The Judge refused to see him.

Then, on the day before the hanging, the governor turned down the appeal.

That seemed to kill all hope.

Lawyer Trencher said nothing more could be done.

Horatio Thomas went to see Kath for the last time, wondering how to tell her.

The jail-house was crowded with guards, both inside and out. The Sheriff wasn't running any risks this last night.

Kath had been washing her long red hair and it fell now over her shoulders. She looked so young and alive that Horatio Thomas couldn't believe she would be dead the next day. He forced himself to break the bad news. Kath listened quite calmly. When he praised her courage, she smiled, telling him, "You forget I've been through all this before. Practise makes perfect. I knew from the beginning there was no hope."

Horatio Thomas replied gently, "Life's never that sure, Kath. Our existence is based on accidents. Even now I hope for a last-minute reprieve. Ram said to tell you that he's confident you will be reunited with your great love."

"In heaven—or hell?" Kath said, thinking of Bo. "In hell probably. How is Ram?"

"His wound's healing fine. That tough little Sikh should soon be back on his feet."

A guard shouted: "Time's up."

Horatio Thomas kissed Kath's hand through the bars.

"What an adventure we've shared, Kath! This can't be the end."

"I was given a second chance—another year of life. Perhaps I didn't make good use of it."

"You made great use of it! Fate's been unkind, that's all."

A guard tapped the English journalist on the shoulder.

"Time to go."

Horatio Thomas walked to the main cell door. He looked so poised and confident in his white suit. He was a master of language in his profession. Yet he couldn't think of how to say good-bye to the young woman he had come to know so well who was to die the next day.

The next time he saw her, Kath would be on the scaffold.

Kath sensed his confusion.

She smiled warmly at this man whom she liked so much without being in love with him.

"When I was in Washington," she called to him, "A Frenchman in a dress-shop said something in French that means goodbye until we meet again. I don't remember the French words, but perhaps we should say that."

Horatio Thomas beamed.

"Au revoir, Kath."

*   *   *

Now she was alone.

She could expect no more visitors until strangers came for her the next day.

But she was wrong.

Out-of-towners, arriving early for the hanging, began to raise
hell in the town and the jail-house soon became so full that even
Kath had to share her small narrow cell with another prisoner—
a little woman with black hair and flashing eyes, who stood at
the bars cursing the guards in a language Kath didn't understand.

"Me, gypsy," the woman told Kath.

Kath remembered the gypsies in caravans, who used to visit
Stockport, especially the one who told her fortune.

"You tell fortunes?"

"You want to know the future?" The woman's eyes flashed
with businesslike calculation and her English sounded better.

"I already know my future."

"No, the real future."

The woman took a small package wrapped in silk out of her
pocket. She began to unwrap the silk.

"Protect from bad spirits, you understand?"

It was a pack of strange picture cards.

"I tell your real fortune. You agree?"

Kath nodded. It would help to pass the time.

The woman shuffled the cards.

"Whichever card you take is your future."

She held out the cards.

Kath studied the deck.

Pure chance, how meaningless it was!

But it would stop her thinking.

She drew a card.

"Look at it," said the woman impatiently.

Kath turned up the card.

It was *The Hanged Man*.

The woman must have known.

Kath said angrily, "I think that's a cruel joke."

The woman looked bewildered.

"I no understand. I do somethin' wrong?"

Kath showed her the card.

"I'm going to be hanged tomorrow. The guards must have
told you."

The woman's eyes showed genuine surprise.

"I know nuthin'. You must forgive me. No joke. The cards know."

Kath stared at her.

"You mean you didn't know about tomorrow?"

The woman made the sign of the cross.

"I swear."

Kath held up the card. It showed a man hanging upside down.

"Why is he upside down?"

"He is still earthbound. He must hang upside down until he has saved himself and accomplished the great work of regeneration within him. *The Hanged Man* has attained some perfection, but not yet complete freedom."

"And death represents freedom?"

The woman's eyes flashed angrily, and she answered as if reciting something she had learned. "No, he is to take his part very soon in the world's redemption, to stand on his own feet. He has nearly completed the stages of man's initiation. Hanging represents a test in one's life, a period of trial which a person must pass through to achieve true freedom. Material temptation is conquered, and you learn what true love is. It is a Tarot card of profound significance. Much of its meaning is veiled for us. But it leads to liberation and love. Everyone who would be free to love must hold this card once in their lives."

"But not twice?"

"Not many are given a second chance."

"But if you are dealt the same card again?"

"Then take it. You are lucky. The meaning may be different the second time."

Kath found the gypsy woman's words strangely comforting. *The Hanged Man* marked a stage of initiation, and she felt it had meaning for her own life.

Perhaps she had been given a second chance to learn how to be free—how to love—how to *live*.

Perhaps she had passed through her initiation—and that was the meaning of life.

But what use had it all been if her life was nearly over?

Yet the gallows now loomed less fearsomely in her thoughts. Now she was ready to live, she was ready to die.

The thought made her feel strong suddenly.

She could take whatever tomorrow brought.

"Thank you," she told the gypsy woman, "you've helped me."

"Good," said the woman. "That will be a dollar."

37

It rained during the night, the first rainfall for weeks, and the parched land of Abilene soaked up the big drops as fast as they fell. Dark, low clouds flashed with lightning, and thunder cracked over the town like shots from giant Peacemakers in a great celestial duel.

The break in the hot, stifling weather helped Kath. The storm reflected her own feelings that kept her from sleep. Standing at the small barred cell window watching the rain pound the main street, she had a sense of release as if the weather was expressing her emotions, and then she could find peace. She wished she could share her feelings with someone, but the gypsy woman was snoring gently on her cot, the Tarot cards, wrapped again in silk, clutched to her bosom. The guards on duty had been told not to talk to her. She was alone with the thunder and lightning.

By early morning, the rainstorm was over. Kath expected the air to be much fresher as in Stockport after rain, but it was even more humid and heavy than it had been, as if the atmosphere was still laden with moisture. Every movement brought out beads of sweat. The jail-house became even more smelly. The buckets that served as toilets needed emptying, and the barrels, cut in half, that were used as bath tubs, were ringed with ancient dirt that had an increasingly strong odor.

But by the time a guard brought in her last breakfast—bacon

and eggs, the same as in Manchester the first time—she was ready for her ordeal, scrubbed, shiningly clean, and wearing her Paris dress that Aunt Martha had brought from the ranch. She had never looked lovelier. The guard paused with the breakfast tray in open admiration. He had brought her the usual plain prison uniform, but made no attempt to persuade her to put it on. With the crudeness of Abilene justice went a comforting informality.

The Manchester hanging had been at eight o'clock in the morning, but here it was to be in the afternoon. It was a long wait—time for the life surging through her veins to harden its resistance to the idea of dying. She felt too much alive to accept it. She had to fight, and she walked up and down the small cell in a fury of restlessness and frustration, watched by the silent gypsy woman.

A local clergyman came for a last visit. A big, well-meaning man, he wanted her to cry for forgiveness for killing her father. She couldn't do it. Her father had killed Bo—and arranged the death of the others. Faced with the same situation, she would have acted the same way again. The clergyman at last went away, shaking his head at her obstinacy. He was used to saying prayers over dead gunfighters. He didn't understand her feelings. The Reverend was the kind of clergyman she needed. She thought affectionately of that shy, vulnerable man with the loud, wild manner. She missed him. She missed them all. That was what made life so hard to give up—you missed too much. And she had to struggle to hold back the tears then, telling herself angrily not to be a crybaby.

At last they came for her, a procession of a dozen armed guards, the fat clergyman chanting prayers, and the bald-headed judge.

The gypsy woman embraced her tearfully, her eyes flashing at the others. "The card, it cannot be wrong," she kept on insisting. Oh, yes, it can, Kath thought. She felt her resistance building up inside. The blood must have been coursing through her veins with the vitality of a fast mountain stream. How could she die when she had so much life? Her whole body rejected the idea of death. Fight for life. . . .

"Good luck, Kath," cried several of the prisoners in other

cells as the procession walked slowly past. They were her people, fellow condemned who recognised a bond between themselves and her. It made her even more determined to meet the
challenge of what lay ahead. Everybody had to live life fully
right up to the end. No giving up.

Then the procession left the jail-house, entering the heavy
outside atmosphere like a huge Turkish bath. The boiling sun
burned with the intensity of lightning flashes. The guards
quickly had dark blotches of sweat on their uniforms, but Kath
in the middle of them still looked unbelievably cool and beautiful. In her Paris dress, she was set apart from the cowboy figures
round her.

The vast crowd let out a great howl as soon as she was
spotted. About seven thousand people had arrived through the
night and early morning, taking over the town, many of them
camping round the gallows. Lines of stagecoaches, carriages,
and saddle horses stretched for as far as Kath could see. In
Manchester, the crowd had been with her, but here she felt a
wave of hostility that seemed to be intensified by the sight of
her cool beauty. They even seemed to resent her fine dress,
preferring to see her humiliated in prison clothing.

As Kath began to ascend the thirteen wooden steps to the
heavy timbered platform, where the hooded hangman was
waiting, drunken cowboys in the audience howled like dogs
and shouted obscene remarks, as if the hanging were some kind
of public rape of her in which they all took part. She was
reminded of what she'd read about the mobs around the guillo-
tine in the French Revolution seventy years before. Public
executions certainly brought out the worst in people.

Kath tried to close out the crowd and detach herself from the
formalities she remembered from the first time. Hymns,
prayers for the dying, and the formal death warrant read by
Judge Drake—she didn't listen to any of it. She sat on a rough
plank bench at the back of the gallows, keeping her eyes away
from the hanging noose. Her hand went instinctively to her
neck and she could feel the terrible burning sensation. Suddenly terrified, she looked desperately round for distraction. Dust
and tobacco smoke rose above the crowd in the misty heat. She
heard the drone of insects. The hard blue sky above was very

beautiful . . . but the shadow of the noose seemed to be over it all.

"Are there any last words you wish to say, Kathleen Tracy?" asked Judge Drake.

She welcomed the chance of action to keep her mind off that hanging rope.

She should say something to show the crowd's abuse hadn't cowed her.

She nodded to the judge and stepped forward, eyeing the thousands of faces that stretched like rows and rows of brown berries almost to the outskirts of town.

They had all come to see her die.

They were obsessed with death—with killing.

How could she strike back at them?

What had been the lesson of her two lives—of *The Hanged Man?*

"Remember, cowboys," she cried in a clear voice that carried across the still scene, "to live without love is nothing. That's the lesson of life—love is everything."

She intended to say more, but loud, obscene howls at once rose from the front rows, drowning her voice. The crowd had expected her to grovel before it and plead for forgiveness like other prisoners who had last words to say, and so people felt thwarted and angry. Several drunken cowboys made sexual signs at her and staggered towards the raised platform. A U.S. Marshal behind Kath raised a shotgun and fired a blast straight up into the blue sky. The noise was deafening. The crowd quietened.

Kath didn't trust her voice to say any more. She stepped back.

Mopping his bald head with a soiled bandanna, Judge Drake told her, "You are now about to be hanged by the neck until you're dead. That fate is inevitable, Kathleen Tracy. But let me beg of you to fly to Your Maker thereafter for that mercy and that pardon which you cannot expect from us mortals."

The Judge then gestured to the nearest guards, and Kath was led to the crack where the planks forming the death trap came together, the noose hanging above her head.

She had a moment of panic then. She was cornered. There

was no way out. She was going to die. Two of the guards held
her arms as if knowing the wild thoughts running through her
head.

The hooded hangman stepped forward. Until that moment,
he had been hidden by the guards.

Kath tried not to look at him.

She struggled, but the guards held her tightly.

The hangman moved closer, only inches away.

She waited for the noose to touch her neck, steeling herself
not to flinch or cry out.

But the hangman didn't move.

He went on staring at her.

At last she turned to face him.

And her heart missed a beat.

Those black eyes. . . .

Her legs trembled and she felt faint.

It couldn't be true.

Not him.

Not Frank.

But she knew those eyes flashing through the holes in the
hood, she would know them anywhere, even in hell.

How had Frank reached Abilene?

And become the hangman?

It was impossible!

Yet there was no mistaking those eyes. And the slope of
those powerful shoulders.

Frank had somehow arranged to be the hangman to rescue
her.

Her heart suddenly began to beat wildly with the hope of
life.

She wasn't going to die.

Frank would save her again!

She couldn't speak to him and give it all away, but she tried
to convey her thoughts through her eyes. Oh, Frank, I'll treat
you better this time, just give me a chance. . . .

She waited for a response—a message from those black eyes
—vibrations of loving feeling from his powerful presence.

But there was nothing.

No reaction from him.

She stared at his eyes.

Then her heart went cold.

The fierce expression in his eyes wasn't a look of love.

It was a look of hatred.

She had fooled herself.

Frank's love had turned to hatred.

Suddenly she remembered the terrible burning sensation in her throat.

For looking into his fierce eyes, she saw that this time he intended to do it.

And it was her own fault. She had done nothing to placate him, even though she had owed him her life. But she must change his mind—his heart—now before it was too late.

"Frank," she murmured so no one else could hear.

Before she could say more, he stepped forward quickly and slipped the noose over her head and tightened it round her throat. At the touch of the rough hemp, the fear surged up in her. She tried to plead with him, but he tightened the rope even more and she couldn't speak. Their eyes met. His seemed to gleam with intense hostility. What hatred he must feel for her! Then he stepped back, away from her. There was no hope. He meant to hang her this time.

Kath braced herself. She had been through this before. She knew what to expect. It lasted only a few seconds. She could bear that. Yes, she could. She understood now the meaning of life—you had to live as if you weren't afraid to die.

Her shoulders went back and she looked challengingly at Frank.

"I'm ready," she said.

38

Frank Butler left Abilene a week later. He told Judge Drake, "You'll have to get another hangman, Judge. I'm through."

"Through?" The Judge's heavy eyebrows shot up. "But I need you, boy."

"Not as much as I need to get home."

"Home?"

"Back to England."

Judge Drake's penetrating eyes studied Frank's tired, haunted face. Later, when the news reached the Diamond Saloon, people who knew Frank, notably Doc Holliday, assumed he was leaving because of Galina's death. But Judge Drake wasn't fooled. He had noted the change in Frank since the hanging of that young woman, Kathleen Tracy. Young men were vulnerable when it came to beautiful young women. Even the Judge had been moved at the sight of such a lovely creature, so full of life, throttling at the end of a rope.

"Very well, Frank," he said sympathetically, "if your mind's made up, I can't argue with you." To show his appreciation of the young hangman's work, he escorted him to the stagecoach and waved him off.

Frank took nearly a month to reach New York by a series of stagecoaches and trains, and then to cross the Atlantic. After paying all the expenses of the long journey, he estimated he had enough money left from his gambling winnings and hanging

427

wages to last a year if he was careful. That was long enough to forget her.

On reaching Stockport, he went to see the black stallion. The still-magnificent horse was in the field behind the thatched cottage as if time had stood still, and immediately came galloping to meet him with the same powerful, graceful stride. The stallion seemed more surprised to see Frank than his old neighbors in the other cottages. They were country people who rarely showed their feelings. They acted as if they assumed Frank hadn't liked America and had come back because he preferred England, and that pleased them. They asked him about his travels, but when he didn't respond, they didn't press him. Soon it was as if he'd never been away. He bought back the cottage and settled down to live the old life again.

But he soon realized that was impossible. He'd left Abilene because everywhere reminded him of her. Everywhere in America would be the same. He had to escape her memory. That was why he'd returned to England, only to discover that everywhere in Stockport was haunted by her, too. Even the cottage. In the evenings, he'd be sitting over a glass of brandy and it was as if she was in the room with him. That face. That long red hair. That body. He was still obsessed with her, even though he'd lost her for good.

In such haunted moods, he'd call the stallion and ride out to one of the old country pubs beyond Rochdale. But gambling and picking up stray women and spending the night with them didn't satisfy him any more. He came back at dawn feeling just as restless and frustrated as when he'd left. He still had the passionate, one-track mind of a gambler. He couldn't get her out of his mind.

He began to drink heavily. His handsome face and figure put on fat, and his normally fine, clear skin lost its healthy glow. His neighbors watched him pass by on the stallion, silent and unapproachable, and they wondered if he had come back because he'd got into trouble in America. Someone heard him muttering to himself when he was drunk, and it sounded as if he'd killed a woman.

So they left him alone. Soon the black stallion was his only companion. They rode for hours together, and sometimes at night people saw him in the moonlight talking to the horse in the field. *Poor Frank,* they'd say, *America and his hangman's work must have affected his mind.*

But then one afternoon a strange thing happened.

Frank was drinking at the time and at first he couldn't believe it. He feared it was the effect of the brandy.

He was sitting at the open window watching the black stallion in the late summer sunshine when suddenly another horse entered the field—a white stallion just as fine as his black one.

The two great stallions came to meet each other, their heads up, alert and challenging.

White and black, both perfect, their movements beautiful to behold, they seemed dreamlike to Frank in his heavy brandy state. He was afraid the white horse was imaginary, out of his drunken mind, and yet he felt he had seen it before—in America.

His mind went back for some reason to Colonel Mosby's camp that time during the Civil War in Virginia.

"Do you recognise him?" asked a soft voice behind him from the open doorway.

He turned quickly, hardly daring to believe his ears.

It was Kath.

39

She had been spared a second time.

She had known that as soon as she awoke in heavy darkness with a burning throat the night after the hanging.

Her eyes had opened on a landscape as bare as the Valley of the Shadow of Death.

But that baked earth was familiar.

She was at the ranch.

Her head moved round painfully and her eyes found Aunt Martha at the bedside.

She tried to speak to the old woman, but the words wouldn't come. Swallowing was a torture. Yet it was more bearable than the first time. She knew what had happened. At last she managed to whisper, "Where is he?"

"Rest, child," the old woman said softly. "Don't talk."

"Where's Frank?"

"He's gone."

"Where?"

The old woman shrugged.

Kath stared out of the window at the distant horizon. He might be anywhere, but she felt she knew where he was. She trusted her instinct because she saw Frank now the way he really was. It was like awakening from a dream. The path of enlightenment had led to the heights of fulfillment as the old

gypsy had predicted so long ago. And on the heights was
. . . Frank.

She knew suddenly she loved him, had always loved him. It
was as if all she had been through was intended to open her eyes
to the truth. Why had she been so blind, so dumb for so long?
She tried to get out of bed, but Aunt Martha held her down.

"I must go to him." Her throat burned, but the pain meant
nothing to her now.

"Not yet, Kath," said the old woman. "Not until you're
well."

She couldn't wait, but she had to. The days dragged, but her
impatience helped her to heal fast. She had to follow him. She
had to tell him how she felt about him. Had she waited too
long? Had his love for her died through her indifference all
these months? Oh, God, let him still have the same feeling for
me. Yet why had he left? Her life had been saved, but it meant
nothing to her now without him.

As soon as she was well enough, she set off for England. He
had to be there. And now at last she had caught up with him.
Now at last she faced him. She tried to read his feelings in his
face. But he was always hard to read unless he was angry. All
that registered now was surprise at seeing her. Was there no
pleasure? Was she too late?

"Why did you leave me?" she asked quietly.

"I didn't want your gratitude."

"For this?" Her hand touched the silk scarf around her neck.
She still swallowed painfully. "My God, it's worse than the first
time," and she laughed.

"There was no way to avoid the pain," Frank said seriously,
trying to explain. "I adjusted the noose the same way as before.
When you lost consciousness, I cut you down. It was even easier
than the first time. Judge Drake left everything to me, not even
bothering to have a doctor there. I took you to the ranch and
left you with Aunt Martha."

"As soon as I could stand, I packed my bag. I had to see you."

"Why?"

Kath said slowly, "Because after all this time I realized I love
you."

"You expect me to believe that?"

His hard tone worried her and made her flare up. "I've crossed the Atlantic to tell you. Isn't that proof enough?" She stood at the open window. "Look."

The two stallions were trotting round the field together in a continuous graceful movement, at peace, their fine skin glistening in the sunshine.

"They accept each other."

"I'm not going to live in Bo's shadow," Frank said.

"Nor I in Galina's."

"How do you know about her?"

"Aunt Martha said it was in the Abilene paper when you left. I knew Galina. I met her on the stagecoach going to Kansas. I liked her a lot."

"She's dead anyway."

"So's Bo. But let's keep their memory alive. They were our friends. They brought us together."

That was true, Frank thought. There had been a time out west when he felt he hated Kath. The hangings had confused his mind. But Galina's death had opened his eyes.

"Let's get married, Frank," she said impulsively.

He was surprised. "We've no money."

"Yes, we have. Aunt Martha's selling the ranch and she's giving me half. We'll be rich."

"That's your money."

"There'll be enough for both of us." She stared at him openly. "But a wedding will take time to arrange. Don't let's wait. We've waited long enough."

"You're right," he said, suddenly grinning at her, his mood changing.

They both felt a great urgency—nothing in their lives was as important as this time together.

They closed the windows and drew the curtains. Frank pulled back the cover on the bed. Then they took off their clothes and lay down. Kath was naked except for the scarf round her neck.

"Take that off," he said. "I want to see all of you."

"Not this ugly wound."

"You forget, I gave it you. It's part of you. I want all of you. I told you that long ago."

She took off the scarf reluctantly. The wound looked like a

black, blood-tinged necklace of death, he thought. Just seeing it made him grateful for life. He leaned over and kissed her neck. "Never hide anything from me," he said gruffly and he took her gently in his arms. *At last,* he thought, hardly able to believe what was happening.

The first time they made love Kath felt as if they were performing a ceremony they had rehearsed with other people. Frank's strength and tenderness reminded her at first of Bo. But Frank had a strange, wild passion of his own.

He cried out with intense satisfaction the first time they came together, as if it was the fulfilment of his dreams—and it was.

He had dreamt of this ever since the first meeting in the woods of Heaton Hall so many years ago.

It was a dream that had carried him to America.

And now it had come true.

It was a long night of love. Frank seemed never to want to finish, his vigor undiminished at dawn as the birds sang outside the window. There would be many other times like this, but this was the first time.

His flashing eyes staring down at her reminded Kath of the last moments in Abilene. She had misread their look then. But now the meaning of those eyes, looking almost as if they were on fire, was unmistakable. It was the intense, passionate love that a boy feels for his first sweetheart.

"If we'd done this after the first time when I brought you back here," Frank murmured in her ear, "We'd have saved ourselves a lot of trouble."

"We weren't ready. I was still a child. I had to find my father to become a woman."

And kill him, she thought.

Or at least the part of him that had become Hugo White.

For she felt that Joseph Tracy was still alive here in Stockport and would never die for her.

It was the old Kath who had died.

She could feel the difference in herself when she came through the center of Stockport on the way to Frank's cottage. The old cotton town was still as familiar as the back of her hand. It hadn't changed. But it was no longer home to her. That had been in another life.

She had already had two lives.

She had escaped death twice.

This is my third life, Kath thought.

The other two were simply preparations for this one. Everything I went through was a test of me.

I'm ready now to stand on my own feet, she told herself.

I'm not afraid anymore.

I have faith.

I'm free at last.

40

Horatio Thomas had also returned to England soon after the hanging. He found his native land strangely different—or was it the effect of his American experience? he wondered. Kath's hanging and America generally had affected him profoundly. But England did seem to have a freer, less tense atmosphere as if the American Civil War's result—the triumph of democracy —really had had a great influence. The crowds in the streets of Manchester were certainly less hostile. All kinds of reforms were in the air. Democracy, having won the Civil War in America, was on the rise in England. The editor of the *Manchester Guardian* was confident much more of the population would soon get a vote and that would be the equivalent of a revolution in England.

Horatio Thomas visited Stockport and walked down the narrow, cobbled street beneath the factory chimneys, where Kath had told him she spent her childhood. It was impossible to associate Hugo White with this squalid industrial setting, and he found himself thinking more sympathetically of Kath's father. What a long way to rise from a factory hand here to a rich Kansas rancher! The struggle for survival had made great demands on Kath's father. A passage from Charles Darwin's *The Origin of Species* came back to Thomas: "Natural selection will not necessarily produce absolute perfection; nor, as far as we can judge by our limited faculties, can absolute perfection be everywhere found." Or anywhere, he thought. What was true of Hugo White—he wasn't perfect—was true of everybody. We were all struggling to better ourselves.

Horatio Thomas spent each day at the *Manchester Guardian* office writing a series of articles on the American west. It made him want to go back to complete his studies and follow what happened to the freed black slaves, but the *Manchester Guardian's* editor was keen he should cover the upheaval in central Europe. "Germany holds the key to the continent of Europe's future for the next hundred years," said the editor. "They will try to unify and expand by war as Napoleon did." But Horatio Thomas's mind continued to turn westwards. America was the dream of Europe—the future lay there. What was going to happen to the American Dream? Would it come true or would it meet the same fate as Kath's dream?

An old gray-haired doorman knocked politely on the door of the office Thomas had been loaned.

"A gentleman to see you, Mr. Thomas."

"Did he give his name?"

But the old doorman was already shuffling away down the dim corridor lined with bookcases.

Horatio Thomas, working in his shirt-sleeves, quickly slipped his white jacket back on, and followed.

A tall, dark, smiling figure was waiting in the lobby.

Frank.

The two men shook hands enthusiastically.

"I've come about our bet," Frank said.

"You've brought your stallion?"

"Come outside."

The old doorman held open the great door and they went into the street.

A closed carriage, drawn by a frisky mare, was waiting. Where was the stallion?

Frank opened the carriage door, and Horatio Thomas suddenly saw a familiar face back from the dead—Kath.

"Good God!" cried Horatio Thomas, an astonished smile lighting up his whole face. "I knew in my heart, Kath, you were still alive." She looked different, he thought, with a new—what

was the word?—serenity. And why not? The woman had survived two hangings!

"Frank saved me again," Kath said happily, embracing the
English journalist with great affection. "I tried to reach you
before you left Abilene."

"I couldn't stand the place after the hanging. I went immediately to Washington and then came back to England."

Frank told Horatio Thomas with a businesslike grin, "I've
come to collect on that bet—your ruby ring."

"Not so fast, Frank," retorted Horatio Thomas. "You
haven't won it until you two are married."

"We've chosen the place and the time," Frank said.

"And we've come to invite you," Kath added.

"I hope you'll have a very quiet wedding," said Horatio
Thomas, suddenly serious. "It could be dangerous if the police
learn you're still alive."

"Don't worry, Horatio," Kath said. "We're going to be
married in the hills."

* * *

The little fourteenth century church was near the village of
Hayfield, about twenty miles from Stockport. Several Catholic
martyrs, tortured and executed in the years of religious perse-
cution, were buried in the churchyard, their gravestones worn
smooth and hardly readable. At the back of the ancient church
were the great heather-covered moors leading to the mountain
peaks known as Kinder Scout, where Kath and her father had
hidden from the police. Kath and her father had once spent a
day walking on the moors. These memories—and the church's
remoteness—were the reasons why she had selected Hayfield
for the wedding. Horatio Thomas and Ram were the only
witnesses when Miss Kathleen Tracy became Mrs. Frank Butler.

The young Sikh, who still walked with a slight limp, said
enthusiastically, "I knew you were both destined to be together. It is your *Karma.*"

"The hangman marries his victim," Frank said grinning.

"That's what I call poetic justice," Horatio Thomas told him.
Thomas slipped his ring off his finger. "Here, the bet's won.

Why don't you give it to Kath for her wedding ring? You can tell your children how you got it."

Frank held up the ring admiringly. The sunlight through the ancient church's stained glass windows made the ruby sparkle.

"It must be worth a fortune," Frank told Kath eagerly. "Guard it with your life."

Horatio Thomas said nothing to spoil the victorious gambler's enjoyment. But he had exaggerated the ring's value in making the bet. He had bought it for very little in India. But why should he tell them? They need never know. Kath would never sell her wedding ring, so it would never be professionally valued, and it was certainly priceless as a memento of their long, arduous courtship.

While a small, rotund parish priest recited the words of the wedding ceremony, Frank slipped the ring on Kath's finger. They smiled shyly at each other.

"Where are you spending your honeymoon?" Horatio Thomas asked.

"We're going back to America," Kath said. "I've grown up. I want the American Dream to come true."

"It's already come true within you," Thomas told her. He held her hand. "Your father was looking in the wrong place."

Her eyes momentarily clouded at the mention of her father. "He tried to make his dream come true at any cost, but he paid for it. I love what he might have been."

"You know what the legends of the Moondancers say, Kath," Horatio Thomas said gently. "You have to earn your dream. That's what you have done, Kath."

She kissed Thomas quickly on the cheek. "I needed two chances. But now I know what I've got." She leaned her head against Frank's shoulder so that her red hair fell across his chest. Horatio Thomas suppressed a slight feeling of jealousy. He thought he had never seen a more handsome couple. Kath's hair and golden complexion perfectly complemented Frank's dark good looks.

And they were so happy together.

That pleased the English journalist, who remembered all the adventures they had shared over the last year.

But as he and Ram waved off the happy couple on their

stallions, Frank on his black one, Kath on Bo's white one, Horatio Thomas felt they had much more in common than their striking good looks.

They had a deep bond that the others had shared, too. Bo and the Reverend and Wash Green, and even Paul in his way.

But how could he express it in words?

He recalled an old Mexican saying he had heard in Kansas, "The earth is our mother, the sun is our father, and the moon is our lover."

Perhaps that explained why people with a great love of personal freedom, with the courage to make their dreams come true, were sometimes called moondancers.

Sometimes, too, he thought, they were called crazy.

But moondancers defined the outer limits of freedom for us, and that was why they were often the ones we remembered—the real survivors.

Kath and Frank and the others were all moondancers, Horatio Thomas told himself, as he watched the two riders in the far distance jumping the dry stone walls separating them from the great heather-covered moors. Ahead of them on the horizon was America. . . .

The sun's haze in the hills blurred their outlines, and for a moment it seemed as if Kath and Frank were not alone. Several other riders had joined them.

Yes, the English journalist thought, and I know who they are. Moondancers never die.

"Best picture of the year."
—National Board of Review

If you enjoyed THE MOONDANCERS, then you will be pleased to know that W.J. Weatherby is also the author of

CHARIOTS OF FIRE

A TRUE STORY

WRITTEN BY
W. J. WEATHERBY

BASED ON A SCREENPLAY BY
COLIN WELLAND

WINNER **4** ACADEMY AWARDS

INCLUDING
BEST PICTURE

"☆ ☆ ☆ ☆ ☆*"

CHARIOTS OF FIRE

The story of two men—Harold Abrahams and
Eric Liddell—who run not to run but to prove
something to the world. They will sacrifice
anything to achieve their goals, except their
honor. Two men, Abrahams and Liddell, one a
Jew who runs to triumph over bigotry, the
other a Scots missionary who runs to glorify
God. Two men eager to face their finest hour
in the 1924 Olympics, two men who race
toward greatness.

*" *'Chariots of Fire' lifts the spirits
to a new high."*

—Kathleen Carroll, New York Daily News

DELL/QUICKSILVER—01149 2.75